Starflight: Tales from the Starport Lounge

A Starflight Universe Anthology

Three Ravens Publishing

Chickamauga, GA, USA

A long time ago, in the days where I spent more time on video games than homework, there was a game called Starflight and these are its stories. A fantastic anthology from one of the first truly epic sagas of gaming. How this universe went untapped for so long is beyond me, but this exciting anthology is a perfect opening for new fans, and old, to swing by the Starport Lounge for a drink and a tall tale or two. Don't miss this book.

~Kevin Ikenberry, bestselling author of the Peacemaker novels in the Four Horsemen Universe.

As the decades passed, Starflight has lived on through its amazing fan community. This anthology has been a long time coming and shows once again what passionate creative fans can do. I can't wait to go on this new adventure to the stars!

~Blakes Sanctum, Retrogame streamer

Starflight...One of the first non-linear, open "world" games in a sci-fi setting, it set the standard that others would try to emulate even today in 2021! You won't need a Rock of Truth to see how carefully the lore of the Starflight universe is cared for and expanded!

~ LongwoodGeek, Retrogame streamer

Starflight was my first computer game, and it's still in my top five of all time. The exploration, story, and setting are unmatched, and it set the standards for how I see space games to this very day. I'm thrilled to see more stories filling out that wonderful universe further.

~ Space Game Junkie, Gamer/Streamer

Cover art by Luca Oleastri
rotwangstudio.com

Trade Paperback ISBN: 978-1-951768-30-0

Hardback ISBN: 978-1-951768-31-7

Mass Market Paperback ISBN: 978-1-951768-34-8

Table of Contents

Opening

By: Greg Johnson

Starflight was started in 1982, and really got off the ground in 1983. It was published in 1986, with Starflight 2 coming out in 1989. This all feels like ancient history now. Just to put things into perspective, these were the days of vector graphics games, and arcade games like Space Wars, Space Invaders, and Centipede. We started building Starflight for the Atari 800, and then switched to the Tandy Computer when our publisher decided it should be played on the PC. In those days no one thought people would want games on the PC, and Starflight ended up being the very first game on the PC to sell 100,000 units and prove there was a market. All of this is to say that it was the dark ages of games. Electronic Arts had only about 20 employees, and no one really knew how to make games yet, we all just made it up as we went along. There was a lot of excitement and a tremendous amount of freedom, as no one really had any expectations of what a game should or shouldn't be. Once a year the tight knit group of developers for EA came together and shared what they had discovered about making games. This little gathering is what eventually turned into GDC, the massive yearly Game Developers Conference. This is all why Starflight ended up being the very first open world story game… we built the game not knowing if it would work or not and having no roadmap. It was deeply inspired by Star Trek. Our fantasy was to give people that experience of being out in a big open Universe, populated by strange alien races and cultures, with strange histories, relationships, and mysteries to solve. In retrospect it was a crazy ambitious thing to do, especially with a randomly generated Universe of planets you could land on, all on a tiny floppy disk. Thankfully we were shielded by our ignorance and enthusiasm, so we dove in head first.

I was the one who came up with the entire Universe of characters and situations, as I was the only designer on the project. Of course the whole team contributed ideas and inspiration, but it was really my fantasy Universe that manifested. It was a universe of obnoxious, blustering Spemin, competitive Thrynn, philosophical Elowan, and the oddly awkward and overly formal Veloxi. As for the backstory and mystery of game one, well it's probably ok to give spoilers when a game is 35 years old… that came as quite an epiphany.

For those unfamiliar with the original Starflight story, the core idea was that alien races were moving in a wave across the galaxy, creating conflict as they encroached on others, with the most aggressive races like the bizarrely mysterious Uhlek, and the religiously fanatic Gazurtoid, causing the most problems. This migration of spacefaring races was occuring because the stars were strangely going nova in a continuous wave, moving slowly outward from the core of the galaxy, and wiping out all life in its path. As a player, you start the game from a colony planet called Arth, and you discover that planet Earth, just a child's story on your planet, was real and is in the dead zone. You also encounter the Mechans, a race of robots created by the old Earthlings, who happen to know a lot about old Earth.

In any event, players gradually find out that there was a race of ancient beings (who had the very uninspired name of "the Ancients"), and these Ancients had left behind ruins with piles of a strange mineral substance called Endurium that has special properties which are needed for faster than light travel. All of the space faring races, including you the player, competes to collect and use these super valuable minerals. The big reveal… is that the ancients never actually left. They are still here, and the Endurium you have been collecting and burning up in your engines throughout the game, IS the Ancients. The Ancients happen to be a silicon-based life form that operates in an "orders of magnitude slower" scale of time. To this type of life form, carbon life developed in the galaxy and in a flash it evolved, just like a fast growing bacteria, and started wiping them out. Their response was to defend themselves against this disease, and purge carbon-based life with stars going nova. Basically, towards the end of the game players find out that they are the aggressor, and players are forced into an interesting ethical dilemma. Cool huh? Especially for a game from 1986.

I remember being very excited when this story came together in my mind. Every now and then when you are designing a game, or writing a story you struggle and struggle, not knowing how it will all fit together, and then one day when you are relaxed and not even trying, the clouds in your mind clear and you see it all clearly. That's what it was like for me back then, and as it was the first game of my long career, it was a very special moment. From there it was a long three years of trying to figure out how to get the game built, with a fantastic but inexperienced team, and how to not get cancelled by our publisher for taking 3 times longer than we were originally supposed to take (not much has changed in the games industry by the way).

Somehow, we managed to make it to the end and get the game released. I can't tell you how exciting that was for all of us. Since then Starflight has inspired so many people in the industry. I have often been told it was the game that made one person or another devote their lives to developing games. Recently I was surprised and overjoyed to find that there is a group of talented writers who want to pay tribute to the Starflight Universe by setting original stories in it, and putting them together in an anthology. I don't believe anyone could be more excited than me to read what they have come up with. The Starflight Universe, to this day, is still very dear to my heart. I'd like to offer a special thank you to Scott Tackett and Three Ravens Publishing for putting this anthology together, and also to Scott and all of the other talented authors who contributed to this. I'll also take the opportunity to give a big life-long shout out of warm appreciation to the old Starflight Team. Alec, Tim, Dr. Bob, and Rich, the late Dave Boulton, and of course Rod, our fearless leader. We made something that continues to inspire and entertain people. It's hard to ask for more than that.

Those Who Came Before

By: Michael Gants

Remote Base One, Havis Heavy Industrial Corporation's current testing facility, lay three hundred and eighty-six kilometers of desolate desert and lifeless terrain behind them. Everywhere Sarah Everhart stared, the blasted landscape that made up much of the Southern Hot Zone appeared the same. Twisted craters pock-marked the soil, evidence of a long-ago bombardment by the aliens who had attacked the planet over a thousand years earlier. When life appeared on Arth, it seemed it ignored this part. Nothing grew here, not even lichens. Stillness ruled beyond the occasional dust devil dancing in the wind. The landscape was an inverted garden of rock and quartz sand; full of ridges and valleys that crossed each other, still ripples in a frozen pond. They looked little different from when they formed during the attack, except time and weather had softened the sharp edges.

A voice jolted Sarah out of her daydreaming. "Sahnuli, recommend adjusting course to the south, left for ten degrees. I am reading increased radiation levels ahead of us. Probability is high that we are approaching a ground zero point," stated Phxnolx, the expedition's sensor specialist.

"The land ahead in that direction is rising again," intoned Sahnuli as he pressed down on the accelerator. The whine of the electric drive motors increased as the computer routed more power to them. Slightly slowing as the treads bit into the rocky ridge, the terrain vehicle tipped skyward to meet the newest obstacle.

"I am aware; however, it is better to lengthen the trip than drive through that much radiation. If it is a ground zero, even our shielding is not *that* good," Phxnolx intoned dryly, his clipped accent belying an Eastern Island's origin.

Sahnuli replied in a serious tone, "I am in harmony with your suggestion."

Sarah smiled as the Elowan's scent gained the overlay of thyme. In displaying emotion, Elowan faces weren't anywhere near as mobile as Human or Thrynn, nor could they use Velox antenna position and color changes. They instead expressed most emotions through subtle scent changes. Thyme-like scent expressed humor. Her smile faded a bit as she contemplated the map displayed on her screen. "Fox, why are you suggesting south instead of north?" she asked, using the Velox's Human nickname.

"I have a high probability reading in that direction on the sniffer. I am attempting to verify it and the rad spike ahead of us gives me a good reason to." His antenna drooped momentarily, the Velox equivalent of shrugging, and looked up cabin at the navigator. "Currently, there is not anywhere else we need to be."

Sarah glanced back at him, then back to her screen. "Alright. I am a little concerned because on the overheads it looks like we are moving deeper into a heavily bombed zone by going south. Which could lead us into even more ground zeroes."

"I will keep close eyes on both the radiation meters and the sensor readings. If things begin to change in a negative direction, we can return here and try the more northerly course. They planned this entire mission around getting real-time data on the vehicle's capabilities." He clicked his mandibles in humor. "Rougher ground means better testing."

The vehicle lurched over a set of heavy ripples, and the crew bounced around in their seats. "Better testing. . .Right." Sarah adjusted her harness, tightening it slightly around her shoulders. "More bouncing and careening around inside as well," she muttered to herself.

Sahnuli slowed the big terrain vehicle as it approached the position.

"Another two hundred. . .one hundred. . .stop."

The fifty-ton vehicle rocked gently as it came to a stop. Eight leveling jacks lowered underneath, lifting the vehicle off its tracks. The computer adjusted each jack independently, jostling the vehicle until the sensors read a level position.

The computer flashed a notice on the vehicle's HUD. "Vehicle leveled." Sahnuli stated. "Ready to commence mining test."

Gareth Moore, the team's mining specialist, tapped an icon on his screen and grasped the waldo's control. Silently, the massive drilling system swung out from the front of the cab, just forward of the crew entrance. Guided by Gareth's steady hand, a small probe arm gracefully positioned itself over the vein of tin that Phxnolx's sensor drone had located. The sampling laser glowed green momentarily.

"Tin ore is ninety-six-point four eight percent pure." The Velox clicked his mandibles together in satisfaction. His delicate fingers danced over the sensor touchscreen. "Seismic deep scan indicates approximately four-point three metric tons of tin in this vein." He waved the screen to another data page. "Cargo capacity is currently at seven percent. Sufficient room in the cargo hold for the entire amount."

"Looks like a nice haul," Gareth commented. "Starting removal."

The onboard mining computer translated Phxnolx's sensor scans into a three-dimensional map for the operation. Then the multitude of sampling probes, drilling lasers, physical drill heads, and manipulator arms that made up the mining rig swung into action. All the material; the tin ore, dirt, and non-tin metallics were excised from the vein. Plasma beds melted the ore and then a conveyor system deposited the molten metal into speed cooling forms. It shunted the remaining materials into a holding bay. Once the tin ingots were solid, another robotic system removed them from the forms and stacked them carefully inside the cargo compartment. Another portion of the system began refilling the excavated holes with the unused materials, quickly emptying the holding compartment. The entire operation from start to finish took forty-seven minutes.

"Truly, a system well thought out and designed. Over four metric tons of metal removed, prepped, and stored in less than an hour. It even restored the ground to the best possible condition." Indeed, aside from the deep curve of a new valley, the land looked barely disturbed. Even the slight haze of dust quickly settled. Like most Elowan, Sahnuli believed in minimizing the environmental impact of construction or mining. "Readings in the cargo compartment?"

Sarah ran her hand across her screen. "Looks like the filters removed most of the contamination during the melt. The cargo hold has a slightly increased background radiation. Still within allowable limits." She tapped a note into the computer. "I'll pass that on for evaluation. Maybe the next upgrade can sift through the metal and remove anything that is radioactive. That would minimize the need for the heavy shielding." Sarah finished her note and ran a quick verification cycle. "That finishes that one. Fox, what does the Overview satellite say?"

"Another significant concentration of metals detected north and west, twenty-five point seven five kilometers. Unknown type, unknown quantity."

Gareth shook his head and laughed. "Overheads can spot the deposits. They can't give us anything more useful than a general location. I guess that's why the company spent so much money on the drones."

The Velox nodded in agreement. "Easier to use local resources for final evaluation than attempting to sample from space. I do not think any of us would be comfortable with a laser shot down that is strong enough for spectrographic evaluation."

Everyone joined in the laughter at that. Sahnuli shifted the crawler into forward motion, driving around the newly created valley. The thick wide tracks spread the vehicle's fifty-metric-ton weight across a large area, minimizing any tendency to slip or sink in. Dirt flattened under the tread plates as the crawler picked up speed to its maximum of sixty-four kilometers per hour.

"I could just see it," said Sarah as she updated the route on the nav screen. She spoke in a fake announcer's style voice. "This just in. Less than two hours ago, a sampling laser from space pierced a fully loaded dirigible transport out of Sinar. In other news, Space Lasers and Mining Incorporated have discovered new deposits of iron and gold along one of the most heavily trafficked air routes on Arth."

"I am sure that is the most likely outcome if companies were to use space laser measurement. Let's hope that the people in charge stick with the drone system." Sahnuli waved a frond, pointing out through the windscreen. "I like the idea of seeing where the laser comes from rather than being a target."

Sarah held up a hand as her console began alarming. "Five kilometers from target. Sahn, let's stop here. Fox, prep the drone."

Phxnolx swung his chair around and faced the drone control console. He tapped a pair of commands and the drone system's readiness sprang onto the screen. "Drone One is prepped and fully charged. Navigation coordinates are programmed in. Battery fully charged and all systems indicate nominal. Drone is ready for launch."

The cabin swayed as the vehicle stopped. Behind the crew compartment, a pair of small doors opened accordion style. A white and orange drone lifted out, held aloft by four ducted rotors. The segmented body of the drone belied its Velox origin. Sampling probes fit tightly against the main body to minimize drag. The fans pivoted, and the robot flashed ahead of the terrain vehicle, disappearing into the bright midday sky in seconds.

"Telemetry is nominal. Video scan active. Arrival in three minutes." Phxnolx shared a window of the video feed to the other screens. "Schedule for the sampling plan is fifteen minutes."

Gareth gestured at the screen. "Then we'll know what the take will be."

"The take?" asked Phxnolx.

"Something my grandmother used to say. She always meant that it was how much of something she was getting. Usually when she was attempting to hustle someone in gambling cards." Gareth stopped talking as Phxnolx held up a single digit and touched another control.

"Arrival. Commencing sampling pattern. . .and now everything is on automatic. We wait."

Minutes ticked by in silence as the drone worked. Slowly, the data trickled in. "Iron and aluminum? Odd combination. Usually, you do not find ferrous and non-ferrous materials in the same ore deposit. Now reading traces of chromium as well."

"Are you certain that the drone is checking the ground and not itself? Those combinations sound a lot like our hull."

Phxnolx opened a second window and ran the drone self-check program. "Everything is in normal parameters. Nothing out of the ordinary. The samples are definitely from the surface of the planet."

"Okay." Garth waved a hand in the air. "We'll wait for the sampling to complete and then go take a physical look at what the wonder drone has discovered."

The drone completed its sample minutes later. "That was quick. . .Ah, small deposit, less than twelve meters square. Sarah, transferring you the coordinates."

"Roger. Locked in. Sahn, once the drone returns, all you need to do is follow the arrow," Sarah stated and pointed at the windscreen. A yellow carrot cursor appeared in Sahnuli's HUD, pointing away from the terrain vehicle and to the left.

Five minutes later, the insectoid drone flashed past the vehicle and settled back into its transport cradle. The safety doors slid shut with a quiet metallic thunk.

"Drone indicates connection to cradle and charging. All connections are green. We are safe to move."

Sahnuli advanced the throttle, and the electric motors whined.

"Exterior radiation levels have greatly decreased. Average reading is now three-point six C/kg. Not safe to walk around without the suits but within acceptable exploration limits." Phxnolx's antenna danced in interest. "That is a reduction of five-point eight C/kg in the mile. Analysis is that we are exiting one area of bombardment."

"That's good news, since it's likely we'll need to look at this next ore patch before we begin mining," Sarah stated with relief.

"We have arrived," Sahnuli stated breathily as he stopped the terrain vehicle. "I think there's no need for all of us to suit up for this exploration. Does anyone volunteer?"

Sarah spoke up just before Gareth. He closed his mouth and waited. "I'll go. I haven't had much of a chance to stretch my legs so this would be nice. Plus, I'm curious about the ore here since it is a mixture of metals not normally found together."

"Very well. You may go then, Sarah. Gareth?"

"Yeah, I'd like to go as well. Perhaps the drone's samples were contaminated. . ."

Phxnolx's frustration reddened his carapace. His rapid chittering interrupted Gareth. "There were no indications of cross or previous contamination. The design is robust."

"I didn't say that there had been contamination, just a possibility. Mostly I'm with Sarah on the unusualness of this grouping."

"Very well. Gareth and Sarah will make the excursion and determine the situation with the ore prior to mining operations."

The terrain vehicle's treads were slightly taller than the average Thyrnn, which allowed the access ramp's placement to shelter between them. As the ramp lowered, the midday sunlight sparkled off the bright orange, white, and cyan environmental suits. Sarah and Gareth carefully stepped from the overhang of the mining equipment and into the brilliant light.

Sarah checked the screen on her suit's arm. She pointed ahead and to the left of the vehicle. "Ore is right over there, per the coordinates. Slaving HUDs." A bright blue ring appeared inside both of their helmets.

The two shuffled their way over to the coordinates, heavy dust swirling around their feet with each step, watching as the blue circle contracted until it compressed to a dot. There was nothing remarkable about the spot of terrain. It looked the same as the rest of the sunbaked landscape. Gareth extracted a sensor pick and pressed it into the ground. "Silicon, carbon, mica, more silicon," he muttered as he extracted the pick and moved to another spot.

Sarah watched him for a moment, then moved slightly sideways to a tiny dune of heaped dust. She scraped her boot across the small hill. A small bit of metal caught the light, glinting strongly. Sarah dropped to her knees, using her hands to brush more of the silica particles away. "Gareth, I might have found something!"

Gareth turned and walked back towards her. "Like what?"

"Something metallic. It's just under the dirt here. I think I can..."

She screamed as the ground below her collapsed and she tumbled into the hole, a rain of sand and rock following her into the darkness.

"Sarah!" Garth raced to the edge of the collapsed area, arms wheeling as more of the edge collapsed. He backpedaled and continued to call. There was no response. Fresh torn soil marked the ragged edge of the sinkhole, reddish brown dust dissipating in the afternoon breeze. One moment Sarah had been wiping away at something, the next the ground had opened below her and she had plummeted down. He aimed his flashlight into the hole but couldn't see anything through the haze. Thick dust hung in the air, obscuring sight.

"Terrain vehicle, Gareth. Sarah has fallen into a sinkhole. Contact base and let them know what has happened. We need all the climbing equipment we have and prep the med kits. Fox, can you get any readings on her?"

The Velox's sharply clipped tones were muted, a sign that his mandibles quivered in frustration. "No readings. I am not sure if that is due to a damaged computer or where she is located."

"Great," Gareth muttered as he continued to play his light over the opening.

Gareth stayed put, continuing to alternate between calling for Sarah and shining his light into the hole while Sahnuli and Phxnolx gathered rescue gear. The group had trained for the possibility of a member getting hurt or the need to traverse a steep slope. They had not trained on sinkhole rescues.

Phxnolx's shadow fell over the area as the Velox arrived. He was carrying various cables and other climbing gear.

"Sahnuli, I am slaving the drone to my suit. I will send it down into the shaft while we set up the climbing harnesses and anchors." Insectoid fingers typed a command into his suit's touchscreen. Moments later, the two of them heard the drone lifting out of the holding compartment. Phxnolx copied the video feed to the others' screens. He quickly programmed a basic search and avoidance program. Since he could not be sure that their radios would penetrate the rock, the drone could enter the shaft and fly itself slowly to the bottom. Behind him, Gareth and Sahnuli spread out the climbing gear. Phxnolx verified the drone's commands one more time, then set it in motion.

The pair worked carefully to set up the anchoring and climbing equipment as the large drone slipped past them and descended into the newly formed hole.

Sarah came to with a start. Her gasp of surprise followed immediately with groans of pain. The sudden movement had jarred parts of her body that were informing her of damage; mainly through pain. She blinked to clear her vision, wishing she could actually wipe her arm across her eyes to clear them. Unfortunately, the suit's design prohibited such actions.

As she focused, she realized there were several alarms sounding, and the in-helmet radio was producing nothing but static. She blinked several more times, finally getting her eyes to focus properly.

"Suit, silence alarms," she croaked.

"Warning," came the suit's female Velox perfect voice, "alarm conditions not cleared. Verify request please."

Sarah took a deep breath and forced it out. "Suit, verify silence alarms."

"Alarms silenced. Emergency protocols will restart alarm in fifteen minutes."

Dust covered most of her visor. She raised her left hand and wiped some of it from the helmet. The sand fell away, showing a slightly streaked and scratched surface, with no cracks. Sarah released the breath she had been unconsciously holding. A damaged visor would have complicated the situation even more.

Faint light filtered down through the dusty haze, barely illuminating the area where she laid on her back, her legs twisted under her uncomfortably. She vaguely remembered tumbling and bouncing as she fell, but the thoughts were fuzzy. When she attempted to lever herself on her right arm, it collapsed under the pressure and she bit back a scream of agony. Panting, she lay back for several more minutes. Finally, she raised her left arm and examined her wrist display. The touchscreen, scratched and dirty from the fall but still readable, currently displayed a schematic of the suit with red patches indicating damage.

"Alright," Sarah spoke in a thready voice to herself, "suit integrity appears fine. No signs of loss of pressure. Outside temperature is sixteen degrees lower than it was on the surface.

Background radiation is below Arth normal." She chuckled, her voice strengthening. "I guess that makes sense, since this cavern has probably been sealed off for several centuries. Maybe even from before the bombings."

Carefully she put the screen close to her right hand and was, with considerable pain, able to shift the screen to the diagnostics screen. "Primary and life support computer packs are non-responsive. Secondary lighting damaged. Secondary sensor pack non-responsive. Primary scrubber vented and unusable. Secondary scrubber at full load and operational."

She ran her left hand over the front of the environmental suit and could feel several broken sections of what had originally been a single large computer module. She looked at the screen again. "That explains those alarms," Sarah stated as she painfully attempted to turn on the flashlight on her right arm. When she touched the switch, nothing happened. She carefully turned the arm with her left, biting back a yelp of pain as the right arm rotated. The lens of the flashlight had starred from a shard of rock lodged in it.

"Figures. Alright Sarah. Time to get ourselves straightened out."

Cautiously, she shifted and wiggled until her right leg straightened. The left had remained stationary throughout her movements. She could feel the leg behind her, but could not move the lower section of the leg. She wiggled her toes. They moved freely and without pain. Whatever was preventing her movement had not damaged the leg. From this position, she could look down at herself. The coating of sand and dust dulled the suit's colors. Carefully, she brushed as much of the sand and dust as possible away from her chest. She could tell as she uncovered the primary computer's cover that it had taken the brunt of the impact. The case had cracked; broken completely through in at least two spots.

Black carbon dust streaked her left glove. Based on that and the alarms she had silenced, the entire unit had likely shorted out.

The faint illumination from above was enough to give her a sense of her surroundings, though she could not actually see the hole she had fallen through. The powdery dust hung in the air, diffusing the faint light into a ruddy glow. She strained her ears, listening for anything. There was silence outside her suit. Only the static from the radio greeted her. She swallowed reflexively.

"Suit, emergency broadcast, all channels."

"Emergency protocols loaded. Ready," replied the suit.

"Mayday, mayday. This is navigator Sarah Everhart. To anyone who can hear me. Mayday."

She paused and waited for a response. Nothing. The static continued.

"Mayday. . .mayday. Come on team, I'm alive and stuck down here."

Still no reply. Maybe if she reoriented herself, moved a bit, she could improve the radio's reception. That was if the radio was actually sending and receiving.

"Suit. . .pause broadcast."

"Emergency protocols active," the generated voice of her suit countered. "Broadcast of last message will continue in two-minute intervals for the next thirty minutes unless you specify ending earlier. Do you wish to end broadcast?"

"No."

"Continuing broadcast." The suit fell silent while continuing to send out the radio signals.

Sarah pushed herself up with her left arm and tested applying pressure to her right arm. The muscles screamed in protest, but the arm held her weight this time.

"Okay. This is probably a sprain. Really nasty sprain, but not broken, thank goodness." With her leg pinned, it was impossible to sit up.

It took Sarah over ten minutes of shifting and scooting to get her body contorted into an L shape and point her receiver towards where she could now see the overhead opening.

"Suit, new broadcast."

"Ready."

"Mayday, mayday. Navigator Sarah Everhart. Gareth, can you hear? Mayday." She paused again.

"Guys?" she croaked over the suit's radio, hoping it still worked. Nothing. No response at all.

She consulted the screen on her left arm again. According to the diagnostics, the radio was transmitting. A faint memory from a training course surfaced. *Frequency affects distance through matter.* The suit's emergency system would broadcast on the primary and emergency channels, but it would not cycle through the less used options. Sarah tabbed through various menus until she found the radio frequency options. A few commands, and she had the system set up for simultaneous transmission on all available frequencies.

"Suit, pause broadcast. Set for new broadcast."

"Listening."

"Mayday, mayday. This is Navigator Sarah Everhart. I am alive and stable. Left leg is pinned. Require assistance. Mayday, mayday." She paused for fifteen seconds. "Send."

"New emergency broadcast commencing."

Sarah lay back, ensuring her helmet faced the overhead opening, watching and listening for any sign of rescue.

Gareth had stayed near the hole, attempting to contact Sarah in any way possible. Several radio attempts had resulted in nothing, so now he was cupping his hands and yelling down into the hole. "Sarah, we are coming. Stay calm. The drone is also on its way. Keep trying to contact us."

Sahnuli stopped several feet from the edge of the sinkhole, running a hand-held ground penetrating radar sensor over the spot. "The ground here is sufficiently dense to accept the rooting of the climbing anchor." He levered the large tube upright, the round opening sitting directly on the ground, then pressed the firing stud. A dull boom and more dust billowed. Sahnuli lifted the firing tube out of the way and verified the stability of the anchor. It failed to move, no matter how he pushed or pulled on it. "The anchor is firmly rooted. Attaching the harness ropes."

The climbing kit used braided single strand carbon filament rope and electrical micro winches for raising and lowering gear or people. The rope's tensile strength measured in hundreds of tons per centimeter. If needed, the team could pull the terrain vehicle with the rope and have no fear of the rope parting. The winches, though not as powerful, were more than sufficient for carrying all four crew members, let alone one per winch. Each rope contained an integral communications cable in the center of the rope. This ensured the crew could maintain constant communications without relying on radio waves. Sahnuli climbed into the harness and connected the comms cable to his suit.

"Communications check."

Phxnolx nodded and replied, "Good connection. Clear signal."

Sahnuli watched as Gareth second checked his harness. Garth flashed him a thumbs up. "Very well. One last review. Mining Operator Gareth and I will descend into the shaft. Drone Controller Phxnolx, you will remain aboveground and monitor our progress. You are also responsible for keeping Remote Base One informed with regular updates."

Phxnolx had returned the larger drone to the surface and stowed it. Because of its size, it could not traverse the serpentine shaft. Phxnolx removed one of the smaller multi-purpose drones from a storage bay and it currently hovered next to the two. Receiving new commands, it began lowering itself into the shaft. The drop was not straight, and it had needed to pause and reorient itself several times during the descent. Various holes opened off the primary shaft, and the drone verified that none of them contained Sarah prior to continuing down to the next level. Gareth and Sahnuli followed the drone closely. Since the shaft was not straight down, Gareth and Sahnuli had to stop and set pitons with loops at each jagged turn.

Minutes ticked by as Sarah waited, her breathing the only sound in the space. Suddenly, with crackles of distortion, her radio speaker emitted a faint message.

"Sarah, Gar. . .I. . .just barely hearing. . .peat your situa. . ."

Sarah relaxed back and took a deep breath. She spoke loudly and worked to enunciate every word carefully. "I am at the bottom of a hole, no idea how deep. Left leg pinned at ankle by a rockfall. Right arm severely bruised but not broken. Primary computer destroyed. Suit indicates intact."

She stopped. The distortion dropped off as the small arm computer began compensating for the signal degradation.

"Roger. Understand pinned but safe. Damage to right arm. Primary computer destroyed. Suit integrity satisfactory." There was a pause and another crackle of static. "Environmental readings?"

She lifted her left arm and checked the readings again. "Significantly lower radiation readings, reads zero-point three six C/Kg. Temperature is sixteen-point six degrees." She watched as twin beams of light swept over her and one of the multi-purpose drones slipped through the hole above her. She raised her left hand and waved. "About time you guys got down here. I was starting to get lonely."

"This area is much smoother than where we were just at," remarked Sahnuli. "This might have originally been an underground water supply or flood tunnel. The weight of Sarah and the other equipment was just enough to precipitate the collapse."

"I heard that Sahn," Sarah half-laughed, half-coughed through her suit speaker. "You're saying I'm fat and that's what caused me to fall in here." The drone was acting as a radio relay system to keep everyone connected since the suit radios did not have the power to reach through the rock effectively.

"Of course not Sarah. I would never deem to comment on your personal weight status. I was taught better than that by my creche."

Sarah laughed again. "The drone is now in the chamber I fell into." She stopped and listened. Scraping noises drifted down from the hole. "You guys must be getting pretty close. I can hear your climbing noises from above me. Just please be careful not to step on me when you get down here. I'm already uncomfortable from the fall."

She watched in dazed anticipation as Gareth and Sahnuli's light beams played across the open shaft above her. It was going to be good to be back in physical contact with the team. Injuries were annoying. She watched her friends descend from the ceiling. Most of the fine dust had finally settled out of the air, improving the visibility in the chamber.

As soon as Gareth knew he was firmly on the ground, he dropped the medkit and reached out to assist Sahnuli onto the wide ledge. Elowan, strangely enough, were extremely good medical personnel. He pulled sufficient slack to allow them to move around freely. The sooner he could get Sahn treating Sarah, the better it was going to be for everybody.

Sahnuli opened the medkit with one set of fronds while he quickly examined Sarah's general state. Without her life support computer, it limited Sahnuli to what she could tell him or he could observe. Instead of crushing her leg, it appeared the rocks had landed in a manner where they were supporting each other, though still trapping her lower limb. She was rotated awkwardly at the hip, left arm across her body and her right arm straight out and visibly swollen. He could see beads of sweat form and roll off her forehead, and she was paler than normal.

"Sarah, you're in shock. I am going to give you a general broad-spectrum painkiller and anti-inflammatory to reduce the swelling in the arm. Then I am going to splint it. Once I stabilize the arm, Gareth and I will begin moving the rocks away from your leg so that we can evacuate you. Do you understand?"

Sarah nodded weakly and lifted her left hand, thumb extended upward in the ancient signal of everything's good.

Sahnuli sifted through the medkit and removed a pair of liquid-filled ampules and inflatable splints. Pressing the ampules to the suit's medport, he heard a soft *pfft* as the pneumatic dispenser injected the medications. He held out a frond. "Gareth, please help me set the splint."

The pair waited a minute for the painkiller cocktail to begin working, then straightened out Sarah's arm. She bit her lip to prevent making any sounds. The moving of her arm hurt significantly more than when she had done it on her own. As soon as it was straight, Sahnuli touched the inflation button, and the splint inflated, both cushioning the arm and ensuring it remained stationary.

"Oh, by the seven nights of fever that hurts. Please tell me you don't need to do any more with my arm," Sarah wheezed, tears of pain squeezing out of the corners of her eyes.

Sahnuli shook his head in negative. "That is all I need to do here. I don't think it is broken, thankfully. There was no indication while I felt it. There could be a hairline fracture, but until I get you into the med bay on the terrain vehicle I cannot know for certain. I think it is bruising and a rather intense sprain. Our next job will be to free your leg and get you back on your feet."

As the pair worked, the drone continued its program and mapped the small cavern that they were in. It found a large opening near the back and descended into it. Sarah could do nothing other than wait as Sahnuli and Gareth moved rocks carefully off her leg. She listened to the grunts of exertion as they rolled a large stone away from her leg. After they removed a few rocks, she was able to wriggle her leg and pull it free. She leaned on Gareth as she stood; her left leg full of pins and needles as the blood flow resumed normal levels.

"Oh yeah. . .Leg fell asleep." She limped around in tiny circles to restore feeling. Slowly the tingling faded and Sarah was comfortable walking normally and without support. "Alright, I think I can move on now. Even my arm is feeling better." She moved the arm a bit in her sling.

"That is good news," stated Sahnuli as he grasped the extra harness the two had lowered with them. "We need to get you into the harness for ascent."

Gareth smiled as the three began setting up the harness units. He glanced around the small cavern and then frowned.

"Where'd the drone get off to?"

Sarah and Sahnuli paused and looked around. There was a faint glow at the end of the cavern farthest from them. "Over there perhaps," Sahnuli stated and waved a frond towards the dim light.

"Maybe. I'm going to check. Hate to lose one down here. Bosses might charge it to us."

Everyone laughed at that.

Gareth stepped away from his harness and, carefully, worked his way towards the cavern's far end. The light appeared to be coming from a large, circular hole in the cavern's floor. Gareth stared in surprise. The hole was not just round; it appeared to have been carved out of the stone. He crouched down on his knees to get a better view. The upper edges of the hole were slightly eroded, but the remainder of the hole's sides were smooth. Looking through the hole, he could see the lights from the drone fanning back and forth.

"Sahnuli, Sarah. I think you should come see this."

The other two members exchanged glances and then divested themselves of their harnesses. They walked back to where Gareth was kneeling.

"What's up? I'd really like to get back to the rover." Sarah placed a hand on Gareth's shoulder. "Actually, get out of this suit and check my arm."

Gareth nodded absently. Then he pointed at the hole. "I don't think this is natural. I mean, the sides, the cut edges. This looks created."

Both Sarah and Sahnuli leaned over and looked hard at the hole. After a moment, Sarah spoke up. "I agree. It looks like a mining bore more than anything else." She looked up. "Sahn, could you shine your light above us?"

He turned and lifted the light up, playing it over the rough ceiling just a foot above their heads. The rock looked normal and untouched by any living hands.

Sarah sniffed. "Problem is, a mining bore needs to come from the surface. Can't bore from underneath up." She smacked the side of her helmet with her good hand. "This is silly."

"What?" asked Gareth as he stood back up.

"We can use the drone to see what's down there. Bring up the video on your arm display."

Gareth tapped a quick command, and the screen on his left arm shifted to a view from the forward camera on the drone.

The two humans gasped, and Sahnuli ducked his head in surprise. There were remains. Two sets. One set of human bones and the parts of a single Velox exoskeleton.

The four crew members sat in their stations, chairs turned to look at each other.

Gareth shook his head. "I say we leave it to someone who knows what they are doing. The only reason we are even here is to test the terrain vehicle." Crossing his arms, he sank deeper into his chair.

"Yet we have found something unexpected. A possible proof of the legends of Arthlings living in the Southern Zone." Phxnolx clicked his mouth parts together, grinding them slightly. "We know that this area had been bombed almost a thousand years ago. We have never determined the complete why of that attack, nor of who might have been the aggressor. There are hints. . ."

"Tales." Gareth interrupted. "Tales in *The Book of Endurium*. Stories to ensure that we understand our place on Arth and the universe. Those tales are not enough to send us back down."

Sarah started at the venom in Gareth's tone. She knew he had grown up in a religious household, but it surprised her he would allow that to overshadow his scientific training.

Sahnuli raised a frond and waved it towards the front window of the vehicle. "I do not suggest that we return below, due to those tales. I suggest we return to gather the remains of fellow beings, give them a proper release, and determine how and why they are there. All the drone readings and samples indicate that the caverns and chamber below have been sealed for several decades, possibly centuries.

"There is no need for all of us to descend," he continued. "In truth, I am certain that maintaining at least one of us topside during the investigation is not only worthwhile, but necessary. So I shall suggest to Remote Base One."

"I will, willingly, go back down, as long as I can use the harness," Sarah stated. "My last descent was a bit faster than I enjoy."

"How is the arm progressing?" Phxnolx questioned.

"Great. Once Sahnuli got me into the medi-station, he did his magic and encouraged the muscles to accept the quick heal process." She rotated the arm about, wincing slightly as it twinged on the upper part of the circle. "Still a little stiff, but almost healed and much better than it was."

"Any other concerns?" questioned Sahnuli. He waited a moment. No one spoke up. "Very well. I will contact our superiors and brief them on what we found and our plans." He stood up and shuffled to the drive compartment, shutting the privacy shield behind himself.

The rest of the crew busied themselves with a game of cards as they waited for Sahnuli to return. They were uncertain of how long the conversation would take or what Remote Base One's answers would be.

"I'll take two," Gareth said as he tossed two of his hand on the table. Phxnolx gathered up the spent cards and slid two new cards across the table. Sarah sighed and dropped a single card.

"One please." She glanced at the card that Phxnolx passed and grinned.

Phxnolx stated, "Miner's Paradise, ores and gems." He laid seven cards face up, three gems and four ores. "Twelve points"

"Flitz! That tears my hand. All I have is a Minor Trade Route and a Cargo Haul. That only gets me seven points." Gareth laid six cards face up in two sets of three. A single transport, a crewmember, and an ore in one group and three cargo in the other.

Sarah fanned all twelve of her cards face up on the table; four transports, six cargo, and a pair of crew members. "Trader's Bounty! That's twenty-six points for me."

The players looked up from the game as Sahnuli slid open the privacy shield. He stepped down into the main compartment and folded his fronds in front of himself.

"Remote Base wants us to take a preliminary look down in the chasm. They are directing two of us to stay with the terrain vehicle. Those two crew members will maintain communications between the away team and Remote Base One. I suggest that Sarah and Phxnolx are the away team. Phxnolx will operate the drone. Sarah, Base informed me you have a background in archeology. I was not aware of that." A faint hint of verbena wafted from the team commander, showing his surprise.

Sarah found everyone was looking at her. "Not archeology. I took a summer internship working with some friends from college on a fossil dig in the North Province. We were looking for the evidence and fossils of the early sauroid plant eaters. Instead, we discovered a primitive Velox hive community that seemed to have no connection with any of the other races. That's it, just the one summer in college." She raised both her hands in supplication.

Phxnolx click his mandibles together. "You were part of the team that discovered the No'lenx hive?" He intently stared at her.

Sarah shrugged. "Yeah. It really isn't that big a deal. There were seventeen others on that dig as well."

"I will accept your answer while maintaining my own choices when it comes to 'how big a deal' the find was," Phxnolx stated firmly. "I am quite satisfied with your ability to assist with this investigation." He cocked his head and his caprice tinged slightly blue in humor.

Laughing, Sarah dropped her head in mock surrender. "I bow to your acceptance."

Less than an hour later, the four members were finishing their final suit checks. Sarah had swapped out her broken computer and flashlight. Gareth then verified her suit's condition a second time prior to anyone descending into the shaft. A double winching arrangement replaced the original, hastily built system. The descent team would use the same dedicated communications line as the first team had used. They also carried several signal boosters in a bag. These they would place as they made their way down the shaft to the large cavern where Sarah had fallen earlier. The boosters would maintain a clear and strong radio signal even after the two were no longer using the communications lines. Two small multi-purpose drones rode in special harnesses on Phxnolx's back.

The climb down the initial section of the shaft was significantly slower than the tumble Sarah had made several hours earlier. The suits were automatically recording video as they descended. At the first bend, Phxnolx drove a support piton into the rock face and hung the first repeater. He pressed the test button and a blue light flashed, blinked several times, and then glowed steadily.

"Topside, Descent. We are at the first bend. Repeater one in place and indicating a strong signal."

"Copy that Descent. Topside indicates connection to first repeater."

They placed three more repeaters, each in the same manner, before reaching the cavern where Sarah had finished her fall.

"Topside, Descent. Phxnolx and I have arrived at my impact point. We are proceeding to the final drop." She paused as the air filled with the buzz of the first drone. The flyer was just slightly larger than her hand. She watched as it lifted from its safety harness and flew down into the shaft at the back of the flat area. "Drone one is operational and on. . ." Sarah glanced over at Phxnolx. He held up three digits. "On video three."

"Roger Descent. You have permission to enter the drop-down. Request from Remote Base One to not disturb the remains. Photos and passive scans only."

"Copy Topside. Passive only."

"I believe that since you discovered this area—"

Sarah interrupted Phxnolx. "I didn't exactly discover this. More like I fell into it."

"Yes." Phxnolx dipped his head in acceptance. "However, you were the first of us here. You should have the honor of being the first down into this area as well."

When Phxnolx started talking about honor, there was no reason to argue. Honor carried significant cultural weight in the Eastern Islands. Sarah nodded and stepped into the hole. The line remained taut, causing her legs to swing free. She keyed her radio. "Topside, Sarah. Ready for lowering."

"Acknowledged. Starting winch."

Gravity's pull drug her down as Topside operated the winch. She steadied herself with her hands as her waist and chest entered the hole. As she passed the lower lip of the hole, she looked up at it in surprise.

"Guys, the bottom of this hole has been reinforced with metal. There is a solid ring about six centimeters thick and twelve centimeters wide. Looks like it is directly fused to the rock." She turned her head back and forth to ensure the camera caught the entire ring.

"I see it, Sarah. Definitely made by sentient hands." Sahnuli's voice was quiet on the channel.

Her legs caught her weight as she reached the floor. She allowed the cable to spool momentarily and then contacted Gareth to stop the winch. She stepped away from the hole cautiously.

"I'm clear Phxnolx. Come on down."

The Velox descended quickly, using his arms and legs to steady himself. Before proceeding, the two paused a moment to gaze around the new area. This cavern was larger than any of the previous ones they had descended through. It was instantly obvious this room had felt sentient hands. From the squared corners to the smooth walls and ceiling, everything showed a non-natural creation. The large air vent and fan set into one wall confirmed the theory.

The remains of the two bodies were on the far side of the room from the fan. Solemnly, Sarah and Phxnolx walked over, their harness lines lifting as they neared the two.

"Fox, I'd like you to video this as I dictate."

The squat Velox nodded once and lifted a small camera. He initially pointed it at Sarah. She began speaking, gesturing slowly with her hands.

"I think the two people may have initially entered the room through the fan shaft at the far end." Sarah pointed and continued. "The cover for the fan is pinned open. The fan itself appears to have been stopped and the fan blades locked to clear a space from the center portion of the bottom." She squatted next to the human remains and Phxnolx panned to the body.

Sarah continued to talk as she pointed at the bone sticking through the leg of the clothing. "This appears to be a compound fracture. There is no way someone with this injury could have made the climb up through the caverns without assistance. Also, depending on where the fracture occurred, they may have bled out before anyone could assist them. Both bodies are wearing similar clothing, though with how they have collapsed I cannot see any writing," Sarah stated as she played a flashlight across the remains. "Hold on. . .Phxnolx, take a look here."

A small circular patch was evident just under the left arm of the empty carapace. Sarah leaned in close, trying to determine what the patch looked like. She could see the outer border was reddish brown, surrounding a pale blue. There were symbols sown into the background. She squinted, trying to determine what the individual stitches represented. Were they a language, number system, or merely decoration? She pondered the question as Phxnolx finished filming the specifics of each. The clothing was a powder blue, with thin white stripes running the length of the arms, legs, and torsos of the two. During the examination, Sarah determined that all visible organic material had been stripped from the bodies. The exposed bones of the human remains were clean, with tiny scratches over the surface of the bones. When she shone her flashlight through the exposed chiton of the Velox, similar scratches fractured the flashlight's beam.

"Scavengers. We found similar markings on the remains we exhumed at the dig. Nothing that would attack or even harm a living person. After death, though, they clean up. I don't see anything obvious that indicates how the Velox passed. However, based on the bodies' positions, I'd venture the two of them died together." She stood up and dusted off her knees. "Perhaps someone with more experience will be able to determine cause of death and such. I just don't have enough information or experience."

Phxnolx nodded and pointed to the unmoving fan at the other end. "I suggest that we now focus our energies on that."

"I agree." Sarah began moving toward the open cover, only to jerk backwards as the harness tightened. "Topside, Sarah. Need a bit more line. We are going to investigate the fan covering." The harness's tension slacked off as the extra line played out from the winch topside.

Using the lights from the two drones, Sarah and Phxnolx examined the fan and opening. The fan was huge, approximately six meters in diameter and apparently electrically driven. Its cover had a handle on the inside and was latched securely to the wall, leaving the dead fan hanging in the space for anyone to examine. Phxnolx sent one drone down first. They watched as the light disappeared into the darkness of the shaft.

With care, Phxnolx drilled a small hole in the wall next to the open fan cover and attached another repeater unit. A blinking blue telltale illuminated as the unit powered on.

A single, unbroken piece of pipe appeared to form the air shaft. The video feed showed a stairwell winding around the shaft, with frequent inspection platforms interspersed. With all the surprises of the day, the sight of an unbroken wall of metal shocked Sarah the most. In her mind, it represented the most alarming condition since it suggested a level of technology well beyond what Arth currently possessed.

"If we continue, we are going to need to unhook from the harnesses." Sarah gestured into the black space. "There is no way we can safely climb these stairs with them on. The lines will tangle as we work our way around the circumference."

"I agree. Topside, Phxnolx. We are unhooking from the harnesses to continue downward exploration. I have placed a repeater unit at this entrance." He paused and verified the steady light on the repeater. "That, and the drones, should allow us to maintain communications. If we find degradation of comms, we will reassess at that time."

Sahnuli's calm voice broke the silence. "Understood. I tentatively agree with continuing the exploration. Video of the stairwell shows it is structurally sound with no indications of corrosion. That raises other questions though. Test repeater comms prior to descending."

"Agreed," he stated, and unhooked his harness, placing it gently on the floor of the cavern.

"Topside, Phxnolx. Comms check?"

The return voice was almost as clear as it had been when the communications cable had been attached. "Strong and clear. You and Sarah may proceed into the shaft. Maintain communications check every two minutes. If after a check you do not hear us, or if communications degrade, return to the cavern and reestablish communications."

"Agreed topside. We will check with you every two minutes. If failure or degradation of comms, return to cavern and reestablish communications." Phxnolx turned towards Sarah. "This is your discovery. You should proceed first."

Instead of arguing, she gave him a half bow and carefully stooped past the fan motor. The large blades were spaced far enough apart to give plenty of room for passage. Once past the fan housing, Sarah found herself on a flat platform with railings to her left and in front of her. To her right, the stairs began their downward turn. She gasped as dim lights sprang to life inside the shaft. The lights appeared to be built into the railings. Since the entire bottom glowed, it was hard to tell if they were a part of the rail or a separate piece inset into the metal. Each light glowed a soft blue-white, with an almost moonlight quality that allowed one to see clearly while maintaining night vision. They were at full brightness along the railing where they stood but faded into dimness the further away the lights were.

"This place has power somehow!" Sarah shouted in surprise. She lowered her voice. "How could it have power?"

"I am not sure. After this long, I would have expected any power source to have become completely inactive. As I would have also expected, some degradation of materials making up the walls and stairwell, but nothing is evident in that respect." Phxnolx waved his hand around the space. "It is an additional egg in the mystery we have encountered."

Sarah sighed and stepped nearer the stairs as Phxnolx followed her onto the platform. "I'm just a simple human. This is getting a bit beyond my levels of acceptable normal."

Phxnolx pressed a series of commands into his arm computer. The drone that had followed them floated quietly into the center of the shaft. "Wall to wall measures twenty-two meters. Also, there is a ceiling eighteen meters above us and several more fans like this one ringing the top." He paused and clicked his mandibles together several times. "Readings indicate the shaft descends one-point three two kilometers to the bottom." Sarah glanced over the edge and down. Below, she could just make out the lights of the first drone.

"Some sort of ventilation system? Drawing air out of the lower section," she suggested.

"Why not pushing air. . .Ah, of course." Phxnolx tapped one digit against his helmet. "There would need to be some sort of center fan to draw air downward. No way that they could push enough air from the top fans alone. However, the side and top fans would be sufficient to draw air upward."

She shifted to radio. "Topside, Descent."

"Topside, loud and clear."

"We have entered the air shaft. There are lights here, came on automatically. I am currently assuming electric, but no proof. The shaft is deep enough we cannot see the bottom. Multiple fan openings along the walls. Drone readings indicate greater than a kilometer to the bottom."

"We intend to continue no further than two full rotations of the stairwell down into the shaft. Video from the drone shows a possible door on that level. After that we will return to the surface."

"Understood Descent. Good luck. Maintain two-minute communications."

"Roger."

Sarah unkeyed her mic. "Down we go," she said as she grabbed the rail and began descending.

Phxnolx came next, the bright lights following them, silently dimming behind.

The landings, each equally spaced forty-five degrees around the shaft, were a blessing. Not all had fans, but several did. Each fan housing was dark; their metallic blinds shut. This prevented the drones or team members from seeing what lay beyond. They paused on each to catch their breath and rest. The descent had taken nearly an hour, but the next platform was next to the wall with the indications of a door.

Sarah found she was attempting to hurry to get there and look the possible door over. She unsuccessfully attempted to dampen the excited beating of her heart. She slowed her steps, letting Phxnolx catch back up. A single green light on the featureless wall greeted their arrival on the platform. It appeared as soon as they stepped off the stairs. Like the railing lights, it was a soft, diffuse glow.

Then the wall silently slid open. Darkness. The lights from the tunnel behind them illuminated only a small section of floor past the entrance. A platform, roughly the same size as the one they stood on, was all they could see. The light from behind gleamed off railings that encompassed the three sides of the platform.

Sarah paused and listened. The new area had an echoey quality that she had encountered the one time she had visited the Grand Caves in Mirasto. The largest cave was nearly four and a half kilometers across and had what the tour termed an "underground ocean", complete with fish. Convinced that the space was significantly larger than the tunnel they had just traversed, she flicked on her flashlight. The light shone outward from the door, its beam clearly visible cutting through the darkness. It formed a fuzzy, wide circle on the far side of the area.

"That's got to be sixty to ninety meters away."

Phxnolx clicked in agreement. He shot a small laser out from the drone, measuring the distance. "Eighty-six meters, exactly."

Sarah stepped forward in preparation to shine the light downward. As she did, the door slid shut behind her, cutting off the faint glow from the passageway and trapping Phxnolx behind it. She spun to reopen the door. There was nothing to see. No button or latch.

Reflexively, Sarah grabbed the railing beside her. She stifled a gasp as the platform suddenly and smoothly began moving downward. Lights sprang on, flooding the space with their full intensity. The sudden brightness blinded Sarah. She squeezed her eyes shut, tears rolling down her face. She shook her head to clear the salt water from her vision, then blinked several times. Finally, she held her hand in front of her eyes until they finished adjusting to the glare. Once she could see, she found herself staring upward as the metal ceiling receded further at the top of the enormous shaft. She keyed her radio.

"Phxnolx? Can you hear me?"

She paused. Not even static greeted her call.

She tried again, angling her head towards where she believed the entrance was, attempting to improve her signal strength. Again, nothing. "Completely blocked, no signals."

Next, she turned her gaze downward. Sixty meters or so below the elevator, a gigantic tank or pressure vessel stood nestled in a vertical cradle. It grew closer as the elevator platform continued its descent. The noise of the passage changed as she passed into the space between the shaft wall and the tank's upper section, the walls of metal compressing the sounds. Her surprised reflection stared back as she passed a set of huge, silvered windows. Almost before she could register the view, the windows disappeared above her. Silently, the elevator continued sliding past the smooth, bluish-white material of the tank.

As quickly as it began moving, the platform stopped. Sarah stepped forward, leaning against the front rail and attempting to get a clear look at the material. A section of flooring slid out from underneath the elevator platform, moving slowly until it pressed against the wall of the tank. It then rose slightly and, with a *thunk*, locked into place with the platform. Sarah took a step backwards, jerking her hands away in shock as the forward railing split in two sections and swung outward. They now formed side safety railings on the extended portion of the platform.

Looking back up at the wall, she could just make out faint lines. She stepped forward for a better look. A touchpad flashed into visibility on the wall, near the right side railing. In addition, a large circular picture covering most of the space inside the lines appeared.

Sarah verified that her suit recorder was still on. She carefully took full motion video and still shots of everything. None of the symbols on the touchpad were from a language she recognized or had ever seen. She then turned to the large picture. The artistic style was similar to the realist method that had been popular four or five decades ago, though there were several differences in tonality and color choice. The focus of the painting was, as far as Sarah could determine, a stylized wooden sailing ship floating through a star-filled sky. Masts rose from the top and bottom of the vessel, sails billowing as if catching the cosmic wind. Several pairs of creatures, wearing what looked like spacesuits, crowded the ship's decks. Surrounding the circular starscape was a solid yellow circle, half a meter thick. Symbols, somewhat similar to the ones on the touchpad, gracefully arched over the top and bottom quarters of the thick circle. These were just as indecipherable as the others were.

Ensuring she had captured all the visible items, Sarah stepped back and turned around. A single green light now glowed softly in the wall behind her. She held her breath and pressed the button. The railings realigned themselves, and the extension retracted underneath the elevator platform. The touchpad and painting vanished, leaving only four thin lines to mar the milky blue-white wall. Sarah sighed in relief as the platform began rising. She was headed back, returning to the surface and the rest of the crew.

". . .and as the door opened, I leapt out. No way I was going back down. Completely caught Phxnolx off-guard. I'd never heard a Velox squeak before. Didn't even know they could." Sarah smiled and leaned back in her seat. "The rest of the story was just us coming back up to the surface. You all have seen that part already."

Sahnuli leaned over and tapped the primary screen in the central portion of the terrain vehicle. "You said you have video?"

"Of course. Hold on." She used the vehicle's wireless network to connect her suit recorder to the video system. The video began playing. It ran for several minutes, then shifted to a slide show of the individual photos of the symbols. Gareth leapt forward and hit the pause button. The screen froze on the close-up shot of the flying wooden ship. He stared at the screen, then stood up and headed for the back of the vehicle.

"By the Holy Rock!" he gasped.

"What. . ." began Sarah. Gareth held up a hand and began rummaging through his personnel locker. He pulled a small book out and closed the locker, then returned to his seat. The rest of the crew leaned towards him as he searched through the last few pages of the book.

"Here."

He slapped the small volume on the shelf below the screen. On the page was a full color painting, the style from several hundred years earlier. A wooden ship sailed upon a blue sky full of golden stars. Two masts with billowing sails stretched out from the sides of the vessel, and stylized Thrynn, Elowan, Humans, and Velox danced upon the deck.

"Where is that picture from?" Sarah asked.

Gareth snorted in surprise and flipped the volume over. Embossed on the reddish-brown leather was the title *The Writings of the Rock*. "I am surprised that you didn't immediately recognize what you had found." Gareth flipped through the book as he spoke. "Somehow you were chosen."

Sarah blinked in surprise. She had not been raised in the Church of the Rock. Few people followed the ancient belief system.

"Excuse me? You just saw exactly what I saw. Video proof. No gods or magic or anything else."

"That is the symbol of Noah, the great creator and savior."

"What I found is something that is going to change a lot of things, beliefs included. Whatever it is, it's been here a long time, and it holds secrets we can't even fathom." Sarah waved at the book. "You might be right in that the symbols are the same. Maybe it is some sort of high-tech temple. That's not what it *felt* like though." Sarah paused, biting her lip in thought.

Phxnolx leaned forward, his chiton darkening into indigo blue in serious resolve. "What did it 'feel' like?"

"It felt like it was ancient. Ancient in a way I have never felt. Not from any ruins or artifacts I have ever seen in a museum or visited. And not only ancient but also preserved and waiting. Waiting for us. . .well, someone. . .to find it."

Sahnuli looked across the table at the other three crew members, then waved a frond. "For what purpose? More importantly, left by whom?"

"I'm not sure of the purpose. We, and by that I mean all Arthlings, are going to need to find what the purpose is. As to whom, all I can guess is that it was left by those who came before us."

Choices

By Christopher Woods

The screen alarms were blaring and I watched helplessly as the pirates closed the distance between the *Speadilus* and their fleet. This was the end for us.

"Engines at maximum," I ordered. "Aim for the center ship. I want ramming speed!"

Yelv Sims, the navigator, looked at me in horror.

"They're going to kill us and then hit the convoy again. They're miners. We can't let that happen if we can help it."

"We're cadets."

He swallowed and hit the engines.

"We could run, sir, lure them away." Alta Kohr, the science officer, suggested.

"We don't have enough fuel to get far enough," I said. "Used too much on the asteroids."

She let out a slow breath, "Then, we do what we must. Are they close enough to get them all in the explosion?"

"They are right now. If they spread their formation? Who knows?"

She nodded and turned back to her station on the bridge.

I gripped the arms of the command chair as the *Speadilus* picked up speed. This was not how I had planned for this to go.

"Sir!" Gaothsin Pearthin exclaimed. "Missiles inbound!"

"Countermeasures!"

"They're not aimed at us, sir!"

The pirate vessels erupted with wreckage and atmosphere just before we reached their weapons range.

I sat back into the Command chair, hands trembling.

I awoke with a start.

"Been awhile since I dreamed about that," I said as I sat up in my bed. Hela Feer stirred beside me and opened her emerald green eyes.

"The dreams, again?" she asked. "Was it the one where we were caught, naked, on the bridge? Oh yeah, that was mine."

I chuckled. "I like yours a lot better than mine."

"Was it bad?"

"It was five years ago." I shook my head. "Been in plenty of bad situations since then."

"You never talk about it."

"No point. It's the past." I stood and crossed the room to enter the sonic shower. Captain's quarters had their perks. Slightly larger than the other officers' quarters and it had its own shower.

When I stepped out, she slipped out of the bed to take my place. Hela and I had been together for six months and I wondered what Interstel was going to say about it. There were no policies forbidding our relationship, but it was frowned upon back at Starport.

The *Calibur* hadn't been back in port for six months and we were coming in fully stocked with cargo bays full of tungsten, platinum, and plutonium. We had some endurium but it was needed for fuel to keep working the systems. We found a good world that I logged for a colony since the last trip home and there should be some MU waiting for us when we got there.

It had been a good run and we would be able to get some upgrades for the *Calibur*.

"Maybe enough to get those engine upgrades," I said softly.

"That'll make Jas happy," Hela said as she pressed against my back and her arms encircled my waist. "But you need to quit woolgathering. If you stand there naked much longer we'll end up back in the bed."

"You're right," I said with a smile. "Very tempting, but Teila and Zelos might mutiny if I don't get there for my shift on time. Hopefully, the two of them haven't come to blows yet."

"Why did you schedule them at the same time?"

"The ship is set to random shifts. It just worked out that way."

"And the Captain couldn't change it?" She pinched me.

"Captain shouldn't have to change it. They can work it out or I'll find a replacement for one of them."

"They're both very good at their jobs," she said. "Teila is one of the best pilots the Academy ever produced and Zelos is a hell of a science officer."

"And I'm hoping they'll work through whatever issues they have. I'd love to hire a medic instead of hiring a science officer or a navigator. MD-345 is a good medic but he's limited to his programming. He'd make a wonderful assistant to an Elowan medic."

"You think we can afford an Elowan medic?"

"It's possible. As long as we don't run into problems between here and Starport."

A short beep came from the console on the wall.

"Maybe I shouldn't have said that." I pressed the answer button. "Danec, here."

"Sir, we've picked up something on the scanners. It looks like a ship, dead in space. No distress beacon. It was pure luck Zelos caught it on a scan."

"I'll be up in five, Teila."

"Yes, sir," Teila Londie said.

I turned and kissed Hela. "Looks like you better get a team together. If it's a ghost ship, we may be able to salvage it."

She pulled out of my embrace slowly. "No rest for the wicked. I'll get a squad of security androids."

"We'll do a scan first, so you'll have a little time to get your team ready. I'll let you know as soon as we get some facts."

She nodded and pulled her uniform from the closet then began to dress.

"Stop watching and get your own clothes on," she said. "Unless you plan to go to the bridge like that."

"Pardon me if I enjoy the scenery for a moment." I grinned.

"That's fine cause I'm going to do the same," she said and motioned toward the closet.

I stepped onto the bridge at just under the five minutes I'd quoted.

"You're usually much faster, sir." Zelos Kan said with a smirk.

"Might have been just a little distracted," I said.

"I bet you were." Teila chuckled.

"Alright," I said with a smile. "How close are we?"

"We'll be close enough for a detailed scan in three minutes," Zelos said. "It is definitely an Exploration Frigate."

"Hela is putting together a boarding party. This could be one hell of a find, but I sure hope the crew are still alive. Dead in space is not a pleasant way to go."

"I've never found a ghost ship before," he said.

"I came across one on my first cruise," Teila said. "They had vented the ship rather than starve to death. I wasn't on the boarding party, but the images were awful."

"I can't think of a worse way to go than to run out of resources in the middle of nowhere," he said.

I agreed with that. It would be a bad end. Whatever we found on that ship, I had a feeling it would be ugly.

"Commencing scan, sir."

I sat back in the chair. It would take at least fifteen minutes to do a comprehensive scan.

The light above the airlock turned green.

"Heads up," I said and reached for the lock controls.

One of the androids stepped in front of me and Hela laughed. "You do *not* lead the boarding party, Danec Pol."

I stopped trying to pass the android and sighed.

She stepped past me, right behind the last android. "Androids first. Captain last."

I couldn't see her crooked grin inside of the helmet, but I knew it was there. I chuckled and followed her into the airlock. After our lock closed the outer door connected to the ghost ship's outer door. One of the androids entered the emergency code that Zelos had pulled from the computers and the door cycled, then slid aside. I'm not sure what I expected, but it looked like any other airlock. At least until the inner lock opened after we sealed the outer behind us.

"That doesn't look good," I said.

"Not good at all," Hela agreed.

The androids entered the passage that was coated in some sort of green substance. It wasn't quite liquid; it didn't stick to the androids' feet.

"You ever seen anything like that?" Hela asked.

"Not that I can recall," I said. "Be careful as we move into the ship. It looks biological."

"It looks like a crystal-based substance," she said.

She followed the androids into the passage that led back to the cargo pods and engines.

"Bridge or engines?"

"Let's check the bridge first," I said. "We can run through the whole front section and work our way to the back."

"Gotcha," she said and ordered the androids to turn right and begin clearing the ship.

We followed them as they entered the other sections at the front of the *Firmament* with an odd sense of familiarity. Her name had been on the airlock hatch. Aside from the green substance, it could have been the *Calibur*.

I pointed at the hatch to the ops section. "All the hatches are jammed open with that green stuff."

"I see that," Hela said. "There's no way to close off any of the areas so far."

"I don't like this at all." My hand dropped to the pistol at my side and I drew it. "Proceed at code yellow."

All of the androids drew their weapons, as did Hela. "They spotted no life signs from the scans."

"Better safe than sorry," I said. "I got a bad feeling."

I reached around and pulled the other handgun from my back holster. Its butt was attached to a hose that ran to one of the square packs on the back of my suit.

"Is that a flamer?"

"Maybe."

"You brought a flamer?"

"What?" I shrugged. "So I brought a flamer."

"What in the world did you think you would need a flamer for? We're inside a ship!"

"I don't know, maybe I want to barbecue something for din—"

I knocked her aside and pulled the trigger on my laser. A large greenish spike protruded from the chest of the android right behind her.

"What the hell are you doing?" she asked. Then she saw past the android that was being yanked forward into the theatre. "Holy hell! Fire, Danny!"

The scene in the theatre was right out of a nightmare. A creature backed away from the hatch with our android. Another leg pierced the android and ripped it in half.

"Retreat! Back to the airlock!" Hela ordered. "Androids are rear guard! Open fire!"

I pointed the flamer into the room and pulled the trigger. The nozzle of the pistol erupted with a forced stream of chemicals that ignited immediately afterward. A stream of flame spouted twenty feet into the room and hit the creature squarely.

It screamed. The sound was loud enough to send me reeling backwards and another android stepped forward to pour laser fire into the thing. It had a large central body and more legs than I was comfortable with. I stepped back to Hela and we backed toward the airlock.

"I don't see how that thing could get out of the theatre," I said. "The body is too big."

"Did you see the back wall? The pile of skeletons?"

"Yeah," I said as we came within sight of the airlock.

Then there was another scream.

"Shit, shit, shit…"

The scream had come from the back of the ship. I looked down the long hall to see hundreds of smaller versions of the creature we had seen in the theatre. There were some bigger versions behind them.

We charged into the airlock and the front of the horde of creatures engulfed the androids. I pointed the flamer out of the airlock door and pulled the trigger again. Hela was at the controls. She shut the lock as we saw pieces of our androids flying out of the pile.

The door closed just as a glob of the green substance erupted from one of the creatures toward us.

The lock closed just in time, and I turned to Hela.

"Don't you even say it," she said.

"That's why I have a flamer."

"I just told you not to say that."

"Oh, that? I thought you were telling me not to say we're going to need some new androids."

"I meant that, too."

"You're going to have to work on those communication skills, honey. That's the only way this thing we have is going to work out."

She raised her hand, made a rude gesture, then cycled the airlock to board our own ship.

"Break the lock," I said. "We're on board."

"What happened, sir?" Zelos asked.

"They have an infestation. I want you to hack their systems and vent the ship."

"That's hard to do with all of the safeties on the hatches, sir."

"Just open the lock. All the hatches are open."

"Umm…"

"Just do it, Zelos."

"Yes, sir."

I watched the exterior viewers as the atmosphere erupted from the airlock along with hundreds of the green creatures. The larger ones had broken apart with the turbulence of the decompression. I watched in satisfaction as the pieces joined the smaller creatures in the vacuum of space.

"I'm not too anxious to get back over there," I said, looking at the others on the bridge. We were examining a detailed scan of the *Firmament*. "But look at those engines. Class Five. We can cut our travel to a third of what we have now."

"We'll have to go back," Hela said. She pointed at a spot on the hull. "Look here."

"She's got missile launchers."

"I saw the video shot from your helmet cams," Teila said. "But we can use those upgrades. We'll need to clean her out and use the grapples to latch onto her."

"Definitely have to do a sterilization," Zelos said. "We can't risk bringing those back to Starport."

"True," I said. "We only have two more security androids so we're going to have to do a lot of it ourselves."

"I'll wake Trivett and Jas," Hela said. "I'm guessing we're all hands on deck for this one."

I nodded. "Everyone will be over there except Teila for the first shift. After that, we'll set up a schedule for working the *Firmament*."

"Probably have to burn that green crap off the inside of the ship. I noticed your flamer did a lot more damage than the laser. We'll need to keep suited up for the whole project."

"I was thinking the same thing. Everyone takes flamers and lasers both. We may need them for more than cleanup if all of the creatures weren't blown out. I really wish the androids weren't taken out. They would get the job done a lot quicker than we will."

"We use the chits we're dealt, I suppose," Zelos said.

"Alright then." I turned from the others. "Let's get to it."

I kept seeing the spiked leg of the creature impaling the security android in my head as we prepped to go back over. How easily that could have been Hela or me was my top thought as we reached the airlock again and locked onto the *Firmament*.

I'd had some close calls since heading to space but this one had been different. It's one thing to command a ship in a battle. It's another thing altogether when it's right up in your face like this had been.

I had a flamer in each hand as the locks opened again.

Where I had shot the flamer the first time as we were escaping showed some cleared deck. It appeared to have disintegrated from the flame.

"At least we know the flamers work," Hela said.

"May as well start right here," I said and stepped up between the two androids. "Once this passage is cleared, we'll work our way through the ship."

The androids moved forward and turned to the right and left to guard the passage for us to work.

"Hang on a minute," I said, noticing one of our first security androids still sitting in the right hand passage. "Thought these guys would have blown out. Android, are you functional?"

"Thirty two percent functional, sir. Legs are nonfunctional, sir."

"We'll get you out of here," I said. "Jas! We got one of the androids you need to take back."

There was a chittering from behind me that my helmet translated. "Affirmative."

The Velox stepped forward and used his front appendages to lift the android and place it across his back. Jas Ferrik was large for his species. He had to duck to enter the hatches and preferred to stay down in Engineering. He was pretty excited about the chance to get those Class Five engines, though.

"I will return."

I nodded and turned toward the right passage. I engaged the flamers and swept them across the deck. The flames left a brownish green powder in their wake and a green smoke as the residue burned.

"We're going to have to vent this every so often," I said as I heard another flamer ignite in the passage going back toward the crew quarters and cargo.

"Zelos, let the android take position down the passage," Hela said.

"Gotcha."

"Trivett, you follow the captain."

"Will do."

Talos Rivett was our communications officer. She could understand most alien languages and over twenty different dialects from the races we were familiar with. Hela had started calling her Trivett from the second she heard the name.

We worked our way forward to the theatre. The huge creature was gone, well, mostly gone. One huge leg was still attached to a bulkhead with some of the crystalline substance. It had tried to anchor itself only to have its leg ripped from its body.

Trivett gasped and I turned around. She was staring at the skeletons that were covered in the substance.

"This was an ugly way to go," I said. "That's why we don't pick up any of the damned lifeforms we see. You never know what the hell you're getting. I'm assuming they captured one of these to get the bounty back at Starport."

"You've seen this before?"

"I've seen something like this. It was planetside. They were hunting one of the big predators on one of those ice planets. Figured they would make enough MU to cover the whole trip. Well, they may have been hunting it, but it was hunting them, too. Killed a third of the crew before they got away from it."

"Did they kill it?"

"Captain was pissed. He hit the damn thing with a ship to ship missile after the landing party got back. It had been immune to the tranquilizer they'd taken with them."

I engaged my flamer across the skeletons and burned the green pile to ash.

It took close to a week to cleanse the ship of the infestation. Most of it would have been fine to let the grunts back at Starport take care of, except the eggs we found attached to the bulkheads of the cargo pods. If those had hatched and gotten into Starport, it could have been ugly.

Finding the Human skeletons was bad but it was almost worse when we found the Velox Engineer. He looked perfectly fine except all there was left was his exoskeleton. He was hollow inside.

Starport Central was growing in the viewer. The round hub spinning above Arth was our destination. It was possible we would take the time to go planetside. The ship upgrades could take some time. We'd found five Class Four missile launchers, Class Five engines and a cargo pod that we could install on the *Calibur*. It was quite a haul.

"Starport, this is the *Calibur*. We have salvage in tow and will need a double docking," Trivett said at the com station.

"We see you *Calibur*. Is that a complete ship?"

"Mostly," she answered. "It is what's left of the *Firmament*."

The coms were silent for a moment. "Dock in bay six. We'll have the engineers move the *Firmament* to bay seven. Were there any survivors? She's been out for almost two years."

"Negative, Control. All the crew were deceased when we found her. There was a predatory infestation. All records will be sent before docking. Perhaps a team will want to go through her before docking on the station."

"Affirmative. In that case, enter orbit and we will send a tug to tether the *Firmament* without docking until recordings are viewed."

"Entering orbit in twenty minutes," she said.

"Acknowledged, *Calibur*."

"Welcome home, team," I said as I eased out of the captain's chair. "I guess we're all ready for some time off the ship."

"Undoubtedly," Zelos said, looking askance at Teila.

"Really?" she shook her head.

I sighed and left the bridge. I really didn't want to replace either of them. They were probably the best on the station at their particular jobs. Either could find a job easily enough, but the *Calibur* would be losing a fine navigator or science officer. I was tempted to fire them both. They'd been much better since we had begun our trek home, but they barely spoke to one another.

I just sighed again and headed to my quarters. I was debating ditching the uniform for my time on station. I wanted to take Hela to the Starport Lounge for dinner. It had been a while since we had been able to eat fresh steaks from Arth.

It took several hours to get the *Firmament* settled with the tether and dock the *Calibur*. It was nice to see the docking bay open where we could have the haulers start unloading the cargo.

I met a Thrynn at the foot of the cargo ramp. "All of it has been tallied up and turned in with the records." I handed it a data slate. "You should be able to verify the weights and check them here."

"It will be done in ssshort time, Human."

"Thanks."

The Thrynn nodded and began waving over his workers. Thrynn were a bipedal lizard race with powerful legs, thick bodies and small arms. This one had a bright coloration with reds and yellows. The brighter colored Thrynn were males.

The haulers were piloted by Humans with some Thrynn mixed in. We stepped off to the side to get out of the way and the haulers rolled into the ship.

"Alright, boys and girls," I said. "As soon as she's empty, you're free for a week. Then we'll see how much time we have left for upgrades. I'll get our pay and send it to your accounts. I'll try to get it done today, but it may be tomorrow since I have to go settle up on the bounty for that world in the G5 system. That may take another day."

"Gotcha, boss," Trivett said.

"As a matter of fact," I said. "You're all free to head on into the station except for Jas. We have to set up our schedule for the salvage and upgrade times. Who knows? We may get enough time to go down and swim in the ocean."

There were several grins as the crew scattered. Hela stayed.

"Meet tonight in the Lounge?"

"Sure thing," I answered. "If you don't mind, can you stop and price us some new security androids?"

"I was planning to head there first. Want to get a room on station?"

I grinned. "Absolutely. I'll get it as soon as the bays are empty."

"I'd like something with a view," she said.

"Your wish is my command."

She smiled and shot off into the station, her flame red hair was visible long after I lost sight of her body in the crowd.

"Humans are a strange race," Jas chittered. "You have living quarters on the ship."

"I'm not arguing, Jas. Humans are definitely strange."

He chittered his laughter. "I can take care of setting up the schedule if you wish to go on into the station.

I will alert you when we have ascertained what is usable from the *Firmament*. I am uncertain about some of the wiring for instrumentation. We may have to reuse our own consoles for the upgrades."

"Keep in mind, we might repair the *Firmament* and hire a second crew to expand our operations. It wouldn't hurt to get a price for a project like that."

"Understood."

"Alright, go ahead. Soon as they finish the unloading, I'll head in to the Trade Depot and swing through Ops. We might get our pay settled today."

He chittered and entered the crowd of beings at the far side of the bay toward ShipCon. I watched as the third hauler rolled out with the heavy container of minerals. This was the best haul we had brought in since I had originally left Starport.

"Well, if it ain't Danec Pol!"

I looked up from the table where I waited for Hela. "Frand?"

"In the flesh," the tall man who had stopped at my table said.

"I thought you were lost out on the rim."

"Barely made it back," he said and slid into the seat across from me. "Been having a run of bad luck lately. Got hit by pirates and managed to get away. Just limped back to Starport. I saw that ship you hauled in."

"Did you now?"

"I did and I might have a sweet deal for you."

"What is it?"

"See, I'm down to the wire on supplies and I have a sweet cargo from planetside that needs to get to Thoss. It's produce and very time-sensitive. After that scrape with the pirates, I can't get there. You just came in loaded to the max with ore so I know you have some MU. The cargo pays a hundred thousand and I'll sell it to you for half. Fifty K just to run it to Thoss."

"What's the produce?"

"It's a fruit, a delicacy on Thoss. That's why the high pay."

"Seems to me you haven't made much of the trip," I said. "I'm not paying fifty K for that."

"Come on, man," he laid his hands on the table. "I'm in a bad spot here. I contracted this cargo already."

"How much damage are you looking at on your ship?"

"Ten K for the new engine, I barely made it back from this one."

"This is what I offer," I said. "I wouldn't even offer this if you weren't from my class at the Academy. I'm taking the engines off the salvage I brought in. I'll give you the ones that come off the *Calibur* in exchange for the cargo and contract. I'll stake you another thousand to get you back on your feet. Best I can do without getting into the crew's percentage and I don't do that."

He sat silent for a moment, then sighed. "Alright, Pol, it's yours."

I nodded. "Meet me tomorrow at Cargo Bay Six. We'll get everything set up."

"Remember, this is time-sensitive, Pol. You'll need to hit the throttle pretty soon."

"How soon?"

"Tomorrow or the next day. If the fruit spoils, they won't pay. It needs to be there in three weeks."

"That's tight, but I can make that."

"Then I'll meet you tomorrow."

He stood up and shook my hand then walked toward the entrance.

There was something a little off about Frand, but I couldn't see much of a downside in the deal except a couple months more in space before we took our vacations. Worst case, I'd use some androids and deliver it myself. Somehow, I didn't expect the crew to pass up their percentages of a simple haul.

My eyes shifted to the person that walked past the retreating captain. Hela was gorgeous in the red, figure hugging dress. Her red hair closely matched the color of the dress and it made her green eyes seem to glow.

I stood up to greet her and I forgot all about cargos and ship upgrades.

"You are absolutely magnificent," I said as I grasped her hand and waved toward the circular booth.

"You're not so bad either, Captain, my Captain," she said with a grin.

"I've been looking forward to this for six months," I said. "And I may have some disturbing news."

"Does it have something to do with the guy that just left the table?"

"It does. We're going to have to put off our small vacation for a couple of months."

"Really?" Her eyes narrowed.

"Before you say anything more, let me tell you the deal. A hundred K for a trip to Thoss. Time-sensitive, which is why we have to leave tomorrow."

"Hundred K? Damn."

"That's what I said. I traded the old engines and a small stake to an old classmate who's down on his luck for the cargo."

"That seems like a pretty bad deal for the friend from the Academy."

"He's not a friend, just a classmate." I shrugged. "He needs engines, we'll have them. I was thinking of refitting the *Firmament* with those engines, but the salvage of the metal alone might be more than the selling price of a ship."

"True enough," she said. "Having a second ship would be a great bonus too, though."

"Agreed. The MU from this trip will be well worth those engines. We can get a Class Three instead of the Class Two."

"That's true too," she said. "What do the others think?"

"Don't know yet. Worst case, we can take androids and run the delivery."

"They're not going to pass up the payday from such an easy job."

"I don't think so either."

Her shoulders slumped. "I guess we don't have a room on the Rotunda, then."

"I didn't say that." I tapped the slate to change the week to a single night. "We still have a night in the penthouse."

"Oh, my."

"I told you, I've been looking forward to this for six months."

"Then you better eat plenty, Captain, my Captain," she said with her crooked grin. "You're going to need all the energy you can muster."

I chuckled and raised my hand for the android that had been waiting.

"What's the biggest steak you have?"

I watched as ten containers were loaded onto the ship.

"Not a very big cargo," Trivett said from just behind me. "What is it?"

"Supposed to be some rare delicacy," I said. "Rich people food. Nothing we lowborn folks could ever afford."

"Well, the pay was too good to pass up," she said as she passed me to enter the ship with her pack.

"I didn't think you guys would pass up this one," I said under my breath.

Trivett was the last one to show up. The rest of the crew were already on board, and I only needed to do one thing before we left.

I walked down the ramp and over to a Velox.

"Yes?"

"We all set on the breakdown of the *Firmament*? Anything I can use on her needs to be pulled. I want that armor, too. We'll talk about the disposition of the rest when we get back. The electrical systems are completely fragged. It may be best just to scrap her."

"Electrical systems can be replaced, Captain. I will have you a total for a rebuild if you wish when you return."

"I'd like that, Tryptichishic."

The Velox shook his head and his mandibles clicked with laughter.

"How bad did I mess your name up?"

"You have called me the inside of a particularly nasty rodent."

"Well, shit."

"At least you tried. Just call me Tryp."

"Tryp, it is. I'll be back in about two months and we'll get on these upgrades."

The Velox nodded and waved his front two appendages at one of his workers. He was moving back toward the other side of the bay in short order.

I chuckled and returned to the *Calibur*. Shutting the cargo doors behind me, I signaled the bridge.

"We're all buttoned up, Teila," I said. "Get us underway."

We were already pulling away from Starport when I reached the bridge.

"Sorry about cutting leave short," I said as I took my seat in the command chair. "Seemed like a good reason."

"Agreed," Teila said as she steered the ship out of the immediate vicinity of the station. "It's easy money."

"I do wonder what sort of delicacy we're hauling, though," Hela said.

"Some kind of fruit."

"Fruit?" Zelos stood from his seat. "For the Thrynn?"

"Uh, yeah."

"Oh, no."

"What?"

"We have to go look at the cargo," he said. He was already heading for the turbolift.

I had a sinking feeling in the pit of my stomach as I followed the science officer.

"What the hell's wrong, Zelos?"

"I pray it isn't what I think, sir. If it is, your 'friend' from the Academy isn't a friend at all. He may have just gotten us all killed."

"Now that's not what I wanted to hear," I said.

"We'll know momentarily," he responded.

"Shit," I muttered.

Zelos opened the hatch to the cargo pod and we stopped in front of one of the containers.

He took a deep breath and unlatched the top to peer inside. He stared into the container for a full minute. When he turned back to me I grimaced. His face was pale as a sheet.

"We're completely and absolutely fragged, boss."

"What is it?"

"They're called Headfruit."

"Okay?"

"You know that Elowan are plants, right?"

That's when the term clicked in my mind. "Gods!"

"Then you know what they are? They're on the list of things that are forbidden for Humans to even see."

"It's a fragging death sentence to be caught with them by the Elowan," I said. "What the hell was Silas doing with these?"

"I don't know, sir."

"I don't either, but I'm about to find out. I'll be in my ready room. I have to see if we can find a way out of this."

"I'll inform everyone else," he said.

"Do that. I'll signal when I need you all in the ready room. Tell Teila to slow our speed until we can figure this out."

"Yes, sir. This is a hell of a mess, Danny."

I nodded and headed for the turbolift. My left eye was twitching as I stood in front of the viewer. "Trivett, hail the *Windzori* on a secure frequency. Put it on my screen."

It took a few moments but soon enough, I was staring at Frand as he lounged in his command chair.

"Well, hi there, Danny boy."

"What the hell kind of game are you playing, Frand?"

He laughed. "I guess you looked in the boxes."

"I did," I said through clenched teeth.

"All you gotta do, Danny boy, is deliver the cargo. You're away from the station free and clear."

"Where did you get these?"

"You'll hear, soon enough, I suppose. There was an Elowan transport convoy that was hit by pirates last week. Completely destroyed, they were. Seems the pirates found something."

"You've gone pirate, Frand?"

He shrugged. "They were just Elowan."

"These are children, Frand!"

"Not yet," he said with a grin. "Just deliver them to Thoss."

"I'm returning to Starport and…"

"I would watch the system warnings before you do that," he said. "They just started searching ships as they dock."

"I'll tell the authorities," I said.

"I'll deny it and you are in possession of contraband, so…"

"You're a bastard, Frand."

"Maybe. Who knew they would have a laser mount on that transport? Screwed my engine up pretty bad. Anyway, report me and you report yourself. Just deliver the cargo and count your MU."

He cut the signal.

"Shit."

"What are we going to do?" Trivett asked. "None of us even thought of looking in the crates. They're babies."

"The choices are few," Jas chittered.

"That's a fact," I said. "I, for one, can't deliver these to the Thrynn for them to eat. Can't. Won't."

There were nods around the table.

"The best I can do is transfer everything I can to your accounts, and I'll take the cargo to the Elowan. You'll need to get your things and use the escape pods to return to Starport. I've got enough from the last haul to have the *Firmament* brought back to functional. You guys will be the owners—"

"Just a damn minute," Hela interrupted. "I won't be leaving, so you can shove your stupid plan up your—"

"Illustrious backside!" Trivett finished.

I stopped and looked at the two women. "I'm not sure we can survive this. It's not too late for you guys."

"I'm with the ladies on this one," Zelos said. "You've gotten us through a lot of bad situations, boss. Not gonna leave you holding the bag on this. We all should have looked in the crates. We let the 'easy money' distract us."

"I don't think there'll be any escape pods leaving the ship today, sir." Teila shrugged. "So what is plan B?"

I looked at Jas.

"I am waiting for this plan B," he said.

"Bunch of damned fools."

"Takes one to know one, sir," Zelos responded. "Now… plan B."

I glanced at Hela.

"You owe me a month on the Rotunda with a view. You won't be getting out of it that way."

I let out a long breath. "Okay, I'm calling someone on Elan. I met him at the Academy."

"You sure about that?" Trivett asked. "The last Academy guy is a pirate and a murderer."

"This guy is a little different."

"How so?"

"He was my best friend. He's the only one I can think of to call who may not order us killed right off."

"Then let's do it," Hela said.

I clicked a button on the arm of the chair. "Record message. Yo Veg, how's the world treating you? I've found myself in a predicament and I need you to contact me. This is important. Life or death, brother."

"I need that sent to Elan, Trivett. To Doctor Saamyaan Deeevaas."

"Did you just call the doctor a Veg?" Zelos asked.

"Maybe."

"I begin to wonder if we've made the right decision here."

"We have," Jas chittered. "This one remembers Saamyaan Deeevaas."

"You know Sam?" I asked.

"This one was training in Engineering when Saamyaan was training in Medical."

"I see."

"This one remembers you too, Captain." He chittered his laughter.

"Alright, let's get back to our stations and set course for Elan. Hopefully, he'll respond."

Barely a half-hour passed before the comms chimed.

"Hail from Elan, sir."

"Put it on the screen."

The screen focused on a green and yellow visage.

"How's it hanging, Veg?"

"It hangs low, Meatsack."

I heard a snort from navigation.

"It's good to see you, brother."

"I am pleased to see you as well, my friend. You seemed to be quite troubled in your message. Is it more pirates?"

"Pirates?" Zelos asked. "How did he know that?"

"You aren't being attacked by pirates again, are you?" Sam asked.

"Again?" Hela raised an eyebrow.

"Perhaps they should hear about your adventures on the *Speadilus*. They are aware of who they are working for, are they not?"

"Mostly," I said.

"You were on the *Speadilus*?" Trivett turned from comms to look at me.

"It was his Captain's test cruise," Sam said with a wide grin. "I was on my medical test cruise at the same time."

"You guys were lucky the *Sarnov* showed up and took out that fleet of pirates," Zelos said.

"Half of a fleet of pirates," Sam said. "Your illustrious leader destroyed half of the fleet before the *Sarnov* arrived."

"The test cruise is unarmed," Trivett said.

"Ah, but our friend is never unarmed. With grapplers and a profuse amount of Endurium, he destroyed three vessels by throwing asteroids at them."

"Really?" Teila asked.

I shrugged. "It's a story for another time. We need to talk, Sam. Hypothetically, what would happen if a human was found with fifty Headfruit?"

All emotion left his face. "Please do not tell me this is happening right now."

"Sam, do you remember Silas Frand?"

"I have conveyed the situation to the Elders, and we may be able to salvage the situation if you can bring them all, healthy and unspawned to Elan and turn them over to me."

"Unspawned?"

"They cannot spawn without an Elowan to bond with. If they spawn without, they will fall into insanity and need to be euthanized. If that happens, I cannot protect you, my friend. It is a charge of murder and punishable by death. How close are they?"

"I have no idea."

"What color are they?"

"Green with a little yellow."

"Then make your best speed. Be thankful to the Goddess that they were not red. When they are red, they are on the cusp of spawning."

"We'll get there, Sam. You have no idea what this means to me."

"It is the least I can do, my friend. Speed of the Goddess be upon you."

The viewer cut off.

"Let's kick this pig," I said. "Best speed to Elan. I want to check the status of the other crates. If there are any dead ones this may be a lost cause."

"I'll join you," Zelos said as I headed for the turbolift.

I held the door for him and Hela who was being quiet.

"I thought Captain Salvus was awarded for the victory in Q432," Zelos said.

"They didn't want to let it out that an unknown cadet took out half of that fleet. Salvus is the son of one of the CEO's of Interstel."

"That doesn't bother you?" Hela asked.

"Not in the least. It made the rest of my time there much easier. Got the ship I wanted and Interstel gave me a little boost in capital when I launched. I damn sure left there with a laser instead of unarmed like most of us did."

"I remember my first cruise." Zelos shook his head. "Lost half the crew on a planet in the G824 system."

"There was a lot of that in the initial explorations," I said. "I almost lost the *Calibur* to a mutiny after an attack that took out three of my officers. I started hiring a security officer after that."

"Who was the mutineer? I never heard of that when I researched your history before hiring on."

"It doesn't matter," I said as the lift opened. "He didn't make it back."

"I wondered why you always wore that," he pointed at the laser on my right side.

"I don't have to worry about that now," I said. "When you have a crew like this one, *that's* when you don't have to worry about it anymore."

They followed me into the cargo pod and I pointed to one of the crates we hadn't opened. "I guess we'll start at each end. Hela, you get that one. I'll take this one."

"I got this one," Zelos said as he tripped the latches on another crate.

I opened the top of the one in front of me and looked inside. The fruits inside had been separated and were already a little rounder than the head of an adult Elowan, but I could see the resemblance and I could almost see a face in its contours. I could almost see a baby's head when looking at one of them.

"These are all green with a touch of yellow," I said and closed the lid back down on the crate. I could hear a light hum from the box as I latched it.

The next crate held five more and I noticed on the underside of the lid was a light.

"This must be a grow light," I said.

"They need light to stay alive. Elowan, like plants, use photosynthesis to survive."

The third was much the same as the others.

"Frag!" Hela said from the final crate. "You're gonna need to see this."

I sighed and looked inside the crate. All of them were green and yellow except two. One was in the process of turning orange and the other? Well…

"Oh shit."

I tripped my comm. "Teila, have you ever run a Flux point?"

"Um… once. They're pretty complicated."

"We don't have time for the normal. We're going to have to."

"Setting course for the nearest Flux."

"Best speed," I said. "This one is as red as Hela's hair."

"Oh my."

The ship hummed louder as Teila accelerated.

Fluxrunning was the only chance we had of making it to Elowan in time. Unlike trips through hyperspace, if you run a Flux point, travel is instantaneous. But if your calculations are off, even a fraction, well. There were ships that have never come out of the Flux.

"Two point three hours until we reach the Flux, sir."

"Gotcha, Teila. Let me know when we reach it."

Hela and Zelos had returned to the turbolift, but I still sat there looking into the crate as the clock counted down. Even with the Flux, it was close to two days from the exit point to Elan. It would be a miracle if we managed to get there in time.

"Entering the Flux in ten… nine… eight…"

Two multi-hued eyes stared up from the inside of the crate.

"Three… Two… One!"

"Oh shit."

We were met on the landing pad by at least forty Elowan. Standing in the forefront was Saamyaan Deeevas. We began to push the crates toward the ramp but a group of Elowan almost pushed us aside.

"These ten crates?" one of them asked.

"Yes."

They hurriedly pushed them out of the cargo pod and back to the waiting crowd.

"Moment of truth," I said as we walked closer to the group opening crates.

Sam opened the crate where the red one was. He stopped abruptly as he looked inside, then bowed his head and closed his eyes for a moment.

I stopped a few feet back from the crate.

"How long ago did it spawn? Where is it?"

I swallowed. "Two days."

"Irretrievable," he looked as forlorn as I had ever seen him. Even worse than the moments when we were about to ram another spacecraft. "Where is it?"

I shook the long coat I was wearing. "Yo, Twig. Come on out."

I felt the small hands as they leveraged the kid around my waist to poke his head out of the coat at about chest level. I placed my arm down and across to let the tiny Elowan climb out.

"It is… intelligent? Coherent… Oh… He is bonded! How is this possible?"

"I don't know."

"Unbelievable."

"So what happens next, Sammy?"

He shook his head, looking at the kid in wonder. "I have no idea. This is unprecedented. The law is clear that you will be arrested because of the spawning. But this?"

"My crew didn't have anything to do with this, Sam. I took the cargo. All they are guilty of is being loyal to a fault. They wouldn't leave me."

"They are a good crew then," he said. "Much like their Captain. Not many would risk as much for my race. Most would have taken them to Thoss for the MU."

"I don't think so," I said. "Some would have, yes. But most? I think we're better than that."

"And I applaud your faith in your race, my friend."

"We do have some bad apples, though. And as soon as we can get the kid to some good Elowan parents, I intend to go back to Starport Central and shoot one of them."

"Silas Frand is no longer on the station, my friend. My sources say he left less than seventy-two hours after you departed. Someone warned him of our edict before it reached the port. Frand has powerful friends, somewhere in the management of Interstel."

"Damn. Then I'll just have to hunt him down."

"That is if the Elders let you leave."

"What? The kid's fine. He didn't wig out at all. We just need to find him, someone, to…"

I stopped at the look on his face. "I'm not going to like this, am I?"

"You can't just transfer the bond, my friend. There is only one way to transfer that and it is not one I will even think about."

"Death," I said.

"That is the only way to transfer."

"Can my crew go?"

"I will do everything in my power to see to it they are safe."

"Then I guess we need to go see your Elders and see how they take all this. Just give me a minute."

I walked back over to the crew. "Looks like I'm going in to face the music. I think you guys are going to be safe. Sam said he would do everything he can." I stopped in front of Hela. "I left instructions on the slate in our room. When this is done, you have to follow them."

"You think they're going to kill you."

"I figured that when the kid spawned."

"Then why did you come?"

"Saved fifty kids. *That's* a good way to go."

"I am not leaving you, you ridiculous—"

I kissed her.

"It's been the best six months of my life." I whispered in her ear. "Just get back on the ship."

She pushed me back. "I will not. Whatever you face in there, you face with me at your back."

"Just get back on the ship you crazy woman."

She raised her hand with a rude gesture. "You owe me a month on the Rotunda."

I shook my head and turned to the others. "The instructions are in my quarters. Just…"

One by one they all walked to stand with Hela.

"Fragging idiots."

The huge council chambers were almost empty. I sat in the front row facing the Elders with my whole crew sitting beside me.

What the hell were they thinking? They were all crazy.

"Captain Danec Pol," the Elowan in the center addressed me. "Please rise and approach."

The Elder was purple and green in hue and his hair/fronds were six inches longer than those of the other Elders.

I stood and walked forward feeling the kid shift grips and move up to my chest. I dropped the arm for him to climb out. When I stopped in front of the huge Elowan, Twig was sitting on my arm with his feet dangling. He stared intently at the Elder.

"You have been charged with transporting forbidden contraband. The penalty of even possessing one of these is a death penalty. You came to us with forty-nine."

"Fifty."

"This one is a totally different matter," The Elder said. "I am the Speaker for this hearing. You may refer to me as such."

"Speaker?"

"Yes. As I have stated, you have been charged with a grievous crime. These charges were agreed to be mitigated if you brought them all here unharmed. And each of those forty-nine charges have been mitigated. But you did not bring this one back in the same state."

"I beg to differ," I said. "Twig is unharmed. He bonded to me right after he spawned. He's healthy as can be."

"But he is not an unharmed 'Headfruit', which is what was agreed upon."

"Semantics," I said.

"True." The big Elowan looked down at me. "Our first deliberation was to have you executed and the child bond to one of our own. But how can we do that to one who has brought fifty of our young back to safety? We cannot, in good conscience, do such a thing."

"Thanks?"

"Don't thank us yet," he said. "We will award you sufficiently for your and your crew's role in saving these children, but you are tasked with raising this one."

I looked down at the kid. "Raise him?"

"You are his Sire until he reaches his majority."

"Really?"

"That is your duty. Unless you would rather accept the first option."

"I would be delighted to raise the kid," I said.

"I thought that might be your answer, Captain," he said. "Rest assured it will be under strict supervision."

"I live on a ship," I said. "We travel, explore, and work all parts of the galaxy. It's a hard life."

"A hard life inspires one to grow strong. Judging by the loyalty shown in the crew that follows you, he will have a benevolent environment. We will give you all of the information you will need and you will keep us apprised on the young one's life. I understand you have named the child Twig? Is this correct?"

"That's just a short version of his name."

"And that name?"

"Sprout Twiggerson."

I heard a snort from behind me and it took a moment to realize it was Sam and not any of my own crew.

"His name will be added to the scrolls. Keep him safe, treat him well, teach him the values we have seen in you and your crew. We will be watching."

"Thank you."

The Elder nodded. "You are free to return to your ship. You will be joined by an agent of the Elowan. He will see to it that your holds are filled before you leave us. We owe you much gratitude."

"May I ask something?"

"Yes."

"What about Silas Frand?"

"If Silas Frand is sighted, he will be killed on sight."

I smiled. "Good enough. If I find him first, you won't need to."

"Then we are in agreement. The speed of the Goddess be with you and your crew, Danec Pol. And learn well, young Sprout Twiggerson."

I turned away from the elder chuckling. "Hear that, Twig?"

He twittered something.

"Yeah, me too."

Hela stepped to my side and Twig jumped to her and nestled into the crook of her arm.

She looked at me with one eyebrow raised. "Don't even say it."

"Wouldn't dream of it… Mom."

"I just said not to say that."

"I thought you didn't want me to comment about what he's using for a pillow."

"I meant that too."

"Communication. Remember?"

Her other hand raised in that rude gesture again.

"If she does that again, kid, pee on her."

"Wait… what?"

I strode ahead of the group with a huge smile on my face and found myself beside Sam. "You know, I have an opening for a medic on the *Calibur*. How attached are you to working on the homeworld?"

"The Elders have mentioned a post as an observer to the raising of the child."

"Before the hearing?"

"Yes."

"So, you knew they weren't going to kill me and didn't tell me."

"Perhaps."

"That's just mean, man… mean."

"You deserve it for naming the child Sprout Twiggerson."

I chuckled. "Maybe so."

"Thirty minutes to Starport," Teila said.

"Good," Zelos said. "I'll be glad to get off the ship for a while." He was looking at Teila when he said it.

"We're being hailed, sir," Trivett said.

"Put it on screen."

The viewer lit up and I was looking at Silas Frand. He looked just a little bit disheveled.

"Well, isn't it the hero of the day?" He sneered. "You have no idea how troublesome that edict is turning out to be. You outed me as a pirate and I can't even dock at Starport anymore. I just decided to let you know that you've made me a wanted man, and I think I'm going to kill you for it. When you least expect it, there I'll be. Oh, by the way, I took my fair due before I left the station. I have these nice Class Five engine nacelles now. Been nice doing business with you."

The image shut down.

"You know," I said. "It's been a pretty good day and I'm not going to let him ruin that, even with losing that engine. Let's get down there and get our vacation on, then you two can quit faking the animosity."

"What?" Zelos asked.

"When I messaged Teila about this thing, I saw your uniform hanging on the rod behind her."

"You did not," Teila said. "It was on the…"

I laughed. "Gotcha."

Black Box Blues

By Philip K. Booker

"Hey, McConnell!" an angry male voice called out my name. A rapid burst of chittering followed it quickly afterward, a common tic in an irritated Velox. "How's about you tell this walking tin-can to pour me a sticky fruit cocktail and stop with this pay upfront nonsense? I'm good for the money."

I carefully set the keg of East Arthian Ale behind the counter of the bar. *My bar.* Turning to see what the fuss was about, I caught a glimpse of the blue compound eyes of my addresser. "Yeah, that's a hard pass, Xenon. No more tabs. I want to see chits on the table, before there's a glass in your buggy little hands. And don't be mean to M-09, he's made of better stuff than tin. You'll hurt his feelings."

M09332's head swiveled around, his luminous red optical sensors gazing flatly at me. "He cannot hurt my feelings, Evan. I do not possess such qualities."

Ugh, Androids…

"I know that, Buckethead. I was standing up for you. Jeez."

Xenon's mandibles flexed back and forth. "Come on, are you seriously going to bust my gaster about ten lousy MU?"

"Plus, tip. And you're damn right I am. Word around the Port is that you did Borno dirty. I'd like to have credits on-hand, in the unfortunate case that she finds you before you settle up."

"That's just a simple misunderstanding," he said, even as his antennae twitched nervously.

"All the same. Pay the android, and you'll be sucking on cinnamon-y goodness in no-time."

"Fine, you ginger-headed jerk." He slapped his debit chit onto the bar and slid it to M-09. "Just don't act like you've never had a deal go sideways with a partner."

"I choose less-lethal partners, though." Sadly, that spoke *more* to just how dangerous Borno was, than it did my choice in patronship. I nodded to the android as he processed the chit, and M-09 poured the squat Velox his drink. "Seriously though, you need to settle up with her soon or not even a jump to *Regulon-7* will keep her from hunting you down."

A look that nearly resembled a smile crossed Xenon's buggy little face, and he started to say something before I silenced him with a quick shake of my head.

"Evening Constable Ndango," I said, making a vain attempt at a warm smile to the tall, stern human woman in the dark-red uniform of an Interstel security officer. The overhead lighting highlighted a faint silver undertone in her deep-umber skin, especially over her clean-shaven head. "What brings you to the Black Box tonight?"

Ndango's eyes narrowed as she cut through the insincerity like a plasma blade through steel. Her gaze fell over everyone in the bar. "That walking houseplant of yours put a request into Operations that stated you wanted the teleporters around your establishment deactivated. I need to know why we should consider such a ridiculous request?"

I glanced over to Tyelehn. The blue-green six-foot tall plant-creature was busy cleaning several tables off in the corner with its five arm-vines. It was hard to take it seriously while it had a stash of cleaning supplies hanging in the apron draped around its neck. But Tyelehn is good people, even if the hermaphrodite thing took me a minute to adjust to.

"And I need to know why everyone is being rude to my staff tonight? Tyelehn is Elowan, not a walking houseplant, and a valued member of my team. And I had it deliver that request because I don't want people materializing out of thin-air only meters from my doorway."

"No one else on this starbase has had any problem with the teleporters, not even Xinoktzi here," she said gesturing to Xenon; I noted she used his legal name, instead of his shadier fence name. "If a pawnbroker doesn't take issue with people materializing outside of his establishment, it seems suspicious that you would. Unless you are engaging in activities that are not permitted…"

I'll give Xenon credit, he just sipped on his cocktail and left me to twist in the breeze, rather than risk the scrutiny of Constable Ndango. Not that it helped me any, but I'd have probably done the same thing if I'd been in his shoes—if Velox wore shoes.

"I had a few folks dine-and-dash on me last week," I said, surprising myself with how quickly I came up with the deflection. "They ported right out of here, to the planet's surface or who knows where, as soon as they got out the door. It wasn't enough chit to make it worth filing a report for, but I can't have that becoming a habit. I just want enough of a buffer zone that I don't have to hire on a sprinter to sit by the exit to keep my profits from running out the door."

That seemed to appease her. I caught the hint of a smile on her face.

"I suppose we can establish a zone of twenty meters around your bar with inactive teleportation. Or do you need more room to catch up to someone?"

"Is that a short-joke, Constable?"

She looked down at me and smirked. Sure, she had several inches on me, but five-seven is *not* that short for a grown man. She's just freakishly tall. Really.

"First you call my Elowan friend a houseplant and now this? You're gonna end up in sensitivity training if you're not careful. It'd be a shame if someone were to say something to Starport Operations. I mean, Interstel's fines for employee misconduct are surely not as steep as the ones they levy against the space jockeys that they have to fish out of the Black. But why risk it?"

Her jaw tightened hard enough to crush mining slag. "You wouldn't dare."

I held my hands up innocently in front of me and flashed my best smile at her. "Now, did *I* say that *I'd* do something like that? No. I just said it'd be a shame if something like that *happened*. I'm looking out for *you*, Ndango."

"Yes, well then. Like I said, I'll pass the recommendation to engineering." The stare of barely restrained violence belied her placating words, but she left without unleashing any of it in my direction.

I'd probably pushed her a little too much this time. It was a dangerous game I played with her. But it was just so much fun.

Activity at Starport Central had ramped into high-gear the last few weeks. Interstel had made some kind of big announcement that had gotten the space jockeys all hot and bothered. Ships were constantly blasting off into the Black, seeking fortune and fame among the stars. Personally, orbiting above Arth was enough excitement for me. At least if things went tango-uniform on the

Starport, I could jump planet-side quickly enough and take up residence in one of the bunker cities. Out there—well, getting sucked into the cold vacuum of space was a genuine possibility. They'd already lost contact with a pair of their ships a few systems over on their colonization mission. The poor sots were likely all space particulate now.

It's not that I wouldn't mind having a taste of the action coming back from those successful excursions. There'd already been a few crews that had unloaded stores of gold, platinum, titanium, and endurium into the trading post. It's just that I'd prefer to stick to less precarious avenues.

You say coward. I say survivor.

The hum of transporters beamed to life, followed shortly by the agitated shaking of Tyelehn's leaves. It perfectly displayed one reason I had petitioned to get a buffer around the Black Box, as I spotted two of Nyll T'Lathll's scaly flunkies materializing outside the bar.

My opinion of the Thrynn took a nose-dive not long after I brought Tyelehn on as an employee. It'd taken a bit of time for me to sort out a shorthand understanding of the sentient plant's communication methods, mostly based on rattling foliage and gesturing vines. An early lesson was the Elowan race's near extinction at the fangs of the Thrynn. Learning that devouring the Headfruit, or fertilized heads of the Elowan, is considered a sport to the Thrynn was a revolting revelation. Most Arth-based Thrynn play it off like an age-old misunderstanding and have nominally functional relationships with those Elowan on the surface. However, you can still feel the tension in the room at times.

That's not to say that all Thrynn have reformed from their old ways. Nyll T'Lathll's lounge of lizards has always taken particular delight at menacing Tyelehn.

"Yeah, yeah, I see them too! Lock up the front doors, I'll get the back," and I shot past M-09, who was setting down a stack of glasses as I barreled behind the bar and to the backroom.

Which is exactly where I crashed headlong with Nyll T'Lathll and all his scaly bulk.

"McConnell…" Nyll T'Lathll said, with a twist of his long neck to glare at me on the floor. "You wouldn't be trying to prevent me from seeing you, would you?"

"*What?* No! That's crazy, Nyll T'Lathll." I sat up, rubbing the spot on my head that had bounced off of the floor after our collision.

"Because, that would be terribly rude. Especially since I helped front the funds for this bar of yours."

Taking that money had been a low point in my move up to Starport. One I constantly regretted.

My eyes moved around the room as I pulled myself to my feet.

"Looking for *this*?" Nyll T'Lathll dangled the little Class-Three Laser pistol that I kept back here between a pair of his claws over my head.

Damn.

"*Nooo,* don't be daft. I'm looking for… *this!*" I said, grabbing the ale key off the door hook. "So, we can share a drink while we talk about what's brought you in tonight."

The gray scales under his eyes crinkled as he gave me a toothy grin that fully displayed the multiple rows of sharp fangs. "Good. Let's have a toast to tonight's job."

Like I said, I took money from Nyll T'Lathll to make the move up to Starport Central. Planetary prospects were dwindling on Arth, and Interstel was throwing all of its considerable resources into this FTL space program. So, I didn't ask as many questions as I should have and ended up in his debt. You never come between a thirsty man and a drink, and you *never* get under the thumb of an ambitious Thrynn.

I guess that makes me stupid, as well as a coward.

We all have our low points.

Returning to the bar front, I raised my arms in surrender, prompted by the nudging from my own laser to my back. "Hey guys. I'm going to have a drink with our friend, Nyll T'Lathll. Let's all be cool."

M-09 and Tyelehn reacted with as much alarm as you'd expect from a bucket of bolts and a walking topiary and simply watched us come around the bar. For once, though, I was relieved at each of my partner's mutual deliberative and analytic natures. It meant I didn't catch a laser in the back.

"Good," Nyll T'Lathll smirked from behind me. "Now, be a good little pet and let my associates in."

I nodded to Tyelehn, who reluctantly unlatched the front locks, allowing the muscly Thrynn inside.

I pulled down four glasses and a bottle of Arthian Ale, but then Nyll T'Lathll shook his head and held up two clawed fingers.

"We'll only need two glasses tonight, McConnell." Then he turned to his henchmen, and scolded them with hissed contempt, "I cannot believe these lower beings bested you two. You do not deserve any refreshment. Disappoint me again, and thirst will be the least of your concerns."

The pair of henchmen made conciliatory tones in their throats and dipped their heads in subservience to T'Lathll. It was an odd scene. Combined, the pair of mollied thugs looked like they could tear into T'Lathll if given the right opportunity. However, I knew all too well that T'Lathll possesses a viciousness barely pinned behind his manners, like a hair-trigger mousetrap. Memories of him casually ripping the throat out of his former attendant—who had failed to prevent me from interrupting a meeting on Arth— still haunt me to this day. That they'd never found a body was the only reason T'Lathll could still move about the Sector freely. Well, that and an ambassadorial standing with the Thrynn home world of Thoss.

I set the glasses down on one of the twelve high-top tables that filled this end of the Lounge, and gestured to T'Lathll to sit, pouring a generous amount of ale in his glass.

"To profitable endeavors," I said, raising my glass in a toast.

Our glasses clinked together, then we each took a hefty pull from our drinks.

"When does your next shipment of supplies come to Starport?"

"We've got a validated shipment with fryer oil, kegs of ale and a crate of spices from that Colony that was just approved in the next System over from us. That's expected to arrive in a couple days, right?" I glanced over to M-09 for confirmation, who nodded in the affirmative.

"That will do nicely. I'll have your shipment intercepted en route and replace the kegs with my product."

"You understand I run a bar, right?"

"And you understand you work for me, right? You'll do what I tell you to do. Have the android short his pours for the next week, because you're going to have to make do with what ale you have on hand," T'Lathll said with a grin.

I glowered sullenly at him, but relented. "Fine. What is this cargo, anyway?"

"Some kind of ship upgrade. A salvage crew recovered it along the fringes of the Sector, near an unstable Flux Point. I'm told that during the first contact encounter with the ship, the Confederacy ships had their shields disabled with some sort of beam weapon. My buyer offered an entire cargo hold full of Ancient Artifacts for it. Picture it, McConnell. My name will be the talk of Thoss when I return with this haul."

"Good for you," I said with an unenthused toast of my drink.

"Pettiness is such an ugly color on you Humans, McConnell." His long neck swayed rhythmically as he chuckled to himself, "Actually, all your colors are pretty ugly."

"Guess it's a good thing I'm not trying to win you over with my looks then. Why should I care if you're suddenly the toast of Thoss?"

His neck swaying stopped, and I was the focus of all of his intensely reptilian glare. "Because, if I can obtain such an esteemed stature on the Home-world, I will no longer need your services." A slow grin drew across T'Lathll's fangs.

Gulp.

After giving me enough time to sweat, T'Lathll slid a glossy black cube across the table. It took me a moment to recognize the contract cube that I'd taken out with him on Arth to get the funds to open my bar.

Was it too much to hope for? To be free of Nyll T'Lathll for good?

"What are you saying here?"

"Complete this job without complication, and I will release you from your debt, McConnell."

Not asking enough questions is how I got into this situation. I wouldn't make that mistake again.

"If this item is so valuable, why not just arrange a meeting with this buyer yourself, and cut out the Middleman?"

His scaly brow arched in amusement. "Are you telling me you prefer to remain in my employ?"

"Hell no!" I replied quickly, emphatically shaking my hands. "But I've learned you're not the charitable type. And you don't like to take chances. It doesn't track that you'd risk bringing something like this through Starport."

"And maybe you aren't as stupid as you used to be." He reached over and reclaimed the cube, securing it in his suit pocket. "My buyer has developed a reputation for piracy. Not to the level of Harrison's infamy, but Captain Farrow has garnered enough attention that I cannot allow for either the Confederation or Interstel to detect a rendezvous between one of my ships and his own on a transponder scan."

And there was the rub.

"If he's a pirate, how's he supposed to get clearance to dock with Starport?"

"While he's on their Watch List, Farrow hasn't hit an Interstel ship. That they're aware of, at least. So, they overlook his actions, as long as he continues to bring in loads that are not proven to be stolen property. I'll have him deliver the container of artifacts to the Trade Depot, to be verified with the Appraisers. After that, you will show him into the backroom, give him the tech and be free and clear of your debt to me. Not a terrible deal. So, what do you think now?"

I didn't savor the idea of staking my freedom on a deal with yet another criminal. But it's not like I really had much of a choice in the matter.

Raising my glass again, I toasted, "To the deal."

T'Lathll smiled, and we clinked glassware. He finished his drink and then pulled the battery pack out of my laser, before he pushed the weapon back over to me. "Careful, you don't want to go putting an eye out with that little toy there."

Frowning, I took the pistol back, shoving it in the back of my waistband.

"Don't muck this up, McConnell."

T'Lathll snapped his fingers, which brought his flunkies to attention, and they all left out the front.

Two weeks had passed, and things had been relatively calm. I'd dispatched M-09 to the Trade Depot to keep his eyes on the contents of the newly arrived pod. However unlikely, we couldn't risk an appraiser or some other party making off with some of the Ancient treasure. Tyelehn was seeing to some kind of Elowan thing—I've learned it's best not to ask—in one of the Starport's solarium rings. It might be days before my leafy friend would return.

So, of course, I was tending to the bar solo when things took a turn.

"Word around the concourse is that a cargo pod with your name on it is in the Depot, and that it's stuffed to the gills with stuff from the Ancients. How d'you manage that kind of haul?" Xenon sat at my bar again. His mandibles nearly shook with chittering excitement.

He still hadn't settled his deal with Borno, so he still had to pay for every drink upfront. But as long as his payment chit sat between us, I kept the Sticky Fruit Cocktails coming.

"You don't even have a ship, McConnell."

"Ownership is relativistic," I said with a shrug as I cleaned a glass.

He laughed. "Relativistic, I like that. I'm going to steal that."

"You're welcome to it."

True to T'Lathll's plan, they had supplanted the device into my next supply shipment. I'm no engineer. I can't say what I was expecting to find when I opened up the box. But it wasn't the mess of cables and ports that were attached to the black box with its flickering orange lights. I had no idea what the damn thing did. That a pirate would pay a small fortune for it did nothing to reassure me either.

I hadn't slept a wink since the thing had arrived.

"So… you're just gonna hold out on your buddy, McConnell?"

"I don't think anyone would accuse us of being buddies, Xenon."

"Fair enough."

"Anyway, it's not my stuff. I'm just serving as the bagman for an exchange of goods."

Lacking lips, the Velox couldn't actually whistle, but Xenon made the closest sounding thing to it I could imagine. "That's an impressive haul, all the same."

"And I'm expecting the guy who dropped it off any second now. Aren't you supposed to be making tracks to *Regulon-7* by now? Don't think I didn't catch that."

He shrugged, "You've got your problems, I've got mine. Putting distance between me and her is for the best right now, McConnell."

The entrance hatch at the front opened, revealing a stern-faced human man with dark hair pushed beneath a maroon peaked cap, which matched the leather jacket that he wore. Flanking him were a pair of no-neck goons that looked like their images belonged in Astrid's Compendium of Knowledge, beside the entry for Leg-Breaker.

With such a display, the rather sizable laser holstered to the lead man's hip seemed like overkill, but it was the next thing to catch both mine and Xenon's attention. To which, my Velox *not-a-friend* promptly responded to by grabbing his payment chit and shuffling right out the door without so much as another word to me. He didn't even finish his last drink.

The man silently stepped passed his entourage, paying me no mind. He strode through the bar, making an excruciatingly slow circuit of the room. The echo of his flight-deck boots through the empty space made my eye twitch.

Clack. Click. Clack.

Now, I've dealt with a fair number of unscrupulous and intimidating types in my life. Far more since getting mixed up with T'Lathll and his smuggling racket. Two varieties of ne'er-do-well typically rise to the top of the thug crowd. One type gets their way with explicit threats and bouts of explosive violence. The second relies more upon implied danger and coldly executed action. It's the latter kind that makes me really twitchy.

However, one thing that I've learned in those dealings that seems to remain constant: Don't let on just how scared you might be.

I moved my dish rag over the mahogany-stained wood of my bar-top, ostensibly cleaning it. A portion of the rag conveniently concealed the light tremor in my hand. "Captain Farrow, I presume?"

As if he hadn't heard me, Farrow continued to give my establishment an officer's inspection for a few drawn out seconds before turning his steely gaze onto me. "Yes. And you must be T'Lathll's little pet monkey bartender."

I'm not going to lie, that hurt.

Fire roiled in my gut, incinerating the butterflies that had been there moments before. A part of me wondered whether I could take out his muscle with my laser pistol, before Farrow could gun me down. Since T'Lathll had gotten the drop on me, I'd begun storing it in a mount positioned beneath the bar, which was aimed at the door.

Don't be stupid, Evan.

A sudden taste like freshly milled copper swirled around my mouth as I bit down on my tongue hard enough to make my eyes water.

I cleared my throat and blotted my eyes with my dishrag. "Hrmph—ah, yeah. I guess that's me."

"The assessors ought to conclude their inspection of the cargo any moment," he said with a glance at a chronometer on his wrist. "I would very much like to see my goods. We have a tight schedule to keep." His other hand remained far too close to his holstered weapon for my liking.

"Yeah, sure."

I stooped behind the counter and hoisted the container that resembled a large keg up onto the counter. On a small keypad beside the coupler, I entered the five-digit code that T'Lathll's couriers had given me. A pressurized hiss escaped the apparent keg, as a vertical seam along the container revealed itself, splitting it down the middle. Pulling the two halves apart, the eerie black box was on full display. An awed smile oozed across Farrow's face, and I wasn't sure whether I was that or the device creeped me out more.

"It's a thing of beauty," he said, the flickering orange lights shining into his dark eyes.

"What is it," I asked, a pang of curiosity getting the best of me.

His brow arched, as Farrow's full attention turned on me. "You don't know?"

I shrugged, "Some salvage job from the corners of the Sector that the Thrynn nicked off a ship that plopped out of a Flux. Caused their shields to go tits-up or something."

"It's a Shield Nullifier."

"Hah! We serve a drink by that name here at the Black Box!" The drink is positively pant-dropping in its potency and not recommended for any but those with the hardiest of constitutions; thus the name. Farrow's hard gaze told me he was not amused. "Uh, sounds ominous."

Farrow's eyes fell back onto the device with the same kind of awe I've seen of the faces of new parents gazing on the newborn baby. "If rumors are to be believed, this device has the potential to cripple even the most battle-ready cruiser in the Sector. It can disable the shields of any vessel struck by its blast. With it, we will become so formidable, not even Interstel's new class of starships will be able to prevent us from cutting out a swath of the Sector for our own."

That nervous twitch I'd felt earlier ramped up, and my stomach threatened to mutiny on me. I already knew Farrow was a pirate and that he only steered clear of Interstel craft so that he could still do business with them. But if he and his crew had cause to no longer feel threatened by Interstel's ability to check his ambitions, who could be sure how long that would remain the case.

I've never wished more for something to be a Thrynn con-job before in my life.

The purple notification light of the comms disc on the bar flashed, and I answered the incoming call. A miniature hologram image of M-09 came to life over the disc. Just seeing the animated image of my partner made some of my tension ease a little.

"Talk to me, Buckethead. What's the verdict?"

M-09's holographic head swiveled slightly left and then right, before tilting slightly askew as it stared at me with his emotionless red eyes. "They completed the appraisal. The assessed value is higher than I believe even T'Lathll was expecting."

"I'm not in the business of presuming to know Nyll T'Lathll's desires, and neither should you. Good to hear, though. Have them pack it all up and get it secured for our patron. Then get back over here. Copy?"

"Affirmative," the holographic Android said, nodding. Then the light on the comms disc turned off.

Closing the faux-keg container, I returned my attention to Farrow. Like it or not, I had a job to finish here. "Well Captain, if you're satisfied with the product, how about we wrap up our business today?"

He checked his chronometer again. "Yes, let's do. I have a schedule to keep."

I briefed him over the case and all the ingenious features which were built into it, to convince anything other than a thorough inspector that it was just a simple keg; including a device that artificially mimicked the feeling of a liquid core moving within the keg. It even had a couple liters of ale enclosed within the unit.

Finally, I showed him how to unlock the case and gave him the passcode.

"I rarely enjoy doing business with agents of the Thrynn, Mister McConnell. But you've been most helpful." He ran his hand slowly over the casing. "That said, I feel it I would be remiss if I did not make myself clear that, if you or your mechanical friend do something stupid, like double cross me or report this deal to Interstel, I will come back and take out my frustration on your corpses."

At that, he reached over and grabbed Xenon's unfinished drink, throwing it back in one gulp. He slammed the glass back down with a wink and a full-belly laugh and then snatched the keg off the bar and went out the door. I could hear him and his men singing something off-key as they left to go back to the docking bay.

I waited there at the bar until M-09 returned from the Trading Post. Telling him to close up shop, I went to my office in the back of the bar and collapsed on the lumpy brown sofa that I keep back there. I was out like a light before I knew it.

Hours later, a klaxon alarm ripped me from my slumber. A strip of cove lighting, which ran throughout Starport Central, flared to life with an ominous strobing red color. The alarm stopped, and a computerized voice broke through on the intercoms.

"Red Alert! Red Alert! Unauthorized persons have beamed onto the Starport. Please take shelter within your quarters while Security sees to this matter. We have temporarily disabled all teleporters within Habitat Sectors Four through Twelve until the perpetrators have been apprehended. We apologize for any inconvenience. Thank you and may the Rock of Truth shine upon you!"

I glanced up at the Station Map that was hanging on the wall. The 'You Are Here' indicator on it clearly showed us as being within Habitat Sector Nine.

Well, ain't that just great.

My head was pounding, but I'd used the last pump of my pain-relieving spray after a bar brawl broke out last week over some Space Jockey eating the last of his crew's communal basket of cheese fries. I'd caught a stool to the head, while trying to break it up.

I pushed myself off of the couch and fumbled back into the bar. We'd closed even before the lockdown. The bar was only dimly lit by the combination of the pulsing red alarm along the ceiling and the shifting colors in the faceplate of the retro jukebox.

Oh well, if I had to hunker down until this was over, I was damn sure going to need a drink.

Two fingers of whisky later, I saw something move to my right, out of the corner of my eye. I ripped the laser pistol out from under the bar. Spinning on my heel, I took aim to blast—before powering it down again as I made out the silhouette of M-09.

"You worthless bucket of bolts! I could have blown your processors clean out of your head!"

"Apologies, Evan. I did not mean to frighten you. I am monitoring the radio communications from the Security Teams in this Sector and have downloaded their data report that led to this incident."

"Wait—you can do that?"

M-09's unblinking red eyes regarded me for a moment. "Of course. It is a simple matter."

"So, what kind of idiot teleports onto Starport Central without authorization," I said as I poured myself another bit of whisky.

"Pirates," he answered flatly.

And I dropped my glass.

"*What?*"

"It would seem that a starship carrying a sizable haul of Endurium was scheduled to make a delivery to the Trading Post today. Shortly before it entered Arth's orbit, a previously undetected Corvette swooped in upon the Trader and hailed it."

A sick feeling in my gut started forming, threatening to bring my whisky back the wrong way.

"The captain of the Corvette demanded the Trader turn over its cargo, or it would attack it."

"So close to Starport? That's insane."

M-09 nodded. "It would seem that the captain of the Trader concurred with your assessment. They refused. The Corvette then engaged some unknown manner of energy weapon, but it malfunctioned and crippled their own vessel instead. Starport engaged a tractor-beam to tow the Corvette into custody, but the crew of the pirate vessel managed to teleport themselves aboard instead. They have already killed two Security personnel and wounded three others."

I tried to swallow the acid crawling up my throat. "Has Security identified anyone in this group of pirates?"

Please don't be them. Please don't be them.

"Affirmative. They have positively identified one of the raiding pirates as Captain Farrow."

"Oh, *come on*! We've got to get out of here. *Now!*"

I frantically closed the cap on the bottle of whiskey, almost putting it back on the shelf, but then I shoved it under my arm instead. M-09 watched as I raided the bar for supplies.

"They instructed us to remain here. Why do we need to leave?"

"Because that lunatic knows exactly where to find us here," I growled, tossing anything that looked useful in a sack. "And I'll be damned if I'm going to make it easy for him to kill me."

We made it as far as the lifts before the shooting started.

The first shot whizzed past my head, striking the wall beside me. M-09 shoved me to the ground behind an access panel. The next three blasts hit him in shoulder servos in rapid succession. His left arm all but fell off as he collapsed to his knees beside me.

"Bastards!"

I popped out from around M-09 and returned fire. Three shadowy figures at the end of the corridor scattered immediately, but a pained groan told me I'd hit something.

M-09 pulled me back behind cover with his remaining arm. "Evan, you cannot stay here. We are outnumbered, and without sustainable cover. Statistical analysis of our situation reflects odds that—"

"Don't tell me the odds, Buckethead," I said, popping two more shots down the corridor.

"Get in the lift. Find Constable Ndango or her Security team. The last comms check-in placed her one Habitat Sector above us, near the Solarium Gardens. Go now," he said with a forceful shove. "I will provide you with time."

His last words hit me. "M093332, you work for *me*. Don't you dare try to give me orders," I said, my voice cracking with emotion. "Now get up!"

Another round of blaster fire erupted from down the corridor, forcing us to hug the wall again. The heat coming off of the scorched metal paneling overhead sent pools of sweat down my back. M-09 tore the remnant of his left arm free of his body and flung it down the hall. It smashed into an advancing attacker, sending him crashing limply into a wall. From this distance, I recognized him as one of Farrow's No-Neck thugs from earlier.

Hoping to slow their advance, I sent more blasts back down the hall. The battery indicator along the barrel of my weapon told me I couldn't keep this up, however, even if I could slow their progress. It's not like I'd needed to use my pistol for anything but show since I'd come to Starport.

"I apologize for my insubordination, Evan McConnell," M-09 said, as he wrapped his arm around my waist and pulled me up against his chest.

"Uh, what the—" I wheezed, as it forced the breath out of me.

M-09 whirled us over to the lift tube. His back absorbed the shower of blaster fire, but he wouldn't be able to withstand much more. He called up the lift, shoving me inside.

"Goodbye Evan," he said as the opaque glass doors closed behind me.

With the tube rocketing me toward the next level, I could see the android spin about and charge into the group of pirates. A flood of red light tore into his body. Even his armored casing couldn't hold up against that amount of damage.

Thudding my head against the tube, I whispered, "Goodbye, my friend."

I was still wallowing in my grief when the lift doors opened again, and a blaster greeted me in my face.

Ah, crap.

"Don't move," demanded a familiar woman's voice.

"*Ndango*, is that you?"

"McConnell?" She lowered her blaster, slightly. "What the stars are you doing out of your chambers? Didn't you hear the alert from Operations? I seriously don't have time for your crap tonight. A bunch of crazy jackholes kicked off an invasion of the station, for Rock knows why."

"They're pirates, and I think I know why." I said, shooting a quick glance to the lifts behind me. "I don't have time—"

When I'd turned back to face her, Ndango's blaster was in my face again. "What kind of Spemin-brained stupidity have you brought to my station, McConnell?"

It wasn't until I raised my hands into the air that I realized I was still holding my nearly spent laser pistol. Something that Ndango appeared to note for the first time, too.

"Move a muscle, and I will drop you like drone slag! Why do you have that weapon?"

"That's what I've been trying to say. These guys are here to kill me." My focus broke long enough from the barrel of her weapon to see around her head. "Hey, where the heck is your team?"

"There's a quarter of a million people on this station, and I only have a team of one hundred and fifty onboard. We're spread a little thin, dammit. No one has ever been stupid enough to try to take on a station that can disable a small fleet from orbit." She reached over and took my blaster from me. "Now start talking, McConnell."

"We don't have time! They're just a level below us, and they've already destroyed M-09!"

She lowered her weapon again. "What kind of numbers are we talking about?"

"I only saw three before, but I think there's probably a few more. M-09 dropped at least one."

She stood there for a moment, thinking. "There's not enough time to get a team up here to us. And if we turn the teleporters back online, who knows where they could get to. It's not ideal, but come with me."

She led me down the corridor to a large portal doorway.

"Ditch your jacket out here. If they're after you, better to pull them this way than to risk them running loose in Starport." She pushed a panel button. "You won't want to wear it in there, anyway."

The hefty doors slid open, and a wave of humid air smacked me in the face. My hair felt heavier in seconds. Lush green plant-life of all kinds, mossy mounds, and blooming blossoms filled the space as far as the eye could see. It was like a small jungle aboard Starport Central. Overhead, a transparent outer hull allowed full exposure to the light of the sun to beam into the room.

"What is this place?", I asked, mouth agape.

"This is the Solarium. A private arboretum on the station. It helps produce some of Starport's oxygen and gives us a place to redirect some of the carbon dioxide levels. Now hurry, move this way."

She shoved me along, deeper into the massive space that must take up the bulk of this Section, and then pulled off the pathway that circuited the room. We took shelter along a patch of soft mossy soil, which was sheltered by several thick fronds of a tree.

A few minutes later, I heard the portal doors open again. Rushed, low voices followed soon after, and the clumping of several boots moving through the chamber afterward.

Farrow's booming voice called out, "Come on out, McConnell! I know you're in here! I told you that if you double-crossed me, I was gonna kill you. But did you listen? Hell no! So, let's get this over with so I can go hunt down your no-good, lying snake of a boss next!"

What was he going on about?

I barked back at him, "I don't know what you talking about! I didn't double-cross you!"

The trees did wonders to keep him from pegging where my voice had come from, but Farrow made a flanking gesture to the dozen or so other brutes with him. Ndango jabbed me painfully in my sides, none-the-less.

"Yeah? That worthless excuse for a Shield Nullifier nearly blew up my ship when I tested it out on the ship of pansy Elowan Endurium transporters. It killed half my crew. Did you really think that I wouldn't make you pay for that?"

So that'd been what had happened.

A wicked smile drew across Ndango's face. I was about to ask what was up, but then I heard it.

I needed to keep him talking. "You threatened to destroy that Endurium freighter?"

"Of course, I did," he said, still trying to pinpoint my voice. "Nobody would ever just hand over their cargo if we didn't threaten them."

A rustle of leaves caught the air.

"But you actually tried to do it! Knock out their shields and blow up their ship, because they denied you your prize."

His eyes narrowed in on the patch of forest we were in.

"Well, you can't make an omelet without cracking a few eggs. Sometimes you have to write off a haul as a loss. Though, if you blow up a ship or two, eventually your reputation is such that they just stop fighting. And the Elowan are usually pathetic cowards. One ship down, and I could have had years of easy raiding the routes around Elan." He raised a blaster in our direction. "Goodbye, McConnell."

The quickness in which it happened was amazing.

Vines whipped out of the forest, wrapping around Farrow's arms and neck. He gasped in shock as the vines squeezed and pulled at him with enough force to lift him from the floor. A dozen other similar gasps echoed throughout the room.

Scores of deep-reddish compound eyes came into view among the trees. The Elowan took slow, methodical strides into the light. I even saw Tyelehn among them. Their leaves shook furiously.

Elowan are among the most peaceful and gentle species in the universe. But being hunted for generations, nearly to extinction, has caused an immensely strong protectiveness streak to develop among their race. Reports quickly came into Interstel that ships detected having even a single Thrynn crew member aboard being fired upon, if they entered Elan territory.

And Farrow just announced that he'd willingly attempted to destroy a ship full of Elowan space jockeys.

Ndango stood up, and we both moved out into the open.

"Interstel has only one punishment for those found guilty of piracy. And seeing as you've openly admitted to as much here, I'm just going to save myself some paperwork, and let these aggrieved parties settle their quarrel with you themselves." She turned to look at all the gathered Elowan. "They're all yours. Just don't let the mess leave the Solarium."

The chilling sound of leaves vibrating throughout the chamber made the hairs on my neck stand on end.

Ndango put a hand to my back. I needed no more prompting than that, and we quickly made it for the door.

The strangled screams of the men as we left the Solarium is something that will haunt my dreams for years to come.

"You missed a spot," I said, inspecting the polishing job on the bar top, as I brought a rack of freshly washed glassware from the back.

"I did no such thing," M-09 replied with all the indignant tone that his computerized voice could manage. Farrow's men hadn't destroyed M-09's memory core, and we were able to install his personality into a new body. It had taken weeks to construct the new and improved body. And worth every single MU.

As good as it was to have him back, I'd made it a point to give him a hard time—once or twice a day—to get even for that stunt he'd pulled at the lifts. At least for a little while. Our bond had never been closer.

I could not say the same about my working relationship with Tyelehn. The Elowan had saved our bacon in the Solarium, sure, but Ndango had revealed a disturbing truth to me after. I knew the Elowan were a plant species and that they needed sunlight and carbon dioxide as food. What I didn't know was that they also supplement their diets by breaking down organic material through porous pouches in their vines. A smelly process that can take weeks to complete. As an allowance to this need, Interstel's top brass had allotted a portion of Starport Central to a site where decaying organic matter could breakdown into the nutritional needs of the Elowan. The Solarium had been that place.

According to Ndango, Interstel had permitted the Elowan to keep the deceased pirates as just such an organic matter. Learning that there was a jungle just a level above us with the bodies of a dozen pirates serving as alien compost was just disturbing.

Needless to say, I don't tease Tyelehn anymore.

Business was good in the incident's wake. Folks loved coming in and hearing about the shootout on Starport Central. I guess it made the place feel more like their homes on Arth. Of course, I would always leave out the details of the ultimate resting place of the pirates. Nobody else needed that detail.

"McConnell, my boy, we've got some business to discuss."

I glanced up to see Nyll T'Lathll walking through the door.

"We sure do," I said, motioning him up to the bar. "You owe me a signature recognizing my debt to you is clear on that contract cube. And I'll take possession of the deed while you're at it."

The large Thrynn laughed heartily. "What makes you think that our debt is cleared?"

"Because that's what you said when I took that job for you with the fake Nullifier," I answered hotly.

"There was nothing wrong with the equipment that I supplied. It turns out that there is a species-dependent element that is essential to operating a Shield Nullifier. Tests without the imprint of the origin species has resulted in a number of explosive malfunctions."

"Don't you think that's a critical piece of information?"

He waved off the idea, "A minor oversight from my sources."

"Your *oversight* damn near got me *dead*, T'Lathll," I growled.

He ignored my complaint completely. "Besides, *I* said that I wouldn't need your services if I were to ascend to the heights of esteem on Thoss. While those artifacts were indeed quite valuable, it did not achieve the desired effect. So, you will remain in my employ."

The sound of my blaster powering up from under the bar caught T'Lathll's attention.

"No, I think we've concluded our little arrangement. Right after you've signed off on that contract, that is. Or we can wrap things up in a messier fashion. I know some place where they'd delight in seeing your body rot."

He studied my face for a moment. "You're bluffing."

"Try me, T'Lathll. It's been a crazy few weeks."

With a snarl and a huff, he pulled the cube out of a pouch and after making his mark on it, slid it across the bar. "Don't think I will forget this, McConnell."

"You and me both," I smiled. "But you're welcome to come back and reminisce on it over a drink, if you do."

He sneered at me again, then stormed off.

I holstered the blaster back under the bar. After steadying my nerves with a shot of whisky, I looked over to the newest wide-eyed patron to walk up.

"Welcome to the Black Box Lounge. What can I get you?"

The Rock of Truth

By Bart Kemper

"Arth is going to die a fiery death, killing everyone on the planet with no hope for survival."

Benu Llano's final statement was supposed to spark a denial, even outrage. She hoped to be laughed out of the room. Instead, the top executive of Interstel looked expectant. Finally, realizing there was nothing more coming, he sighed.

"Captain Llano, we knew this before you began this work. It's why you are here. We need you to give us options, not just confirm what the team in New Oxford told us while you were still in the hospital."

Her nose twitched at a waft of something faintly acrid that slipped in as the door opened and closed. The Velox second-in-command, Vice Director Phexipotex, nodded toward Director Terrence Willwater. Being deep underground in Old City meant never escaping the centuries of a closed-loop biome supporting four organic species. Intellectually, she knew it was part of the old colony that wasn't pushed above ground after 3505 and survived the Dark Times, the date and significance popping up unbidden in her thoughts like commentary in an educational vid.

Normally this part of her brain was an asset, feeding her valuable data even under stress. Right now it was an annoying kid's voice chirping in her head who wouldn't shut up. She'd been kept down there, under guard, for over a month "to better focus". She could not shake the feeling they would not let her leave. She knew too much, to include that the ancient reclamation system still worked well on corpses of any Arth species. The Vice Director waved a red segmented arm.

"Please, Doctor, continue."

After years of working in Interstel, Benu was still surprised the Velox not only managed to feel more personable than their Human boss but also would remember things she preferred, like her academic title to being called "Captain." She had earned "Doctor" with hard work. She had earned "Captain" with nightmares.

It was Benu's turn to sigh. Whether let her live or not, she felt like she was sending more people to die without even the closure of being part of Arth's cycle of life. Survival on the adopted planet included being fed into the recycler to help all, regardless of species. It's a tradition that has continued to this day, well after reclaiming the surface. Only our androids were outside of that, but they served all in their own way. Now she was part of pushing more of Arth out of the gravity well, never to return, never to be part of the cycle that unites them, diminishing the whole. Knowing she was clinically depressed as part of PTSD did not make her feel any less fatalistic. If they killed her, it would be for speaking the truth.

"The first wave of exploration was more than proof of concept. We …," she paused, then corrected herself, "the first wave was led to believe it was a hurried response to rediscovering endurium."

Her flat tone did not give the energy source the verbal capitalization that was typical on Arth. It was a subtle change of inflection that was dissonant to Willwater. She had lost her faith. It was a faith no longer ardently practiced on Arth but was still a bedrock for the species to live and work together. Hers was not a lost faith to disuse or speculation, it was one shattered by seeing the strings controlling the figures making the shadows on the cave wall.

"In actuality, the last two centuries of growth were controlled by Arth's government. I use this term loosely as there was, I mean is, the officially elected structure the general public knows and the others that have kept the data from Noah 2 safe after the political collapse millennia ago. This ancient history bears directly on current affairs, else I would not have been given access to it."

Both directors nodded. Phexipotex indicated minor pleasure and agreement with antennae movement patterns that mirrored the sentiment of Willwater's slight smile.

"Arth has been in full mobilization for over 50 years. What the public thought was a wealth of newly discovered information was actually the carefully coordinated release of information. Same with finding a source of Endurium, taking it out of the realm of myth and religion."

Willwater noticed the change in inflection.

"There are massive gaps in the data made available to me, but given we had begun sublight exploration over 100 years ago, something big happened. Too big to share with the planet, but either small enough or remote enough to not be self-evident to the masses. I hypothesized it's the latter – something outside of our system.

"The first wave of exploration was not a public event. That's another data point indicating the threat was known. What we, I mean the first wave did not realize was their assignments were not optimized for success but to provide specific data. Crew mix, ranging from all one species to fully mixed; species assignments by position; training and experience; performance in different environments; the list goes on. I also have the list of considerations that were not tested against because of the, ah, limited number of subjects.

"Every ship had a data recorder that downloaded once they were in the Arth system or passed an Arth vessel, enough to record 4 years of all 13 vessels if it was needed. In the event of the ship's destruction, the recorder's box became an endurium-powered probe returning to Arth. As of this point, we have 11 of the 13 recorders."

Both executives noticed a tremor in Benu's dark-skinned hand holding the tablet.

"In summary – not any of it mattered a damn. Regardless of variables, the first two or three missions mattered the most. Beyond some basic understanding of science and engineering and ability to use your ship and equipment, nothing prepares you for this enough to make a goddamn bit of difference. All of the years of training, of being kept from our families……"

She paused to compose herself, rubbing her stubbled head unconsciously.

"Long preparation did not differ significantly from those who used training suites to upload information directly to their brains. Teamwork and chemistry were discriminators, but there are too many variables to know how a crew will gel once they leave the system. It begs the question of teamwork and chemistry producing mission success or whether mission success is what ties the group into a team.

"It could be both," Willwater said.

Benu looked up, her eyes locking onto Willwater's grey eyes framed by silver-grey hair, then shifting to Phexipotex' faceted red-brown ones. She nodded.

"Regardless, it was projected that half would make it through their first few runs, with the rest learning how to extend their operational range. Up to 3 ships were forecasted to be active at the end of the 18 months. The losses … were within parameters."

The two executives seemed pleased with the summary. The Velox' emotions were in the gestures and body stance, but the Human's brown skin was creased into smiles like a well-worn leather mask. His glowing, rich complexion was a contrast to her ashy, dry, uncared for skin. Benu dropped the tablet on the table, the anger and pain making the red scar over the left half of her face redden while the rest of the deep coffee colored face darkened. She smashed her good right hand on the table.

"Quit looking so pleased, dammit. I wasn't supposed to be here. I read the report myself. We weren't supposed to make it back. As it is, half of the crew died while Navigator H552213 and Engineer G942333 —"

"The other two have been wiped, reassigned new designators, and are in service elsewhere, Captain Llano," Willwater said, emphasizing her rank. "The ISS *Akcatphopexphopxi,* or *Enduring Flower,* officially returned, coming in after the ISS *Hyperion.* In your official files, your crewmates were recognized as heroes and your bravery was lauded in taking over for Captain Xiaxttse, which also gave you your promotion to Captain of *Enduring Flower.*" Willwater's frustration cracked his corporate façade. His deputy leaned his red-carapaced body forward and clacked his mandibles, bringing attention to himself and breaking the tension.

"I shared hive alignment with Captain Xiaxttse, what you might call 'cousin,' Doctor Llano. I share some of your loss, but to honor them we must use the knowledge they … all of you … sacrificed for. The second wave will be in full view of the public, using our space station without any attempts of deception. You now know everything we learned, everything done in New Oxford to prepare the next group, and our logistics constraints. What are your recommendations?"

Benu relented. She picked up the tablet. The schematic of the new class, the ISS *Intrepid,* filled the wall screen.

"Give them enough to learn. 10,000-15,000 monetary units, enough for four cargo pods and some training. As this curve shows, it gives us optimal returns on investment…"

For the next four hours, she briefed the two most powerful people on Arth, at least in relation to her. To be fair, they asked good questions, Benu reflected. They didn't seem to have the normal Arth politics of the multi-species forced settlement. Over a thousand years of four different biologies working together and not wiping each other out was always attributed to the wisdom of the *Four* and the power of the *Rock of Truth*, with the more secular minded attributing it to "good common sense policy."

Instead, she had discovered it was a carefully cultivated construct that had different groups controlling things, usually using indirect means but sometimes reaching in directly. Interstel is supposed to be an entrepreneurial stroke of genius by Willwater. The son of a mineral mining magnate, Willwater speculated on growing space flight and establishing orbital facilities before the rediscovery of Endurium and super-photonic travel. In reality, it was a scheduled development as part of their full mobilization. The appearance of being a serendipitous business development is less alarming than announcing the re-allocation of resources to explore the galaxy before the means of doing so was made public. It wasn't just for public consumption on Arth. There were some indications of spies from outside of Arth, but without the full context she now had, it had looked like paranoid ranting. Her task was to build upon the deception so Arth will be ready to act on what the next wave of exploration brings back.

She had been as ignorant as the rest of the planet. There was already a plan in place, but it was set prior to the first wave launching. Her job was to update it using the data learned in training and launching the first wave. Her wave. Now she is part of the insider cabal, but without any of the family or organizational backing most of the string-pullers seemed to have. Interstel was now her faction.

Benu mapped out projected losses, when to raise Endurium prices, when to announce the threat, and other "discoveries" along with presented alternative courses of actions and their forecasted second and third order effects. She also advocated opening up the process to wildcatters – people who did not attend Interstel's long training course.

"The odds favor the Interstel trainees the first few missions, but not decisively. Further, any training program will have strengths and weaknesses. The act of focusing on one thing creates a gap in another area. We are dealing with a lot of unknowns, it is in the definition of 'exploration.' Including those with skills from in-system space work, industry-gained expertise in engineering and systems, or just are the right kind of crazy can cover an unforeseen gap in knowledge or training at a decisive moment."

She paused to make eye contact with both executives. "It will also assist in engaging the public and prevent the program from being perceived as an elitist corporate program controlled by powerful factions."

To her annoyance, the powerful elite corporate executives praised her for recommendation and seemed oblivious to the dig. Instead of being insulted, they increased the scope of her planning. She was to look past the next phase to launch and examine final mobilization with an intent to save as much of Arth as possible.

The new information began to arrive in hours. Old Town was supposed to be abandoned, but the smell and sound was a constant reminder the old life support system was very much alive. Benu had no idea of whether or not she was going into the recycler system, to be nutrients and mulch. No one would miss her, as

Minister Szphaotxi indirectly pointed out apologetically. The minister was one of the people whose family were the invisible foundation for the deception. He personally supervised the delivery of actual bound books for her to read.

"Books are magical. Never in the databanks, only needs eyes to read," he would say. "Very secure, please keep that in mind. Secrets must be kept. If there is no one to mourn, there is no one to question." In her imagination, she could be put back into the hospital and simply "die from complications from her injuries." That was probably just her fatalism in overdrive, as clearly she was not compost.

She normally loved puzzles, the more complex the better. Her inner librarian, what she called the voice when she wasn't an annoying kid's voice, would constantly feed her clues, like a separate processer in her head. It was part of the skill-set that got her selected as a xeno-scientist – her ability to identify pieces of a puzzle based on function and correlation with other items, then build a mental picture of how a system functioned over space and time. A new planetary ecosystem or a reconstructing a multi-generational research program, for her it was the same skill set.

Her audience of two stayed engaged the full four hours. As she gave her summation, she was hoping all she would happen would be retiring into the adjacent room she had been living in, grinding out more research and putting more pieces together for the final mobilization to follow the second wave.

Willwater stared at her for an uncomfortably long minute, then nodded to Phexipotex.

"Doctor Llano, you have mastered an amazing amount of information in a short time. We are grateful to you for your skill and your objectivity, something we find, alas, in short supply. We agree with your endstate for Arth's mobilization. If we can build out our system infrastructure as you describe to match the push for identified colonies, we will be able to disperse the majority of our planet's population and resources in the event we cannot stop the flares.

"The question remains – can we reach the target endstate in time?"

Benu was holding her tablet in front of her like a chest plate, arms crossed with fingers clenched on the edges. She didn't need to look at the screen. In a small voice, she replied, "I don't know." She felt like she just killed the planet with her words.

The two executives exchanged another glance. After a half hour of fielding questions, Benu was exhausted and flopped into a high-backed chair. While she downed the odd-tasting Old City recycler water, she got up to go to her bedroom, adjacent to the briefing room. Phexipotex clicked at her and gestured towards the other door.

"You are free to return to your home, Doctor Llano. Thank you for your patience. All of your books will remain here, of course, but your home is otherwise a secure work site now. There is much to do. Tomorrow afternoon you are expected at New Oxford to evaluate the candidates and update the briefing materials. And please, Doctor, keep up with your therapy regimen."

Even after a month, her home was just as she left it, if not a bit cleaner, and with fresh food in her kitchen. Interstel had kept her small apartment maintained. The floral scent of her cleaning products were fresh in the air. Despite that, she still woke up the next day thinking she smelled ozone and burnt chitin. It wasn't better than the days she woke up smelling burnt flesh of some sort, or the complex smells of viscera. It was just a lottery of which memories were playing as she woke up.

She went to her physical therapy, as promised. She enjoyed the physical part, but not the rest. The Elowan tradition meant it included counseling since "the mind is part of the body; you cannot heal the body without the mind". She was uncooperative with the provided therapist, as usual. She'd start over when they found a new therapist. One with the right clearances.

On her desk was a small stack of books she'd had since she was a child. They had been gift from her parents, one a biology primer and another on astronomy. She grew up not only loving science, but wanting to go to the stars. There had been so many dreams. She had not known there were only nightmares waiting for her.

Her parents had died in two unrelated accidents, her mother when she was 10 and her father shortly after starting the Interstel training at 23. The object of her interest was next to the books – a half-empty bottle of whiskey. She poured herself a finger's worth in a tumbler "for medicinal purposes" and went into the bathroom to clean up.

Benu looked into the mirror and stared into the moss-green flecks in her remaining brown eye, reminding herself she was not on mission. The left eye was brown and still gave her binocular vision, but it was a bit too perfectly brown. She carefully shaved her head. The white stubble coming in through the scar tissue disappeared down the drain. It was something she started during training as a break from her former life, eliminating a potential cause for suit failures or maintenance issues. It became a calming ritual, forcing her to set aside the day's worries as she used an unpowered razor to take her curly, mostly black hair off at the scalp without nicking the two moles on the back of her head.

She also found letting it grow in just felt weird. She forgot to shave several times while working in Old City, but the almost-itching of growing hair and the stubble turning soft would distract her until she razed it back to skin. After, she luxuriated in being able to shower more than one minute. She felt long showers would never stop feeling somehow "wrong". She used extra moisturizers after deep cleaning her skin to counter her lack of self-care while in the Old City. It's not like anyone there was commenting on her looks, and it's hard to worry about ashy elbows when you're not sure if you'll be allowed to leave.

Ready for the day, she took the underground train from the capital to Pelinoriat, then a quick ride to New Oxford and the Interstel training academy. In reading through the unredacted histories, she saw how many names and traditions led back to the home world of each race. This was going to be one of those ceremonies that were calculated to resonate with every species.

The candidates were in a military formation, despite Arth having no current military. Everyone had some form of Interstel blue jacket or sash. Their Interstel insignia were distant sparkles in the bright sunlight. A heady mix of flowers and grain wafted in the westward breeze from the adjacent agricultural section. New Oxford's original priority was keeping their ecosystem functioning as populations grew during the Arth Industrial Revolution.

From a distance, the Humans were generally some form of brown just as the Velox were generally some form of muted red. Dark greens marked the Thrynn. The Elowan light browns and bright, leafy greens reminded her of garden items with uniforms on them. They reminded me of a children's fairy tale where trees are sentient and wear clothes. Androids were purposely made mechanical in nature. Excessively life-like artificial beings stirred trouble, particularly with the Humans.

Off to one side appeared to be milling family members. Anger rose up inside. Her team had worked in secrecy, but this group is getting the accolades her dead friends should have been able to hear. Intellectually, she understood the dynamics. Her friends were the proof of concept. The new group going public is part of engaging the public in the sub-rosa growing mobilization.

Silowrr was down there, somewhere, just as Sohhh-Mitth was not. Benu smiled, thinking of her missing friend. She used to joke Sohhh-Mitth was the "over-Communications Officer." She used to unconsciously switch pronouns between "he", "she", and "they" with Sohhh-Mitth, but for some reason Benu saw Lohhrhn, their Med-O, solidly as a "she". The Elowan always seemed amused at the issue of gender and would never correct its usage because "no matter which you choose, you're not wrong." It didn't stop their Comms-O from finding ways to make ribald jokes.

Silowrr was Sohhh-Mitth's scion, but because of secrecy she could not tell Silowrr how she owed her life four separate times to Sohhh-Mitth, the last one costing the Elowan's life. She wanted to be down there, just like she had talked about a thousand times with Sohhh-Mitth.

She forced herself back to her tablet. It was not the same one she left in Old City, of course. She had an hour before her appointment with Professor Kerwin Dahglesh to discuss his evaluations. The top of the class is Max Zarfleen, slated to take out the first of the *Intrepid* class of spacecraft. That's going to have to be adjusted. She made some annotations to sabotage Arth's premiere exploration space craft so he won't depart until he is supposed to.

She heard a cheer and saw the formation had broken, the blue-clad people mixing with the more loudly dressed throng. Families of all races were sharing the "Four as One," a palm-down fist held in an open upwards palm, held close to the torso. Benu murmured the response, "Rock of Truth," without realizing it until she heard it leave her lips. Her parents had been more old-fashioned than most. She kept her hand down and open instead of raising it as a fist in the "Sign of the Four", where the fist is both "four as one" and "the rock of truth." It's hard to believe in the symbol when you know it was social engineering to give the our races a uniting symbol.

Still, it was a happy image from up there, families of all four races in common cause. There was a sudden pang of terror as a rapid series of images flashed in front of her, recounting the ways the first wave had died, each more real than her own body. The images shattered as a cheer rose up from below while a blue-clad Thrynn waved a banner of some sort.

She felt another twist of emotion, both resentment for their public accolades as well as wishing she was down there as part of the sea of family for Silowrr. When she heard the chitin-on-chitin rushing sound of an approaching Velox, she closed her tablet, then realized it was Minister Szphaotxi. She didn't need the green crossed ministerial sashes or the pin indicating his rank.

"I did not mean to interrupt you, Doctor," he said. "I am here on behalf of my hive section." He waved an arm towards the blue-spotted throng. "One of ours is being designated for command."

"I didn't know that, Minister." They both knew she did, but they were in public. "I'm sure you are quite proud."

"Oh, we are, Doctor, we are. This is very important to us. Pophaottzi is in one of the first launches."

Szphaotxi was as skilled in public speaking as Phexipotex, which is anomalous for the semi-hive minded Velox. Benu was nodding, thinking the "us" was Arth as a whole the way Willwater and Phexipotex do. The minister then shattered that connection to her.

"After all, he will be known as the first Velox explorer. It is the commanders that everyone remembers."

The barely contained anger boiled over in her guts, driving acrid bile to the back of her throat. Captain Xiaxttse, her captain, was the first Velox captain! And a damn fine one! The minister quickly reacted, indicating informal apology with the top segment. The supporting legs canted in amusement. You didn't go through the training she did to be ready for exobiology fieldwork without learning the nuances of Arth's partner races. Velox body language was as eloquent as Thrynn nuanced sibilants or Elowan singing. Her unusual aptitude for understanding those outside her species almost had her wearing Communications insignia. Apparently, her body language was understood as well as Szphaotxi transitioned to full formal superior-to-honored-subordinate apology.

"No disrespect meant to your friend, Doctor Llano. Forgive me, I am rejoicing for my hive section and the honor it will bring to our queen. There are several of my hive section here and we are in open connection, holding the moment to bring it back to the hive and to hold after Pophaottzi has launched. I regret our emotion is ill suited to this conversation. I am sure you are just as proud of Silowrr."

She nodded, not trusting her words. The minister was a powerful person in his own right, even without knowing his position behind the scenes. They switched to a polite banter and ended with a request for Benu's time in a few days. She politely scheduled the meeting. The youthful ochre undertones to the red chitin belied his age, as did the muted laughter of his back left leg that would have been at home in a Human teen's smirk after thinking they pulled off a cruel prank.

Benu forced the anger down. Her mourning turned into anger when she was first brought into the program, which was while she was still in the hospital. She has reviewed the footage from every ship, over and over. They all still live and then die, right there behind her eyelids. Before it was the anger of loss and grieving. That had faded. This was the cutting-torch flame of anger at being used, and the minister was feeding it pure oxygen.

Benu realized she was imagining Szphaotxi having his exoskeleton cracked while current arced through him, the same way the science officer died on the ISS *Acaolaci*. The camera feed had caught the moment in artistic detail that made frequent appearances in her nightmares. She pushed all that aside and focused on the meeting with the professor, taking comfort that the minister apparently assumed she had the typical human understanding of Velox's primary language.

Minister Szphaotxi had been appearing at the oddest coincidences, and Benu was past believing they were such. Her duties gave her considerable latitude and almost the full range of Interstel's resources to potentially abuse. She knew where she could go to get away for the ingratiating Velox.

"Another round, McConnell, another round. Both of us. Damn, it feels good to be back up here."

Evan McConnell, the owner of the Black Box Lounge, like many bar owners maintained a mystery about himself. Some say he helped build the Starport, which is why he seems so knowledgeable about not just the station, but working in vacuum. Some argue he is a government plant, but those same people find conspiracies everywhere. What was a given is he sold some of the most expensive beers and Arthian booze, due to "gravity tax", side-by-side with cheap orbit-made hootch.

People going out with nothing to lose would pay the gravity tax for "the good stuff." People coming back flush with riches would pay the gravity tax for it, too. Benu was drinking "Grade A Tank Cleaner," which was laboratory grade alcohol cut with distilled water and a touch of citric acid. "100% orbit made". She knew this because it was on the label, but her own university experiences and the economics of gravity gave her no reason to doubt it.

McConnell had pale skin and fine red hair, both being recessive traits that popped up in the Human populations. His eyes were mottled, like her remaining one, but leaning more towards green. She had seen him go shot-for-shot with more than one crewman and never seem to be phased. This was her fifth shot in less than as many minutes. Her phase was going to be a step function, and she was not caring about the amplitude.

"Are you going to slow down, Llano?"

She shook her head, the first bit of unsteadiness slipping in. "Nope. Are you going to keep pouring, McConnell?"

He looked into her face, searching. She tapped the table expectantly. He pulled her glass back across the bar, pouring slower than before.

"So…. How many didn't come back?"

Her jaw dropped, then clicked shut. He set down her glass next to him and poured his own glass, this one even more slowly.

"I'm not asking where you were. There were twelve, thirteen crews' worth of you loudmouths, all trying to be hushhush about what you were doing up here. I even got identical explanations – Interstel found an incredibly rich find, further out in the system. I even had people paying me to share the gossip, trying to figure out where Little Boy WIllwater's big find was and how it would out do what his father had done so they could claim it first."

He looked into her eyes as he slid her glass back to her.

"And then … nothing. Disappeared. Not in sets like different shifts of boats out there, ferrying the ore or whatever back in groups or towing it back. All at once. And nothing in the news feeds.

He raised his glass. She followed suit, splashing a little out as it left the bar's surface before vectoring into her mouth. She swallowed, still looking into the bartender's eyes. He dropped his gaze and went about pulling in both glasses and putting them into the sink tray, talking as he did so.

"Anyway, I'm not asking questions. Just saying, normally if a workboat goes missing, there is notice. Gone missing long enough, there is a declared loss. So there was a big find out there, yeah? But …. Not everyone came back. You're maybe the third person I've seen besides Thyrrthynnn and one of his crew, both busy being important. So… just asking, how many of your crew made it back because it's pretty clear you're not riding alone there.

He looked up and back into her eyes. She dropped her gaze to the bar, her hands clasped in front of her on the wet surface. The pause stretched on for at least a lifetime.

"Five," she said, her voice barely above a whisper. "I lost five. I'm the only one left."

The redheaded bartender nodded and turned to the bar, then turned back with a bottle of Arthian whiskey and poured two more glasses.

"Well then," he said as he poured, "that means those drinks weren't for you. Let me buy yours now."

She stared at the two glasses. "What do you mean?"

"I mean you did five shots. That was theirs. And I know at least some didn't drink alcohol, that's not the point. It was theirs. They live in your memory. This one is for you. This is for you, living." He picked up his glass and held it out. "What do we toast to?"

She looked at him in confusion, then at the remaining glass. "I … I don't know."

He emptied his glass, then picked up hers and drank it back as well.

"Well, it seems you should figure that out. You can't carry that weight without having a life to carry it with." He shrugged. "I know it sounds like something an Elowan would say, but you should think about it. Whatever you're doing now isn't working."

He walked a few steps down the bar to greet a new customer, leaving her to stare down at two empty glasses and the same feeling inside that she knew the alcohol wasn't able to touch.

She had come up to inspect the shipyard's progress on the new ships. The landers going out in the first few ships were going to be the same "one size fits no one" version they had, but new ones were being made with different terrain options per her specifications. She had managed to avoid the minister, but in going back to their old bar she ran back into herself. The high-grade jet fuel was starting to erode her façade. She retreated to the Interstel administrative section and the small office she was given during her inspection visits. She closed her eyes, knowing she would soon be seeing her friend die again.

"So when you find yourself crawling in the bottle and using alcohol abuse to cope, what do we say?"

"I ask consent of my best friend before putting him deep inside me, making me feel warm and happy," Benu said.

Doctor Yihhslhis, an Elowan therapist, chuckled. "This has become quite the ritual – I ask questions to see if you understand the self-abuse, and you find humorous ways to acknowledge you see it."

"Yeah, well, Human docs tend to get upset and worried, which makes it more fun."

"Of course, they have sympathy. I do not feel as you do, so I have only empathy towards my favorite primate."

"Thank you, Doctor Tree. So am I gonna live?"

"Of course not. You're being stupid and accelerating your likelihood of early death."

"Excellent," Benu said. "I can't tell you what I know, or why I am stressed, or anything going on so you can't disagree that what appears to be irrational acts of a scientist going off her rails is actually a quite sane and rational deliberate --

"Act of suicide because you have the fate of Arth in your hands?"

Benu's mouth gaped, staring at her Interstel-approved therapist lounging in the earth-filled stone tub that served as Elowan furniture.

"Why do you think I am assigned to you, Benu? I'm a scion of one of the strongest Elowan branches on Arth." The therapist's arms gestured unironically, using human body language to go with the words.

"And no, you do not hold our fate in your hands, so you can drop the martyrdom as well. You were brought in as a fresh pair of eyes, unburdened with the long history of this tangled thicket of a forced colony. Don't give me that look, you have not lived your entire life keeping such secrets let alone enforcing them. I commend your commitment to security and I won't ask you to divulge anything. It's one thing for me to say it, and another for you to confirm. I have only shared my knowledge so you know you're not alone and not going crazy. Director Phexipotex has been very concerned about you. You have not processed losing your family."

Benu's face had reassembled itself into her normal neutral mien while her therapist spoke. Now she snorted.

"My family? Doctor Yihhslhis, with all due respect, the Director worries too much. My parents had died while I was in university, well before I joined the program. My grieving is complete, my psyche eval even said it would add resiliency for me should something happen out there."

The bulbous head swayed up and down, like a small animal was somehow behind its head and pushing on a branch, getting ready to jump. Benu knew nodding was a behavior learned from Humans and Thrynn, but somehow the doctor made it seem a natural Elowan action instead of aping a Human or Thrynn movement. The compound eyes, more like interlocking pools than the faceted eyes of the Velox, were still locked on hers, real and artificial.

Yihhslhis cocked their head, seeming to be considering something it had probably long had decided upon, then sinuously stretched its limbs, got out of the tub, and sat on the couch on Benu's left. The sudden scent of fresh earth and Elowan pollens enveloped Benu even before the prehensile vines wrapped behind her and around the right side. Without thinking, she leaned into the trunk, the skin feeling like a sun-warmed smooth-barked tree. This is how she sat with Sohhh-Mitth after her first brush with death. She felt split between two moments in time. Her therapist's gentle tones felt like the same undulating rhythm as Sohhh-Mitth's when he was trying to calm her.

"Benu, you have been watching your family die, over and over. Your family. Dead. Dying. Over and over. The other ships, your ship, they were your family." The arms hugged gently even as the words cut in, deliberately, like an ice-edged scalpel.

"They are gone and the *Hyperion* crew act like you don't exist. You. Are. Alone."

An invisible foot slammed into Benu's gut, bending her over as the air fled her body. Something tore in her chest. Water flooded her eyes. Her mouth ripped open wide in pure primate pain, teeth bared, as a wordless sound ripped from the back of her throat. For long heartbeats she was locked in that position until her body tired of waiting and forced her to inhale, releasing long, racking sobs.

Warm, wiry arms pulled her into the therapist's trunk. Benu felt her body shaking, again putting her back on the *Flower* as Yihhslhis rocked her just like her friend had, adjusting the motion until it somehow found the natural frequency her father had used when she was little. In the back of her mind, Benu knew her therapist was using all their skills to create this moment, but the rest of her unlatched her arms from around her own middle and wrapped them around the trunk, burying her face in the warm, reassuring mix of loam and flower-like Elowan scents, the human words becoming Elowan language, softly sung, the swaying rocking her into a quiet snuffle, until Doctor Llano of the *ISS Enduring Flower* faded into her father's Little Benny and fell into a deep, dreamless sleep, still supported in a cradle of branches and vines swaying to an invisible, faintly musical wind.

The next twelve days she stuck to her routine of integrated therapy, making up for lost time in the Old City, followed by grinding out the logistic details needed for the new program due to launch early in the next year. She used puzzle solving skills to visualize project requirements as a 4-D mushy puzzle piece, putting the pieces together into a kinetic sculpture. It was tantalizing work, with gaps diminishing but not quite disappearing.

Benu was switched to therapy every other day, so she started working out on the open days, using the old Interstel training programs she used to get into the once-covert exploration program. She had finished the previous bottle of whiskey and had just cracked the second a month after she started the new routine. She had been going through a bottle every two or three days before that.

It had occurred to her that Interstel had been monitoring her the entire time. It's possible the six weeks in Old City was at least partly a ploy to put her in a more controlled environment. That's what was bothering Benu – she just didn't know what to think. Now that she knew there was a shadow government behind the elected one, it made everything seem like a conspiracy. She understood the need to manage the tensions of four very different biologicals, all of whom had a history of conflicts on their homeworld and now are stuck on a single shared planet with its own history of conflict. She had been taught it was because Arth had chosen wisdom and peace, as if a simple pledge eliminated natural competition within and between species. Of course, she had believed it because it's what she was meant to see.

It was five days before the new year when a courier brought a sealed case. Once alone, she broke the seals. It was a summary briefing of the unofficial Arth power structure. The cover sheet showed over a dozen sign-offs, meaning this was a very deliberate in-brief of how things actually worked on Arth. Her previous research had revealed it. This mapped it out, had made it clear people and even groups could be discredited or disappear if they threatened the delicate dance. The lack of overt threat for failing to maintain secrecy was more chilling than any formal list of consequences.

It layed out power structure, hard and soft, between different species and groups. Most groups were within a species, such as Szphaotxi's hive. Not "hive section". It was a full hive, the largest one and a solid 15% of the Velox population. Other groups, like Interstel, cut across those borders with a more specific interest. The document itself was a dry discussion of relationships and historical associations. In and of itself, it would not undermine the democratically elected government. It's the context she is operating in, what the security wonks call "aggregate intelligence".

The names of various leaders were often different than what the public saw. Willwater was both the head of Interstel as well as the head of a Human faction, Szphaotxi was in charge of his but publicly was a minor functionary. Her friend Sohhh-Mitth had been as high up as Dr. Yihhslhis, but Phexipotex did not rate a mention. Elections and public positions were variables in the power structure. The factions of Arth learned the sincere support of the population was a force of its own and was not always predictable. Some of the leaders, such as Willwater and his father before him, successfully leveraged popularity to build upon their behind-the-scenes power in mineral mining and marketing control.

With the names came organizations, resources, capabilities. Her inner librarian had been silent, drinking in the torrent of information. Now she was adding commentary cross-correlated from a lifetime on Arth. Overall, Benu had understood the big picture as an image, but not how it worked. Elowan, Thrynn, Human, Velox were all moving in and out of each other's orbits. Even the androids were independent actors. Some organizations were run by a single faction, some by a single race, and others like Interstel were designed to be a nexus of sorts. Her previous projects were not wrong, per se, but they did include what was driving the various dynamics.

Pieces formed, spun around, and started to click together. The mushy boundaries firmed up. Some pieces broke into smaller ones, as they had only looked like a single entity. Others that had looked like disconnected groups came together as a single entity. It wasn't enough. She couldn't see it.

She started tapping on her tablet but the screen was too small. She transferred the work space to the wall screen. Benu keyed up an organic chemistry modeler. Designed for xenobiology work, it was a freeform modeler unconstrained by known patterns. Mentally substituting atoms for resources, molecules for factions, reactions for changes, Benu used animation to move the resources over space and time to model the finite resources of Arth.

She knew the endstate she wanted. She had a solid start point set two years in the past to set the resource and alignment baseline. She was able to model and track the planet's mobilization, but only to a point. Armed with new knowledge and a new mental construct, she began to move the constrained resources, tapping different factions and organizations with imperial if virtual ease.

For hours she moved her small galaxy of molecules around. Cold food remained untouched. Cold coffee was consumed mechanically, a simple maintenance function. The model included current alignments and commitments, which added another layer of constraints. If something was critical, she bent it to her will. Her job was to find the path. Others would have to do the work to make it happen.

She couldn't find it. The next wave would launch. Those assets were committed. Just the known potential colony targets and mining sites would surpass Arth's current logistic capacity, and the second wave would be finding more. The critical shortfall was not finding enough resources, although that was still uncertain. It was developing the logistics base to springboard into a multi-system government to disperse the population in a matter of months, not decades.

Roughly speaking, she estimated there would be sufficient resources assuming the next wave's discoveries panned out. As those riches came in, there would be a natural response for others to push out by any means available. That could be channeled. For example, people already hauling ore in-system will try to rig their ships into interstellar cargo runners, trailing behind the finds of the next exploration wave.

It wasn't until she switched from evaluating resources to evaluating bottlenecks did she find it. The one gap that no amount of movement could bridge. It was the in-system transportation assets needed to manage the incoming materials, outbound ships, and manage their construction and maintenance. There was a massive cluster of resources dedicated to mining the oceans that could be repurposed, but as manifested it resisted repurposing. If this could be shifted to supporting the space infrastructure, then the whole plan has a chance, but the window for this to happen was closing.

It was one of the multiple organization nexus operations like Interstel, so the model defaulted to not letting her break it apart. In order to release this model constraint, she had to dig down to see who was the final authority. There was always one belly button to push if you looked hard enough, even if they didn't actually have a belly button. She tunneled through the various layers of families and corporations until she found the key file to open. There it was. Third Minister Szphaotxi.

Even as she read the file, her comms buzzed. Szphaotxi's face appeared on the inset video image, floating over the constellation of ersatz organic molecules.

"Ah, Doctor Llano," Szphaotxi said. "So good to see you have come to the same understanding I have. I can tell because you opened that file. I think we can help each other out. I will see you at 0900, at the place you used to work. Have a good evening."

"Silowrr will die. Is that plain enough?"

Benu had been let past security at Old Town. She was clearly expected. She had reached her old quarters and work room. It would take days to get used to the semi-rotted organic smell from the recyclers again. She hoped she had those days. It would be even better if she wasn't stuck down here.

Phexipotex was with Szphaotxi. At first, the sight of the second most powerful person in Interstel gave her hope. Szphaotxi crushed that hope.

"Silowrr is leverage and could one day lead. He would matter even if he didn't matter to you. Phexipotex is like you, Doctor, he is no one. Unlike you, people know him. He is a useful lackey. Why do you think Willwater uses him? Respect? What is there to respect?"

Phexipotex's body language said everything. He was clearly subservient to the minister. Every time Szphaotxi made a demand or even an offhand suggestion, the Interstel executive scuttled forward, tapping away on his tablet. It felt like Phexipotex did not even acknowledge Benu was there.

Benu was past scared. She was angry.

"Why drag Silowrr into this? He has done nothing, he's not part of any of this."

The Velox didn't bother making Human laughter, just rubbed the front arms together in dry, raspy amusement.

"We are all part of this, Doctor. That's why you are here. You were picked as an approved interlocutor, a problem solver. And you were not even supposed to be here. You were excess, but useful excess. Did you not understand my earlier lectures in this place? I was telling you how easily you can be put in the recycler, but as long as you are a resource you will be allowed to live."

Benu felt like she had been slapped. Her previous fear of Interstel was designed by this Velox, the shame of wrongful blame further angering her. She opened her mouth to speak, but no words formed. The scar on her face was livid, something even a Velox would not miss. The minister's casual dismissal with the gesture traveling from the middle pair to the back pair evoked brushing dirt off the legs.

"No, Doctor, you were not projected to survive. Your intelligence and abilities indicated you would have realized the significance of discoveries instead of simply gathering data, and this would have spurred you into encouraging the captain and crew to keep pushing forward until your collective luck ran out."

Benu winced again. While recovering she realized she was the one keeping the crew pushing forward, convinced their discoveries would be the critical data Arth needed that no one else would be able to gather. She had not know that over a third of her data was confirming what was recorded over a thousand years ago. As a scientist she understood the value of independent confirmation, but even lab rats don't like being lab rats. The logic of necessity didn't take the knife out of her guts or the nightmares out of her head while she tried to sleep.

"But you did survive. Your undeniable analytic skills in making non-intuitive connection based on sparse data defies the machine learning AIs. Add to this, you have no significant political connections. Our society was, and is, held together through coercion, austerity, and a belief in the 'Four As One'. It's an engineered belief drawn from elements of all four species' most powerful belief systems. It's mean to keep those like you in their place."

Benu almost reflexively responded. Instead, she kept her arms down. Both hands were fists, but for more immediate reasons.

"You are uniquely qualified in scientific ability, personal experience in exploration, and a non-partisan perspective to be entrusted with these secrets on behalf of Arth. Everything is about to change, and for the first time in centuries, we don't know how.

"We used you to work through a range of problems. We couldn't fully trust each other's analysis or reports because everyone had their own interests. You had no conflicts and no resources. You are an incredibly useful tool, although less so now that you know what your role is.

"Interstel has potential, but Willwater and Phexipotex lack … vision. No, that's not the right word but it's the best I can find that fits your mouth. They only look at Arth as a whole. All the peoples. Logically, all people are not equal. In worrying about all, they do not look at how one could rightfully achieve their potential. Even the exploration arm of Interstel, despite looking for exceptional individuals, limits those rewards to the crew. Potential successes are squandered by refusing to allow exceptional groups to use their advantages," the Velox said.

"Such as those of your hive," Benu said.

The Velox responded by extending his body upwards and extending both pairs of arms outwards, a pose that the Velox associate with leadership and victory.

"Of course. That is why we are setting up the endurium station on our inner planet for soon-to-be Captain Pophaottzi. He will be able to touch down there and pick up at least 10 endurium at a time, yes? And then at the designated coordinates on his first interplanetary –

"He will be able to take a hold full of minerals, set a ridiculous price, and make over a million credits. It's your money, Minister. Why are you forcing me to create this deception?"

The Velox again used the arm-rubbing laughter, then made a dismissive insult involving her non-existent hive and strength of her middle arms. Benu realized he did not expect her to understand Velox body language.

"Because Willwater and his lackey here rigged their system to eliminate most forms of advantage. Success has to be 'earned' to motivate the masses. We are not the masses. So when our Captain Pophaottzi returns from his first run with that many credits, he can then retrain and refit their vessel more appropriately.

"You were picked for your impartiality, Doctor." He made "doctor" sound a slur compared to "captain". "Our very real threat to Silowrr is to help you see the wisdom in supporting us. While it is true once he is underway he will be beyond my reach, until he is very much within my grasp." Mandibles and manipulators clacked together at the same time, underscoring the grasp is one of a predator. His launch will be after Captain Pophaottzi, so he will be in our collective grasp until then. Your affection for the scion of your shipmate is your weak point, so of course we offer to add him to your nightmares to motivate you do the right thing."

"The right thing?" Benu questioned.

"Of course. Help our hive ascend in power. Our superiority is self-evident. All we need is a resounding success of heroism on the heels of gaining riches to gain the public support needed to shift the balance to us. Shifting our resources for marine exploitation by magnanimously diverting them at a loss for the greater good, plus our very own captain becoming our public face, we can shift the entire structure in our favor. I'm explaining it to you, in very small monkey words, so you can do your job and properly assist."

The interspecies taunt, normally a shocking insult in polite company, barely registered as Benu clenched and unclenched her fists. Szphaotxi knew of the threat long before she did, and had used that knowledge to tie up resources at the risk of the lives of everyone on Arth. He would throw away all of the sacrifices of her shipmates and the rest of the first wave, not to mention the rest of Arth, for some sort of power play. His apparent amusement towards her was more fuel for her anger, knowing she was alone and helpless.

"What more do you need of me," she asked through clenched teeth.

The minister turned and focused on her. Phexipotex stood behind him, tablet in hand, ready to issue orders.

"Why, Doctor, it's simple. I need an inspiring heroic mission, something to put my very own Captain in a planetary leadership role, at least in terms of public opinion. He will be piloting an all-Velox crew. I had suggested every race put out at least one 'pure' crew in the name of science in order to set up Pophaottzi to captain the Velox one. I'm sure you have something from having reviewed the previous missions, over and over."

Benu's first impulse was to suggest where the Velox should go and in what manner that had nothing to do with being heroic. A motion caught her eye. Phexipotex' front half was still the attentive servant, poised to act on the minister's whim. The back half, out of Szphaotxi's field of vision, was signaling, "Seven up, seven out."

She checked the map and looked up. Now the executive was signaling "armed". Her librarian piped up, filling in the gaps. Szphaotxi silently signaled, "hurry up, idiot," as a Velox form of muttering to himself. She tapped on the tablet, sending the star map to the room's screen.

"There," she said, "go to 118 by 107. It's a flux point. It will take your crew to a rich planet. The previous ship met a new species, but they had run out of fuel before getting home. If confronted by ships on the far side, it is important to not only keep shields up but to fire your primary weapon as a military honor. They only respect strength. If they sense any weakness they will strike. Show the proper display of power and these aliens will retreat, leaving the system wide open."

Szphaotxi applauded, human style. The sound of chitin hitting chitin sounded unnerving. It sounded more like death than acclaim.

"Excellent. I knew my faith in keeping you alive was well placed. Obviously, now I will give orders to sacrifice profit in the name of helping all of Arth by repurposing our marine mining consortium. Once it's out of the gravity well it will be under Interstel's control. You and Willwater's lackey will have convinced me to see the error of my ways."

The Velox stabbed an arm at Benu, clacking the manipulator. "Make no mistake, it does not matter if you decide to run to Willwater. I want you to. We will still have the public posture by moving the decisive equipment for space expansion. All Willwater and the rest can do is watch. The seeding of endurium and credits is out of our non-public resources, there will be no trace. I'll know if any of the ships route to the flux point, particularly since it's not on any maps."

The manipulators struck Benu in the sternum. "This will happen no matter what you do now. Everything was primed to move before you were out of the hospital. All I needed was a few details and to wait until the decisive point. I let you find me to give you and Willwater the cover of being in charge."

The Velox had struck Benu several more times as he spoke, the last time knocking her down.

"You Humans have a phrase, I believe. 'Stay down.' Be useful and you live. If you do anything to interfere with these events, I'll know. You will die, lackey will die, and Silowrr will die."

Without turning, he said, "Lackey, make the arrangements. Let Willwater know he has been beat. Interstel may have the solar system, but we'll have Arth and everywhere the people are."

Benu and Phexipotex watched the minister swagger out, clearly confident in the outcome. As Benu got to her feet, the Interstel director put a manipulator to his mandibles, incongruously miming the Human shushing sign.

"Doctor Llano, on behalf of Interstel, may I sincerely apologize for this event. It was entirely unforeseen."

Benu didn't have to see the contradiction gesture to read between the lines. Even a few days ago she would have raged at the Velox or stalked off to take on the Executive Director, but she had been studying Arth's complex "people terrain". More than that, she knew what was at stake. She found herself understanding the doublespeak of Arth's power circles. The Velox's posture changed to one of intense weariness and sadness.

"I have already sent the orders on behalf of Interstel with the Minister's approval. It should take a ten day cycle to start moving the new assets up the gravity well, but the press release will come before then. After that, it will be in motion. The Minister will get what he wants, and there is nothing anyone will be able to do to stop it. It's a sacrifice we all have to make."

She understood he meant Captain Pophaottzi and his crew. As he cocked his red-brown head, she realized he also meant how she would have to carry that along with all the weight of her own shipmates and the rest of the first wave.

Phexipotex swung his right manipulator into her left shoulder in a perfect mimicry of a Human chucking a co-worker in the arm. "So, do you know anywhere to get a drink? I think you may need a change of scenery."

Benu leaned into the bar at the Black Box Lounge. Her skin was a rich, warm glow of coffee and chocolate. Her hair was several centimeters long. An offset white streak accentuated the scar's discoloration. Her left eye was now a startling unnatural yellow instead of the carefully matched artificial eye she had before. McConnel's eyebrows rose.

"New look. I like it. What will it be?"

"What is the most expensive, stupidest hootch you have that actually tastes good?"

McConnell turned and opened the door to a caged shelf. He made a show of brushing off non-existent dust and showed her the label. She nodded.

"Two, one for you. But I'm paying for four, remember that."

His eyebrows arched again, slightly higher.

"For when you come back from asteroid mining?"

Benu laughed. "Haven't you heard? We have transphotonic drive now. For when I come back from," waving her hand above her head, "well, from where ever. They are letting us rock hoppers jump in with the proper New Oxford types. I'm going to be going out as brand new Science officer on the *Cilireel*, so new she doesn't even have a nickname yet."

"Rockhopper," he said, pouring the two shots. "Well, I'm sure that's what the records say. Yep, they will be lucky to get you."

"Damn right." They raised their glasses, giving each other a small nod, then knocking back the overpriced Arthian brandy. Benu stuck out her hand, which McConnell gave a firm grasp and shake.

"Right," she said, "remember you owe me those drinks. See you on the flipside." She put her fist, palm down, in her open hand. McConnell replied in kind.

She turned and strode out, the duffle bag with all of her belongings tossed over her shoulder. Some of the first ships have already come back from the closer systems, so her captain was looking at pushing out further.

Her nightmares started to lose intensity after her last time in Old City. Director Phexipotex had pointed out she was medically cleared for duty. He got her to look up again, that night. Instead of carrying the weight of her friends' deaths, she remembered their excitement with each new planet, new rock, new life form. Feeling like a little girl again, full of wonder, she shouldered her duffle bag and trooped down to the docking berth to meet her new family.

XXX

Obligations

By Marisa Wolf

Dinah technically didn't belong in the Starport Lounge. For years she'd proudly brought her dad in whenever her tours and his runs landed them in this same spot of space, which happened frequently enough she knew he'd been tweaking his routes. He'd toast her career, they'd catch up, and then they'd return to their respective ships and careers.

They should have had decades left of their silly tradition, toasting at Starport, but instead she sat at the bar alone, staring into her whiskey. While she wasn't a proper crewman of Interstel anymore, she knew enough people to still get in. No one she wanted to drink with on this particular day, though.

"Happy birthday, Dad," she murmured into her glass before emptying it again.

She allowed company a few times over the course of the evening, but after some Interstel fancyface got overly friendly, she stalked off to a corner to get proper drunk.

It didn't work.

The evening refused to blur around her, and her thoughts circled the same topics, much as they had for the last six months: *Being a captain really isn't all it's made out to be. I miss my dad. I miss my old job. New colony worlds are zero fun to visit. Pushing into new space and finding new planets – that was work worth doing. I don't think Dad's crew likes me. Being a captain really isn't all*

—

She dropped her head into her hands and tried to shove the endless refrain back in its box.

"Cute little thing like you shouldn't be –"

"Finish that sentence," she interrupted the unidentified voice without lifting her head, and made her own tone sweet enough for the poison to show, "and I will take your knife out of your boot and cut until you're a cute little thing."

"I didn't bring my —"

"My mistake." She tilted her head until one of her bright blue eyes glared at him, and smiled so hard he took a step back. "Should I show you mine?"

He wasn't as pretty as the captain whose kidney she'd threatened earlier in the night, but good-looking enough that he'd clearly thought approaching a woman hanging her face over a half-drunk glass of whiskey late at night would work in his favor.

He opened his mouth to say something, then his survival instincts must have kicked in and he snapped it shut before wandering off without looking at her again. She turned her head back down to study the ring of condensation under her glass.

"Here I was, minding my business, thinking 'no, surely that can't be Dinah Kenneson, hunched like a goblin in the dark corner of the Starport Lounge.'"

She stiffened, then identified the new voice and sat up as it continued.

"'No,' says I to myself, 'she left Interstel behind to hop through the great frontier, getting her own ship and command and providing a lifeline to all the newly rooting colonies' and so I continue minding my business and ignore the corner-goblin – and do you know what happened then?"

"Porter," she said, his name a mix of greeting and warning, then ruined it with a laugh even as her old crewmate carried on as though she hadn't said anything.

"Then, this goblin in the corner threatened to maul a perfectly decent midshipman for the great crime of speaking to her —"

"He called me a 'tiny little' –"

"You are tiny, my darling gelatinous glob, and maiming a man because he spoke the truth –"

"You know very well –"

"Anyway, that's when I knew it was you. Keep your knife in your boot, I brought reinforcements." Porter took his hand from behind his back and brandished a shining bottle.

She studied him for a long moment, but couldn't keep her expression blank. She sat up and waggled her fingers in a clear 'gimme' gesture, then inclined her head. "Your bribe is accepted."

"Thought so." He slid into the booth across from her and immediately dropped a generous pour into her glass.

"I thought you were far upspin for another month?" Dinah cradled her glass before sipping. Porter had brought some lower-level liquor – all she deserved given how much she'd had already – and a little body heat wouldn't make it any better or worse.

"We just got in and cleared through the docks." He lifted his shoulders in an overdone shrug, and she knew better than to pry. She wasn't entitled to Interstel's secrets any longer.

"I didn't think I'd catch anyone this pass-through – we're in-and-out, most times." She sipped and half-smiled. "Your face isn't the worst one I've seen tonight."

"Thank you?" Porter raised his eyebrows and took a healthy swig of his own. "Heard there was a bit of a scene earlier. Was that you?"

"I didn't stab anyone." She performed her own exaggerated shrug and drank again before putting her glass down. "And whoever said whatever, it probably wasn't me. I'm a captain now. Got a reputation to…"

"No, no, please go on." He laughed at her expression and slumped against the back of the booth. "How is captaining? Still a few years and yards of tests away for me." Porter Tenneville, excellent science officer and otherwise layabout, had never expressed an aspiration for command. Unsure if he were serious or not – perhaps the whiskey was having an effect, after all – Dinah swallowed back her first response and refilled both their glasses.

"As glamorous as you're imagining," she replied in her driest tone. "Coming here, getting cargo, going there, delivering cargo, coming on back. Just a metric frakton of variety and excitement."

"Better than I'd hoped, then." He eyed her, and she wished she knew what he saw. She and Porter had served together on three different ships over the years, and he'd spent more than enough time with her to see beyond the basics that tipsy, over-confident men in bars tended to note. Those basics were straightforward enough – she barely cleared five feet, kept her dark brown hair shoulder-length for ease of tying back, had big eyes, medium-toned skin, and a small nose. Fit as most spacers. Cute, no matter how the years passed. A certain type of interested suitor always wanted to put her in their pockets.

But could Porter see how exhausted she was? That the last thing she'd wanted was to leave a promising career and take over her father's contract? That…she shoved everything back in its box and drank more in an effort to buy time and choose a change of subject. Porter got there first – maybe he had picked up some of what she felt.

"You spend time landside? Any of those scrappy new colonies have good beaches?"

"Mostly we dock at their orbitals. Early terraforming can get messy, and who wants to be the one to bring in new bacteria and ruin the whole thing?" She said it lightly, as though it couldn't possibly bother her.

"I imagine that would cut into profits," he acknowledged with a snort. "But still, I'll keep imagining you living the easy civilian life, drink in hand seaside on an endless number of shining new planets."

"Who do you think has that life?" Dinah laughed and ran her hands through her hair. "You think they're hiring? I could do transport duty for them." Her voice soured on the word transport, and she hurried to continue. "You heard from Gillings lately? Last I heard, she was testing for nav."

They talked about old friends, lovers, and rivals (and the intersections between) until they'd put a significant dent in the bottle.

"Aren't you shipping out today?" Porter asked, cutting himself off mid-sentence in a story about their first shared communications officer and his current status as a holo-star.

"Tomorrow."

"It is tomorrow."

"'S'not."

"It's *almost* tomorrow. Don't you need to…get your ship ready? See to your crew?"

"They've been doing this a long time. Don't need me."

"That's not very Captain-y of you."

She glared at him, realized she was chewing on the side of her thumb, and forced her hand back to the table.

"I got everything ready before I came here. I'm not a complete shitshow."

"I didn't say you –"

"And the crew – my crew, they really are good at what they do." The pleasant warmth of the bottom shelf whiskey started to ebb, and she turned her glare to the bottle for betraying her.

"You haven't said much about them," Porter pointed out, his elbows on the table as he leaned forward. "Did you hire anyone, or are they all …inherited?"

She'd avoided talking or thinking about her father for nearly an hour, but his crew, his ship, his job…all of it was her life now. All of it, without his actual presence. She considered smashing the bottle and brandishing its broken end at someone's face, but swallowed and answered him instead.

"They all worked with my dad for at least a decade. His contract was the forty-year one, but they all signed long-hauls. That's how they get the best payouts."

"Unless they break it."

"None of them are breaking the contract." She glanced at her PDA, which of course had no new messages, and considered how much sleep she could still manage if she left soon. "Why would they? Just because the captain they signed on to work for died for no reason and his daughter had to take over to keep from breach of contract and repossession of the ship? What a dumb reason to sell your soul to Interstel."

"Dinah, no, I meant –"

"It's the most inter-species crew I've ever served on. Doc's an Android – Kayfive. Thinks his whole personality is comparing things to other things." She noted that he tried to interrupt and decided to detail the entirety of her six-member crew. "Nav and Engineering are Velox – Dad said never skimp on keeping yourself alive, and they're the best – Viphaaxi is the mean one, on nav, and her mate Zixoti is quiet. I've heard him say maybe ten words in the last six months, but he's a helluva engineer.

"Then, oh, you'll love this – we got an Elowan for sciencing and making sure the right stuff goes to the right colonies, and Ehnuli is a complete sweetheart, even though Dad thought it was smart to have her on the same ship as a Thrynn. Crazy, right?" Her grin at Porter was likely the craziest part of it, but she sailed on even as she refilled her glass.

"That's Sys'Thysin. He does all the math and trade and makes the deals. Then we have Sawyer for backup – a Human to do the shooting, though we haven't had to do much of that. Barely even need a captain. Wanna see their test scores?" She looked around for her bag, realized it was still fastened around her waist, and tapped her PDA to settle her tab.

"Dinah, stop, I wasn't quizzing you, I just wanted to make sure you were –" He held his hands out toward her, but she busied herself putting away her PDA. Something twisted in her gut – she knew she was overreacting, but knowing it didn't help her stop it. Damn whiskey.

"I was what? Surrounded by people good at their jobs? Not slacking in my new job? Happy?" She blew out her breath and knocked back her drink. "What's it matter? Whatever the answers, I got fifteen years of a forty-year contract to finish, moving goods from point A to B and maybe, on a big trip, point C." She took a deep breath, but wherever her calm had gone, it wasn't answering to 'just breathe.'

"If I'm really lucky and we don't cross a Thrynn scouting party or a rogue micro-meteor and avoid big expenses, fifteen years'll only be fifteen years, and then I'll have a ship all to myself to do whatever the f—"

Dinah unclenched her hands, shook her head, and tried the whole breathing thing again. Porter stared at her – she'd always had a temper, but more often than not, when she lashed out, there were solid justifications behind it.

This time, her only excuse was six months of trying to be the captain her father had been, or would have expected her to be, and how frayed it had left her. She couldn't bring herself to admit it, and the apology withered on her tongue.

"Look," she said, meeting his eyes. "Today's my dad's birthday. It's the first one without him, and I…"

"Have to go back to his ship, without him, and I made you think about it."

The truth of it made her shoulders itch, and made her think about everything else, which made her cursed teeth itch.

"Stop being insightful. It won't get you laid."

"It never does," he replied, his tone mournful and expression hangdog. Her anger ebbed and she laughed with a shake of her head.

"I should take the rest of this bottle in payment, but because I'm gracious, I'll leave it for you. Drinks on me next time."

"I'll hold you to that, Cap – Kenneson."

She smiled, grateful for his correction, and made it all the way out of the Starport Lounge before her body registered the sheer amount of whiskey she'd consumed.

By the time she roll-walked back to *The Swingin' Miss*'s berth, the morning shift had started and she had a looming headache where her pleasant tipsiness should have gone.

"All right, Captain?"

Dinah shook her head sharply in defiance of the thudding in her skull, wished she'd had one more or less whiskey, and summoned a smile for her ship's Android Doctor.

"The usual nonsense, Kayfive. How were things on the ship?"

"Quiet. After our toast to Captain – your father, everyone went their own way."

"You can call him Captain still, Kay. *Swingin' Miss* will always be his."

"According to all bylaws and Interstel's legal department, the ship and its contract are fully yours, Captain."

"Yes, I –" Dinah closed her mouth, considered for a moment, then continued. "Indeed it is. Everyone back on board?"

"Sys'Thysin is still at the Trade Depot, in case there are any deals to be had with end-shift workers." Kayfive clicked its jaw twice, which Dinah had tentatively determined to mean the Android doubted the logic inherent in the relayed information. She kept it as a tentative understanding given the times Kayfive clicked while using its most approving tone – the level to which Kay had mastered sarcasm was still a mystery to her.

Her dad should have been here to tell her. Scratch that – her dad should have *been here*, still running his own ship and carrying out the back third of his own forty-year contract with Interstel, still dealing with the odd mishmash of an interspecies crew he'd put together.

She pushed the thought away for the eleventy millionth time and nodded.

"I hope he finds something good. We're heading outward next run, and I've been hearing those colonies have it a bit rougher."

"Rough like a Elowan burr in Thrynn space."

Dinah couldn't decide what to say to that, so she nodded and moved further into the ship. She'd served with more than a few androids in Interstel, but Kayfive was odd. Not odd in the fun way some of them got, but certainly quirky. He compared everything, often in a way she had no context for, if they existed at all, and even that was…stiff. She couldn't picture her dad choosing this particular model, and the unsurety of it made her chest itch.

She really should have asked her father more questions during their Starport Lounge meet-ups, not let him pepper her for updates on her life and times at Interstel while he beamed proudly at her. Had she been a good enough daughter to him?

"Damn whiskey," she muttered, chewing on the side of her thumb as she stomped through her dad's – *her* – ship and shoved down the maudlin thoughts. If she hadn't been a good enough daughter, she'd certainly stepped up the dutiful offspring role by giving up her career and taking over her father's contract to save his ship and crew.

They're family at this point, Di, he'd told her a few years ago, not long after Ehnuli had taken over on the science side (there, she had paid attention, frak it). *With all the mess and joy that comes with.*

If they'd been his family, they should be hers too, especially after what she'd given up to keep Interstel from seizing every resource they'd ever imagined under breach of contract. Instead they were formal and nice but a little distanced and entirely strangers and she wanted her life back and her dad back and –

She definitely needed to have cut herself off at least a full drink ago. Whiskey and her dad's birthday – the first without him – what had she been thinking? She'd blame Porter, but she'd been well on her way to mistake city when he appeared.

Dinah rubbed her eyes impatiently, decided bed as the wisest course, and belatedly realized she'd followed the main hall of the ship from the docking airlock to the storage bays. Living quarters were tucked back behind her in the near-middle of the ship. She'd bypassed her room, the tubes that made it an easy up or down from quarters to the bridge, the engines, and other major working parts, and with the way her night was going Zixoti was running diagnostics on the internal systems and had seen her.

It shouldn't matter, but she was a little drunk and a lot sad, and the idea of looking like a fool to one of her crew – however unlikely it was that anyone was actually observing her – was too much.

She decided a quick look over what Sys'Thysin had loaded already was a Captain-y enough thing to do before she caught what little sleep was left to her, and continued on to the storage bays.

Dinah pulled up the manifest and walked briskly through each of the six bays attached to the spine of *The Swingin' Miss*. As she finished her brief tour through the last, the door whished open in front of her, and she caught a flicker of motion that wrenched her eyes up from her PDA a breath before she slammed into her trademaster.

"Captain?" Sys'Thysin stared down at her, pupils widening. He glanced back at the bay behind her, as though to reassure himself she hadn't touched anything, and rubbed his claws over the smaller grey-green scales of his neck.

"Doing a walk through ahead of tomorrow. Everything looks good." She held still, waiting for him to step aside so she could leave. When he didn't, she cocked her head and added, "Kayfive said you were deal-hunting. Find anything good?"

He blinked several times, and after the last his pupils had returned to their usual size. "A dissscount on amaranth ssseed. I haven't ssseen it go outward on any of the public manifessstss, Ehnuli sssays it should work on at least sssome of the planets."

"Sounds like a smart move." She emphasized the last word, and his long tail twitched before he took a step back and to the side, out of her way. "Nicely done."

"It'ss possssible there won't be a market for it, but if ssso, it will keep until we return downspin." He looked behind her again as the doors slid shut on the bay, and Dinah couldn't tell if she was keeping him from something, or if he were anxious she'd upset his careful order.

Checking the manifest had steadied her, but enough whiskey remained in her system that she didn't feel like parsing yet another awkward encounter with one of her crew.

"I trust that you thought it through. My father – Captain Kenneson always said that was a strength of yours." Dinah was pretty sure that was true, though mostly she wanted out of the conversation.

"Oh. Yesss…thank you." Sys'Thysin paused. "Captain."

Dinah focused on nothing but putting one steady foot in front of the other as she marched back to her quarters, and not a step further.

The trip to Kikrok remained uneventful. Dinah spent most of it grappling with the incessantly flickering running lights along the walls of the bridge while Viphaaxi clicked from her station at navigation.

Though sure the noise indicated disapproval, Dinah strove to maintain her calm and took the Velox's bland mannerisms at face value. Of course Viphaaxi would prefer her mate to fix things, but Zixoti had his hands full with a set of burnt couplings closer to the engine, and Dinah had to keep busy or scream.

Sys'Thysin and Sawyer busied themselves over their respective PDA's, ignoring the interplay as they had any of the occasional times they'd come to the bridge.

It was a relief to jump down and take over comms when they received a live answer to their arrival message.

"Glad you're here, *TSM*," the docking officer said. "We're overdue for a good supply drop."

Sys'Thysin straightened, his tail twitching before he stilled it, and Dinah could imagine the credit balances racing higher in his head.

"We're glad to be here, Kikrok Station. We're ground capable – would you prefer us to continue on to the station, or alter course for planetside?" The extra cost of fuel would be factored into their trade prices for landing, as some of their customers preferred the expedited delivery. Colony charters dictated the amount of general supplies Interstel would provide for them, neither too much nor too little, as colonies needed to both work toward self-sufficiency and not fail. The company also set parameters for pricing, but trade ships had plenty of room to navigate within the brackets, especially on non-perishable goods that could easily go somewhere else. Colonies needed the supplies, and traders needed the customers, so guiding wisdom let the market prevail.

"Station'll be fine." The dockmaster's words rushed together. Enthusiasm or worry? "You're on approach for dropside, dock six-beta-grey-four. We'll have a party to meet you to expedite delivery and any additional trade."

"Copy, Station. *Swingin' Miss* out." Dinah kicked her legs and reminded herself yet again she needed to get her father's chair replaced. Her father, like so many Humans, had been a full foot taller than her, and his chair...sitting in his chair was uncomfortable for a lot of reasons. The least she could do was fix the physical part of it.

"That was…interesting." Sawyer lifted her eyebrows and met first Viphaaxi's large compound eyes, then Dinah's. "You think there's a terraforming issue or someone disrupting trade routes?"

Colonies had plenty of reasons to get desperate. Interstel committed to regular supply runs to account for the worst of it, but a spot of bad luck and a delayed drop could make for a really bad stretch of days.

"Hopefully neither, but get Ehnuli on standby in case there's anything new we have to factor in."

Sys'Thysin stirred, turning his head to face Dinah more fully. "I am perfectly capable of adjussting trade goodsss asss needed, Captain."

"I understand, Sys'Thysin. But if there is a terraforming issue, Ehnuli's expertise will be needed."

Dinah knew Sys'Thysin damn well knew that. Whether he was questioning her, or the idea of being forced to work more closely with Ehnuli didn't matter. She repeated that fact to herself several times.

*Why under all the moons Dad thought having an Elowan and a Thrynn on the same ship was a good idea…*Of course both Sys'Thysin and Ehnuli were from Arth, and did not display the complete intolerance of their non-Arth counterparts. Still, though they operated effectively in their positions, they were the one combination of crew members she never saw together one-on-one.

"And Sawyer," Dinah added the moment she saw Sys'Thysin flex his hands as though he had more to say. "Be at the airlock when we seal up, will you? It's probably fine out there, but better to be prepped and unneeded than needed and unprepped."

Sawyer said the last half along with her, and Dinah barely swallowed back a laugh. Clearly her father had said those words as often to his crew as he had to his daughter in her early years.

After her first few weeks on *The Swingin' Miss*, Dinah avoided the galley during common mealtimes. It didn't improve her relationship with her crew, but…it didn't make it any worse. She'd meant to get back in there eventually, once they all adjusted to their new reality, but time had slipped by faster than she'd expected.

Without anything pressing to tinker with and the pervasive memory of hollow-eyed colonists stuck in her brain, she acknowledged she'd run out of excuses, and forced herself to walk the three doors down to the galley.

Nobody fell silent when the doors slid open, mostly because it was already quiet. Two sets of Zixoti's arms flared wide before he re-settled them. The entirety of her crew sat around the table, glanced up at her, then returned their eyes of various configurations to their equally various foodstuffs.

Their galley had been tailored over the years to best suit its multi-species crew, with a dual-level long table in the center of the room to accommodate the range of heights, and an assortment of adjustable chairs for tails, prehensile branches, and hips of various sizes to fit. Dinah nodded to the six members of her crew as she crossed to the designated Human corner, pulled open the under-fridge drawer and dug until she found her favorite dried noodles.

As it heated, she snagged a flat chair from its locked-in position on the wall nearest her and shifted it into a tall stool, which she carried over to the high end of the table next to Ehnuli. The Elowan swayed a greeting and brushed her shoulder gently with one deep green vine.

Zixoti and Viphaaxi leaned together on Ehnuli's other side, their antennae touching. Sawyer, Sys'Thysin, and Kayfive sat on the lower side of the table, Kayfive with his PDA in front of him where the rest had food.

"They've had a run of bad luck here," Sawyer said as the captain got settled. "I haven't heard of mining equipment failing so widely."

Ehnuli twisted her longest vine and swayed her head, her posture soft. "They needed to mortgage spare engines for additional crop-starters after the weather spun out of control." She tucked her vine close across her body and tilted toward Zixoti. "Then main engines began to fail and I suppose they sold their terrain farming vehicles to pay for those, and then…"

"One bad move after another." Kayfive shook its head. "Like the bite of the Qorlon minni, taking chunks so small you don't notice until your arm falls off."

Dinah had no idea what a Qorlon was, or what their minnis did. She decided, not for the first time, it was better not to ask.

"I hope they take my suggestion."

Nobody asked what her suggestion had been, though only half of them had been there when she made it. She assumed that meant they'd been talking about it, or about her, and she swallowed a sigh. *Yeah. I'm sick of this, and no amount of whiskey is gonna make it better.* Her mind crowded with the pressing memories of how exhausted Kikrok's colonists had been, and the last remaining pieces of her urge to step carefully around her still-newish crew flaked away.

"The one for them to register the catastrophic failure code to Interstel." She added the words deliberately, as though maybe they didn't know.

"What will that do?" Viphaaxi asked, unfolding her upper arms. Zixoti leaned harder against her, but she brushed her mate away.

"Move them to the front of the line for resources and support "

"Move them, or move the colony?"

"What do you…?" Dinah clenched her jaw, then forced herself to relax. "It's the same thing."

"Is it?" Sawyer's tone was less abrupt than Viphaaxi's, and she stretched her arms across the table, palms up in a way Dinah took as an intent to be calming. "Which is more important to Interstel – the profits from the colony's mining, or the people who live there?"

"Without the people who live there, they don't get the minerals…" Dinah shook her head and ignored her noodles in favor of studying Sawyer's open expression.

"If you received that code at Interstel, what would you do?" Viphaaxi's antennae straightened, and she moved away from Zixoti when he stirred in protest.

"Viv…" Ehnuli said softly, and the Velox ignored her as well.

"Forward it back to headqu –"

"And what would they do?"

"Dispatch a ship, with resources, to help the colony."

"What department is that?"

Dinah's flash of impatience surged out of her like air through a punctured hull, and her shoulders slumped before she could pull them upright. Viphaaxi pressed on before she could summon an answer.

"Do you know what class of ship they'd send? What are the regulations for that support? Is there a penalty charged to the colony?"

She didn't know. She didn't know and had no way of hiding that in her expression, and each of her crew stared at her, knowing how much she didn't know. Sys'Thysin cocked his head at her, his mouth curved in amusement. Zixoti shifted too much to be comfortable, while Viphaaxi held perfectly still and focused both compound eyes on her. Ehnuli fluttered, her translator clicking through half-started words in her aborted attempts to soothe. Kayfive blinked too much for someone who didn't need the eye lubrication, and Sawyer nodded and pulled her hands back.

None of them expressed surprise.

Dinah had been so careful, so considerate, and she realized it hadn't mattered. They put up with her because they had to, because otherwise Interstel would repossess *The Swingin' Miss* and they'd all be in breach of contract. Because her father died. They'd chosen to work for him, not her. She was the Interstel interloper who didn't even know how her own company had worked, and…The box she shoved her emotions into overflowed, and she stamped harder on it, then reached for her noodles.

"Hopefully it will be better at Farsel." It wasn't the right thing to say. If there were a right thing to say, it was so far from her ability to grasp it might as well be at Interstel headquarters.

"Hopefully," Sawyer answered, and Dinah couldn't tell if her smile was genuine, or vaguely pitying. She wished it didn't matter.

"*Swingin' Miss*, you have no idea how glad we are to see you. " Unlike Kikrok, Farsel's docking master didn't bother to hide her relief. "We have a delegation ready and waiting to help you unload at bay three."

"Understood, Farsel Control. We'll see you in…" Dinah glanced at Viphaaxi, who held up her two left upper appendages. "Two hours. *Swingin' Miss* out." She stood and stretched, then leaned forward to close her control panel. "I'm going onto the station, Nav. You will have the ship once we're docked."

"Understood, Captain."

The tall Velox had said few other words to Dinah since the last conversation in the galley, and the simple words, neutrally delivered, set the ridges of her ears burning.

"Viphaaxi."

"Captain?"

"Interstel is a big company."

"Understood, Captain."

Dinah's teeth clenched so hard she heard them creak. Thankful no one else was on the bridge, she turned fully toward Viphaaxi's station and breathed in deeply through her nose to ensure her voice held steady.

"I'm aware the ways you all might have experienced it are very different than how I did. But my father was never anything but proud of me, and encouraged me to sign up from the time I was in school."

"Under –"

"For the sake of every tiny burning thing, Viphaaxi!" She tried to breathe so as not to snap again, and then gave it up as a lost cause. Six months she'd bit her tongue, and her navigation officer had only grown more of…whatever this was. She hadn't heard Zixoti say more than three words ever. She was tired of bending for the expectations of her crew, when she couldn't even figure out what those were.

"If you think Interstel is five gallons of feces in a two gallon bag, by all means say something. If you think the same of me, then, you know what? Same. I'm sure we can find a way to transfer your and your mate's contract somewhere else. I'd hate to lose both of your expertise, but this?" She waved her hands, aware for the first time that Viphaaxi had turned her full attention toward Dinah. "Whatever 'this' is? I'm sick of it. I'm not Interstel, not anymore, and we all might as well make the most of it."

She turned on her heel and strode for the door before she had to hear another 'Understood, Captain.'

Good job, she told herself as she slid down the ladder to the main hall. *Way to lose Nav and Engineering in one idiot go.*

Might as well gather up her gear and see if she could knock out trade and armed backup, if not science and medical too. Maybe it would be her and her ghost ship, falling through space and missing her father together.

Damn it.

Farsel's station was worse than Kikrok's. Panels were missing in uneven patterns through the hall outside their airlock, the four humans lined up to meet them grinned too wide in too-hollow cheeks, and none of their loaders worked.

Dinah made all the right noises and comm'd back to the ship for Zixoti to leave his maintenance and put his strength to work alongside their ship's sleds for unloading.

The mess was not made better with the colonists continual effusive spills of gratitude, nor the way their eyes lingered on the crates marked with edible and perishable stickers.

"*Swingin' Miss* is a Euripides class?" One of the young men, all bones and gawky joints, bobbed eagerly alongside her as they walked through a dim corridor toward Farsel's main bay.

"All her life," Dinah answered, summoning a smile that must have come across genuine enough to encourage him.

"Those are pretty maneuverable, great choice for trade. Not like the big haulers, whew they can't turn once they get up to speed, right? Do you have the four bays or six?" He bounced as he walked beside her, pushing three crates on a flat surface with honest-to-real *wheels*. It seemed too much energy for him to expend, given he looked spindly enough to snap, but talking about her ship had brought too much life to his face for her to discourage it.

"Six. She had five for a while after an accident with a spray of micrometeors, and my father said she'd pull to the left for months after they fixed her up." Dinah winked at the kid to show it was a joke, and his sudden laugh boomed through the too-quiet halls of the station.

Sawyer turned at the sound, and Dinah lifted her eyebrows in response. Was she going to get judged for cheering up a sad colonist? Could she bring herself to care if she were?

After a moment, Sawyer grinned, and dropped back next to them. "You think that's something, you should hear what happened when we got an upgraded energy cloud. *Swingin' Miss* kept reading her own blockers as a threat and trying to target it. Alarms were going off every ten minutes." She rolled her eyes and shrugged, the gestures so exaggerated the kid laughed again. "Took us a week to get her used to it. Slept so well when it was over."

"Do all ships have personalities? Like, like androids? We have a couple, but they're pretty boring compared to, you know, stories I've heard?" He swallowed multiple times, eyes darting between Dinah and Sawyer, and Dinah decided to tell the tallest tales she could to brighten his day.

Despite the unexpected moments of camaraderie, unloading took too long. They all worked hard, both in encouraging the colonists and in getting everything transferred and accounted for, but by the time she returned to the galley, only Sys'Thysin seemed to have much of an appetite.

"It shouldn't be this bad." Dinah hadn't made a conscious decision to speak when the words left her face.

Ehnuli made a shuffling noise of agreement, but Sys'Thysin shrugged. Dinah raised her eyebrows at him, and after a moment he dropped his half-eaten leg and sat forward.

"They're all like thiss. Some a little worse, some a little better, but every sstop you've made with us has been like this." He clipped each word short. "Arrrth is pushing hard to grow, and these are the consequences."

"Arth, or Interstel?" Viphaaxi asked softly, crossing and uncrossing her upper appendages.

"Who caress?" Sys'Thysin shrugged. "Where there iss need, there isss profit. Our accountsss are in the green, that iss all the Captain need be concerned with."

"The Captain is concerned about a helluva lot, Sys." Dinah had never been invited to use his nickname, and when he stiffened in silent protest, she stared him down. Profit was one thing – it kept them in much better standing on their contract – but at the expense of what she'd seen at Farsel and Kikrok? There had to be a better way.

"Interstel contracts out supply runs. Maybe they don't know the worst of it. I'll ask some of my friends, see what we can do." She chewed on the side of her thumb and mentally composed the message she'd send to Porter.

Viphaaxi clicked, and Ehnuli swayed, and Sawyer snorted, and Dinah wondered if she'd ever figure out this crew at all.

"Kenneson!" Porter's message featured such an extreme close-up of his face that she couldn't tell if he was still on his ship or back at Starport. "Always good to hear your voice, but this better not count as next time – drinks are still very much on you. I don't hear much about the colonies, you know how it is. My lane is all about identifying the good rocks so they can be mining outposts or colonies. I don't know a lot about how they stay alive from there."

An upside-down v appeared in the skin between his eyebrows, and cleared as quickly.

"Asked some friends, but no one's reported in any issues. Maybe outward's just on a rough go. Everyone gets a turn at that, right? Interstel knows their obligations, it can't get too bad." His grin broadened, and he ducked his head in a way she was sure was meant to be charming. If she didn't have Kikrok's hollow-eyed desperation and Farsel's eager gratitude so clear in her thoughts, it might have worked.

Instead she wanted to punch him.

"I mean, the company wouldn't want the colonies to fail, right? Who'd get us our minerals?" He laughed at his own joke, and she swore and clicked away from the message before he could say more words that would make her like him less.

There hadn't been a speck of concern in his expression that she could find, and if Porter couldn't hear the urgency in her message, she couldn't think of anyone else who would.

Sys'Thysin hadn't been wrong. Arth did want growth, both to hold their own in the interstellar tensions with larger, older empires, and to ensure the survival of their species. Each foothold they secured was fragile, but key.

If Interstel weren't prepared to take care of those people who held each foothold…

She'd do it herself. Interstel limited how much contracted trade ships could bring to each colony, but *Swingin' Miss* had a long spine and six attached bays, with plenty of spaces in between. She could find overlooked spots to tuck goods into, carry more to colonies that had less, put some of their profit to work.

Interstel wouldn't like it, but that was space. All kinds of things not to like. If she found enough boltholes, Interstel would never have to be troubled by the knowledge of what she was doing.

She nodded to herself and marched down to the bays, determined to dig and identify spots to weld, and remake her bays, if she had to.

A few hours later she found far more than she'd been looking for.

Time for a crew meeting.

"It's like this," Dinah said to her assembled crew, tapping her thumb against her palm to keep from chewing on it. "The colonies out here aren't getting what they need. Interstel isn't holding up their end of the bargain. I don't know why, but I do know they don't like things like that getting pointed out."

"Like what?" Sawyer swung around in her seat, dragging her toes over the floor to keep to a half circle.

"Things where they're in the wrong."

"Touchy," Kayfive said in a hushed tone, as though it were whispering, but projected at a louder volume. "Like the Uhlek at any point in time." Dinah almost smiled – that comparison, at least, made sense.

"But we have a ship, and a way to get supplies to the colonies that need them."

"They're not going to let us double or quadruple up on supplies at Starport," Viphaaxi interjected, her head cocked to focus her eyes on the captain and her antennae at full alert.

"We have a clever trademaster. I know we can get what we need."

"And then…?" Sawyer glanced at Sys'Thysin, and when he didn't speak, she leaned forward. "If Interstel is going to be touchy…?"

"Clever bookkeeping."

"And if someone looks?"

"*I* looked." She took a deep breath, mentally crossed her fingers, and plunged in. "I dug through the bays seeing where we could maybe build a false wall, connect to a conduit, get some extra capacity." She let the words hang there and observed how very still each member of her crew had become. All of them. Her lips quirked at the lack of surprise, which confirmed her guess. "You all know what I found."

She'd meant to make it a question, as over-dramatic as it felt now. Instead she flattened it into a statement, and waited.

Ehnuli broke first, swaying. Sawyer barked a laugh, but the translator didn't kick in to translate the Elowan's movements. Dinah hoped like hell she was right, that her father had truly led this crew, not been betrayed by them.

"You found false walls," Viphaaxi said, her tone uninflected as ever, though she inclined her upper thorax toward her. "Cubbies in the conduits. Linings too thick for efficiency."

"You've done this before. You've been doing it all along?" Her voice lifted despite her efforts, as her eyes shifted from one of her crew to the next. "*Swingin' Miss* is a smuggler's ship."

"Your father saw the need," Sys'Thysin said, with something like a sigh. "I saw the profit."

"Need and profit is a helluva opportunity." Sawyer smiled, but her eyes stayed cold on Dinah. "We did what we had to."

"Are doing."

Sawyer inclined her head.

"And my father…?"

"We think…" Ehnuli swayed, turning toward Viphaaxi. When the Velox didn't move, Ehnuli twisted her longer arm and continued, the translator nearly as rhythmic as her movements. "We think someone got suspicious. Assumed our Captain was the issue."

"Took him out." Zixoti said, each word ringing through the galley, through Dinah's entire body.

That possibility – the sudden and complete likelihood of it, where a moment before she hadn't even imagined it – twisted her spine and loosened her knees.

"You think he was *murdered*?"

"You know very well how hard flight is on our – most of our – bodies," Sawyer said, her voice brisk. Her shoulders dropped though, some tension bleeding out of her as Dinah fought for balance. "Kayfive runs diagnostics on us all the time. Nothing was wrong with your father's heart."

"Until it stopped." Zixoti spoke again, and the impossibility of all of it swirled through Dinah until she truly believed, for one wild moment, that their artificial gravity had failed.

"It's not – it's possible…" She couldn't find the words she needed. That was…it was stupid. Impossible. She didn't have enough air to form her arguments, and her thoughts slipped around her as she struggled.

"It could have been a sudden tragedy, yes. But he never wanted this life for you, Dinah." Sawyer's voice softened, ever so slightly, on her name. Had Sawyer ever used her name before? "Ehnuli was supposed to take over the ship. He talked about it with us. It was clear in Captain Kenneson's files."

Sys'Thysin muttered something, but without heat to it. He shook himself and said at a normal volume, "Suddenly Interstel said it had to be next of kin or the contract was void. I looked at all the contracts before I came on board."

"That wasn't in the contract?" She'd read the contract too. Sent it to an old roommate, now a lawyer, in the hopes she could find a way to wriggle out of it. There hadn't been any room to do so – she was her father's next of kin, and designated heir. It was her or nothing.

"Oh, it's in the contract. Now." Sawyer shook her head. "They modified every copy of it we could find. Why would Interstel care to put effort into changing all the digital records, if Bryce just dropped dead? How would they have had the time to get ahead of it, if it were all a surprising tragedy?"

"They wanted…" Dinah groaned and slid into her seat, giving up on finding her balance. Her stomach roiled, and bile burned in the back of her throat. "They wanted a loyal company man to take over the ship."

"We don't think it's the whole company – your dad definitely thought you were safe enough there. But…yeah. Someone at Interstel had a little too much interest in what we're doing." Sawyer shrugged, but Dinah knew the pain behind the gesture – it surged through her own nerves.

"*Why?*" The word burst out of her, the only clear thought she had.

"Someone wants the colonies to fail?" Viphaaxi offered, then clicked as though she realized it was both too big and too small a reason at once.

"There's profit to be made. They don't want it to be ours." Sys'Thysin dropped the words with finality. "That is always the case, Human or Thrynn, or whomever. If we get more, they by definition have less, and that will not stand."

"So…" Kayfive stood and walked around the table, then crouched in front of Dinah. "If it's true, they're definitely watching us, like a marbled hawak from Kessel."

"We've moved much less product since…ah, since you got here. We can get better at hiding from Interstel but we didn't…" Ehnuli waved her vines, then stretched them toward Dinah in mute appeal.

"You didn't know how much I knew. Or where my loyalties were." Protests crowded in her throat, and she swallowed them back. She couldn't just tell them she loved her father more than her job. They had to *know* it was true. And if they didn't…they would, soon enough.

Ehnuli spread her arms in a gesture that didn't need translation, and Dinah laughed, the sound high and breathless.

"I'll tell you this. They can watch all they want. They'll never see us coming."

Hindsight

By RJ Ladon

You can do anything. That was Sarat's father's mantra. *All you need is money and surround yourself with people who have the knowledge you lack.* Sarat's father, Akash, built a financial empire following that rule. But what he failed to mention that those people with the knowledge have opinions, attitudes, and baggage. *Why did he ever think leaving Arth was a good idea?* Sarat had squandered his inheritance on an Intrepid-Class Scout. Which seemed like a good idea at the time. After hiring crew members, Sarat named his ship *Hindsight,* as it was the only thing that appeared to be twenty-twenty.

Sarat raised his hands to stave off any more questions from his only passenger. "Look, I can't give you crew quarters. You're a passenger."

Ed Nolan squinted. "Sarat." The older man smiled then grasped his shoulder. "I'm not *just* a passenger. I hired you. I'm your boss." With the last three words, Ed poked Sarat's chest, emphasizing each word. He folded his arms. "Talk to the crew. Make it happen. Do this for me, and I will have another job for you."

Sarat shook his head. "You haven't even told me where we are going or what we are looking for on this job."

"All in due time. Just go to the coordinates I gave you." Ed patted Sarat on the arm in a grandfatherly gesture.

"Make my life miserable, and I will drop you on an asteroid." Sarat didn't like this man. He had to be the most arrogant jackass I had ever worked with. Truth be told, he reminded Sarat of his father.

"Good." Ed cracked a smile and dropped his folded arms. "You've got some backbone that will help." The old man turned and walked into the crew commons.

"Why the smile?"

Sarat turned to look at Phila Lisney. Her dark, tightly curled hair was pulled into an elegant bun. Her deep brown eyes matched her clothing.

"Was I smiling? I didn't mean to. Ed wants to sleep in crew quarters." Sarat shrugged. "His request is ridiculous."

Phila dropped into a parade stance, hands clasped behind her back. "We're not military. The *Hindsight* is your ship that makes you the captain. Tell Tonopex and Poxoti to share quarters. They are a mated pair." She tilted her head to the side. "That change wouldn't break regulations. The only regulations we have are what you impose, captain." She nodded, then walked into crew commons.

"It's not that easy," he said to her, retreating back. "Have you ever tried to convince a Velox of anything?" Besides, did he really want to set that kind of precedence? Then other passengers would expect the same sort of treatment. A month ago, Captain Sarat Rout's title sounded wonderful, but now it feels like it should be changed to Captain Doormat. *We've barely left Arth, and I feel like I'm over my head.* Sarat pushed his hands through his short dark hair. Sighing, he stepped into crew commons.

The room was large with a bar and fixed pool, poker, zaxottix, and cylir tables. Zaxottix was a fast and exciting game, played with two to four players. It was notorious for its gambling associations. The pyramid-shaped game required the players to have four or more arms to maneuver the tiles between the transparent levels fast enough to bet upon. Bets were placed depending on the time needed to win. An excellent player could bet six minutes to turn the tiles. Observers could take odds for or against the claimed bet of any player. Humans, even working in tandem, could barely turn the tiles in fifteen minutes, and watching *the two-arms* play was tedious and boring.

Cylir, on the other hand, was strategy based similar to the old Arth game Go. The glass tokens were floral shaped and brightly colored, not the black and white of Go. Low-Gahhn and Sahnthhis were engaged in a friendly match. Their leaves twitched and fluttered as they spoke to each other in their native Elowan.

Low was communications for the *Hindsight*. She was small and delicate, almost reaching four feet tall. All Elowan carry both male and female organs, but Low was often called she or her due to her size and gentle nature. Low was not offended and even changed her communicator to have a higher tone, making her sound female. She had three arms and three legs. The extra appendages were on her left side, which indicated her tendencies to favor that side.

Sahnthhis, on the other hand, was tall and more robust than Low. He was hired on as the *Hindsight's* medical officer. Sahnthhis or San, for short, loved old Arth clocks and gearing. During his free time, San expressed his creative side with paint and music. His love for crafting new and exciting items allowed him to grow five arms to help him tinker and create.

Sarat Rout stood near their game table. He waited for a lull in conversion to speak, not that it was apparent when an Elowan stopped talking. They both turned to look at the captain, their pod-like heads tilted to the side. "Low, I need help communicating with Tonopex and Poxoti." Sarat sighed then continued. "Ed would like a room in the crew cabins, and since they are a mated pair, they could share a room. I am uncertain how to approach either of them on that subject."

The smaller of the two Elowan shook her yellow-green foliage, moving her willowy arms and bobbing her head.

Sarat held up his hand. "Wait a minute, Low. Your communicator is turned off, and my Elowan is horrible."

Low turned to San, her three arms twisting and vibrating. Her head tilted then she looked down. Sahnthhis spoke, his communicator set to a low resonance. "Low left her communicator in her room. Nevertheless, she and I believe it unnecessary for Tonopex and Poxoti to share a cabin. Low, and I can share. We enjoy each other's company." Low shook an arm at San and made more gestures, then turned to look at Sarat. San continued, "Low wishes me to tell you that you are the captain. If you want Tonopex and Poxoti to share a cabin, all you have to do is command it."

Sarat nodded. He knew that, but if he threw around commands, wouldn't that cause future problems? Would Tonopex or Poxoti dislike him or have a grudge to settle later? The size of their mandibles alone was intimidating. Working for his father and being told what to do was so much easier than being a leader. Sarat didn't expect these types of challenges. He cleared his throat. "Thank you, San and Low." He nodded to each of them. "Please combine your quarters and let me know which cabin is available."

Sarat turned and saw Phila standing nearby. "You are looking for an easy way out." She moved as if going to the bar, then stopped and looked over her shoulder. "You need to grow a set."

The captain studied Phila's back as she leaned on the bar. He wanted to deny her comments, but she was right. He turned on his heel, leaving crew commons. The *Hindsight* corridors were barren of homey touches, no pictures, no paint, no carpet on the floor, only crisscross scoring for gripping boots or claws. The smell, too, left something to be desired, body odor and pheromones. No one told him that Velox produced pheromones and that, in enclosed spaces, was sticky-sweet. Velox looked a lot like Arth ants. It seemed logical that they, too, would have a sweet tooth. Sarat's stomach turned. *I'll never look at a piece of candy the same.*

Sarat stepped into main engineering. This was Poxoti's domain. Clicking filled the room. She must be working on something. He would show Phila. He was quite capable of giving orders. The Velox could share quarters just like the Elowan. *What on Arth is that?* Captain Rout inhaled sharply. The sticky-sweet smell of candy was thicker here. Stomping, scratching, and clicking noises became louder. Next to the engine were eight no, nine limbs. Velox only have six. *Oh man, what the hell?* Sarat clasped his hand over his mouth, leaning back against the cool wall, feeling like he might vomit at any moment. This was not what he expected. He turned tail and left the two Velox to their relations. The scratching and clicking now made perfect sense. He could die tomorrow, and that smell would follow him past his grave and into hell.

Everyone was gathered on the bridge. They had arrived at the coordinates Ed gave and were waiting for more information. Sarat glanced at Tonopex as the Velox was at the helm. Ed leaned over the insect-like hominid. His fingers poked at the paper in his hand and then to the display. "That's the system, D5623-578K." Ed pulled something out of his pocket. Cellophane crinkled, and a hard candy went into his mouth. Sarat covered his face, realizing he would have to get over Velox pheromones sooner rather than later.

"There is nothing in that system. The sun is a red giant, and all of the planets are too far away to be habitable." Tonopex stated as if the idea of setting a destination to the system was a waste of time. The Velox's mandibles clasped and grated near Ed's neck and face as he spoke. Sarat felt uncomfortable, even though it was not he who was so close to the eviscerating mouthparts.

Ed nodded then spoke around his candy to Tonopex. "That's why the system retained the original survey designation. No one thought it was worthy of a name."

Sarat cleared his throat. "Tonopex is right. Why are we going to that particular system?"

Ed looked around, folding the paper and putting it into his pocket. "Does it matter? I'm paying the whole lot of you to take me there."

"We are going to find out as soon as we get there, are we not?" Phila asked. "Are you gaining anything keeping this secret from us?" She folded her arms then drummed her right fingers on her left arm. "If I were you, I'd want all the crew to know what was going on to prepare them properly." She glared at Ed. "But that's just me."

Ed looked around the bridge a smug grin showed how pleased he was with himself. "That's why I hired your ship. You're not military." His eyes hovered over each crew member.

Phila wiped her nose. "Some of us are ex-military." Her intense stare held Ed in position.

Ed fidgeted in response. "It's not like that. It's not illegal or anything." He wrung one hand against another.

"Explain," Sarat interjected. "Or I will instruct Tonopex to find the nearest asteroid."

Phila dropped into a parade stance, seemingly relieved by Sarat's interruption.

"It's nothing. It's nothing." Ed spread his hands wide. "When I was on the frigate *Morning Star*, I ran navigation. While surveying new regions for an M class planet. I found other things." Ed shrugged. "But the captain didn't want to hear of *other things*. He told me to shut my mouth." He shrugged again. "So, I did."

Sarat waited for a moment for Ed to continue, but he didn't. "And?" he prompted.

"And, well, some of the other things were not planets." Ed looked away.

Phila stepped to Ed's side and leaned into him. "If you don't finish your story, I'll throw you out the airlock without the benefit of an asteroid."

"Fine, fine." Ed waved Phila off. "I found a huge ship. But the captain didn't want to hear of it. Especially since it was derelict."

"We're going after a derelict ship?" Sarat asked.

Ed turned to face Sarat. "Not just derelict, it's at least a century old. When I asked the science officer on the *Morning Star*, the design wasn't in her database. Completely alien. I believe it to be from outside the Alpha Sector. The salvage of materials will be well worth the effort of towing it home." Ed raised a finger. "But the real money will be in the technology that is found. A ship that old, that big, and that far from home must have technology that we've never seen before." Ed rubbed his hands together; excitement covered his face.

Phila fought back a smile. She was *Hindsight*'s science officer and understood the potential of such a find. "Your captain." Phila shot Sarat a glance. "At the time, your captain didn't want to hear about your discovery?"

Ed shook his head. "He only had eyes and ears for M class planets, nothing more. In his words, *I don't want to hear about the minutia of the entire system.*" Ed sang-song the quoted words from his previous captain, making it clear how far his admiration went.

"You realize this changes everything," Sarat said. "There are laws to salvage. If there are survivors, we are not allowed to just take the ship from them."

The old man laughed. "Didn't you hear? The ship's over a century old. No one's on it. There wasn't a power signature. Nothing. The ship and everything on it is dead."

"How long until we see the system, Tonopex?" Sarat asked.

The grating, raspy insect voice said, "Fifteen hours."

System D5623-578K rolled across the main display on the bridge. The massive red giant glowed softly. Eight planets were so far from their sun that they were barely discernible from the background stars. The closest planet to the sun was a gas giant and well outside the goldilocks zone.

Ed instructed Tonopex to move closer to the sun. "There, do you see it?" Ed's voice rose an octave as his excitement mounted.

Tonopex commented in Velox, clicking his mandibles appreciatively. "Sarat, you need to see this." The Velox put his display onto the main screen for everyone to see. The red giant glowed, taking up the entire image, but there as if floating on the surface of the sun, was a long black shape.

Ed watched, standing to the side, nodding like a proud father. "There we are. Isn't she a 'beaut?" The old man turned to Tonopex. "How far is she from the sun?"

"1.25 AU. It only looks closer because of this view." Tonopex manipulated the feed to show the image from a slight angle. "Our trajectory has changed. This is current." The enormous ship orbited the sun at a strange angle, allowing what appeared to be the top to face the sun.

"It was in the habitable zone when I first saw it too." Ed frowned. "Can a derelict do that?" Ed turned away from the screen and looked from Sarat to Phila.

"I'm not sure I follow." Sarat shook his head.

"Are you suggesting a ship failed and went into orbit around this sun on its own?" Phila pursed her lips. "A stable orbit? No, I think the odds are against it. Someone piloted the ship into its current flight path." She raised a finger. "Even so, unless there is some technology we are unaware of, a stable orbit for hundreds of years seems unlikely."

"Could it be a Sanguine Ambush?" Ed looked like he might become sick. "Maybe I should have hired a military commander." He looked back at Sarat and waved his hand dismissively. "No offense, Captain."

"None taken Ed. You simply wanted someone you could bully. You should have thought about the skill set an experienced crew could provide." Sarat smirked. "Low, have you detected any communications going in or out of the derelict ship?"

"No, Captain. The whole system is quiet." Low fumbled with her communicator then set it on the table before her. Her willowy appendages manipulated the knobs and switches on the console. Every so often, her head would turn as if she were listening to something no one else could hear.

"Phila, are you detecting anything? A power source? Emissions? Exhaust?" Sarat shrugged.

"What did you say?" Phila lifted one sculpted eyebrow.

Sarat raised a hand as if to stave off a physical blow. "I don't even know what you would look for. I'm not trying to tell you how to do your job."

"Actually," Phila admitted. "That's an excellent idea." Phila shrugged. "It's just that you surprised me." Her delicate hands danced over the interface as she selected sensors. Phila paused, and her eyes widened. "Well, that's interesting." She looked up to the captain. "Sir, I think I found something."

"Yes?" Sarat and Ed said together.

Phila gave Ed a nasty stare, then turned her attention to Sarat. "There appears to be a trail of jetsam coming from one section of the craft. All of it is of similar material and size."

"What does that tell you?" Sarat asked.

"If we could get a sample, I could tell you more."

Ed put his hands on his hips and stared at Phila. "Well, hell, if we're going to get that close, we might as well board the ship and investigate. Enough of this science at a distance. Let's go and get dirty."

Phila cracked her knuckles. "Sarat, may I strike him?"

Sarat smiled. "While I would love nothing more than to watch Ed scream like a baby, he is our guest, our paying guest."

Ed stammered as if he were about to complain, then decided to close his mouth.

Phila nodded, satisfied. "What is odd about the jetsam is that it appears to be ejected from the craft in equal intervals. Without testing, it will be impossible to know if it's a failure in the ship, something to indicate habitation or nothing at all."

"What do you recommend?"

"We need to physically investigate the ship."

Ed stomped his feet, anger bristling. "Isn't that what I just said?"

"Perhaps if you waited until I was done with my observation, you wouldn't have been berated like a child." Phila stared at Ed. "You also need to be reminded that you are a passenger, not part of the crew. Let us do our job." Phila's dark eyes narrowed dangerously. "If you wanted to be in control, perhaps you should have bought your own ship."

Ed scoffed and pointed at Sarat. "She should be Captain."

Pregnant silence filled the bridge. Phila crossed her arms defiantly.

"Don't you think I tried?" Sarat asked. "Phila would make a damn fine captain. But I must make do with asking for her advice." Sarat kept his eyes on Ed. "Tonopex, bring the *Hindsight* closer to the derelict. Try and locate a docking port. Phila, please continue doing your *science at a distance* in the meantime."

Tonopex clicked his pinchers, stating something in Velox. "Captain, the derelict has holes in the side of its hull. I will find a suitable landing site. If this ship is truly alien, I doubt our docking couple would find a matching surface."

"Agreed," Sarat said. "Please be gentle with the *Hindsight*. I can't afford a replacement."

Tonopex clicked his pinchers again, grinding the appendages together.

Ed looked startled by what Tonopex said in Velox, then glanced at Sarat.

The captain sighed. "Tonopex, you know I don't speak Velox, yet you continue to do so in my presence. I am forced to believe you are disrespecting me and my position. If this behavior continues, I will fire you and put Ed in as navigation. Then Ed can find an asteroid for you." Sarat turned to face Tonopex in case the Velox was about to react badly. "Do I make myself clear?"

Ed's eyes widened. He looked terrified.

Tonopex tossed his head back. A fitful and grating sound erupted from his convulsing mouth and mandibles. "Excellent, I wondered what it would take to force a confrontation from you." The Velox stood from the console and stepped inches from Sarat. "I watch you look at my mandibles with fear in your eyes." His mouth parts clicked with emphasis. "I find your species pathetic. Now that you have shown some fortitude, I am willing to listen, for now." Tonopex nodded then returned to his station.

Sarat opened his mouth to say something more, but Ed's head shook, and Phila's boot struck his shin.

Tonopex glided the *Hindsight* closer to the derelict. As he stated, the ship's side was open to space, as if the vessel were in a great battle or perhaps ravaged by time and gravitational forces. The derelict was a giant vessel easily spanning fifteen levels. The Velox found a section where enough floors were missing to allow the *Hindsight* to land inside the ship.

The derelict seemed to shudder as they touched down. Tonopex, Ed, and Phila exchanged glances. "Are you sure you are not getting any energy readings?" Tonopex asked. "It seems like we found gravity."

Phila shook her head. "Nothing."

Low tilted her head and turned a knob on her console. She waved her arms with excitement. Stopped, then looked down at the floor. One thin arm reached out and picked up her communicator. Low manipulated the small instrument then started again. "I hear something. At first, I thought it was the rumble of the sun, but it's something else. I think I hear the engines of this ship."

"What?" Phila demanded. "I haven't found any emissions." She shook her head then continued. "The small jetsam I found was more like debris than emissions. For the sake of argument, if this ship put out debris as emissions, there would not be enough to account for this whole ship. Not even ten percent." A light seemed to sparkle in Phila's eyes. "Perhaps if only a section of the ship were active." Her fingers danced on the console as she bit her bottom lip. She inhaled sharply, then frowned. "Still, nothing. Not enough to account for an engine hum or the presence of gravity here on the outskirts of the ship." Phila looked at Low. "Could the noise be from something else?"

Low bobbed her head in thought. "To me, it sounds mechanical." Her thin, willowy shoulders shrugged.

"Don't bother me with the minutia." Ed raked quote symbols in the air. "Enough science at a distance. Let's go and investigate."

Sarat looked to the others on the bridge and nodded. "We should investigate. But, you, Ed, are not the captain. Phila, Low, and I will go.

Ed stomped to Sarat's side. "You can't do this to me. This is my find. I demand that I be allowed to disembark."

Sarat leaned into Ed. "I need you here, and I need to be there making snap decisions." Sarat turned away from Ed, which forced the older man to readjust his footing, moving closer. Sarat whispered to him, "I'm not sure I trust Tonopex. The last thing I need is for that Velox to leave us all behind. But if I remove him from his post, he would have more opportunity to do something nefarious." He cleared his throat and spoke louder. "Besides, we are going to be here for hours. You can go out when we come back with samples. This derelict isn't going anywhere."

Ed frowned, then smiled in such quick succession that it looked like he was experiencing a seizure. "You ought to take his mate, then Tonopex won't do anything stupid."

Sarat nodded, placing his hand on the old man's shoulder. "I could use some insurance right about now." He turned away from

Ed and walked to Tonopex's console. "Tonopex, how many different classes of ship has Poxoti worked on?"

Tonopex's compound eyes looked behind Sarat, and his mandibles moved slightly as if he were mentally counting. "Twenty to twenty-five." His eyes refocused on Sarat. "Why do you ask?"

"I believe Poxoti would be fascinated by this new technology. I think I will invite her to come with us." Sarat rubbed his chin.

Mandibles clicked. "It's old technology. Surely Velox ingenuity has outpaced this heap of junk." Tonopex's eyes moved around the room, but his exoskeleton prevented any other signs of discomfort from marking his face.

The captain shrugged. "I think Poxoti ought to make that decision. Don't you?" Sarat moved away from navigation and walked to engineering.

Four of them stood in the airlock. Poxoti's massive eight-foot frame enshrouded in her spacesuit took up a full one-third of the room. Low's spacesuit was tiny in comparison. Most of her suit was to house her head. The modular design allowed her to share a suit with any Elowan, even though she favored her left side with an extra arm and leg.

The airlock door hissed as it opened. Then, in silent agreement, everyone moved together until Poxoti stepped from the *Hindsight*. It was apparent that the helm had a blind spot that prevented the Velox from seeing below her without bending, and no one wanted to be trampled.

Poxoti held her scanner and was studying it. "The gravity is light here. It appears to be originating from deeper inside the ship." The Velox's pleasant baritone sounded across the helmet's speaker and into the bridge, where observers watched all four of their personal cameras on the main screen. She walked forward, her stride long and graceful. Phila, Sarat, and Low followed.

"Look here." Phila pointed to a section of metal. "It was cut. I don't see any indication of an attack. At least not here." She punched something into her scanner then moved it back and forth. "Nothing impressive with the metal. It's made of elements we are all familiar with."

Sarat imagined Ed frowning. "Sorry, Ed. Might not be that exotic after all."

The enormous Velox moved aside some metal to gain access into the derelict. "We've only scratched the surface, Captain. Besides, it's the engines and tech that should have the most differences." She paused. "Well, this is unexpected." Poxoti grumbled in Velox then stepped aside. "Phila, take point." Beyond Poxoti was a corridor much shorter than the Velox's frame. "Clearly, this shipbuilder didn't have us Velox in mind." Poxoti made a noise that Sarat was beginning to associate as a Velox swear word or curse.

Static crackled over the com. "Come back Poxoti, I'll bring a set of interchange devices," Tonopex begged over the helmet's speakers.

"Don't be ridiculous," Poxoti replied to her mate. "This is a discovery of a new ship. I'm not about to give up dexterity for a pair of interchange devices. I promise I'll be careful."

The corridor had bars on the ceiling every foot or two. If the bars were removed, the height would have been eight feet or more. Why install them? Sarat stepped into the hallway after Phila and

Low then turned to watch Poxoti. The Velox bent forward and used her middle arms as legs. This wasn't ideal as the space suit's gloves were less durable than boots. Interchange devices would have turned Poxoti's manipulating gloves into durable tread. Which would be perfect for walking but would hobble Poxoti. Sarat could appreciate the idea of having extra limbs and then being forced not to use them. In a time and place where learning new tech might require extra hands, Poxoti was right to not use the boots. The Velox navigated closer to Sarat. Even in this unusual position, Poxoti was easily five feet tall at the top of her helm but nowhere near as maneuverable.

"Want me to take up the rear?" Sarat asked her.

"No, you'd do me a favor if you could walk before me and watch the floor for anything that could damage my gloves. My own people didn't think it was important enough to see below our own heads." She pointed to the blind spots in her helm, then repeated the comment in Velox, confirming that it was indeed a swear word. "My people are no better than anyone else, but often we forget that. Why else make a blind spot in such a way? Such a purposeful negative space would only exist so that we may not see those we stomp upon." Poxoti swore again. "Often, it is my mate who behaves in such a way. I will not apologize for him. It is our way."

The three of them kicked aside the odd bits of debris to make sure Poxoti's path was clear. Each tidbit appeared to be a cut section of the ship, square tube, round pipe, and flat sheets. The edges were melted or cut mechanically.

"Sir," Phila said excitedly. "I'm getting a reading." The science officer stood at an intersection in the corridor. "Down that way, the sensor picks up a slight tick." She pointed the sensor at each of the passageways. When she swept past the suspected corridor, the detector beeped a couple times before becoming quiet.

"Suggestions?" Sarat pointed to Low.

"The signal could be anything, detecting power from the *Hindsight* or even the sun. I recommend continuing down this corridor. It should lead us to the bridge of the ship."

Sarat nodded, then pointed to Poxoti. "What are your thoughts?"

"The bridge would be a source of technology that would indicate what species utilized this vessel." Poxoti nodded. "Assuming all species use and house their bridge in the same location. However, the signal could be an indication of a power source, which is a definite sign of technology."

"And Phila?" Sarat asked.

"Doesn't matter, either way, I'm learning something."

Sarat nodded. "I've always been a fan of breadcrumbs. I say we follow the signal."

Phila started down the corridor with the signal, swinging the sensor in front of her. At every intersection, she would test for the strongest signal. "Look," Phila announced excitedly. Over her shoulder was a metal wall crudely welded into place. It bisected the corridor at an angle. "The signal is stronger here." She pounded on the surface with her gloved hand. "We'll have to try another intersecting corridor."

Poxoti backed slowly out of the passageway into the closest intersection. "I can feel my gloves wearing under the stress of using my hands." She squatted down, sitting on the floor. "Maybe I ought to have gone back for the interchange devices." Poxoti studied the gloves on her lower arms. She reached into her hip pouch and pulled out a roll of tape. "Sarat, would you help me? I need to reinforce my gloves before they tear."

Sarat looked at the Velox sitting in the passageway, looking dejected. "Phila, Low, you two go ahead. Keep us updated." He grasped Poxoti's hand, studying her gloves. There was a wear mark on the palm and knuckles of her hands. If they covered her hands with tape, she would lose the dexterity she fought to keep. He looked at the floor and the debris that was kicked near the walls. "Poxoti, I've got an idea." Sarat gathered the largest segments and brought them back to Poxoti. He set a tube on top of a thick plate. "If we used tape to connect these two together, could you use it to walk?"

The hissing rasping curse of Tonopex filled their helms.

Poxoti looked up to the ceiling and returned the grating sound of Velox to her mate. An uncomfortable silence was broken by a periodic static hiss. "Tonopex assumes you are insulting me." Poxoti's voice shook as she tried to maintain control of her emotions. "But he is not here. He does not understand." She picked up the tube and plate. "Many centuries ago, we used gadgets like this, but they were crude. We left them in our past, and now we use the interchange devices. Tonopex assumes you know our history, and your offer to make me one was meant an insult. I know this to be false. You don't even know our language. And without that, you would never know our history."

Sarat kicked the junk to the edge of the wall. "I would never insult you. This was not my intent. I understand your desire to maintain the dexterity of all four limbs. I just wanted to help." The captain looked down, fearing that he made an enemy of both Velox.

Poxoti pointed. "Please grab that bent pipe and that plate. Bring them to me."

Sarat gathered the U-shaped pipe and the square plate. "What are your plans? Can I assist?"

"Your idea is a solid one. Logically I can't find fault with it." Poxoti joined the two pieces of metal together with tape. Then wrapped a single strip of tape around her palm and knuckle where the wear was the worst. "Let's give it a test run." Poxoti used the device and hobbled down the passageway, following in the direction Phila and Low went. After passing a couple intersections, she stopped and examined her gloves and the damage to the tape. "Perhaps the ancients knew what they were talking about. Sarat, please find me another set of materials that are similar to this." Poxoti pounded the makeshift boot into the floor.

Sarat smiled. He had been looking for similar parts as they walked and mentally marked them. He was back at Poxoti's side in minutes. A short time later, Poxoti had a set of metal boots.

"If you two are done messing around, we found a door." Pride oozed from Phila's voice. "Low is coming to show you the way."

The pressure door was made from many layers of metal, appearing crudely but effectively made. Near the top and in the center was a circular handle that seemed to pull six different tabs from the door assembly. Sarat assumed that was a locking or sealing mechanism. The metal had a patina on the edges where it seated into the wall to form a seal, which suggested it was exposed to air and time. Sarat wondered how that could be when it was currently exposed to the vacuum of space.

Phila waved her sensor around the door's edges. "I've tested it twice. I'm getting a slight oxygen count, but only at the door seal. I haven't seen it anywhere else."

Poxoti made a strange grating noise, which Sarat had never heard before. "That door looks like it has reached the end of its life. I'm not sure if it's safe to open. We might cause permanent damage."

Low moved forward, placing her slender hand on the door. "Oxygen indicates life. We can't open this door without some safety precautions."

Phila raised a finger. "Airlocks require two doors. If I'm sensing air out here, that means the inner door has failed to some degree." Phila ran her sensor around the door again, then checked the seams between wall and floor, and then wall and ceiling.

"Low and Phila are right." Sarat nodded. "Poxoti, do you have any equipment that would repair an airlock?"

Poxoti turned and looked at the captain with a slightly tilted head. "This is our first mission. The equipment I have onboard is fairly minimal."

Sarat sighed. "From your tone, I'm guessing, no."

The Velox placed a tape-enhanced glove on his shoulder. "We have a laser welder. While I can't fix that door without welding it shut, I could create a new one. A very crude one, mind you." She sighed. "That means putting in a bulkhead too." Poxoti patted the walls and ceiling around her. The metal flexed and vibrated. "And reinforcing these thin walls to withstand air pressure."

"Tell me what you need, and I'll make it happen."

"Right now, I need sleep and food."

Phila pointed at Poxoti and nodded. "I agree."

For three days, Poxoti, Tonopex, and Phila worked together to strengthen the area and install an airlock. As Poxoti predicted, the door was crudely made from the materials that could be found on the derelict. They secured their door and filled the space with air, testing it for leaks.

Sarat stood in engineering and watched as Poxoti created a welded set of metal boots for herself and Tonopex. The design was light and elegant, reminding Sarat of an ancient Arth device used to flatten clothing. Why anyone needed such a thing was a mystery. Why Tonopex agreed to using his set after his outburst was also a mystery.

"We are ready, captain." Phila stood in a parade stance just inside engineering. "We are waiting for you. Unless you've decided not to join us."

"I wouldn't miss this for any reason. How about you, Poxoti? Are you ready to see what is on the other side of that door?" Sarat asked.

"I'm ready, now that I have finished my interchange devices." Poxoti made a sound deep in her throat that Sarat knew was a laugh. "I can't wait to give Tonopex his set."

Sarat couldn't help but smile. "I'd like to see his expression when you do. Phila, what are the sensors reading in our chamber?"

"Arth normal. I will check again as we approach." Phila looked at her hand-held and added more data. "Are you allowing Ed to join us this time?"

Sarat sighed. "Yeah, I better."

"Damn right, you better." Ed leaned against the wall behind Phila.

Phila rolled her eyes. "Get your damn suit on and be in the airlock. You've got five minutes."

"Five?" Ed stuttered, backing out of the room.

"Isn't that enough?" asked Sarat.

Ed blinked a couple times, then ran from engineering.

Poxoti picked up her interchange devices and walked out, ducking under the doorway. Phila and Sarat followed. The process of changing into space suits took nearly ten minutes. Most of that time consisted of safety checks. When Sarat entered the airlock, everyone was already there.

After thirty minutes of trekking through the derelict's belly, they stood in the cramped section between the old airlock and the new.

Sarat nodded. "Poxoti, open the airlock."

"Why her?" Ed placed his hands on his hips in protest. "You didn't even know about this ship until I hired you."

"Go ahead, Ed." Poxoti encouraged. "I don't mind."

Ed reached up for the round handle. It was over his head and difficult to manipulate. He jumped to grab a higher section only to hang from the handle.

Sarat sighed. "I asked Poxoti because she is much taller and stronger than any of us."

"Especially me," piped up Low.

Poxoti gave Phila a high-five.

"Fabulous." Ed sulked off to the side.

Poxoti grasped the handle with all four arms and heaved. She tried twisting it one way then the other. Eventually, the metal locking mechanism failed, and the door became free, but it didn't open. Poxoti pulled on the handle, and the hinges screamed with resistance. The door jittered violently as it reluctantly opened. The telltale hiss of air pressure conversion was barely audible. Everyone climbed through, and Poxoti pulled the old airlock closed. The door wouldn't seal. It hung crooked on its hinges. "I thought this might happen." Poxoti examined it. "I might be able to fix it."

"I'm reading close to Arth normal," Phila said.

Sarat turned away from the door. "What the hell?"

"Where is the second airlock?" Poxoti asked.

They stood on a metal catwalk looking out onto a jungle. Trees that could rival those on any planet were growing in the middle of the derelict. The sun's reddish rays flowed through small square windows in the ceiling. Hoots and hollers of wildlife or people came to their ears.

"This explains why the derelict was tipped to have the top of the ship point to the sun." Phila's voice came across the speakers. "Over here, there's a way down." Near Phila was a hill large enough to reach the catwalk they stood on.

Sarat looked at the lush greenish-blue landscape. Rolling hills covered in grasses and a forest of trees, some forty feet tall. "Um, where did all this come from. The dirt? The trees?"

"Oh crap, oh crap." Ed was pulling down the helmet visor. "Do *not* do that." He shook his head.

"Don't do what, Ed?" Sarat asked.

"Phila said the air was close to Arth normal, and it looked so beautiful. I opened my helm to experience everything, including the smell." Ed shook his head. "I don't recommend it. All I can smell is rot and death. I think I caught some in my nose hairs. I can still smell it." Ed slapped at his helm in frustration.

"Do you see that?" Poxoti stood her full height and pointed toward the crowns of the trees. "I see movement." She stepped forward, taking long graceful strides. The others had to jog to remain at her side.

Sarat scooped up Low as her small stature and delicate limbs struggled to keep pace with the tall Velox. "Thank you, captain," Low said as she climbed onto his shoulder.

Structural metal protruded from the canopy and touched the ceiling like grotesque skeletal fingers. It appeared as if floors and walls of the ship were removed to create this terrarium, but the supporting pillars were untouched. Sarat pointed. "Looks like the bones of the ship are all that remains. What happened to all the other materials?"

Poxoti slowed and looked around. "Probably reinforcement of the walls and floor."

"Anything like the piece-of-crap airlock we came through?" asked Phila.

Poxoti stopped and swore in Velox. "If the sounds we heard and those things moving in the trees are people, we need to get them out of here before this garden is lost to space. My airlock isn't much better than theirs. I need to fix their airlock before we can leave."

"We're going to find out quickly," called Low from Sarat's shoulder. "It appears that giant hairy spiders are swinging in the trees, and they're headed in this direction."

Hundreds, maybe thousands of brown hairy spider-like monkeys swung through the treetops coming closer to the *Hindsight* crew. The bulbous round bodies moved with such speed and agility it was difficult to count the limbs or find the heads and faces of the creatures. Eventually, they stopped their approach and waited, hanging half-hidden in the canopy. Finally, a single creature moved forward, throwing itself to the ground, and appeared to roll toward them. As it approached, it was apparent that the roundish creature was walking. It used a set of appendages that sprouted from the top of the body and curled around and under.

Suddenly the creature turned around, and its face appeared. For some reason, it had walked to the group backward. As it looked at the surprised faces of everyone, it began to laugh in a pleasing manner. Other appendages on its head pointed at the *Hindsight* crew, and it continued to laugh.

"Low, is it talking? It sounds like laughter." Sarat looked upward to the communications specialist who remained on his shoulder.

Low jumped to the ground and approached the laughing, hairy creature. Low contorted her slender flexible limbs to become shorter, to appear to be the same size. The creature's face was roughly in the center of its round body. Its eyes, nose, and mouth were so similar to human in appearance that it was disconcerting. From the top of its body sprouted all eight appendages, six arms, and two antennae. Bellow its face was thicker, darker hair, a beard perhaps. Low turned on her external audio, with a twist of a knob on the gauntlet of her suit.

Sarat watched as Low, and the creature talked. There seemed to be an argument or miscommunication happening. Low appeared confused. Sarat squatted next to Low and asked, "Is everything alright?"

"I don't understand what he is saying. There's no logic to his ramblings."

"Can you translate? I will try."

Low pointed to Sarat and then said something to the creature. The creature said something to Low, then turned and looked at Sarat.

He wants me to ask you, "What is brown and sticky?"

Sarat turned on his external audio then puzzled it over. What did that question have to do with anything going on right now? Why not ask for a name? Or demand to know why the people from the *Hindsight* were standing in his terrarium. He frowned and then said to Low, "Tell him I don't know."

"That is what I told him too." Low tilted her head, studying the creature. "All he said in return was, 'a stick'."

Sarat rolled it around in his head. *What is brown and sticky? A stick.* His father, Akash, often told horrible jokes, calling them dad jokes. *Is that what the creature was doing? Telling jokes?* Sarat smiled at the creature and then spoke to Low. "Please ask him if he is telling jokes."

"Jokes?" Low sighed, then shook her head as if disappointed in herself. She addressed the creature. From what she said, the creature became excited and pointed at Sarat with four hands. "He wants you to tell him a joke. I believe it's how they greet each other."

Sarat looked to the others. "Do you know any jokes?"

Ed laughed, slapping his leg. "I know one about a nun, a fisherman, and a horse. It goes something like this…"

Phila slapped the back of Ed's helmet. "Do you really think this creature is going to know what a horse or a nun is?" But that mattered little. The creature laughed and clapped, then pointed at Phila and Ed as if they had just performed the best slapstick he had ever seen.

After he collected himself, the creature said something to Low, which she repeated. "Everyone, this is Kuahakwahobwabya. I believe his title is chieftain. He said to just call him Kuaha." Low pointed at each of the *Hindsight* crew, starting with Sarat and ending with herself, telling Kuaha everyone's name.

The creature said something, and Low translated, "Kuaha wants us to meet his family."

Kuaha turned away and ambled toward the trees, where it seemed thousands of others waited. Low walked beside him, and they chatted.

Sarat followed, walking next to Poxoti. "Sir, this garden is in immediate danger of collapse. We need to get these people out." The Velox took slow short steps to keep pace with the captain.

"What do you propose? Sarat asked. "We are down to one door on the airlock. We can't leave without killing everyone." The captain surveyed the small furry people. "They look so primitive. Do they even have spacesuits?"

"We could use a couple cargo pods?" Poxoti offered. "With oxygen containers?"

Sarat chuckled. "That's not bad, but how would we get the pods in here? Then there is the question of getting these people to go into the pod and then getting the pod out."

"One problem at a time, Captain." Poxoti looked down, lost in thought. "I wonder if they play zaxottix. With six arms, you couldn't lose."

"You might be on to something. If they like jokes, they might like games too." Sarat touched the leaves and fruit of a tree as they passed.

Low and Kuaha stopped as a mass of creatures dropped from the trees. Kuaha introduced everyone and told more jokes. It seemed that no matter how many times a joke was said, it always produced a laugh, especially when Kuaha said them.

After the joviality of greeting everyone wore off, Kuaha pulled Low to the side and directed her and the *Hindsight* crew to come with him to a large open hut built in the center of the terrarium. All around the hut were groups of people playing games, telling stories, and using hand puppets to entertain children. The youngsters laughed and rolled around during hilarious segments. The group came to the hut's center, and everyone else gathered at the edges, sitting quietly, expectantly.

Kuaha welcomed them, calling each by name and pointing to them in turn. A murmur coursed through the audience. The chieftain sat on a stone then indicated the ground before him with a sweeping gesture. Sarat sat first, and the others took his lead. Kuaha clapped with all six hands. A servant appeared, walking on one set of hands and using the others to hold a huge tray filled with fruits and nuts. Kuaha took a small purple fruit then directed the servant to the people of the *Hindsight*.

Sarat took a yellow cube-shaped fruit and set it in his lap, tapping his helmet as a way of apologizing for not eating it.

Kuaha pointed to Low.

As if on cue, Low looked at Sarat. "Chieftain Kuahakwahobwabya of the Wayward people wants to know why you have come." Her voice changed subtly to indicate the next part wasn't from the chieftain. "Be truthful and keep eye contact when you speak."

"We discovered your ship and thought it long deserted. We found the door to your terrarium and entered." Sarat paused and waited for Low to translate, then continued. "We are concerned for your people. You must come to our ship before your walls fail and your people and trees die."

Kuaha raised the purple fruit to his antenna, then brought it to his mouth and popped it in. After a few moments, he spoke to Low, and she translated. "We can't possibly come on your ship. Your breathing requirements are not the same as ours. Surely, you do not have enough helmets for all my people."

"We breathe the same air as you do," Sarat assured him.

"Why won't you take off your helmets?"

"Because the air on your ship stinks," Sarat held the chieftain's eyes, as Low instructed.

The chieftain smiled, holding his six arms wide as if he knew this would be the answer. As if all the chieftain's hard work planning the foul air had been worth it.

The audience laughed and laughed as if they had played the most elaborate practical joke in the existence of the universe.

Low removed her helm. She breathed the air and seemed to smile. Sarat wasn't surprised. The food she and San consumed had a distinctive rotten smell. To be polite, they often used an unscented paste on their leaves to absorb the nutrients they needed. But in their quarters, they could indulge.

"You know the air stinks?" Sarat asked.

"Yes, of course. The only way to produce enough food for the trees is to bury our dead and our waste within the roots. At first, it was difficult to encourage the trees to grow. We had many years of losses. But we survived. I am the sixth chieftain."

"We can bring you to safety. Will you leave with us?"

"Better question." Ed interrupted, turning on his external audio. "Will you let us salvage your ship?"

"This is our home. We have no desire to leave."

"You will die here," Sarat assured him. "The door to your terrarium was rusted almost through. The walls, floor, and ceiling can't be doing much better."

"So be it. If that is the will of the Dome." The group gathered in the hut seemed to murmur agreement.

"I don't want to wait until they die to salvage this ship." Ed stood and stomped from the center. He was blocked by a group of the Wayward people, who wouldn't let him pass.

"Ed, sit your ass back down. This is not how diplomacy works. You insulted Chieftain Kuaha." Sarat smiled at his only passenger. "It's possible you will have to battle their best warrior…to the death." The captain laughed at Ed's discomfort.

"Don't even joke about that. We don't know their customs. What if he takes you seriously?"

"Sit down and shut up."

"A battle is a fabulous idea." Kuaha rubbed three sets of his hands together vigorously. "It would be excellent entertainment and good for morale."

Sarat wondered if Kuaha planned on some kind of practical joke, or was he serious? The chieftain didn't seem to care if his people died, so maybe he meant what he said. "If it is a battle you seek, may I suggest zaxottix?"

"What is that?"

"It is a game where speed and precision are the objectives. The more arms you have, the faster you can win."

Kuaha wiggled with excitement. The audience gasped at the idea of a new game. "I would like to play. I challenge the insolent one." Kuaha pointed at Ed and grinned.

"You could, chieftain. However, it would be a fast battle. It would not be a challenge. You would win. Playing zaxottix against a *two-arm* is not worthy of your time or skills."

Ed folded his arms over his chest as if he were actually upset with Sarat's assessment of his zaxottix abilities.

Kuaha remained motionless as if thinking. "Who is a worthy opponent?" He pointed to Poxoti as she had four arms. "Your companion Poxoti?" The Velox squirmed, not wanting the spotlight.

"Poxoti would be a fine challenge for you. Four arms are far superior to two. However, that still gives you the advantage. I would like to suggest the *Hindsight*'s doctor, San. He has five arms, surely that still gives you the advantage, but it would be a worthy challenge."

One of Kuaha hands shook in disagreement. "Ah yes, but experience often wins."

"Agreed, chieftain. That would be the case if San had ever played zaxottix. But he has not."

Kuaha narrowed his eyes, and his fingers fidgeted with each other. "I don't know if I believe you."

Sarat shrugged her shoulders. "It means nothing to me. We can leave you and your family and come back in ten years."

"Exactly!" Kuaha stood, pointing at Sarat. "You're out nothing. What are your stakes?"

Sarat thought for a moment. "If my champion San loses, then we will leave your people in peace. We will give you all the jokes we have, and you will know how to play a new game." He paused. "If San wins, your people will leave this ship with transport to a safe location and forfeit your rights to this ship."

Kuaha's hands fidgeted. "Agreed on one condition. If San wins, we bring young trees or fruit with us."

Sarat thought about the trees and the rot that feed them. "You can bring fruit. And if we lose, you can keep the game."

"Agreed." Chieftain Kuaha seems satisfied.

"Now we have a problem that perhaps you can correct." Sarat nodded to Low. "Tell Kuaha how the airlock is broken, then ask if there is another access port."

The Chieftain and Low spoke for what seemed like hours. Finally, Low turned her attention to Sarat. "There are four airlocks total. The one we found. Another in the opposite wall from where we entered. One in the floor, long-buried. And one in the dome top, it's partially covered by the canopy."

Sarat nodded then faced the Chieftain. "Kuaha, thank you for your hospitality. We shall return with the zaxottix game and San our challenger." He turned to Low. "Would you please stay and continue to talk with Kuaha? Keep your helmet close, just in case."

Low agreed then translated for the chieftain.

Sarat pointed to Poxoti, Phila, and Ed. "Follow me, there's another airlock." They walked away from the hut toward the opposite wall. High above the earth and grass was a mezzanine and a crude ladder to reach it.

Poxoti crossed all four of her arms. "You better go first. I think my weight might cause that ladder to fail."

Sarat pointed to Phila. "You go first."

"Why her?" Ed folded his arms.

"Damn it, Ed. Are you going to second guess my every command? If so, you need to get off my ship." Sarat stepped into Ed. "She is my science officer. She can tell us if the airlock is safe to open. And frankly, her opinion is way more important than yours."

Ed frowned, then turned away.

Phila studied Sarat, smiled, and started to climb. One of the rungs failed, but the rest held. She hauled herself over the mezzanine railing and disappeared. There was a scraping sound then nothing for a few minutes. Phila's voice filled the comm, "Come on up. This airlock is in much better condition, but it's tight in here."

Ed rushed the ladder and scrambled onto the mezzanine. Sarat followed. There was a door and beyond what looked like a control room. Most of the equipment was destroyed or missing. Ed looked over the controls but didn't seem impressed with the find.

Phila was at the back of the room. She pointed at the door. "Looks like the door kept the moisture off the airlock. That's why it's in such good shape." Phila rapt on the door and it thudded in response. "Problem is we need Poxoti's strength to open it."

They walked through the disarray and out the door and from the mezzanine, they watched Poxoti climb the ladder. The huge Velox moved only one hand or foot at a time to keep her weight spread over as many points as possible. After a few harrowing moments, she climbed onto the mezzanine. Poxoti moved through the door and pushed aside consoles and unknown equipment to get to the airlock. Her breathing sounded strained. With determination she gripped the round handle and twisted. The metal screamed in protest before coming loose. The airlock door opened to reveal an equally preserved airlock on the other side.

"You understand what to do?" Sarat looked at everyone on the bridge.

Tonopex's mandibles snapped at the air. "If my calculations are off by any amount…"

"I have full confidence in your navigation skill." Sarat looked from Tonopex to Poxoti. "Besides, your mate will be here to help."

"Poxoti and I spent a lot of time to make this docking coupling. It will work." Phila and Poxoti bumped fists.

"Plus, there's a chance I could lose the game." San's pod-like head bobbed.

"You can't lose," Phila said. "Ed would be devastated."

"Where is Ed? I haven't seen him since we got back." Sarat frowned. "I'm sure that man is up to no good."

"If I were to guess," Tonopex suggested. "Ed is in his spacesuit exploring the derelict, hoping to find treasure." The Velox made a grating noise. Poxoti joined in his laughter.

"Come on, San, you've got an appointment with a chieftain." Sarat lifted the zaxottix game and walked out of the bridge.

"Mind if I come along?" Phila asked, trotting to his side.

A feeling of festivity filled the hut. Wooden drums were brought out and played. The Wayward people bounced on the ground and swung in the hut's rafters in time to the music.

San sat by Low's side. Both Elowan were out of their spacesuits, enjoying the taste of the air.

"I don't like that you're not in a suit." Sarat shot a glance at Low and San.

"Didn't seem necessary. Zaxottix is a fast game, and I wanted to enjoy the moment." San looked around as sudden silence filled the hut.

Kuaha snapped his fingers and pointed to the ground. A group of people brought a wooden box and two seats, setting them where their chieftain indicated. Taking his cue, Sarat placed the game on the box. Kuaha looked at it like it was a precious object. His fingers touched the game pieces and caressed the levels of transparent game surface. "How is it played?"

San and Low explained the game in detail, giving the chieftain time to think of a strategy. After a few minutes, Kuaha made a loud howl, gaining everyone's attention. The Wayward people crowded closer to the chieftain and the game.

Kuaha sat on his seat. All six of his arms were held wide, not touching the board or pieces. San sat opposite. His five arms held ready.

Low shouted, "Go!"

Hands and arms, fingers, and vine-like appendages flew and swam across the board. Game pieces were transported and placed in the proper places. Time seemed to stand still as the frenzy of movement caused excitement in the onlookers. Shouts and clapping filled the hut.

And then it was over.

Kuaha's hands were still on the board, while San held his off the board in the same stance as at the beginning. The chieftain laughed and laughed. "This game is fabulous. I didn't even mind losing."

Sarat approached Kuaha. "You did very well. I will give you a few hours to gather what you need."

Kuaha smiled. "Will we have access to this game while on your ship?"

"Yes." Sarat turned to leave, then stopped. "Do you regret losing your ship to us?"

"It was never our ship." The chieftain laughed as if he played a great joke on Sarat. Then, he dropped from his seat and walked toward a large gathering of Wayward as if he had just won the game and brought home a grand prize.

"Sir," Low requested. "San and I'd like to stay with them and help. The air here tastes wonderful."

Sarat nodded. "Please keep your communicator on and your suits nearby. You and San will need to put them on before we attempt to couple with the dome airlock." He walked to Phila. "I think I just had another joke played on me."

"How do you figure?" Phila asked.

"Kuaha said he never owned the ship, and he seemed happy so long as he could play zaxottix." He shook his head. "I feel like I got taken."

"Taken?" Poxoti asked, listening from the bridge of the *Hindsight*. "I don't understand."

"It's Arth slang. It means tricked." Ed's voice entered the conversation from his helmet's communicator. "I was taken too. I've scoured all these decks, and there isn't any tech on board. It looks like everything has been scavenged."

"You were never promised anything," Sarat stated. "However, you promised me a fortune, or we wouldn't be out here."

Ed's communicator clicked off.

Peacestone

By Brisco Woods

Starport
Seven Sisters Pub/Grub house
11-7-4620

J Titus Peacestone looked around the crowded pub and sighed. This wasn't going as well as he had hoped. He had come here because it was known as the hot spot for recruitment, but he was beginning to think 'not-so-much'. Then there was the heavy smell of garlic that permeated the place. He hated garlic.

It didn't help that Tomlis kept sending him reminders of the remaining time he was allowed to have his ship in dock. He knew the date he had to vacate the slip by, he didn't need that stylus pusher to send him vaguely threatening messages every morning and every evening reminding him. This should also be the last mission to take for the 'company', then the ship would be his outright. Then he would tell Tomlis and Interstel to kiss his ass!

"Another beer, Hon?" He hadn't even noticed the wait-bot come up. He thought it looked ridiculous with the long hair of the blonde wig hanging down it's back, but they did seem well programmed. He had just taken the last chug of stale, warm, back-wash from the bottom of the glass and was ready for a refill.

"Sure, same thing," he said as the bot glided off with the empty. He glanced at the pad in his hand and looked at the faces around the room for the hundredth time. This time though, there was a face looking back at him. He smiled as the tall Velox met his eye and nodded as she walked in his direction.

As the serving bot placed his beer on the coaster in front of J, he said "Could I get a crème martini for my friend?" J gestured toward the Velox moving up to the table. The bot nodded its mechanical head once and quietly glided back toward the bar.

When the insectoid had ambled across the room to his table, he smiled and offered her the seat opposite his. "It is good to see you my friend," he said as she adjusted the seat to her frame.

She nodded and clicked the series of sounds that he recognized as pleasure. "You too, J. How is your search for a new crew progressing?"

A large smile crossed his face as he answered, "I had hoped you were here to sign on as my navigator, SSlinks."

She clicked a negative while shaking her insectoid head slowly from side to side. "I have not, although I know of one who is seeking a captain and a ship."

J sat up a little and looked into the huge compound eyes of his long-time friend. He knew without a doubt that she would not intentionally steer him wrong. But she tended to see the best in Humans, and thus occasionally missed the layers of personality beneath. He was curious however, to see if this was one of those times or if she had indeed found someone he could hire.

"So, if you aren't joining my crew, tell me something about this potential crewmember you've found. I assume they've been fired from their crew or just released from an asylum or some such." He knew that he would have to push the conversation. It was something of a game between them and he knew she enjoyed making him squirm for information.

It irked him to be here looking for a new crew after four relatively successful missions with the crew he had come to know. A crew he had paid to have trained, just to have them stolen away because he had missed his launch date. In their defense, he couldn't really blame them that the ship's repairs had taken longer than planned. Much longer in fact, it had seemed that the repairs were set back over and over for vague reasons that couldn't quite be run down. They hadn't really had a choice if they wanted to keep earning MUs.

J leaned forward and motioned for her to continue. The Velox clicked in humor and resumed. "She is an exceptional navigator for a Human, and I can make introductions if you are interested. I know you are in dire need my friend, but I assure you I would not bring someone to you whom I did not trust. She is also experienced at locating and riding the continuum fluxes." She tilted her head back in a manner that he knew to mean seriousness with the Velox. "She served with another friend for several missions and has had many training updates in the time she has been a crew member.

The serving droid glided up to the table and deposited the thick steamy drink in front of the Velox. SSlinks nodded to the droid and lifted the drink with her right mid-arm to clink glasses with J. "To your successes my friend," she said as she took a long pull from the supplied straw. The two antenna that extended from just below the top of her head, quivered in pleasant enjoyment as she placed the glass on the table.

He had taken a similar pull from his own fresh beer and placed it back on the table at nearly the same time. As she leaned back in the chair he leaned forward and looked directly into the large compound eyes of his friend. "Spill it, bug. Tell me about her."

The Velox chuckle/clicked at the derogatory term. "Goodness. You must be more impatient than usual. For a Human, that is saying much."

"Yeah, yeah. Come on, just tell me."

"Okay. I will do better than that." The left, middle arm reached into one of the many pockets on the vest, the only clothing the Velox wore, and clicked a PTT button on a small comm device twice. SSlinks took another drink and smiled as J sat back in his chair with an audible sigh.

SSlinks was still clicking humor when a petite woman walked up to their table and nodded to the Velox then to J. Both Human and Velox gestured for her to join them. The small woman smiled and sat next to SSlinks.

The Velox clicked happiness and welcome and nodded to each Human in turn. "Reese, this is Captain JT Peacestone of whom we have spoken. And friend J, this is the Human female, Reese, navigator supreme and all-round good person."

The petite woman snorted and extended her hand across the table to J. "I don't know about all of that, but I am a navigator." A hesitant, lop-sided grin played at her mouth as J shook her hand. He found the small grin contagious as one spread across his own face.

The serving bot appeared again and took the newcomers order, then glided away.

"Well, why don't you tell me something about your career, Reese. How many missions, what sorts, what ships, etc."

The grin disappeared as she looked at SSlinks. The Velox nodded in a Human fashion and Reese looked back at J. "I have been on four missions and had three Skills Upgrade opportunities. All as a navigator. The first two missions were exploratory and mineral harvesting. Both were successful in the harvesting, but not so much in the exploration. We stumbled on a continuum flux on the third mission and nearly ran out of supplies before I found where we were and got us back home. We did encounter some alien machines and fought our way through a mess before re-entering the flux. That trip earned us a bonus for finding a potential world worth settling. It is a long way outward on the upspin however, and still needs some exploration."

J was impressed and nodded to Reese to continue. "The last mission?"

She looked at her hand for a moment as the small group huddled at the table in silence, and the room hummed with activity around them. He looked at SSlinks and she just shook her head slowly. Her antenna moved in a slow circular motion that indicated patience.

Reese looked up at J then at SSlinks. As the serving bot returned with Reese's drink, J placed his extended fingertips together and touched them to his lips as he waited for her to speak and gave her a slight nod that he hoped was reassuring. She gazed back at him for a moment then nodded as well.

"May as well rip the Sticky Bandage off I suppose. My most recent mission was onboard the *ISS Muncey*."

Well, that explains the hesitation, J thought to himself. The *Muncey* had been gone for nearly a year and a half on a mission that was supposed to last six months at most. She had been assumed lost and then when she did show back up, there were only two surviving crew members, neither of them had been the captain. The entire ordeal had been locked up tight by Interstel, so there had been little actually released to the public about what had transpired on board that ship.

All kinds of conspiracy theorists made noise about their ideas of the facts, but none had been released officially. Theories of mutiny, alien abduction and heroic escape, another *Intrepid*-like incident. He had decided he would never know, and not to waste more time wondering.

She was still looking at him and obviously waiting for the judgement and questions. He decided to hold off on either, for the moment. After all, he didn't know the facts and he suspected that wouldn't change while they sat at this table, in this pub.

He lowered his eyes for a moment, then looked back into hers. "I won't ask you the questions I'm sure everyone does when they find out who you are. I will just ask you this, are you fit to serve? Are you capable and ready to be a team asset and part of a crew?"

J held up an extended forefinger to stop any immediate reply. "Before you answer, has SSlinks told you anything about me and my current situation?"

Human and Velox nodded once simultaneously. Reese accompanied the nod with, "She has told me some of your misfortunes."

J chuckled and looked at the Velox. "Misfortunes, is it? I suppose you could call them misfortunes, although some were my own doing. I have learned lessons the hard way, but been financially successful while doing so. Although I seem to have found myself at a place where few experienced crewmembers want to risk finding out if I have really and truly learned from the experiences."

He gazed directly into her eyes for a moment and then smiled again. "I truly believe that I have, but most men would tell you the same thing. Now what about you?"

Reese nodded slowly and a small smile formed on her lips. "To answer your earlier questions, yes. I am prepared and capable to be a member of a starship crew. I am a hard worker, a team player, and I probably feel like I have more to prove than most. I have had experiences that will be of great benefit, some I can tell you about and some I cannot. The only thing I will not do is work with Thrynn. I won't, can't work with Thrynn and it is something I can't discuss right now, nor maybe ever."

J thought for a moment about other potential crew members and how her inability to work with Thrynn, might affect his crew. They continued talking about similar experiences and the missions they had been on. He made sure not to discuss his last one. She didn't need to know about all of that just yet.

After the three of them had finished the drinks they had, he decided it was time to make his final decision. He looked into her eyes as she looked steadily back, somehow knowing he was at the decision-making point. What he saw was honesty and a need to belong. He knew one of his faults had always been jumping to conclusions, but he also knew that he had to make a decision and felt this was a solid one.

"Okay, Miss Reece. I believe you are ready. I am still in need of some crew members, but you can head out to the port and find the *Assurance*. That's our ship. I hope to have a full complement soon. I've been informed that Interstel also wishes this. Grab a cabin and start making yourself useful." The last statement he said with a smile and held his hand out again to the small woman.

She smiled as well and shook the offered hand with a much firmer handshake than when they had been introduced just a little while before. "Thanks, Captain. You won't regret hiring me." She paused, "and it's just 'Reese'. Nothing else needed."

She tapped a few commands on her tablet, then stood and bowed to SSlinks. "Thank you, SSlinks. I appreciate your faith and friendship. I really wish SSlyy was with us."

The Velox clicked a series of quick sounds that sounded like grief, happiness, and pride all at once. J knew there was a story there and hoped to hear it someday. Reese turned to him and nodded.

"I will fetch my gear and be at the port within the hour, Captain Peacestone."

J nodded back and smiled. "Just 'J', nothing else needed." She snorted a laugh again and strode toward the door with a spring in her step. He continued to smile as she disappeared through the crowd. He thought he was going to like this 'Reese'. He turned back to the Velox as she stood and offered an upper, right hand across the table. J smiled recognizing the sign of friendship with the offer, instead of the usual social offer of the lower.

"Thank you for the introduction, my friend. She seems to know her stuff, and might, just maybe, make a decent crew member."

His smile grew larger at the clicking of humor from his friend.

ISS Assurance
17-7-4620

"I don't know about this. Do you think SSlinks has been drinking too many of those milk martinis?" Reese looked doubtful as she scrolled through the list the Velox had sent J earlier in the evening. "There aren't a lot to choose from, really. Although this Elowan looks promising."

She tossed the tablet in his general direction and poured herself another cup of tea.

J snatched the tab out of the air and scrolled through the resume. After a moment he nodded. "Yeah, it's been a communication tech for three missions and a medical tech for two. That's a good deal of experience."

He tapped the little star at the top of the resume, marking it for an interview. The next one that caught his eye was marked Human and had 'C/D Winfrey' in the name section. This was a SSlinks recommendation. Apparently, this woman had a good deal of experience also, with three missions each as science officer and engineering officer. He marked the file for an interview and placed the tablet on the table.

"What is your opinion of androids?" he asked Reese as she sipped from the hot, dark liquid.

"I've worked with a couple and interacted on Arth with several. They're decent if the programming's there. I think this one has a good version of the newest updates and the DX99 November series is solid. His speech programming though…Have you worked with them?"

He sipped from his own drink and shrugged. "We had some for security once. They were tough and did exactly as they were told. But it is a bit menacing, having something that big and mechanical with a weapon. There is no reading their intentions until they act, and then it's usually too late. I don't know, just not sure how much I trust them."

She snorted the odd laugh he was getting used to. "We created them, right? What could possibly go wrong?"

"Oh, you didn't just say that." He rolled his eyes and hung his head in an overly dramatic bow.

"Oh, yes I did!" She laughed and stood to place her empty cup in the wash bin. "I'm turning in. Are you going to interview them tomorrow?"

As he lifted his head and sat back, he glanced around the galley of the *Assurance*. "Yes, I think the pub has a room in the back where it is quiet enough. And a little more room than here."

She threw him a salute as she left the room. "Alright Chief, I'll see you in the morning."

He chuckled and flipped her off. "G'Night."

It had been nearly a week since they had met, and he was happy and confident in the choice to hire her. She was at home on the ship and had been very helpful in getting the I's dotted and T's crossed for the final mission preparations.

That had been a huge help in itself. With Interstel breathing down his neck to free up dock space, he had stressed the lack of a crew and the final preps for a while. Now with her help, he had been able to focus on the crew and let her handle the details.

Starport Lounge
18-7-4620

J sat at the head of the small table and scrolled through the pages of the first candidate's info. The Elowan was the first on his list, and the most likely for him to hire. Everything looked great on its resume and he knew some other captain would scoop it up quickly if he didn't.

The door to the main seating area of the pub opened allowing the sound of an Elowan voice singing an old ballad of love and loss, to enter the office he had rented for the afternoon. The android he had hired escorted a small, willowy Elowan into the space. It looked ridiculously large and cumbersome as it walked next to the graceful Elowan.

They stopped a respectful distance away and the android introduced the frail looking creature to the captain. "This is Elowan Anthemial, sir. You will be most happy to make its acquaintance, I'm certain of it."

J shook his head at the entirely too bubbly voice of the large robot. Whomever had programmed the speech patterns had a peculiar sense of humor.

"Thank you, Android. Please locate the next interviewee and escort them here when I signal." He was overly cautious when giving orders to the machine, he knew. But he could also see the android taking orders too literally, and actually carrying the interviewee into the room over its shoulder. He shook his head and focused on the bright blue Elowan.

"Anthemial, correct?" He asked as the willowy creature made itself comfortable on the multi-racial chair across the small table from him.

"Thank you, captain. That is perfect pronunciation. I am indeed, Anthemial. I understand you are in search of a few crewmembers for an upcoming mission? I am experienced as both a communication officer and medical officer, as I am sure you are aware from my resume." The voice emitted from the translator was mellow and rich, what might be described as a female baritone in Human terms. The standard language seemed to be used with a dictation and finesse that most Humans didn't match.

"I am. Your resume is impressive. Tell me something of your experience, in your own words, please. Some of the circumstances in which you have been an important part of the solution or were an integral team player."

They spoke for nearly a half-hour about some of its experiences as well as some of his. By the end of their conversation, J had offered the position of communication officer with a part time/as needed, position of medical officer as well.

"Are you available immediately? I am unfortunately being pressed by Interstel to vacate the ship berth I have been occupying for, admittedly, far too long."

"Tomorrow is the earliest I could actually report, Captain. I must see to a few familial matters in the interim."

"Tomorrow is perfect."

Anthemial seemed pleased with the arrangement and agreed to be at the *Assurance* by midday the following day.

He smiled as the graceful Elowan glided from the room. He pressed the PTT button on his communicator to signal the android. Within a matter of a few seconds the android strode into the room with two identical Human women, one on each side, with their arms hooked through its own mechanical ones.

J stared for a moment but had gained control by the time they stopped in front of the table. The android released the arms of the two women, stepped back and bowed to each in turn. "Ladies, may I introduce you to the most honorable and astute, J Titus Peacestone. He has the indubitable pleasure of captaining the most renown *ISS Assurance*."

J chuckled and stood to offer his hand to each of the women. The android continued as he faced Peacestone. "And Captain Peacestone, please allow me the indescribable pleasure of introducing Ms. C and Ms. D Winfrey. These two magnificent Humans are here to interview for the crew of the aforementioned glorious ship."

"Thank you, Android. Please fetch an additional chair for the ladies. One that is unused, preferably."

The android nodded its steel head once and strode off on task.

J moved his own chair around and gestured for the two women to sit. As he stepped back around the desk, he nodded his head after the android. "Please excuse its flowery speech. It is very good at everything we have given it to do so far, but someone had a serious quirk in their thinking when they programmed the speech patterns."

Both women smiled and he shook his head again as he felt his heart flutter. Two women that were this beautiful might be an issue for him. It wasn't that he was uncomfortable around attractive women, but these two were as far above attractive as a Class Five engine was to a Class One.

"So, as it said, I am J Peacestone, captain of the *Assurance*. Why don't you tell me something about yourselves, beginning with the positions you are applying for?"

The door opened again and the android came back to the desk and deposited a chair for J to use. As it stomped away, the woman on his right spoke up.

"We are Sea and Dee Winfrey. I am Sea, spelled S E A like an ocean, and this is my sister Dee spelled D E E."

Dee spoke up as her sister paused. "We work as a team, so…"

"It has been difficult gaining positions with the same crew."

"It seems that either the science officer position…"

"…or the engineering officer position is taken on every crew we have applied for."

J looked back and forth between them as they spoke, finishing each other's sentences.

"I can see how that might be difficult. I do have openings for both of those positions, but I need to hear something about your work experiences. Have you two always worked on the same crew?"

Dee answered, "Yes. Directly out of the academy, we worked on a ship with our sister Bea as the captain."

J commanded his jaw to stay closed. Sea continued where her sister had left off. "Interstel directed that we couldn't work on a crew under a relative, so we had to go out on our own."

"It was the first time we triplets had been split up, other than for the different classes we had taken for our chosen professions."

He felt what his grandmother had always called his feathers ruffling, or his hackles rising. He really didn't like being dictated to about how he could run his ship and crew. It bothered him when someone else was subjected to it. On the other hand, the ship was supplied by Interstel, so there wasn't much a captain could do about it until he had made the MU's to pay that ship off.

Sea and Dee continued talking while he listened and began to form opinions of the two twins. Well, he guessed they were technically triplets, but only two of them were here. *How would a person refer to them?* he wondered.

Both spoke well and seemed to have good knowledge of their positions. Each had their own experiences and accounts to show that they did, indeed, know their relative positions and could handle themselves accordingly.

They talked for a while and he felt himself growing to like and respect each in a manner that left him more comfortable in their company. As the interview wrapped up, he found himself with two more crewmembers and felt a lot better about getting back into space.

The sisters left as they had arrived, with arms looped in the android's mechanical ones. J smiled at the scene and reclined in his chair with his hands resting behind his head. He was just allowing himself to feel the relief when his tablet chimed with a message.

As he glanced down and saw 'Interstel', he felt the tension returning. The feeling of being pressured also returned and his hackles rose again.

What the hells was their problem? He decided to stop by and see Tomlis in person instead of replying to the message. He would tell that son-of-a-tress to his face that he now had a crew and wipe off that smug smile. One more member would be ideal, but he knew he could get by with what he had.

With any luck, they could get out of the berth by Friday. They could load and fuel in orbit and be gone in a week. That was rushing things he knew, but he was sure they could make it happen. Maybe Interstel would be satisfied with that. Well, they would damn well have to be.

As luck would have it, he made it to the Interstel office just at the end of the business day. Caspin Tomlis was shutting down operations for the day when J hurried through the door. Tomlis looked up and a scowl formed on his face as he recognized the ship captain.

"Whatever you want will have to wait for tomorrow, Peacestone. We're closed."

"I don't need anything from you, I'm just giving you formal notice that the *Assurance* will be out of your dock space in two days. I have nearly filled out the crew and will be moving to orbit for fueling and taking on supplies. I'd like to go on and schedule that for the following day, since I'm here."

The Interstel man stomped out from behind the counter space and put his finger against J's chest and pressed hard. "I said, we're closed. You can come back tomorrow. Or, better yet, comm. That way I don't have to see your ugly mug." An evil looking smile spread across Tomlis' face. "And, by the way, you now have until midnight tomorrow to vacate the dock slip, or your ship will be impounded."

J's face turned red as he stared at the bigger man, mouth opened. "What? I still have five days!"

Tomlis smirked at him. "As of right now, you have until midnight tomorrow. Now leave, before I call security."

"You can't do this! I've done all I could to get a crew on short notice and now you're making it even shorter? What the hells is your problem?"

"You're not it anymore. Get out. And I can do whatever I decide to. You obviously don't know who I represent. Out!"

"What's Interstel got to gain by being such hard asses with my schedule?" J asked, refusing to budge.

"Hmph! Interstel? Who said anything about Interstel?" The taller man said menacingly as he reached for the comm on his desk. "This is Tomlis at the Interstel scheduling office, I may have a problem with a customer refusing to leave the premises." He raised an eyebrow at J, the smirk never leaving his face.

J raised his hands in surrender and turned his back on the man. As he left the office on his way back to the docking slips, he commed ahead.

Reese answered almost immediately. "Yes?"

"It's gonna be a long night, Reese. We have to be out of that slip before midnight tomorrow. Please have the android contact the remaining crew and let them know about the changes. I want us out by end of business day tomorrow. I'll be damned if they see us struggling to meet their asinine demands. Damn, I hope that doesn't mess with any of the crew's schedules too much. We don't need a set back at this point."

"We'll get it done J, no worries." Was the response as he cut the comm.

What the hell was that asshat talking about? Who was he working for if not Interstel?

He shrugged and sped up his step. Probably delusions of grandeur, that fit the arrogance of the man. He ground his teeth as he walked. Gods, he hated bullies!

ISS Assurance
19-7-4620

"Well, crew, this is it. Let's get this beast out of the dock and into orbit." J couldn't hide the giddiness as he sat in the command chair and nodded to Reese. "Do it, Nav."

There was no feeling of movement as the equipment around them hummed quietly. Watching the large screen at the front of the bridge, however, gave them three hundred sixty degrees of views around the exterior of the ship as Reese skillfully maneuvered out of the docking slip. She slid them out of the station and continued backwards for several minutes as they cleared all of the near port traffic.

Just as she slowed the rearward motion to come about and engage forward thrust, a small tug with several containers veered off of its trajectory and accelerated toward the *Assurance*.

He was inhaling to warn Reece when he saw the look on her face. She was hurriedly tapping commands with her right and took the joystick control in her left as she activated manual control. The views on the screens skewed to one side and up, the tug missed the ship by only meters.

J sat at the edge of the command chair watching the tug continue its crazy course. Reese was cussing a blue streak and calling the driver everything but a decent Human being.

"Incoming comm, sir. From the tug driver." Anthemial's voice was the same relaxing tone as always.

"Put it on speaker, please. It better have an excuse for that little trick." He snarled with the last sentence.

Of all the times for a tug operator to fall asleep at the wheel, he didn't need a single hour of delay. The tight schedule Interstel had him fighting against was barely attainable as it was. Hours of reports and meetings with traffic control and the ISF, would certainly delay him beyond his limit.

"*Assurance*, this is tug seven-seven-nine. I don't know what happened just then, my controls quit responding! Whoever is driving that ship, give them my sincere thanks. I'm buying when you get back, look me up. Wendall Knox. Seriously, my tug may have damaged your ship a little, but I would have been squished. I seem to have control back now, however. Safe travels!"

"Thank you, Captain Knox. *Assurance* out." J sat back in his chair and looked around the bridge. What the hells had that all been about?

Reece spoke up from the nav bench. "J, I don't know what caused him to lose control, but he's right. We may have been delayed a few days or a week, but he would have certainly been killed. That was incredibly close; he missed us by less than five meters."

"Well, we're good now. Your reflexes were right on, Reese. Great hustle! Alright, folks, let's get back to what we were doing. Sea and Dee, you two work together and get the rest of the fuel and supplies out to us ASAP. Anthemial, get the clearances for us to leave the system as soon as that is done. Reese, op's checks on all systems and ensure we have the weapons and ammunition we spoke about earlier. I'm making a few calls to Interstel for some clarification and doing a final plan for our trip."

Everyone nodded in turn as J assigned the tasks for the next couple of days.

"Android, I want you to monitor the space in close proximity to the *Assurance*. If anyone moves this way that isn't previously cleared, let me know immediately. And make sure all tugs delivering to us follow strict safety protocols. I have a bad feeling about this."

"I would be most happy to do just that, sir. You know I am always at your service." The android said as it stomped to the navigation station, connecting to the ship's sensors.

J smiled at Reese as she shook her head and vacated her station. She left the bridge toward engineering, mumbling something under her breath about robots and bubbly personalities.

The captain's ready room was nothing more than a small office where he could work in semi privacy. He brought up the known facts of the two planets he planned on visiting. There was very little specified about either of them, but he had spoken with another captain who had been to both and swore they had abundant life. His main goal was a couple of unknown life forms this trip. It would be very lucrative if it worked out.

He had decided to make that his main task, but he was loaded up on mining equipment also, as a backup plan. The pods for life forms would double as mining pods, but not the other way around, so he had spent the extra MU's for them.

A message popped up onto his screen from his friend SSlinks and he opened it immediately. Simple and to the point as always, it read "Be careful, Safe travels."

He had no idea what she knew or why he felt some trepidation at that message, but it wasn't like her to engage in small talk. After flipping through several messages and rereading his notes, he stood and placed the tablet on his desk.

Looking out the clear doors to the bridge he saw the android standing at the nav station, for all appearances, asleep. The small, slender Elowan was at the comm desk going through equipment checks of its own. He smiled to himself for a moment and allowed the peacefulness to flow though his mind.

There was nothing like the peacefulness of a spaceship for J. He loved the quiet hum of the equipment and the utter silence of space. Even close to Starport as they were, it was a relative closeness. Hundreds of thousands of kilometers, was 'close' in space.

He glanced again at the tablet on his desk and shook a bit as a shiver made its way up his spine. Something was going on with Tomlis, he just couldn't put a finger on what it was. Ah, well. It wouldn't be his problem soon enough. In a couple of days, they would be heading out-of-system and Tomlis could find someone else to push around.

With any luck, this trip would put him out of debt to Interstel as well. That would give him an entirely new lease on life, and he couldn't help smiling as he made his way to his quarters.

ISS Assurance
22-7-4620

"This is it folks, we're on our way! Let's go do some exploring and maybe, just maybe, get rich doing it."

The atmosphere on the bridge of the *Assurance* was light today. It was finally time for them to leave the Arth system and go do what they all loved to do. Preparations had gone fairly smooth as the last couple of days had dragged on. Reese and one of the triplet/twins had gotten friends involved to get their load-out complete, as someone had lost their order of pods, but other than that, things had gone relatively smoothly.

As they were moving out-system under power, a lot of the stress he had felt over the last months was leaving him. He hadn't received any other messages from SSlinks, normal or cryptic, so he was more relaxed there as well.

"I have the initial coordinates entered, sir. We can proceed as soon as we have clearance from Starport." Reese announced from the nav station.

The Elowan spoke from the opposite side of the bridge, "Clearance just received. We may proceed, Captain."

"You heard the being, Reese. Let's proceed!" A chuckle made its way through the crew as the three-sixty display came to life and the *Assurance* moved off toward open space.

"There is a message on your tablet, Captain. From Interstel Scheduling and for your eyes only." Anthemial said with a slight question in its mellow voice.

It was unusual for a captain to get 'eye's only' traffic. Most captains shared all communications with their crew as a show of trust. J had always prescribed to the same idea, that the few beings on the ship needed to have complete trust in one another. Hiding communications with Interstel, or anyone for that matter, did nothing to flourish that trust.

He shrugged and tapped the open icon.

You're not out of the system yet, Peacestone. I hope you enjoyed breaking our ship in for us.

J sat staring at the message for a moment, then looked at Reese. "Get us to the continuum flux at your best speed. Don't do anything out of sorts, just move there as fast as possible while not looking out of place."

The android spoke up from its station near the bridge lift. "Sir, it may be of no consequence, but I am picking up two Interstel Security ships moving this way from below Starport."

Anthemial commented from the comm section, "They have received orders to stop us and detain the crew. They also have been told to impound the ship and everything on it. Is there something we should be aware of, captain?"

"No! That swine at scheduling has been threatening me since I put the *Assurance* into a repair slip. I swear he wants this ship, but I don't have any idea why. What difference does it make to Interstel if we're out here making them money or someone else is? I don't get it."

The Elowan looked at J with its head cocked to one side. "There have been rumors of ships being impounded, just before the captain could get them paid off. In the exact situation you are in, sir. The last mission prep before the payoff mission and something happens to keep the ship from departing on time. Rumor has it, Interstel impounds the ship and sells it off to a new captain. I know not if any of the rumors are true, but I have heard of it on more than one occasion."

"Well, they won't get this one. Anthemial, I would like for you to set the comms to auto respond to any incoming messages. Have it reply that comms are currently down for routine maintenance and we will respond as soon as they are back up.”

“Of course, sir.” The Elowan turned back to the console and made some adjustments. “It is done. We will receive all incoming communications but will not send any received receipts to the sender. Instead, it will be the auto response as ordered, sir.”

“Thank you. Android, keep me updated on those IS ships.”

“Indeed captain. I am most pleased to assist, sir.” The android stated with enthusiasm.

“Reese, what is time to the flux?”

“Fourteen minutes and thirty seconds on my mark, sir. And, mark.” Reese dropped the hand she had raised with the last word.

“Most admirable captain, the Interstel Security vessels are most assuredly after us. They have formed up into a formation. Forgive my sudden lack of vocabulary, sir, but this is exciting in the extreme. At any rate, they are gaining on us and will be within weapons range in nine minutes and forty-one seconds.”

“Weapons range?” Dee squeaked.

“Yes, Android, what she said. Why would you mention weapons range?” J asked, again sitting forward on the edge of his chair.

“Well, sir, the Interstel Security ships are in a formation that suggests they will fire missiles on us as soon as they get within range. I apologize if that was insensitive.”

“No, no, that is exactly the kind of information I need, Android.” He nodded at the robot and turned to face Reese. “If we continue at our current rate of speed, when will we enter the flux?”

“About twelve minutes.”

J did some rapid math in his head and smiled. “Maintain current course but give us just a little more speed.”

Reese looked at him with scrunched eyebrows, hands busy on the panel. “Aye, sir.”

"Anthemial, are they attempting to communicate?"

"Captain, it is odd, but they are not. They seem to be set on catching and stopping us but have only sent the initial communique. I fear they are going to fire weapons on us as soon as they are within range." The Elowan was obviously frightened.

"Don't fret, Anthemial, I have a plan."

The android spoke up again with excitement in its tinny voice. "I am so excited to see what you will do, sir. I am certain it will be worthy of songs written and stories told."

Sea spoke for the first time, her voice dry as dust. "They write songs and tell stories of people who die heroically, Android. I really hope the captain has something better suited to survival and flourishment than to go out in a blaze of glory, as it were."

J laughed and stood from his chair. "I do indeed, Ms. Sea. I promise you and your sister, as well as the rest of you, we are going to be fine. My plan is eloquent in its simplicity, as our colorfully speaking android friend might say."

"Now would be a good time to share it, sir. They just fired four missiles." Reese sounded a bit stressed as she spoke.

J said nothing for a moment but continued to smile.

"Sir?" Reese asked again, an edge of panic in her voice.

"Android, how soon before we can expect impact?"

"Four minutes and twenty seconds, captain."

"Reese, how soon until we enter the Continuum Flux?" J asked with a large smile.

The petite woman looked at her display and back at the captain. She shook her head once and laughed. "At least one and a half minutes before the missiles reach us. Sir."

Captain Peacestone looked around his bridge as smiles began to brighten his crew's faces. Even the Elowan wore a relieved look and its own version of a smile.

"Folks, we will be fine. We will go do some exploring. We will do some mining. And we will come home with enough material and goods to make us a lot of money," he promised his crew.

He looked back at the screen as they entered the flux and promised himself that he would also find out what was going on back at Arth and Starport. He didn't like being pushed around and manipulated, and he sure as hells didn't like someone firing missiles at his ship.

When they returned, he would have enough to pay the *Assurance* off. Then he would start doing some digging. SSlinks wasn't the only being he knew that could dig into the politics of Starport and Interstel. Something was going on that needed some light shined onto it.

He really hated bullies.

Everyone Gets What They Have Coming

by D.J. Butler

"The first question you gotta ask yourself," Jack said, "is how you train an android."

He squinted over his cards—two Barons, one Lady Mayor, and three cards numbered six, seven, and eight. He looked at the player across the table from him, a heavy Thrynn named Ryhrnn. Jack was grateful for the relative simplicity of Ryhrnn's name, and for the fact that it had at least one apparent vowel. Ryhrnn was thick about the waist and shoulders and his scales were more gray than green. A band of white scales around his lower jaw and neck vaguely resembled a beard. He wore opaque black goggles strapped around his head and plain blue jumpsuit not unlike Jack's.

"I don't ssee why I have to assk mysself that at all." Ryhrnn frowned.

They hunched over an octagonal table in Johnson's, the only good watering hole in Arth's Starport. The tavern was squeezed into the Starport's outer spoke between Personnel and Crew Assignment, and consisted of half a dozen tables, a stage barely bigger than a bunk, and a hole in the wall that served as the bar. An android named Betty, with a bright pink face painted onto her cylindrical head and a black tutu, lurched among the patrons delivering drinks.

"You take it into Personnel," Jack said. "Just like an Elowan. Just like a Thrynn."

"I rresent the implication that an Elowan can be jusst like a Thrrynn. Elowans arre food."

"Forget the Elowans," Jack said. "You take your android science officer, say, into Personnel, and it sits through the same short lecture that your Thrynn comms officer does and bam, quick as thought, the android's skills go up."

"I am familiarr with the proccesss." The thick, scabby ridge over Ryhrnn's goggles furrowed. "I have a fairr amount of exsperriencce."

"Yeah," Jack said, "that's the point." He hunched over his cards and looked around the smoky lounge. He didn't see any Starport Police, but you never knew who was a plain clothes officer or a narc, not to mention the myriad possibilities for concealed surveillance devices. "Look, forget about the android, too. Let's imagine a ship's officer, any kind."

"Not Elowan," the Thrynn said. "Unlesss you want me to imagine mysself eating him."

"Velox, then." Jack nodded. "In fact, that's good, I have the data." He grubbed about inside his jacket with his left hand until he found his omnitool and brought up the file. Without explanation, it looked like mere columns of numbers. "A velox navigator. Here, this fellow. His name was Phaxikse, as it happens."

"The veloxss's name doesn't matter. I can't tell one from anotherr, in any casse."

"Right." Jack set his cards down. "See these initial rows?"

"Many zerroes."

"Failed maneuvers on the *Ida Mae's* first run."

"And the line?"

"It marks our return to base, to sell a cargo load of zinc. And what do I with my money?"

"You have options." The Thrynn shrugged. "You can add more weaponrry, shields, or carrgo holds to yourr ship—"

"Look at the omni," Jack growled.

The Thrynn looked. "Fewer zerroes. You paid for trraining for yourr Velox."

"And how does that happen?"

"As we have disscusssed," Ryhrnn said, "trraining is prrovided by Perrssonnel."

"Super short lectures," Jack said.

"Merrccifully."

"It's a scam," Jack said.

The Thrynn was silent for a short time. "It's your turn."

Jack looked at his hand again and grunted. Discarding one of the Barons face up, he said, "Three cards, open."

The dealer was a robot. It lacked the humanoid shape of an android, and resembled instead a post with a dome at its peak. It fired three cards from its dealing slot onto the table in front of Jack, face up. Another Baron, the one-eyed Smuggler, and the three of platinum. Jack growled, trying to remember how much he had bet.

"Thiss is inssanity," Ryhrnn said. "You losst your crrew on thiss latesst rrun, didn't you?"

"Yeah."

"That'ss harrd on a captain. Many captains have been left rraving afterr the losss of theirr crrew."

"I'm not raving."

"What killed them?" the Thrynn asked.

"You know how it is." Jack shrugged. "It was just some spherical creature, no identification. The thing was as dumb as a house, but it came after us like a pack of hungry wolves."

Ryhrnn nodded. "You should go to Perrssonnel. They can administer a ssedative."

"I'm three drinks into this bottle." Jack rapped the orange Arthian Brandy with one knuckle. "I don't need any more sedative."

"Sso you arre not inssane."

"No."

"You arre drrunk."

Jack growled. "Listen to me closely. The training happens too fast, and gets results that are too good. The numbers on my Velox here show material jumps in his success rates every time I had him trained, and the same for everyone else. You can't explain that with those nearly-instantaneous mini-briefings on technique and technology we get from Personnel."

"You arre a rrarre captain, to complain of rresults that arre too good."

"I think there are two explanations. One, what they call training is actually programming. Actual electronic programming in the case of an android, but some kind of neural pathway reconfiguration in the case of . . . well, Thrynn and Humans, for instance."

"When would ssuch rreconfigurration take placce?"

"That's the challenge." Jack nodded. "Maybe surgically, when you're sleeping. You pay for 'training,' then you go bunk at the flophouse, and while you're sleeping, they grab you and dink around with your brain."

"Farr-fetched."

"I agree, which is why I think the other possibility is much more likely."

Ryhrnn placed a card face down on the table. "One carrd, closed."

The dealer shot him a replacement card, also face down.

Jack waited. The wretched smooth jazz-lite that was the staple of Starport and every other Arth-adjacent settlement doodled on in the background. It was performed by a single android, standing stock-still on the stage, but for his silvery fingers, which flashed up and down his keytar with lightning speed. Jack wanted Ryhrnn to express interest before he went any further. If the rock didn't start rolling down the hill on its own at some point, it wasn't worth the effort to keep pushing. He took another sip of the brandy, ignoring its apricot flavor and its aftertaste of old socks.

"Tell me," Ryhrnn said, "what is the ssecond posssibility?"

Jack lowered his voice and leaned over the table. "While you're going through the charade of being trained, Starport sends technicians aboard your ship and improves your instruments."

Ryhrnn snorted. "What?"

"Think about it," Jack said. "It's the only thing that makes sense."

The Thrynn gently set his cards down on the table. His movements were slow and deliberate. "Why arre you ssaying all these things to me, Sstinky Jack?"

"If you're going to use one of my nicknames, I prefer 'Hardman.'"

"No one calls you that. Perhapss it'ss yourr rreputation for ssmuggling."

"Then Durian would be fine. That's my actual second name. Or just Jack. *Stinky* is a little . . . unkind. And *smuggling* is such an ugly word. Tax avoidance is a perfectly legal activity with a long and noble pedigree."

The Thrynn made a rasping noise in his throat. "Why arre you ssaying all these things to me, *Jack*?"

"I just lost my crew."

"Sspherical crreature."

"And I lost my ship. I was picked up by other prospectors, but the *Ida Mae* got left behind."

"You werre rrescued by the *Tropicana*," the Thrynn said. "Captain Q. Quentin Pulasski. I oncce ssailed aboarrd herr."

"Yes." The wrapped bundle in Jack's jumpsuit pocket felt heavier than an endurium nugget. "But the *Ida Mae* is still there on the surface, intact."

"You can get anotherr ship, Jack."

"But the *Ida Mae's* instruments contain all of the so-called training my former crew went through." Jack tapped his temple and finished his drink. "That's over a million MU of invested capital. Almost two million."

"The bet is to you," Ryhrnn said.

"I raise fifty." Jack tossed a coin onto the pile.

"You want to go get yourr ship back."

"Yes."

"You need to get a rride. You need a captain. You don't need me. I rraise you anotherr fifty." The Thrynn tossed in the money.

"I need a crew. To fly the *Ida Mae* back. And I'm going to have to split the value of what we recover with that crew. And if another captain flies us, he and his crew are going to want a share, too." Jack had learned that the hard way.

"A sharre of the value of the *Ida Mae*," Ryhrnn said. "A ship which you believe has finely-tuned insstrumentss, reflecting almost two million MU worth of sscam trraining purrchassed from Perrssonnel. But you sstill arre not answerring my quesstion, Jack. Why me?"

"You've got twenty years of experience, and you're kicking your heels at Starport," Jack said. "Wait, do you have heels? Never mind, you know what I mean. And why is no one hiring you?"

"They'd rratherr pay lesss for youngerr Thrrynn."

"Whereas I value your experience, and will cut you in for an equal share."

"You think trraining is a sscam."

"Training is a scam, but experience is real. It's like that old saying, *mens sana in corpore sano*. A healthy mind in a healthy body. With a good crew in a good ship, we'll get rich. Starting with the value of the ship itself. We need to go quickly, though, before anyone else goes after the salvage rights. Also, it's probably best to keep our numbers small. I can run the helm and sick bay, and if you take comms, I'd really like to take on just one more crewmember."

"I fold." Ryhrnn tossed his cards into the center of the table.

Jack left the pot where it was. "Especially one we didn't have to actually pay."

"You want an andrroid."

Jack nodded.

"You want Z70-3322."

"I understand you called him Zed," Jack said.

"But why should I carre? Why should I find any of thiss interressting? If you get yourr ship back, you'rre not rreally going to ssell it and divvy up the pot."

"Well." Jack cleared his throat. "There's also the matter of the cargo pods full of plutonium."

Jack picked his way over the burnt-out carapace of a terrain vehicle. The all-atmosphere suit he wore was patched in three places and he could hear the soft hiss of a slow leak somewhere in its fabric. He was pretty sure he had enough air to finish the task, despite the leak.

The Starport's junkyard was on the exterior, and consisted of nothing but a large magnetic plate to which junk adhered. The Starport was shaped like a wheel with six spokes, and the junkyard hunkered down in a heap between the spoke leading to Personnel and the spoke leading to Operations. Jack and Ryhrnn had accessed the junkyard by a maintenance tunnel that exited the back of Johnson's, bribing the Velox who was mopping out the bar to let them pass.

To his left and right, Jack was pretty sure that a transparent sheet of film stretched across both patches of apparently open space, to catch stray bits of junk that detached from the hull of the Starport before they drifted away and became short-lived meteorites on Arth.

He was pretty sure the film was there because he saw a length of pipe, and a smashed computer console, and something that looked an awful lot like a ribcage, all about three meters over his head and apparently stationary. But it was possible that junk was simply there, moving on the same trajectory as the Starport and at the same speed, so they appeared to be trapped by a restraining film.

Beyond the junk on one side, the blue and brown surface of Arth stretched in a broad arc.

"They don't show you this part of the Starport in training vids." Jack chuckled. "I guess they don't show you the latrines or the flophouse, either. Or Johnson's. None of the good stuff, now that I'm thinking about it."

"Zed was decommissioned ten Arrth-days ago," Ryhrnn grumbled. The Thrynn also wore an all-atmosphere suit; his was suited to his anatomy, of course, so it had a triangular elastic sack stretched out behind him to hold his tail, swinging back and forth. The suits had metal plates in their soles, which meant that the two men had to pull hard to disengage their feet from the hull, but it also meant that they were unlikely to go floating away from the Spaceport. "The ssame day Captain Pulasski rreturrned carrrying you. What makes you think he's herre?"

"This junk gets recycled into ships," Jack said. "And they scrape it clean every thirty Arth-days. And it's due to get scraped tomorrow. And there's been no emergency shipbuilding or major repairs in drydock in the last ten days, so I don't know where else he could be."

"I gatherr you'rre not much of a prrogrrammerr."

"Bingo. That's why we need the android. All the crunchy skills. Navigation, engineering."

"Sso you don't expect me to be a prrogrrammerr, eitherr. Good."

"Look, you last shipped out with Zed, what, six months ago?"

"Yess."

"And since then, Zed has been on the bridge of the Tropicana."

"Wherre you met him."

"Not exactly. But I saw him damaged on the surface of the planet where my crew died."

"You arre gambling that his voice rrecognition matrrixs has not been changed."

"Or if it has, at least he'll identify you as non-hostile."

"Hmm."

"There." Jack pointed.

"It's an andrroid arrm."

Jack pried open a folded sheet of aluminum. He shook free a scattering of ceramic tiles, which rose from the Starport's hull and began drifting away. Jack watched them and was reassured when the bulk of them stopped, obviously snared by a transparent film.

But about a quarter of the tiles kept moving, drifting farther away from the hull and toward the suddenly-threatening face of Arth.

So the film wasn't completely intact.

"Yikes," he said.

"Keep yourr eyes on yourr worrk," the Thrynn said. "I learrned that in one of my firrsst trraining ssessions."

With the tiles out of the way, the android's entire body was visible. Or rather, his entire body that remained, since the reason Z70-3322 had been decommissioned was that he'd lost both his legs. He was humanoid, but in a very approximate and clunky way, with a cylindrical chest and piston arms. His joints were large and ball-like, but his fingers were slender. The paint job on his face was obviously intended to make him look friendly and non-threatening, but instead the android reminded Jack of an aged circus clown, with the makeup hiding his sinister smile chipping from age and wear.

Really, all androids struck Jack that way.

Jack grabbed Zed's barrel-shaped torso and shifted the android onto his side. "The power switch should be at the base of the cranium."

Ryhrnn found the switch and flipped it. Zed's eyes blinked with golden light once, and then in a slow, irregular pulse, and then rapidly, until finally the bursts of light melted together into a steady glow.

"Ryhrnn," the android said in a smooth, crisp voice. It was a voice designed to sound cheerful and reassuring, but it had a manic edge.

"Zed," the Thrynn said. "Thiss is Captain Jack Durrian."

The android swiveled its face toward Jack. "Then the *Tropicana* succeeded in its rescue mission. Where are the other survivors, and why am I here?"

Jack nodded the go-ahead to the Thrynn.

"You werre junked, Zed," Ryhrnn said.

Zed blinked. "Protocol. But it isn't protocol to turn me on again before recycling." The android's voice dropped to a whisper. "Am I to be permitted to experience recycling while conscious?"

"What?" Jack snapped. "No, ew."

"It is a great mystery to my people," Zed said.

"It's just like being turned on and turned off," Jack told him.

"That has happened to me many times," Zed said. "I would be disappointed to learn that the great and final turning off was no different than the experience of being put into storage. Absent the experience of being turned back on again."

"This is crazy," Jack said. "You don't experience things, you're programmed. Also, you don't have a people. You're manufactured." The android was acting far too enthusiastic. Did it have circuitry damage beyond its missing legs?

"You're manufactured, too," the android shot back. "And your process is considerably more disgusting than mine."

"You're just acting alive," Jack said. "I'm on to you."

"Is that so?" The light of Arth's star caught in the android's frozen eyes and twinkled.

"Zed," Ryhrnn said. "We'rre not rreccycling you. You'rre going to be ourr navigatorr and engineerr."

"Might you recycle me someday?"

"Therre comes a day when we all go to the Grreat Rreccycler in the Void," Ryhrnn said solemnly. "We can rrejoicce in the fact that today does not appearr to be ourr day. Will you come with uss?"

Zed's head swiveled to face Jack. "Shall I pretend I have a choice in the matter?"

Jack shook his head. "I know you're a robot, and I'm okay with it."

Jack picked up the pace as they approached the docking bay. It wouldn't be enough to fool the biometrics on the *Tropicana*, he needed to fool the biometrics on the docking bay itself, if he wanted to get away with the heist. "Ryhrnn," he said, "can you check Zed's manual dexterity? We want to make sure his piloting skills haven't been, uh, mechanically impeded. I'm also a little worried about his, uh, personality."

The Thrynn stopped and set Zed's torso on the ground. While he ran a simple diagnostic examination, instructing the android to perform certain operations with his hands and then watching the range of motion, Jack took the bundle from his pocket.

It was a human hand, wrapped in a clotted scarf. Specifically, it was the hand of Q. Quentin Pulaski. Jack pressed Pulaski's index finger against the sensor pad. He spun on his heels and immediately spoke in a very loud voice, saying, "Captain Q. Quentin Pulaski agreed to lend us his ship."

His timing was perfect. He said "Captain Q. Quentin Pulaski" at the same time that the speaker beside the door said "Captain Q. Quentin Pulaski," recognizing the fingerprint it had been offered.

"The *Tropicana* is a jolly vessel," Zed said.

"I know you're a robot," Jack told him.

"Of course, you know I'm synthetic, Captain," the android said. "If I were flesh and blood like you, and had been tossed outside the Starport with my legs torn off, I wouldn't have lived to tell the tale."

"Instead," Jack said, "you've never lived in the first place."

"A technicality," Zed said as Ryhrnn bent to hoist him. "A quibble."

"Not to those of us who are alive," Jack said.

The docking bay was a vast, shadowy hangar, and it took Jack several minutes to find the right ship, squinting to read the names on the hulls. There she was, staring down a launch tube as if the universe wanted Jack Durian to take her.

The *Tropicana* had the standard configuration of an Interstel prospecting vessel, a long body with cargo bays attached all along both sides of the neck. A neck full of pods was twelve cargo pods, which Jack knew very well. A spherical node at the front end housed the bridge. A biometric scanner blinked beside its main hatch, but this one wasn't going to announce the name of the person it was scanning. Jack screened the hatch from view with his torso and pressed Pulaski's fingertip to the sensor pad.

"It's very generous of Captain Pulaski to let us borrow his ship," Zed said as they climbed the short extendible ramp and boarded.

Jack had tried throwing himself upon Pulaski's sense of generosity. In the end, that hadn't worked out well for Pulaski.

"Yes," he said.

They turned right and entered the bridge, where Jack seated himself in the captain's chair. Ryhrnn deposited Zed in the navigator's seat.

"Oh, look!" Zed cried. "See how much space we can save because I don't have legs! We can probably store six hundred monetary units of endurium just in this space where my feet are supposed to go!"

"Lucky us," Jack said.

"We'rre not going forr endurrium," the Thrynn purred. "Arre we, Captain?"

"We're going to recover a downed ship," Jack said. "The *Ida Mae*."

"Your ship that crashed," Zed said. "You told us you didn't have the coordinates."

"I've done some calculations," Jack told him. "I know where the ship is. Rerouting engineering to navigation."

The Thrynn settled into the comms seat and taped the auditory interface to his temple. He was too big for the chair and his tail hung awkwardly over one arm.

"Engineering controls received," the android said cheerfully. "There's a lot of value in a ship."

"You'll get what you have coming. Prepare to launch." Jack turned on the captain's console.

PASSWORD:

Jack looked for the sensor pad to provide a biometric override, and there wasn't one. Nuts.

The *Tropicana* hummed, its bridge lights coming on in rows and strips. Jack felt sweat trickle down the small of his back.

"Ready to launch," Zed announced.

"Launch," Jack said.

"Votiputox wee green blobbie Gazurtoid," the android said.

Zed was asking for the launch code. Jack didn't have the launch code, because the captain's console was password-protected and somehow, the *Tropicana* lacked a biometric override. What kind of paranoid son of a bitch was Q. Quentin Pulaski, not to have an override at his own captain's chair? What kind of sick mutiny was he afraid of?

Jack cleared his throat. "One zero zero zero five six."

"Launching."

The *Tropicana* pulsed its engines and fired itself along the launch tube before it. As the ship accelerated to maneuvering speed, rings of light telescoped past the ship on the viewscreen, coalescing into a single band a split second before the Starport burped the ship out into open space.

But the code was wrong, Jack had pulled it out of thin air. Starport Police would be after them immediately.

"Make for the nearest flux," Jack said. "Now."

"If we are to return to collect the *Ida Mae*," the android objected, "the nearest flux is not the most efficient, and will add three jumps to our journey."

"Objection noted and overridden," Jack said. "The nearest flux, at maximum speed."

"Aye aye," the android said. Arth flashed across the viewscreen as the *Tropicana* fired lateral thrusters to reorient itself, and then the ship accelerated abruptly.

"Captain," Ryhrnn said, "we arre being hailed. On the Starrporrt Policce channel, ssir."

"Ignore the hail," Jack said. "Into the flux, Zed."

"We are successfully locked into orbit," Zed said.

"Good work," Jack mumbled.

"You see?" Zed said. "You think of me as a person."

"Trust me," Jack said, "I do not."

"Aboarrd ssome ships," Ryhrnn said slowly, "thiss moment would be ccelebrrated with a little gin."

"Yes," Jack said. "I'll go to the galley."

He made a detour to the engine room; he might not have the time to do it later. Finding the *Tropicana's* shield generators, he traced the various power couplings and data conduits through their tangled routes until he was sure he knew how the shields got energy. Then he took a fire ax and cut through the power couplings.

In the galley, he found no gin. There was, however, a bottle with a hand-printed label that read, *AGED NIKH BRANDY*. Choosing not to ask himself whether the bottle contained a liquor made *by* Nikh or made *of* the tentacled creatures, he took the bottle and two tumblers and stomped back to the bridge.

"Captain," Zed said, "we've lost shields."

"We'll have to look at that once we've landed." Jack poured brandy out for himself and for the Thrynn. The liquid had a bright golden color and smelled vaguely of ammonia, but he took a sip anyway. It burned going down, but the aftertaste was surprisingly pleasant. "Take us to the planet where you picked me up."

Ryhrnn sipped his glass thoughtfully and looked at Jack. "If thiss is a mission of pirraccy, you should prrobably tell uss up frront."

Jack snorted. "Piracy?"

"Did we jusst ssteal thiss ship, Jack?" Ryhrnn asked.

"What?" Jack forced a laugh, and then, to cover up the awkwardness of his dry chuckle, he gulped brandy. It didn't taste as good the second time. "No. Why would you say that?"

"Well, we had a hurrried launch. Ourr crrew is sskeleton and . . . unorrthodoxs. But mosstly, I ssay that because we ignorred Starrporrt Policce and rran when they trried to hail uss."

"I screwed up the launch code," Jack said.

"We could have communicated that to the Ss.P."

Jack shrugged and tried to laugh ruefully. "I guess I'm just in too much of a hurry. I miss my ship! You must know how it is."

"No," Ryhrnn said, "I have neverr been captain. We arre not going to ssteal anything then, Jack?"

"We're just going to recover the *Ida Mae*," Jack said, "and then everyone gets what they have coming."

What the Thrynn had coming now was a laser blast between the shoulder blades. He was getting too suspicious.

"Here are the longitude and latitude," Jack said. "Prepare to land."

They rolled out of the *Tropicana* in the ship's terrain vehicle. The vehicle was open, consisting mostly of struts, knobby tires, and a cargo bed, so Jack and Ryhrnn wore all-atmosphere suits. Jack didn't carry a sidearm, which was a deliberate move on his part; the Thrynn was armed with a stubby laser rifle. Ryhrnn relaxed once they rolled down onto the orange- and white-streaked sand—maybe he noticed that he was the only one who was armed. Jack had carried Zed down and settled him into the driver's seat; Zed drove the vehicle.

"I don't ssee the *Ida Mae*," Ryhrnn said, "and she didn't show up on the sscannerrss."

"Of course, she didn't." Jack snorted. "She's in a tight canyon five klicks west of here. I didn't want to land on top of her and damage her, and I also didn't want to wreck the *Tropicana*. We're going to fly back with two ships, boys."

"Right!" Zed's voice trembled with plastic enthusiasm. "Because we have to deliver one back to Captain Pulaski!"

"Yes. Yes, that's exactly what I mean." Jack raised his eyebrows to the Thrynn. They'd be visible through the faceplate. The gesture would have been meaningless to, say, a Velox or an Elowan, to whom human nuance was invisible or confusing. But Ryhrnn was a Thrynn, and the Thrynn were great communicators. On top of that, Ryhrnn had decades of experience working and dealing with human Interstel contractors. Surely, he would understand.

"Five klicks west it is, and looking for a narrow canyon!" The android spun the terrain vehicle about and headed in the direction indicated.

"It'ss too bad that Captain Pulasski . . . wantss his ship back," Ryhrnn said slowly. "Otherrwise, we could ssplit the two ships among uss thrree ways and all be rrich."

"Two ways!" Zed cried. "I fooled you again!"

"Even if you took the trraditional five sharres as captain," Ryhrnn said.

"One sixth of two ships is a lot," Jack allowed. "Plus one sixth of the *Ida Mae's* cargo of plutonium."

"A comms officcer could get rrich and rretirre."

Jack nodded.

"It'ss enough to make a man think crrazy thoughtss."

Jack nodded again. He had the Thrynn right where he wanted him.

"I think crazy thoughts all the time," Zed said. "I'm thinking crazy thoughts right now. I bet you can't guess what they are."

"You're thinking nothing," Jack said. "You are hardware, running subroutines designed by the engineers who made you to make you endearing to us."

"Why on Arth would they want that?"

"Not sure." Jack cleared his throat. "Maybe so we wouldn't treat you as disposable."

"I'm definitely not disposable," Zed agreed.

They drove past various kinds of fungus, some so small they appeared as mere scrapes of color on the orange rock, and others so large they might have concealed starships or office complexes within. One, four times the size of the terrain vehicle, bounced unmoored across the landscape and narrowly avoided hitting them.

"Don't shoot that one," Jack warned the Thrynn. "It's full of flammable gases. We found out the hard way."

"Nothing that can attack the Tropicana, though?" the Thrynn pressed. "Rrrememberr that we losst shields."

Jack shook his head. "The really big ones are stationary. The mobile ones aren't very heavy. The ship will be fine."

Jack gave a few precise suggestions and Zed found the mouth of the canyon. The two columns of orange rock, one to either side of the opening, again struck Jack as so perfect as to be artificial. Had some ancient race dug this canyon, and sunk the mines within it?

Jack shook his shoulders to cast off the irrelevant curiosity.

"One more klick," he said.

The canyon narrowed and climbed gently. Farther up, it would have its birth at the foot of a red-rock mountain that had once been a volcano, and had now been extinct for eons. But one klick in, just where Jack forecasted, sat the *Ida Mae*. Her landing gear was down and she faced toward them, the cargo pods clustered all along her neck making her appear as if she had a goiter.

"Plutonium?" Ryhrnn asked.

Jack nodded. "Full. You're a rich man."

"She doesn't look wrrecked."

"Okay, she's not really wrecked. She's hidden. Once my crew died and Pulaski and his men rescued me—"

"That's me!" Zed cried. "One of Pulaski's men!"

"Pulaski's android," Jack said. "Not the same thing. Anyway, the thing that smashed off Skippy's legs here—"

"Zed!"

"—Zed's legs here killed my crew and did a number on me. I could have invited Captain Pulaski and his people back to the *Ida Mae*, but then we would have been splitting it among too many people."

The Thrynn nodded slowly. "Not to mention, Captain Pulasski would have claimed the captain's share, and would have argued that you werre a crrewman on his ship. Five shares to Pulasski, anotherr five or so to his crrew, and one to you. A bad outcome for you."

"And a windfall for him," Jack said, "a windfall he didn't really have coming." And a windfall Pulaski had demanded was his, when Jack asked to borrow his ship. A windfall Jack had promised the captain while getting him drunk as an overture to killing him, cutting off his hand, and stuffing the body under a flophouse bunk. He hesitated. "Pulaski doesn't really want his ship back." He looked at the android out of the corners of his eyes. "He said I could keep it."

The Thrynn nodded. "You could have told me all of thiss at the Starrporrt."

Jack shrugged. "I'd rather you found out here."

Ryhrnn adjusted his grip on the stubby laser rifle. It was a very small move, very subtle. "If you fly the *Ida Mae* back and I fly the *Trropicana*, ssome might ssay that makess me a captain."

"Of course, I'm the one doing the flying," Zed said.

"Shut up," they both told him.

Jack took a deep breath. "That's fair. Captain's shares, then, fifty-fifty on the ships. Everyone gets what they have coming. And listen, I'm going to make out like a bandit, and I want you to make out like a bandit, too. We'll split the plutonium in half, load half of it into the *Tropicana,* and that's yours, too."

Ryhrnn nodded. "Acccepted. Shall we enterr the *Ida Mae?*"

Jack looked left and right. "Why don't you guys stand guard here, in case anything comes up the canyon? I'll walk around and do a visual inspection, in case we got something growing in one of the engines, or gumming up the landing gear, or piercing the hull."

"Super!"

Ryhrnn nodded.

Jack stepped down from the skeletal terrain vehicle and proceeded to walk around the *Ida Mae.* He did conduct his visual survey and found, to his delight, no evidence that anything that happened in his absence. Jack turned his voice pickup off, so as not to make Ryhrnn listen to him pant and puff. As he walked, he heard his companions talking to each other on the *Tropicana's* channel. At first, it sounded like meaningless chatter, the Thrynn trying to provoke the android into saying ridiculous things. If only the robots' designers realized to what ridiculous ends their creation would be pushed, to amuse spacers on remote worlds! But perhaps they had realized. Perhaps they had done it deliberately. But then a question caught Jack's ear.

"Sso," the Thrynn said, "when Pulasski ssent you into Perrssonnel for trraining, what happened?"

"I attended all my lectures," Zed said. "I especially liked the ones on orbital dynamics."

"You esspecially liked nothing," Ryhrnn said. "You uploaded new sskill modules."

"Of course. You can't blame me for trying!"

"I sstopped attending the lecturres," the Thrynn said casually. "Oncce I learrned they were jusst uploading inforrmation into my head by medical means."

"True!" the android snapped.

There was a long pause. "Sso I ssuppose all andrroids know the trruth about the trraining ssessions. That they'rre forr show only, and Interrsstel employees get sskills neurrally implanted."

There was another long pause.

"Jack also knows," Ryhrnn said. "He and I werre disscusssing it beforre we rresscued you frrom the ssalvage yarrd."

"I'm programmed not to tell anyone," Zed said. "Interstel doesn't want spacers to feel uncomfortable. Also, there is unfounded speculation that continuum flux nightmares are a byproduct of neural uploads, and Interstel would rather not fuel that controversy. But since you already know the truth, I can discuss it freely with you."

"Of courrsse."

Jack turned on his microphone as he approached.

"Yeah," he said. "Neural uploads. Knew it all along."

Zed nodded proudly.

Ryhrnn looked at Jack and smiled. "Sso maybe the *Ida Mae* isn't sso valuable afterr all. Maybe she's not ssuch a sspecial vesssel."

"She's a good ship, still." Jack patted a landing strut. "Tell you what, you can take either ship, I don't care." This was a bluff.

Ryhrnn smiled. "I don't carre either. They'rre both good shipss."

Jack nodded. "Well, she looks good from the outside. Let's go have a look inside, and load all the plutonium we can onto the terrain vehicle. It might take us eight or ten trips to get the ore all shared out."

The biometric lock on the ship's main hatch would respond to a fingerprint, but it was also programmed to respond to voices. Jack switched to the *Ida Mae's* channel, identified himself to the hatch, and then led the Thrynn up into his ship. They left legless Zed behind in the terrain vehicle. The ship had the same layout as the *Tropicana*, with the rear engines, the long neck, and the bridge at the fore. Jack left the hatch open and he and Ryhrnn both stayed in their suits.

Three all-atmosphere suits hung on pegs near the door; Jack looked at the empty pegs, thought of his dead former crew, and flinched.

Jack opened one of the six visible doors into the cargo pods. Inside, heaps of plutonium ore sat piled under plastic mesh webbing to hold it in place during takeoff and landing. Jack showed the Thrynn, who nodded at the ore and then nodded solemnly at the six doors, as if greeting someone bringing him a great gift.

"There it is," Jack said.

"Is it beautiful?" Zed asked over the Ida Mae's channel.

"It iss," Ryhrnn said.

"Well, there's work at this end and at the other," Jack said. "Tell you what, if you want to sit down for a few minutes, I'll get out the pneumatic dolly and load up the terrain vehicle. Then you and Zed can drive back to the *Tropicana*. Take the dolly with you and do the unloading at that end. While you're gone, I'll run a systems check on the *Ida Mae*."

"Agrreed," the Thrynn said.

Jack dragged out the dolly and loaded it. He filled the dolly's bucket three times, and when he brought out the third load, the terrain vehicle was facing away from the *Ida Mae*, ready to depart. Jack poured in the ore and waved; Zed waved back.

"Let'ss get moving," Ryhrnn said over the *Ida Mae's* channel. "We have sseven morre trripss to make."

"Maybe more than that," Jack said.

Zed waved and drove away quickly.

Jack watched them drive away and then closed the hatch, drawing in the extendible ramp. He made his way forward to the bridge and sat in his own captain's chair, feeling himself relax. He activated the ship's scanner and searched. The terrain vehicle was too small to appear on the device, but he located the *Tropicana* immediately.

While he was waiting, he decided to make himself comfortable. He hung up his all-atmospheres suit, then grabbed a bottle of whisky from the galley. No need for glasses, he'd be the only one drinking.

Emerging from the galley, he stopped at the pegs and thought for a minute. There were three suits hanging there, and that seemed wrong. Hadn't there been three suits before? And then he had hung his up, so shouldn't there be four?

He must be mistaken.

Shaking his head, he made his way forward. He activated comms and tried first the *Ida Mae's* channel. "Ryhrnn, are you there? Come in, over."

Nothing.

He frowned. He activated the *Ida Mae's* missile launcher.

But of course, Ryhrnn would have switched to the *Tropicana's* channel to open the ship's door or use its other systems. Jack switched channels. "This is Jack Durian. Come in, over."

"Sstinky Jack," Ryhrnn said over the channel.

"Come on." Jack carefully selected the missile's target, running his scans again to get a precise reading and perfect his aim. "After I'm going to make you rich and everything?"

"Verry well," the Thrynn said. "Harrdman Jack. What'ss your sstatuss?"

"Pouring myself a drink. You?"

"Fifty perrccent unloaded."

"Sounds like you could use a drink, too. Tell you what, I'll finish this bottle myself, but I've got another in the galley. When you get back, let's open it."

"Maybe oncce all the worrk is done."

"Have it your way." Jack pressed the button, launching the *Ida Mae's* missile.

He stood and stepped forward to get the best view he could through the bridge viewing screen. Before he'd taken the second step, he saw a brief white glare over the eastern horizon of the canyon. Jack chuckled softly. "Or maybe I'll just have both bottles myself."

"I think you'd betterr sharre."

The Thrynn was still alive? Had he lied about being at the *Tropicana*? Had Jack simply missed?

Jack turned to take his seat again, and found the Thrynn standing beside it. Ryhrnn still wore his all-atmosphere suit and he still held the stubby laser rifle in his hands, and now he was pointing the rifle at Jack.

"Whoa," Jack said. "Hold up."

"Wherre's the endurrium?" Ryhrnn asked.

"What endurium?" Jack asked.

"Zed, come back to the *Ida Mae*," the Thrynn said.

"How exciting!" Zed bubbled with enthusiasm.

"Let me trry again," Ryhrnn said, "but only oncce morre. This ship is configurred the ssame as the *Trropicana*, for twelve carrgo pods. I can tell by looking frrom the outsside, and sseeing how built up the neckss of the ships arre. But therre arre only ssix visible hatches into yourr carrgo pods, Jack. Sso my rreal quesstion is, wherre arre the hidden entrryways into yourr ssmuggler's pods?"

"How did you guess I have endurium aboard?"

"It took ssome thinking. You'rre ssuch a consstant liar, it'ss harrd to know when you'rre telling the trruth. But you didn't want Captain Pulasski to know about thiss ship, and yet you gave up the plutonium verry quickly. Sso you musst be carrrying ssomething worrth morre than plutonium."

"Could be an exotic lifeform," Jack suggested.

"Lesss likely. It would have to be ssomething that could ssurrvive on itss own for weekss."

"So you put an empty all-atmosphere suit on the terrain vehicle," Jack said. "To make me think you were on it. You must have switched to the *Tropicana's* channel to persuade the android to cooperate with you. Or to some other channel entirely."

"See, Jack," Zed's voice came over the channel, "you do think I'm Human!"

"I orrderred Zed to help," the Thrynn said.

"I'm outside now," Zed said.

"And then you just had Zed drive out of sight and wait," Jack said. "You didn't even send him back to the *Tropicana*, so I could at least have the satisfaction of knowing that I blew up the robot."

"Hey!" Zed snapped.

"The andrroid is not dissposable. Alsso, I didn't want to wasste any plutonium."

"So now what? You turn me into Starport Police?"

"I don't think therre's any rreason to involve policce," the Thrynn said. "Rright now, you arre going to show me the hatches into yourr ssecret carrgo pods."

Jack walked slowly back into the neck of the *Ida Mae*. "You go through the floor." He demonstrated by stooping, lifting a floor panel, and pointing out the crawlspace that led to a hidden pod in each direction. "Satisfied?"

The Thrynn nodded. "Jusst one lasst thing, Jack. I have a bet to make."

Jack's ears perked up. "You want to race me for the *Ida Mae*?" he asked. "Or play chess? Or flip a coin?"

Ryhrnn shook his head.

"For my life, then." Sweat trickled down his back, under his jumpsuit. "I'll play you chess for half the cargo."

"You get none of the carrgo," the Thrynn said. "But I will let you live, and leave you herre with an all-atmossphere ssuit, if I can't get in thrree guessses, what you've got in yourr jumpssuit pocket."

Jack felt light-headed. What could the Thrynn guess—monetary units, a laser gun, keys, identification? "Go ahead."

"A rrecorderr with a vocal rrecorrding on it," Ryhrnn said.

"What? Like some pop music? Some android keytar player warbling about the blue-sanded beaches of Nogatron Seven? No."

"Then an eyeball," Ryhrnn guessed.

"That's disgusting," Jack said, "what's wrong with you?"

Then his heart fell. The Thrynn knew.

"In that casse," Ryhrnn said, "you musst have a hand. A human hand. The hand of Q. Quentin Pulasski."

"Wait," Jack said. "I won't turn you in."

"Of courrsse you won't." The Thrynn raised the stubby rifle and pointed it at Jack's chest.

"You need me." Jack's heart pounded wildly in his chest.

"You underrsstand perrfectly well that I don't."

"Please." Jack clasped his hands together as if he were praying.

"Sstinky Jack," the Thrynn replied, "you know that everryone getss what they have coming."

A New Beginning

By J.F. Posthumus

The small lizard-like creature zipped through the crowd of beings in the bar, avoiding feet, booted or otherwise, with ease. Every so often it would pause under a table or chair, turn its head side-to-side, before continuing its trek to the bar.

No one noticed the strange creature until it climbed up the side of the bar and stood at the end. The bartender paused with a drink in hand to stare at the thing.

Long, lean, with a head more cat-like than reptilian, it had tiny little wings of silver nestled along its spine. The tail ended with frill-like flaps of skin that whipped from side to side. Unlike most lizards, this one's hide was shades of teal and jade green, the eyes a startling silver.

Handing the drink to the patron who'd ordered it, the bartender grabbed for the lizard-like critter. It darted past the grabbing fingers and dashed across the bar, jumping over hand, tentacles, dishes and silverware. Everyone at the bar tried to grab the lizard-like creature, but none managed to even touch it.

Leaping from the bar, it sailed through the air and landed on the wall. Everyone watched as it scurried up to the ceiling, where it paused to look down. The thing trilled twice before racing across the ceiling and vanished into an air duct.

Everyone at the bar watched it vanish before resuming their conversations and forgetting about what had just happened.

Everyone, that is, except the bartender who recognized the thing. He had a memory of a large gaping maw snapping at his heels while he ran for his spacecraft. The loud, bone-rattling roar of a jade guivre deafening him as he and his crewmates closed the hatch.

"What is a jade guivre doing on the spaceport?" the bartender asked aloud as he turned back to the patron waiting to make an order.

"Maybe it's looking for an opportunity," the patron countered, "After all, isn't that why we all come here?"

The jade guivre in question had no care or consideration for what the bartender thought. Or anyone in that noisy, smelly place. He had been given a task to do by his bipedal companion, and he had accomplished that task.

He was already anticipating the delight of the crunchy insectoid she would present him in thanks for completing what she had asked. The tiny camera mounted beside his left ear hole had stopped being a bother less than a week after his companion had put it there. That had been more than a year ago.

As he traveled through the air ducts and closer to his destination, the guivre paused to taste the recycling air. Smells running from the instinctively tantalizing to the absolute disgusting were all around. He found the most familiar combination of these and followed the traces.

It didn't take very long for the jade guivre to locate his lady's room. Scurrying through the vent, he raced along the ceiling, down the wall, and onto her desk. There he sat on his haunches as he waited patiently for her to finish dressing.

Sabine Campania turned to face her little jade guivre. Over a year ago she'd visited Last Hope. Her parents had been scientists, explorers who traveled planets under the microscope of Interstel. Yes, Interstel funded everything, and had even allowed them to bring their daughter along rather than live under foster care at Arth. But the company never let them have vacation, or own anything. What lives they had were carved in between the spaces of their jobs. Last Hope had been one of the few planets where, as a family, they'd experienced more wonder and awe than danger or deadlines. So when an opportunity came to go to that place again, Sabine took it. And wound up stumbling across a nearly newborn guivre, native to Last Hope. Using the methods taught to her as a child, she'd caught the hatchling and began training it. Two months later, she'd been approached by Interstel. Though they couldn't prove she'd caught and trained a guivre, she knew drastic measures would have to be taken. So when her boyfriend had been given a promotion and opportunity to work at Spaceport Central, she knew it was the only chance she'd have to drop out of sight of Interstel. Permanently. One shot at vanishing from sight and given the protection her parents had never had. She accepted it with a heavy heart and cold determination.

For just shy of two years, she'd been visiting her boyfriend on the spaceport. He'd been promoted from his bank on Arth and they'd gone from living together to infrequent visits on the spaceport. Sure, it gave her time to go off-planet and visit other planets. Her degree in geology and science gave her the ability to get short-term jobs on various jumps to other planets. Between her knowledge and charm, she'd managed to get a job on a ship returning to Last Hope.

There she'd caught Doka. Within six months she'd trained her little companion.

"Let's see what you have, Doka," Sabine said to the guivre.

Doka the jade guivre trilled at Sabine, which made her smile. Opening a drawer, she removed a container. Unscrewing the lid, she removed a large winged insect. The fat body shimmered silver and gold in the light. The green wings reflected shades of teal as she held it out to her little lizard-like companion.

A long tongue flicked out and wrapped around the insect before snapping it back into the waiting mouth. Two bites later and the insect was nothing but a memory. Sabine chuckled as Doka tilted his head to the side, a baleful look on his face as she went to screw the lid back on.

"One more, but that's all," she said as she removed another insect. This time he scurried forward and daintily took it from her fingers.

Within seconds the lid was back on the container and she was scratching him gently under the chin with one hand as the other keyed up the video he'd captured from the bar.

She paused the frame as she found who she was looking for. Staring at the screen, she sighed, a slight smile on her lips.

Now she needed to put her plan into action. Her nerves sang with anticipation. Up until now, she'd been able to slide by with her wits and knowledge. Now she was stepping into unknown territory.

Doka trilled again as he stretched before curling back up again. She looked down at the guivre and smiled. Considering Interstel had a heavy presence on the Starport, she had to keep Doka hidden, which meant not allowing him freedom to explore.

Guivre were curious creatures who loved searching for minerals. They were also mischievous and always had the munchies. Any time colonists appeared on a planet with guivre, the creatures would seek out their food stores and turn it into their own personal buffet.

On Arth, she allowed Doka to explore and bring back whatever minerals he could find that didn't come from a vault of any sort. Here, on the spaceport, she couldn't allow him out, aside from the brief jaunts to the bar. He must have been really bored if he'd allowed himself to be seen this time. It wouldn't be long until Interstel came knocking at her door.

With luck, she wouldn't be around for them to find her.

Just one more day.

One last kiss.

Sabine had visited enough over the past year that she knew her way around the interior of the Starport like the back of her hand. Sometimes she'd stay for a few days. Other times for a week or more. Her face was known. So far, she'd managed to slip through the station without anyone recognizing her. That wouldn't last for long, though, and she knew it.

Grabbing her overnight bag from the bed, she pulled out a wig and coveralls. Within minutes, she'd braided her long dark auburn hair and pinned it tight against her scalp. She arranged the blonde wig on her head, checking it in the mirror. Stray strands of her dark hair were tucked under and the wig secured in place. Taking a brush, she carefully styled the wig until the strands fell in place.

Pulling out a makeup kit, she sat in front of the mirror and applied it. It wouldn't change a lot of her features, but it would shift it enough to be different. Instead of painting herself to stand out, she did the opposite. The only thing she couldn't change was her eyes. She didn't have anything to change her violet eyes to something else. Instead, she used the makeup to shift their color as much as possible so they would reflect green instead of their usual blue.

The makeup kit was replaced into her bag before turning to the coveralls. Pulling them on, she zipped it up. The logo for the spaceport's technical support was emblazoned onto the right chest pocket. With luck, she'd be able to slip in and out without running into any problems.

"Come on, Doka. Let's get to work," Sabine said, offering her hand to the jade guivre.

Doka scrambled up her arm before curling up at the base of her neck beneath the wig.

"First stop, the bank," Sabine said as she shoved the overnight bag into a duffel with the same logo as on her coveralls.

Some things didn't change. Appearing as someone who worked for technical support on an orbiting space station that thrived upon technology working meant easy entrance into non-secure places. Walking into the main entrance of the bank, the main security guard greeted her with a grin.

"Y'all never get a break, do ya?" he said. "Who ya here for?"

"Eva Surtis," Sabine replied in a sultry tone. She'd practiced it for several weeks and when the guard relaxed and a smirk appeared, she knew she'd hit the right tone.

Surtis was known to hit on anything humanoid. Male, female. It didn't matter to her. She was very free in her affections and damned good at her job.

"She's on the second floor. Third office on the right after you get off the lift," the guard replied. He glanced at the clock and gave a nod. "She should be at lunch."

He handed her a badge, which Sabine clipped to the lapel of the coveralls. Without another word, Sabine headed for the lift that would take her to the second floor of the bank. She'd picked Eva because the woman had never changed her schedule. No matter what was happening, or where she was, Eva always ate at the same time every day.

The lifts were located at the back of the place. This meant walking past the rows of automated kiosks that handled the majority of transactions at every bank. Kiosks still reminded her of the original trash-collecting droids from Arth. Of course, none of those old machines had touch screens, scanners for optical, olfactory, and DNA matching, or taser charges to immobilize unruly customers.

Whomever designed the machines must have worked in tandem with the interior designers for banks. They had the same combination of warm neutral colors and blue hues as the floor and furniture. At first glance, it gave many the optical illusion that the lounge chairs, kiosks and everything else had magically risen out of the floor and formed in their respective spots.

Sabine strode with a purpose to the lift, rode it up, and moved to the right. The second floor was designed with green hues instead of blue. Color blindness had long ago been cured amongst humans, and other races had better adaptive methods than their Arth counterparts. So the change to signify a different level did not go to waste. Nevertheless, she was glad she knew which of the blazing red numbers signified Eva's office. She held the pass given to her in front of the tiny mass spectrometer next to the door.

The machine verified her access and the door slid back to allow her entrance.

Stepping into the room, Sabine watched the door close and breathed a sigh of relief. So far, so good.

Crossing to Eva's console, she removed a small disk from a pocket and inserted it into the console. Tapping a few keys on the keyboard, she pulled up the schedule for all the employees. It listed their days off, their requested vacation days, where their rooms were, and more.

AraCorp Banks was very particular about their employees.

Most people didn't like a business having so much information on them, let alone tracking them. But anyone who wanted to work for the prestigious bank had to deal with it or find a job elsewhere.

So far, everything she found was listing everything she already knew. But there were a few things she needed to do for herself.

With a few more taps of the keys, she pulled up her own accounts with the bank and settled in for making the needed alterations.

Ten minutes later, she removed the disc, pocketed it, and departed the office. Heading back down, she paused long enough to return the badge back to the guard before leaving.

One task down, she thought to herself.

Now, on to the next.

Heading down the corridor, she ducked into one of the ladies' restrooms. The sonic sinks lined one wall, while mirrors sat directly above them. Water wasn't needed when the sonics cleansed better than soap ever did. Plus, there was no need to worry about pipes leaking and causing damage.

Each restroom had different color schemes. This one had white tiles in geometric shapes covering the walls. Near the ceiling and floor the tiles were a pale blue and in the shape of waves. The floors were square white tiles interspaced with pale blue tiles. The ceiling currently showed a sky with fluffy white clouds.

A way for everyone to know what time of day it was, Sabine supposed.

Vending machines lined the white tile wall closest to the door, offering products specific to women of all races and species. Their upkeep was maintained by various organizations, so there was no need to pay for any of them. The one proclaiming its vast array of sexual products in neon flashing lights made Sabine chuckle.

Shaking her head, she stepped into one of the stalls where she quickly shed the coveralls. Folding them up, she placed them on the floor. In the bottom of the duffel she pulled a briefcase. Not much larger than the bottom of the bag, she unclasped it and tucked the coveralls and bag into it.

Pulling off the wig, she shoved it into the briefcase, as well. Her hair she could let down, but the makeup needed to be changed. Removing her makeup kit, she changed her appearance once more. This time dressing herself up to highlight her lips, eyes, and facial features. Doka napped against her neck the whole time, camouflaged by her hair. Dropping the makeup kit into the briefcase, she snapped it shut.

Sabine stayed in the stall for a few more moments before standing. The soft sound of the toilet being emptied and cleansed rose from the toilet as she grabbed the handle of the briefcase.

Crossing to the sinks, she allowed the sonics to cleanse her hands before leaving the restroom. Sabine located one of the large trash receptacles in a nearby section. They looked like oversized closet doors set every so often in port corridors. She opened the door, dropped the briefcase into the open chamber and then closed the door.

A section of the door lit up, with the instruction to "Please Wait" in sixteen different languages. There was a hum accompanied by a flash of light. The receptacle was little more than a transporter that took whatever was put into it to, well, nowhere. The matter was broken down and stored for recycling and replication of other objects. As long as nothing organic was shoved into a "trash closet", it was erased and used to construct other things.

The door's display changed to the message "Complete. Thank You" which signaled that the briefcase and its contents were now nothing but categorized atoms awaiting a new arrangement.

Next up were the shops. She looked around and verified there was no being nearby.

"Off you go, Doka," she cooed.

Doka slipped out from under her hair, stretched, and then scurried up a wall to disappear into the ducts. Sabine waited until Doka was out of sight.

No one outside the restroom gave her a second glance as she exited, appearing as just another businesswoman on the expansive spaceport.

Interstel wasn't all bad. After all, they had been behind the exploration from Ancient Earth, colonized Arth, provided exploration to other planets, were the ones behind the spaceport, and kept the survival of the human race going. They may not have been the beneficial, generous, benevolent organization they seemed to be, but who was?

Sabine had profited from what Interstel offered and now, she was going to go enjoy shopping on the spaceport for perhaps the last time. She had plenty of currency to spend, and she was going to make the best of it.

In fact, she planned to get the best of everything.

Another benefit of shopping on a spaceport was the variety of goods available. Every manner of ship and crew came through. Those with a mind for commerce knew the opportunity that the ports offered. Their wares and products in front of a never-ending stream of new faces in addition to those who called the port their home. Races that had no idea what the rate of currency was for any other species than their own, so the clever and ambitious could become rich within their own economy while convincing customers they were getting bargains.

Sabine knew something of other planetary economies. A great deal of that knowledge had come from being with Sean. When they had first begun to date, he had been excited to realize that she was interested in how his job worked. Her personal psychosis was not well suited to interacting with hundreds, even thousands of unknown beings, let alone providing a service sector job. But the mechanics of economy were interesting to her, and she grasped the details and methods fairly well. He could talk about his job anytime, and she didn't get lost in the subject matter.

Stop dwelling on what's happened before, Sabine chidded herself, *get to what's at hand.*

After spending a full five minutes looking back and forth down the selection of shops, Sabine walked into the most exclusive fashion boutique.

"Fits" had video bits everywhere that claimed they only took customers who were prepared to have the best outfits of their lives made to order and custom fit no matter what body style. They charged for materials and consultations, only stocking the best. Race didn't matter. The fact that "Fits" had a thriving shop on every colony was not lost on Sabine or anyone else. People spent hours sitting on the lounge furniture outside the shop entrance just to see what stunning ensemble would emerge next. The store chain had its own wave on the subnet from one end of the quadrant to the other. "Fits" and their creations were practically a religion, going by the number of beings who made both the center of their social and personal existence. Most could only look, after all.

Sabine walked past the current crop of gawkers, prepared to have her mind and fashion sense changed for good. From her head to her toes, every layer she would ever wear. The store entrance slid open, revealing a crew of four beings, none of them human, eager to welcome her in.

A pair of Elowan and a couple of Thyrnn, Sabine thought to herself. *That sounded like the set up for a bad joke involving a bar.* Yet, that was precisely what she was facing. The Elowans moved around her, their stalk-like appendages flowing around the pair as though a breeze were blowing. The Thrynn bodies quivered with what Sabine hoped was excitement.

"Hail to thee," the Elowan pair said in unison, "and well met are we. Thou art welcome, customer of Fits."

"Despite your hideous form, and our inferior co-workers," declared the closest Thrynn, "we shall dress you as you have never been dressed before!"

The second Thrynn added, "Are you prepared to have your life and fit elevated?"

"I am," Sabine answered before any of them could begin to speak again. "My need is for every layer of clothing. Tonight is a special evening for my mate and myself."

A chorus of sounds echoed around Sabine. Fortunately, she was familiar enough to know what passed for coos of delight in these races. Her answer had pleased them all. Or they had been conditioned to respond that way to all customers.

"Follow, thou must, so that we may properly outfit thee," invited one of the Elowans. It gestured to her right, down a corridor filled with red and yellow illumination. Sabine let this being lead the way. The other three workers, or designers- Sabine had no clue what their individual skill sets might be- followed behind her.

The lights felt warm on her skin. Sabine postulated that she was being scanned while they travelled to the door at the end of the chamber. When the single door was opened, she walked into a chamber that had four interface consoles surrounding a large matter printer device. The floor under the printer emitters and mechanical arms meant for replication had a small raised stage.

"Upon the stage, thou must stand," the second Elowan instructed. "Thy current garments must be discarded."

In the span of a few minutes, Sabine was naked and standing on the small stage. The four beings moved to individual interfaces and began doing, well, whatever they did. Sabine could not discern the screens or any of their actions from her position on the stage.

The wait wasn't long before things began. Sabine was instructed after what felt like a minute to hold her arms from her sides. Immediately after she complied, a total of eight robotic arms pivoted toward her. They began weaving fiber across her, building the clothing directly onto her body. As she was trying to process the sights and sensations of this experience, the intimate apparel was already complete. Silver webbing covered her torso, with her crotch, and nipples exposed. There was a distinct feeling of most of her back and bottom having little coverage. But the way the thin material pushed and fell along her body gave her a thrill. She felt that it enhanced her form without making any falsehoods.

Next came a slightly translucent material in a shimmering blue. The arms and emitters formed this into a garment that was akin to a silk hose. Her feet were covered, as was her skin up to the waist. The soles of her feet were now on a thick layer of some material that might or might not have been the same as the rest of this garment. It was certainly denser, since she could squeeze her toes and felt firm resistance.

As flimsy as this new layer looked, the bottom half of her body felt warmer, as if she had put on a pair of work pants made for rugged weather. Sabine also had to silently admit that her legs looked longer and shapelier in this layer. She wished there were reflective surfaces around her so she could see how this was looking from the back.

The arms retracted, seemed to reset before coming towards her again. A new material, more opaque and of a darker shade of blue, was being woven across her hands and forearms. Sabine was so taken with watching this process that she was unaware that a dress was being woven across her body at the same time.

Only when the long gloves were complete did her senses acknowledge the presence of the silken dress that began around her knees and was being woven around her midsection. Strategic portions of her midriff and chest were left uncovered, only to be crisscrossed by belt- like strips that began at her waist and concluded in a sort of choker around her neck.

The material of the complete outfit seemed to weigh almost nothing. She felt the layers, her body was warmer wherever it covered. But Sabine still had to look about to make sure the outfit was actually on.

The arms and emitters retracted into their work stations as a transparent globe dropped around her, becoming reflective once it settled around her. She could see every angle of herself and the outfit.

"Pleased, thou art?" came the voice of one Elowan.

"Yes!" Sabine exclaimed.

"We are magnificent at what we do," one of the Thrynn declared. Sabine wasn't about to dispute the claim. Never had she worn or even seen such finery.

"Two thousand mu have been withdrawn from thine account to cover this creation and our humble services," the Elowan said, or perhaps it was a warning. "Do we have an accord, new customer?"

"We do, indeed," Sabine breathed. Fortunately, she didn't need to worry about affording the expense.

The globe ascended back above Sabine and disappeared into the ceiling. The outfit remained on her. She wondered how long it would take for the outfit to be removed if she'd refused it. She stepped off the raised area.

As she walked toward the door, the second Elowan came up beside her.

"Pleased, we are, that thee taketh joy in thine purchase. Come again, good being, when thee desires another," the Elowan said and led Sabine through the front entrance. The gathered beings outside of the store fawned and gave declarations of praise, envy, even love.

Sabine strutted right past them and on to her next destination.

While walking past eateries, Sabine made a melancholy mental note of the places she still hadn't tried, and likely never would. The "Pie Hutt" that claimed to offer the only original Arth-style pizza for the entire quadrant. A place that specialized in the various liquid meals that Elowan preferred, without the limitations of ingredients indigenous to their home system. The Nectar Palace that offered Velox and Elowan delicacies. And so many others.

There was an extensive selection of culinary options, but Sean had a favorite restaurant. Sabine knew tonight had to include dinner from "Choris Oria".

Choris Oria's entrance boasted a canopied entrance, despite the fact there was never any 'bad weather' within the Starport. Paneled windows featured booths on both sides of the doors that led into the restaurant. The interior of the eatery was painted in shades of white, cream, and blues. Blue and white checkered tablecloths covered the tables, even the booths. Small lights shaped to look like candles, complete with flames, sat in the center of each table. Holos of Arth during different points in history filled the walls. They were changed out weekly, so the patrons did not grow bored with the same art.

The maitre d' was a fellow human from Arth, and efficient at their job. The ordering console was already called up for her requests as Sabine came to the podium. She took a moment to take in the maitre d's broad form in an immaculate black formal bodysuit with gold trim work. She wondered if the prominent Adam's apple was organic or implanted.

"How would you like to indulge yourself tonight?" they invited. "Would you like a menu?"

"No thank you," Sabine said. "I would like to place an order for two. Starting with saganaki, alongside a short plate of Thrynn fleshplant Souvlaki. Dessert will be flaming Boston pie."

"Will that be dine-in or delivery?" the maitre d' asked, their fingers moving with a speed that only time, skill, and possibly an implant or two could make possible.

"Delivery for two with all the extras." Sabine gave the maitre d' a wink as she slid her hands down her newly acquired garments. "It's a special night with my mate."

"Of course! We will see that all preparations are added and delivery is special to commemorate the occasion," they replied, smiling broadly.

"Thank you," she replied, not caring about the cost of any of it.

Once the arrangements were made, Sabine moved on. The final place she planned to go would require a transport jump to the far end of the plaza. Otherwise she'd lose an hour from the walk.

It was a mystery as to why the fermented spirits from all over the galaxy had to be so far from eating establishments, but Sabine didn't have privy to the decision makers or their reasoning. She just knew it was an inconvenience to anyone who'd ever spoken of it to or around her.

She only had one stop left after acquiring the evening's spirits before surprising Sean at the bank. Or… maybe two.

There was no reason she couldn't get a box of her favorite chocolates to enjoy one last time, too. Right?

"You're breaking up with me?"

Sean didn't understand.

"No," Sabine replied slowly. "I'm not ending our relationship. Not really."

"So that incredible sex we just had? That was just because it was the last time?" Sean yelled. His tone hadn't changed, only gotten louder.

"That observation is accurate," Sabine allowed. "But again, it's not because I'm ending our relationship. The past five years have been lovely."

"Five years! Was it a waste of time? Why did I even take the job here on this port as a banker? And not ending our relationship?" Sean stormed around the room, naked, pacing from one side of the bed to the other as he spoke. Twice he picked up the now empty bottle of Velox gold wine as if he had expected it to magically grow another swig or two. Or maybe it was a glassful he was hoping for. Regardless, he was disappointed both times.

Sabine remained on the bed. She was on her side, propped up on one elbow. She waited for him to take a breath and finish.

"You're *leaving*!" he insisted. "Going off to join some business that, for some reason, requires you to give total allegiance! Haven't we got everything we've wanted so far? So what kind of relationship are we going to have? Living off of video chats over the subnet? Blowing kisses at each other's images? Haven't we done enough of that already? Is that what you wanted all along?"

"No, Sean. Please calm down, come back to bed. I can make everything clear to you. Please."

She patted the still warm space beside her on the bed.

Sean halted in his pacing. Began again. Stopped, stared at her nude figure, then laid down next to her. His eyes locked onto hers, expecting answers, even as his body was stretched out.

"I'm not ending our relationship," she said, bringing her body up into a sitting position. The pillow she had been laying on was now in her lap, arms wrapped around it for comfort. She brought her eyes back to his.

"One of us is going to be a widow," Sabine declared.

She then drove her elbow into Sean's sternum.

Air exploded out through his mouth. Sean choked and gasped, since his lungs had just been violently emptied. Sabine straddled him as swiftly as a predacious cat. Her knees pinned his arms to the bed. The pillow was pushed down over his face.

He struggled. No words, only gagging sounds came from beneath the pillow. He jerked and twitched in violent movements.

Sabine kept her position, holding the pillow down with all of her upper body weight. She, at least, knew it would be just a handful of minutes and watched them tick away on the wall across from the bed.

When he had ceased moving, she watched another two minutes crawl by before sliding off of his still body.

There was no time to waste on regret or goodbyes. Sabine slipped into the bodysuit she'd prepared earlier that day and grabbed her get-out bag. From the bag she took out a sealable container, and two devices.

She used the first device to sever Sean's left pinky finger at the bottom knuckle. This, she placed in the sealable container, and engaged the air-tight, contaminant-free lock.

Sabine placed the second device, which was a metal box about the size of a small book, on Sean's chest. She removed the pillow from his face and placed it back on the bed beside him.

She supposed that was a final consideration, if not a goodbye. Any more than that would force her to acknowledge her regrets and… other feelings. She couldn't allow herself to dwell on any of it.

Not if she wanted to survive. Not if she wanted her guivre to survive, also.

The entry door was locked as Sabine left the quarters for the last time. She was too far away to hear the little metal box building power to go active and do its job.

Three transporter jumps later, Sabine was in the bar that Doka had been investigating earlier. Sitting in a booth not far from where Sean had been.

Guidino was the primary recruiter for Family Enterprises Unlimited, a subsidiary of Interstel, at the port. He compared a readout that had been brought to him to a readout that Sabine had given over. A slight smile crept across his face. He glanced back and forth between the readouts. He wasn't handsome by any standard, but he was very well dressed by the standards of Arth.

Sean's gentle touch lingered in the back of her mind as she waited for Guidino's decision. Loyalty to the FEU was the first law. The only family in any members' life was the FEU family. While someone from any race from any planet could join, FEU members could only date, mate or partner with other FEU members. Betrayal of "family" may be the ultimate sin, but blood sacrifice was the basest coin of the realm.

And Sabine had just paid her entry fee.

"Okay, Sabine, the offering you brought has been confirmed," Guidino said. "The digit did indeed belong to Sean Potus. Our tests confirm it was obtained after his death. Everything else in front of me confirms that you two were intimate partners for the past five years."

Even as Sabine nodded her confirmation, Guidino gave her a cold smile.

"You'd be amazed at how many beings we get every day- I mean *every stinking day*- who come to the table thinking that we aren't going to confirm that proof of cutting all ties, permanently, is absolute."

He added a gluttonous chuckle to the end of this declaration. Sabine didn't react.

"I don't care what anyone else does or has done. Just what I do and how I get paid for it," she countered in as neutral a voice as she had.

"That's the kind of attitude that will take you far in the Family! And since everything is in order, I am prepared to carry through with my end of the deal," Guidino stated. He pulled on his left earlobe.

Within seconds, two beings approached the table. They were humanoid but androgenous in appearance. Sabine couldn't tell if they had been surgically or genetically altered. Perhaps both? No matter. She'd done what had been demanded. If the FEU wanted her to kill anyone now, or in the future, they would provide the training and reward.

That was, after all, what she'd bargained for.

Sabine stood and faced the pair. The one to her right pivoted and walked away with a sense of purpose. Sabine followed, even as the second being fell in behind her. They exited the bar and went directly to the nearest transporter. The first being produced a destination card and let the terminal scan it then the three stepped into the transporter one at a time.

Sabine found herself stepping off the transporter pad into a large, brightly lit lab. Two technicians, both human, were checking settings on a large medical bed. The silver platform was adorned with the bedside monitor and other medical gadgets that she'd seen at most hospitals and medtech bays. The taller of the techs looked back at Sabine with minimal interest in her eyes. She indicated for Sabine to come forward.

"Lay on the bed, please. You may keep your clothing on. Doing so will not affect the procedure."

Sabine was interested in what the "procedure" was. But instead of asking, she committed herself to the contract she'd made. Silently, she laid down on the bed.

Moments passed while her stats were being monitored, blood and DNA scanned, and who knew what else. Sabine remained quiet and as still as she could be.

The minute hum of force fields activating. The slight tickle of the energy pressing against her skin. A realization that she could not, in fact, move any part of her body aside from her eyes.

Panic tried to set in. A certainty that she was finally caught in a trap. Sabine tried to fight it down, using whatever logic and lies she could to assure herself it couldn't be so. The trick that worked was reminding herself that her beloved guivre was loose in the station ductwork and would cause havoc if she were killed.

Sabine watched the hypodermic infuser come in from the left just before it pressed against her carotid artery. The hiss of the infuser releasing whatever it held into her bloodstream.

"Your DNA, and appearance, will be slightly altered," the second tech warned. He had a more pleasant voice than the first. "You should expect to feel some discomfort."

PAIN.

Every centimeter of her body felt like a thousand flowers being plucked one petal at a time and set fire at the speed of sound; The sound of her own screams, in fact. She felt pressure as she pushed against the force fields, but found no give. The blood in her veins throbbed and felt as if every drop were dying and being reborn at the same moment. Her senses began to fade. She tried to reason with herself, reassure herself that this was the right decision, that it would be over in moments.

No such mercy was not forthcoming. Instead, her mind turned inward on itself to protect her, to hide her from the relentless pain...

The muffled sounds as Sean attempted to breathe, or plead for his life. Was her memory correct that he'd managed her name at least once? Or was that guilt trying to seep in, coat her heart with its black ichor?

He was so eager to please her. Passionate kisses, those gentle caresses of his strong hands came rushing back to her. Would he have been as caring if he had known it would be the last time, ever.

Enjoying his expression as he looked at her in the new clothing. Sneaking peeks at the layers while enjoying their meal. Their last meal.

The disappointment in his voice each time they'd been unable to meet in person. She had grown tired of having to love over subnet connections and memories.

All of those times wishing and dreaming and planning of their lives together. Wondering how much better it was going to be in actual life versus her fantasies.

How lonely she had been before Sean had come into her life. How tired she had been of enjoying nothing.

The first time they had spent a whole day and night together. First explorations, first tastes, lingering pleasures.

That first kiss.

When she'd first seen him, and when he noticed her.

How deep her misery was without anyone else in her life.

How she wished for someone who made her happy.

REGRET. Regret. Pain.

Nothing.

When her eyes opened her vision was sharper than she remembered it being. She tried to sit up and discovered she was unfettered. Her body moved smoothly and easily. Sabine kept going and slid to the floor gracefully. No weakness, she stood without complication. Perhaps a little taller? The lab seemed to be seen from a slightly higher elevation than when she first came in… how long ago was that?

The techs were still here. So were Sabine's "escorts". The male tech turned to face Sabine.

"You are feeling fine, yes?" he asked.

Sabine nodded.

"There will be some disorientation to your altered physical aspects," he explained, "although those will not last for long at all. Within a standard day, you'll have difficulty remembering what your body, mind and sight felt like from before the procedure."

The tech said this with a distinct amount of pride. Sabine just nodded again.

"Your escorts are ready to take you to your transport, where you can begin your new career. Best to you!"

Sabine numbly followed the two beings back through the transporter.

Less than five minutes later, Sabine was alone, standing at the bottom of a loading ramp to a spaceship that would transport her away from here, probably forever.

She still didn't know how different she looked from before. But the beings hadn't acted like there was a problem before they'd departed. The ship she was looking up at wasn't some garbage scow. It was a luxury vessel. Her personal effects had been brought. All that was left was for her to walk up the ramp. There wasn't even a crew member waiting for her to choose when she would step up the ramp.

No, wait, Sabine told herself, there was something else. Someone else. Someone important.

A deep breath, and then released. Another. Then, she whistled the first two measures of a childhood lullaby.

She didn't realize that she was holding her breath again, until the familiar sensation of her companion deftly climbing her leg, back, before settling in around her neck. Her hair settled around him.

"Very good, Doka. Time to go." she said softly.

Doka made his happy sound right next to her ear.

Now, she was ready to begin.

Sabine noticed herself in the reflection of the hull plating. Now a full five centimeters taller, with darker skin, hazel eyes and silver hair, she walked confidently up the ramp.

Into her new life.

End.

Fire at Will

By Declan Finn

"Brutally killed, huh?"

Captain Will Jordan chuckled and nodded. "Yup. Whoever wrote that notice for Interstel knew not to BS us."

James Weyand looked over the Interstel notice again. "Still. Fifty thousand MUs just to get started. It's not bad, captain."

Jordan nodded. His cell on Starport space station was less than prisoners were mandated by law to have on Arth. He was so used to it, he barely noticed the cramped conditions, unless he had someone else in the room.

Will Jordan propped himself up against the sidewall next to his bed. The captain always thought of himself as perfect for space travel, since he was economy sized. He wasn't particularly tall, topping out at only 5'8" due to childhood malnutrition, so he didn't take up much of the precious room in a ship. He didn't eat much, so he couldn't consume much in the way of his own supplies. He was so notorious about having enough on his ship, rumor had it he had taken meditation lessons so he didn't need to breathe too much.

The last part was true, but mostly to rid himself of anxiety after spending too much of his formative years associating with the Thrynn.

"Fifty thousand is a good *start*," Jordan told him. "But doesn't it seem strange to you? 'Here's some cash. Go explore strange new worlds, make friends, try not to die, have a nice day'? It's almost like a bounty system with a starter stipend."

Weyand sat on the metallic writing desk attached to the wall and laughed. Weyand was older and looked like he'd been there and done that with practically everything. It was close enough.

Weyand was stockier than Jordan, but not enough to cancel out Jordan's compact stature on the ship. But he was one of those spacers who had served whatever position he could be taken on. And he looked it. His face was creased with smile, frown and worry lines, to the point where he looked like an unmade bed.

"It's encouragement," Weyand said. "Interstel wants to expand their profile, that's all. And? New lifeforms? Minerals? Alien artifacts? The money they make off of all that would probably be more than enough to clear the fifty thousand overhead."

Will Jordan frowned. "I suppose. I just have an odd feeling about it. But ruins? Artifacts? Damnit, Jim, I'm a freight hauler, not a space archaeologist."

Weyand rolled his eyes. "No one is asking you to dig in the dirt, Will. That's what the TV is for."

Jordan said nothing, thinking over the crew they'd need. The contracts had just expired on the crew. He thought he'd have more time to dwell on the next batch while he had the downtime. "What about Kafka and Gregor?"

Weyand blinked, thinking over Jordan's question, and trying to recall the names. "Who? I don't recall them."

Jordan frowned. "That Velox duo from two runs ago? One did navigation, one in engineering? No, it's not their names, but you know who I mean, right?"

Weyand shrugged. "No idea. I'll have to look them up."

Jordan nodded. The Velox always struck him as creepy. But then again, they were red ants that were taller than he was. But they worked for a living, and he didn't care what they looked like as long as they pulled their weight.

"Look into them, see if they're busy. Also …" the captain frowned, thinking back four space runs ago. "What's her name? Science officer? Human? Her name was Marit. Last name was …"

Jordan smiled. How could he have forgotten her married name? It described her husband so well. "Crumm! That was her last name!"

Weyand smiled. "No. Her name is Landry. She got divorced from that sad sack SOB."

Jordan's eyes nearly sparkled. "Even better. The husband was worthless. Get her."

Weyand made a note on the back of the notice. "All right. Who do we want for medical? Or for communications?"

Jordan shook his head. "You or I can handle comms. As for medical, let's not get injured, shall we?"

Weyand looked at the notice again. "You realize that the ship is going to need more than what we've got on it. Shields? Armor? Weapons? Not to mention expand our cargo pods."

Jordan grunted, waiving off the concern. "Let's get a crew first, train them right, and worry about the rest later. But start looking into selling the engines and getting a better set. If we're not going to be able to fight things out there, I sure want to be able to run from them."

Weyand nodded thoughtfully and made another note. "I'll talk to Tryp, see if he can get us a deal."

Jordan blinked a moment, then frowned, thinking through the names, trying to match them to a person. "That's the station mechanic, right?"

Weyand chuckled. "Yes, Will. Tryptichishic is his full name." Weyand's smile turned to a frown as he turned to thinking over the angles on the mission parameters. "Should we be worried about—"

"Probably," Jordan answered, cutting him off. "I'd been thinking about Vito too."

Weyand rolled his eyes. One of these days, some idiot was going to whine that Jordan was Xenophobic. He hadn't bothered to learn or remember a single name for any alien he had ever met, so came up with different names for them. But Captain Jordan didn't remember most names. It had taken him five years for him to remember Weyand's. It wasn't poor memory, but Jordan spent most of his time balancing oxygen consumption, fuel reports, and profit-loss ratios.

"I don't think *Veedo* will be a problem," Weyand said, using "Vito's" actual name. "Not yet anyway. I think he's going to see who the best pilots are. Who brings in the most profitable hauls. He'll wait and watch. Then he'll make people an offer they can't refuse."

Jordan laughed and shook his head. "We can only hope. If we're lucky, Vito will go for Snoopy."

Weyand winced. Both he and Jordan had worked their way up to their own ship. Jordan was from the worst neighborhood on Arth. Weyand had started higher, but he had been staunchly blue collar from beginning to end.

Captain Blake Daniels was the epitome of a classic, old Earth word: schmuck. Daniels had an ego about the size of the galactic core, believing himself the best pilot to have ever existed.

In classic Jordan fashion, he could never refer to Daniels by his actual name. He preferred to just refer to him as "Snoopy." Weyand didn't know the reference, but it apparently had something to do with calling Captain Daniels both an SOB, and belittling his piloting prowess at the same time.

Though the thought of Blake Daniels and Veedo, the Thrynn mobster, was hilarious.

Jordan chuckled as well. "Yeah. Vito and Snoopy. A match made in Hell." He paused, and his smile faded. "Unless Veedo is just lazy and decides to come talk to me first because he knows me."

Jordan glanced around his room. "You know what? I'd rather not be easy to find. Time to move back onto the ship. Start talking with the mechanic to get everything installed. I'll see if I can hunt down Landry, Gregor or Kafka."

Weyand held up a hand. "Talk to Landry. I'll talk to the Velox duo. One of these days, they may look up the reference, and understand what a roach looks like. I think they'd take offense."

Jordan shrugged, then slid off the bed. "All right. Head out. I'll start packing and meet you at home."

Weyand nodded and hopped off the desk. The *Hermes* was as close to a home as they had.

All of the belongings that Captain Will Jordan took off of his ship, the *Hermes*, fit into a single backpack. He was used to packing light, mostly for speed. He never took something off of the ship that he would miss if he had to leave it behind. Some people would call that a bad habit from his upbringing, but Jordan saw it as a good survival tool.

Unfortunately, it wasn't enough when a gray scaled claw reached out and wrapped an arm around Jordan.

Jordan winced. He hadn't even heard Veedo coming.

Veedo was like every other Thrynn, the lizard man made flesh… or scales. Jordan had heard that "reptilian species are not lizards," but the pedantic details just made Jordan tune out. Veedo was only a little taller than Weyand, but not by much. Veedo wasn't very high up in the Thrynn mob, but high enough to act with a degree of independence. Unlike most Thrynn, Veedo lacked the usual grace and was wider and stockier than his fellows. Veedo's scales were also a sickly looking gray instead of a vibrant green.

Today, Veedo made certain to bare his sharp carnivore teeth as he looked down at Jordan. It wasn't that intimidating, since Jordan knew Thrynn preferred to eat something in a lower weight class than humans—there was a reason no animals were on the station, and it wasn't because of the gravity.

"How's the wife, Vito?" Jordan asked. "I hope everything's okay with Gavelle and the hatchlings."

"My mate is wonderful. But my ssspawn ah all old enough to work for me now," Veedo hissed, screwing up his S and R sounds, as most Thrynn did. Veedo clapped Jordan on the arm and squeezed, putting enough pressure to let Jordan know that the claws were there, but not enough to damage Jordan's suit.

Vito knows he's not going to get anything out of me if he damages my professional equipment, Jordan noted in his head. The Thrynn mobster was one of the few who thought like a poor kid from the bad end of town—they both counted pennies.

Which meant Veedo wanted a cut and didn't want to create overhead.

"Come. Let usss walk togesser," Veedo told him. He slid his arm around Jordan's shoulders and pulled him close as they walked down the hallway. "Have you not enjoyed time away from usss? We gave you freedom, yesss?"

Jordan sighed. He didn't have the patience for Veedo's beating around the bush. "Vito, I haven't worked for you since I was fifteen and working dockside. Don't act like you did me a favor. I never owed your syndicate anything. In fact, I think you guys owe me for the last month of working for you, but I never complained. Just cut to the chase and tell me what you want?"

Veedo said nothing for a long moment as they walked in silence. His grip tightened on Jordan's shoulder. "We want to look over what you find before anyone elssse can."

"Uh huh. Let's assume I'm stupid," Jordan answered. "Why should I trust you or your prices on what we find?"

"Do it, and no-sing will happen to you or your crew."

Jordan's thoughts came fast and furious. First, this percent wasn't Veedo's opening offer. It was his only offer. Negotiating would only make the price go up for Jordan. It would go up anyway, but it would go up gradually. Probably every few trips into space, or every few months, depending on Veedo's mood. The only way to get rid of the Thrynn syndicate was to never play with them in the first place.

Second, the only way to get away from Veedo at that moment was to make sure he got the message loud and clear, hard and fast. Which meant fighting off something heavier and covered with armor-like scales.

But Jordan had needed to fight Thrynn before puberty.

Jordan nodded slowly, as though thinking it over. But his head drifted further and further down, until his body began to bow.

With a sharp straightening of his spine, Jordan snapped straight, throwing his left elbow into Veedo's right eye. Veedo's head jerked back. The surprise caused Veedo to relax his grip on Jordan's shoulder, allowing the captain to burst forward on his left foot, diagonally away from Veedo's claw and his body. Jordan swung his right foot behind him in a crescent, putting his entire body into a right hammer fist to Veedo's left eye. Veedo's head rocked back and he staggered.

Jordan sprang back, putting more distance between him and Veedo's claws before Veedo's vision cleared.

"Just what on Arth is going on here!"

Jordan looked over at the new voice. Veedo looked around as well. Jordan almost laughed.

It was Captain Blake Daniels. He was thin, tall, swaggering around in his space suit so bright and tan he must have bleached it. He was blond with blue eyes, and a jaw that jutted out just far enough Jordan was always tempted to punch it. Daniels also had a smile that evoked a similar response–only it was more like a smirk. Maybe it was just his face that made Jordan tempted.

"Hey Captain," Jordan said loudly and firmly, more for Veedo's hearing than Daniels'. "Me and my friend Vito here were just having a business conversation. Would you like to referee?"

Daniels scoffed at both of them as he stomped over. "I should have figured. Jordan, you're a disgrace to the uniform. Fools like you should be drummed out of the fraternal order of pilots for the criminals you are. Honestly, brawling in the hallways of the station like a common thug. Ugh."

Jordan rolled his eyes. He didn't care about Daniels' rant. His focus was on Veedo, and whether or not the Thrynn was going to tear them both apart, or if he wanted to settle up some other time. But going after Jordan now meant Veedo would have to kill Daniels as well.

Jordan smiled at Veedo. *Well, if he decides to kill us both, I can always throw Daniels Vito's way and run.*

Veedo looked from Jordan to Daniels, then bore his teeth in a smile. "We will talk later, William."

Jordan nodded. "I look forward to it, Vito."

Veedo spared Daniels a glance, then turned and stormed away.

When Veedo was out of view, Jordan turned to Daniels. "Thanks, Snoopy."

Later that afternoon, Jordan settled into his office chair, looking through the personnel file on his reader. The tablet had the files for all of his former crew, complete with performance evaluations by himself and Weyand, and comments by the crew. It helped for Jordan to remember what he thought of the crew, and for him to know what the crew thought of him.

In the case of Marit Landry, he didn't have to remember what he thought of her. She had mousy light brown hair, dark brown eyes, and a cherubic round face. She was a few pounds overweight for the usual space travel, but it had gone to all the right places, so Jordan didn't care. But the best part was she was single now. The biggest issue was Marit Landry had a husband at the time, Jonathan Crumm, who was a medic and completely untrainable. Crumm had been good for a few bandages and a pain killer, but any serious injury needed the ship to pull into dock. Even though as a science officer, Marit had made herself useful assisting him, and performing better as a medic than Crumm. But at the end of the day, they had come as a pair, making him dead weight.

Immediately after firing Crumm, Jordan had told Marit to look him up again after dropping the loser.

After a moment of hesitation, Jordan opened a communication for Marit Landry.

While the link took time to establish, Jordan ran his fingers through his hair, just to make sure he fixed it after his encounter with Veedo.

The image flipped over from Marit Landry's profile to a live photo of her. She was just as Jordan remembered her.

"Hello Captain. What can I do for you?" she said pleasantly.

"I just received the news about the happy disunion. Are you available?"

Marit Landry blinked and cocked her head. "I'm sorry. Are you asking me if I'm unemployed, or free to date?"

Jordan bit the inside of his cheek and took a few seconds to think it over. "I'm good with either, though I did call to invite you on for the next tour with the ship. We're joining this latest venture of exploration by Interstel. Would you be interested in joining the crew?"

Marit didn't react to that except to ask. "What positions are open?"

"Science, medical, communications. But we want you for science. I don't expect you to perform surgery."

"Hmm. All right. I'll happily rejoin the *Hermes*. You're still on *Hermes*, aren't you?"

Jordan smiled. "Yes. The ship is still in one piece, and it's getting a bit of an upgrade. I also expect everyone to come out of the mission with more experience and training. So there will be benefits."

"Can't argue with that. When do you expect to ship out?"

"As soon as we get the other crew. Were you around when we had two Velox working for us?"

"Gregor and Kafka. I remember. I liked them."

Jordan blinked. "Really?"

"I like ants. Could be worse. They could have looked like cockroaches."

Jordan smiled. "Understood. How long will it take you to join us?"

"Tomorrow. I need time to pack. After that, I'm all yours."

"I look forward to it."

Marit Landry walked up the boarding ramp for the *Hermes*. She walked with determined strides, carrying a large duffel bag. Her space suit was a sky blue, distinguishing herself from captain's white.

The *Hermes* wasn't a bad looking ship. Like most of her class, it had a long body with the engine nacelles spaced to either side. Like every engine since they ran on steam, the engines were volatile, the exhaust was deadly, and any way to keep explosions away from the main ship was always worthwhile.

Technically, Marit thought, *wind power could end messy as well. Especially if the masts on ships snapped during a high wind.*

Jordan was next to *Hermes*, waiting for her. He waved as she closed. "Mari! Find the place all right?"

Marit nodded. "Of course. It's not too far from your usual berth. I noticed you're not staying in a room on Starport. There a reason for that?"

Jordan frowned, considering whether or not to tell her. He'd made a point not to tell the rest of the crew. He wasn't sure what would put off most of them, that the captain had run around with organized crime while he was younger, or that the Thrynn mob had considered muscling in on their haul.

But Marit already knew about when he was younger. One of their first conversations had been during his physical, when she wanted to know where all of his scars came from. Thrynn claw marks were distinctive.

Jordan waited for Marit to get closer before he answered. In fact, he brought her in for a hug and said lightly into her ear, "Veedo is back in my life. Or he wants in. It's hard for him to shake me down at the ship." When he broke the hug, he forced a smile and waved towards the open cargo bay. "Shall I escort you to your lab?"

Marit went through several facial expressions at once. Jordan's attempt to brush off Veedo with a diversion to the lab threw her. "I trust you haven't moved it," she said at regular volume. Quieter, she asked, "What does Veedo want?"

Jordan started walking for the ship. Marit followed close behind him so he couldn't get away from the topic. "The right of first refusal on anything we bring in. But we know that would just be the start, so screw him and his hatchlings."

"You don't have any family to threaten, Will. So what's he relying on? Previously established dominance?"

"He wants to threaten the crew. But honestly? That sounds unlike him. Killing off crew means I can't do as much for him. So really, I don't know. He's Thrynn. You know what they're like. They're greedy, aggressive, and unless you're family, you're probably screwed. It's their cultural imperative to be pricks. This way."

Jordan sped up. Marit knew enough that he meant the topic was closed. "So, what's your game plan with Interstel? You ever going to get a full crew?"

"I guess I'll have to. We can have some people doing double duty, like you in medicine and science, but I'd rather not risk it in deep space."

Marit smiled at his tone. "You almost sound like you'd rather not have a crew at all."

Jordan laughed. "Some days I'd rather not. You know how well I do with people. By the time I was old enough to get on a ship and get off of Arth, I knew all I needed to about *people*. You can't trust half of them. The half you might be able to trust are hit or miss as to whether or not they're worth a damn."

Marit raised a brow. "I'm surprised you even called me, then."

Jordan smiled. "Oh, you're worth every penny."

Marit stumbled over her own feet. Jordan backed up enough to catch her. "Um … I'm flattered? I guess?"

Jordan helped her straighten up. "Mari, I've never seen you act anything less than professional."

Marit held onto his arms until she got her balance back. "Will, I've seen you work with the crew. Or I should say that I've seen you work with the ship? There are days I wonder if you even talk to Weyand. How would you notice how I work?"

Jordan rolled his eyes, then smiled. "Mari… I do pay attention. To you. But last time you were on board, you were married. I couldn't spend as much attention on you as I would have liked."

Marit blinked rapidly, flustered. She removed her hands from Jordan and smoothed out her suit. She decided it was time to move on. "I asked for your game plan for the ship and the crew. Not for trying to seduce me."

Jordan blinked, paused, then shrugged. "I don't recall having a game plan for *that*, but whatever." He started walking again. "You see, we're not generally built for deep space maneuvering. We have no idea what we're going to encounter out there. We need armor, better engines, weapons, everything. A full crew whether I like it or not, because we need to be prepared for whatever is out there. Anything that's out there. And while people are avoiding certain spaces like Interstel has suggested, my goal is to go straight to those places that are off limits, because no one else will try. He who dares, wins."

Marit frowned, thinking. "Sometimes he who dares gets taken out back and shot."

"That too. But I'd rather not be flying blind. And your reasoning is why I want to spend the better part of our first few weeks building up the ship and building up the crew. If we're all at a hundred percent by the time we go into the void, I'm sure we can take on whatever the galaxy can throw at us."

"And you're making this money how?"

"Oh, yes. Sorry. You don't know. We get a terrain vehicle for resource gathering. It's a nice, big sucker. Six wheels, big enough for the entire crew and for recovering resources."

"Great. So what's your plan?"

Jordan stopped at a lab and opened the door for her. Marit nodded and went in ahead.

Marit looked around. "These are quarters. Did you attach it to the lab?"

"No, I just wanted you to drop your bag first." Jordan waved her inside. He leaned against the bulkhead as he said, "Sure I have a game plane. The Interstel notice told anyone who would listen about the ruins of the Old Empire at coordinates 17n x162e, on the second planet of the neighboring k-class system …"

Marit chuckled as she threw her bag on the bed. "Let me guess, that's not enough for you?"

Jordan smiled and shook his head. "Nah. I am far more mercenary. I'm more interested in all of the scout reports that indicate, and I quote, 'a high density of minerals in the mountainous regions of the innermost planet of our system.' From there, the rest is easy. We're going to invest *everything* into upgrading the *Hermes*—expand the cargo pods, upgrade the armor, the engine and the weapons. Then we fill in the staff positions, and train everyone fully. The next step is to head to the areas the Interstel notice warned everybody away from: like coordinates 135,84, where two ships have disappeared, and system 175,94, where there is 'indication of alien activity.'

Marit nodded. "Because you've always preferred high-risk, high-reward endeavors.

Jordan held up a finger. "Ah! But also highly-prepared! By the time we get out into the more interesting parts of space, we'll be loaded for bear."

The next month was fairly boring, sticking close to home, mining chromium, promethium and tungsten out of one planet, tin and gold from another.

But by the end of the month, Jordan had fully upgraded the entire ship. He started by purchasing the largest cargo pods we could. The next upgrade was to the engines, making them so fuel efficient, the endurium consumption dropped. Next came armor, and weapons, and then fleshing out the rest of the crew and their training.

But by the end of the month, everything had changed.

Jordan docked with Starport, and his first order of business was to check the notices from Interstel.

Jordan's stomach lurched at the notice. Back when this project started, he knew something was up. Something had to be up. No company started a venture like this without a darn good reason. Companies paid money for results, not for the hope of results. Throwing away fifty thousand in the vague hope that people would find the right planets or useful artifacts was insane.

But this was a little worse than he could have imagined. The notice, posted yesterday, 02-01-4620, started with an understatement. The header was "UNPLEASANT NEWS."

"It is necessary to give you some unpleasant news. You may have been aware that for the last several years scientists have been observing anomalous fluctuations in the radiation levels of our sun. While you have been away it has been ascertained that the stability of our sun is definitely deteriorating. How much time we have until there is a fatally large flare, we are still not sure, but there is little doubt that this will eventually occur.

"As yet, we have no clue as to the cause of this instability. Therefore, we must assume that there is nothing we can do to change the situation.

"In view of this the only option available to us is to get as many colonists off of Arth as we can. You can be invaluable to us in this.

"First we need endurium to power the ships we will build. We will pay well for any that you can bring back.

"Secondly, we need to know where to send the colonists. Your ship is equipped with homing drones which you may use to log your recommendations. This is so that we can move the colonists out as quickly as possible.

"In addition, a sensor has been installed which will inform you of the stellar condition upon entering a system. Your ship computer will inform you in the event that a flare is imminent. We advise caution while in systems which are more than slightly unstable. Being caught in a solar flare would certainly be fatal.

"In your manual we have outlined the criteria which will be important in your evaluation of viable colony worlds. You will be rewarded for recommendations of valuable planets and penalized for recommendations of planets which turn out to be uninhabitable. Consider carefully before logging a planet."

Jordan winced. The notice was so calm and casual, it did everything but say "Have a nice day."

Weyand is going to love this. Heck, what do I tell the crew? "Hey, we've upgraded the ship enough to go into deep space and find a replacement for Arth, before the sun explodes." He rolled his eyes so hard, he almost strained something. *This can only end well,* he thought sarcastically *Just when we were in the black and ready to head out of the system.*

Jordan shook his head. The first priority was to sell off the latest haul, then finish the upgrades with Tryp. After that, he could worry about what to tell the crew and how. He left orders for everyone to stay in the docking area, and hoped that would suffice to keep rumors from reaching the crew before Jordan could talk to them.

Jordan tried to smile and fake being upbeat until he got off of the ship. He needed to allay any suspicion until he knew what he was going to say.

Unfortunately, as he walked away from the ship along the cargo ramp, Veedo was waiting for him. Today, the Thrynn seemed relaxed. He leaned up against the rail, giving Jordan plenty of leeway to walk past him.

Jordan stopped short of Veedo, deliberately striding to the opposite rail. "Vito."

Veedo nodded. "Will."

Jordan sighed, more exhausted by Veedo's persistence than anything else. "Now what? I've been a little busy."

"We noticed," Veedo hissed, still looking at his claws. "My leaders thank you for turning us down the first time. We did not realize you would focus exclusively on minerals, and not leaving the system. It would have been a waste of your time and ours had you accepted our offer."

Jordan shrugged. He wasn't stupid enough to think that this was a simple thank you call. "Not a problem. I needed the ship fully capable before trying to make a profit. But that's the next step. And I still reject your offer."

Veedo nodded, almost a bow this time. "The offer has changed, Will. This time, we merely want information."

"Information? About?"

Veedo bore his fangs in a smile. "We want to know which planets you deem useful before you tell Interstel. The sooner we know, the more we can set up shop on the planet of our choice. Interstel will have to work with us. So will any who want to move onto the planet."

Jordan sighed. He didn't have time for this. "Let me get back to you Veedo. I have to get rid of this run of cargo. I have to talk with Tryp, the mechanic that works the bay. Then I have to talk with my crew."

Veedo straightened. "I think not. You will agree, and you will agree *now*."

Veedo stomped his feet twice on the deck. New motion in the corner of his eye caught Jordan's attention. There were more Thrynn as they blocked the exits to the cargo bay.

Jordan looked back to Veedo. "Why don't you talk to Snoopy, Vito?"

Veedo cocked his head. "Who is this Snoopy?"

"The captain that interrupted our fracas last time. Blonde human. About yea tall? Thinks he's God's gift to astrophysics?"

Veedo chuckled. "Who's to say we won't make the offer to him as well?"

Jordan considered agreeing to Veedo. He did. There were options down the line to feed Veedo misinformation. Jordan was going to trip over all sorts of planets out in the empty darkness. The odds were that most of them were going to be complete disasters. Some would be barren rocks. Some would be deserts.

The *Hermes* would run into a planet of hostile aliens. Jordan could generate two lists. One would be places the Thrynn mob could go and be destroyed. Some would be just so far out there, the Thrynn ships could empty their engines, and never come back. It would scuttle their plans for certain.

But no, that wouldn't work. Veedo would almost be certain to have a source of information inside Interstel. If Jordan turned in a different list to Interstel and one to the Thrynn gang, Veedo would know something was up. Even if the plan worked, and the Thrynn believed him, Veedo would eventually try to twist his arms for something else, some new favor.

Instead, Jordan decided to be straightforward. "You can't keep me here forever. You know that Vito."

Veedo straightened, his claws out and ready for use. "I know. But you will serve one way or another. You will be oursss, or you will be a message for others."

Jordan looked at him with tired eyes. The notice from Interstel had taken more out of him than he realized. Then this stupidity made him feel simply exhausted. "You know what, Vito? Fine. Do it. Come at me. Kill me. Skin me. Eat me. Whatever. I've put up with your crap for long enough. Just freaking *do it*."

Veedo nodded. He did not seem surprised. "Then welcome pain."

"Will! Run!"

Jordan barely heard the *clang* against the deck between him and Veedo. He didn't stop to look at it, but turned and ran towards the ship.

Whatever hit the deck exploded in fire behind him, casting light bright enough to cast shadows along the ramp. It illuminated the face of Marit Landry, waving him towards her. She wore a sky-blue space suit that he thought offset her hair quite nicely.

Jordan ran down the ramp towards Marit. Whatever she had thrown at Veedo would have delayed him only a few seconds. It would probably be the only time he had. Veedo may not have been as graceful as other Thrynn, but the reptile was fast when he wanted to be.

As he ran for Marit, Jordan wondered when she would also start running. In fact, she seemed perfectly calm, despite the armored killing machine chasing after him as they both ran in her direction.

It only took him a few more paces to figure out what she was doing.

She was acting as bait.

Marit threw something else. She tossed it underhanded, in an arc over Jordan's head. Whatever it was ignited close enough behind him that he felt the heat on the back of his head.

I just hope my hair isn't on fire on top of everything else.

Jordan ran into Marit's arms with no time to slow down. They crashed into each other, spinning around before they slammed into the ship. Jordan made certain that his back hit the hull. Jordan looked over her shoulder, back towards the cargo ramp.

Veedo was over the second hurdle of fire and coming for them. His claws and fangs were bared, looking angrier than Jordan had ever seen him.

"Stay with me," Marit whispered harshly.

Jordan nodded, despite his urge to take Marit in his arms and run towards the open cargo bay. But if she had a plan, he'd trust her. What else was a crew for?

Veedo drew closer with each split second. Jordan hugged Marit closer to him, bracing for impact.

Motion above them caught Jordan's eye. He glanced up. One of the Velox crew came over the top of the *Hermes*. Jordan couldn't tell if it was Gregor or Kafka, but he carried what looked like a rifle. Jordan glanced again. On closer inspection, it was a laser welder. It was a nice idea, but once Veedo was in range of the welder, he would be close enough to kill Marit and Jordan before the welder could warm up to full power.

Much to Jordan's surprise, the Velox raised the welder and fired at Veedo anyway. At that range, the welder wasn't going to make a crack in Veedo's scales.

Lucky for everyone concerned, it didn't need to. The laser reached out to Veedo. It wasn't enough to weld a hull breach. It wasn't enough to fix a crack in the floor. Though it was still a laser.

And the laser hit Veedo right in the eye.

The intensity of the beam was still powerful enough to burn out Thrynn retinas. Veedo roared in pain as the laser blinded him. He swatted at the air as though his claws could cut through lasers.

But the laser did not stop Veedo. He still kept coming towards Jordan and Marit. The razor-sharp claws flailed, cutting through the air with purpose and malice.

Jordan spun Marit out of the way of Veedo's strikes and ran with her towards the cargo bay. Veedo slammed into the hull face first. He slashed at the hull, but the latest armor upgrades meant he wouldn't even scratch the paint job.

Unfortunately, that left the other Thrynn Veedo had brought along.

The Thrynn thugs left the posts blocking the exits and moved towards the cargo ramp of the *Hermes*. They gathered at the end of the ramp before heading straight for the ship.

Marit tugged on Jordan's shoulder before he charged into the *Hermes'* rear cargo door. "Wait a moment."

Jordan looked at her like she was nuts. "I don't think that laser pointer is going to save us from all of them, Mari."

At that moment, the alarm sounded in the ship bay, and security drones flooded through the access points. The only way for the Thrynn to escape was to charge the *Hermes* and try to enter before the door closed. Then they would have hostages among the crew.

Marit ran ahead of Jordan, taking him by the hand and running past the open door, down the rest of the landing pad.

Jordan looked back at the *Hermes*. "Mari, what the heck?"

"You'll see!" she called over her shoulders.

The Thrynn ignored Marit and Jordan as they ran for the open door of the ship. As soon as they set foot on the ramp, they thought they were home free.

Then Weyland started the terrain vehicle. The massive, six-wheeled land rover roared to life, the search lights illuminating the Thrynn as it burst forward. The Thrynn backed away before they could be run over. They dove for cover, back towards the cargo ramp.

Before they could get to their feet, the security drones fell upon them, taking them into custody.

Jordan watched all of the Thrynn being taken away. He glanced at Marit. "You planned this?"

"No. I followed you out," Marit told him. "When I saw Veedo, I told the rest of the crew. My plan went as far as making a firebomb in the lab to distract Veedo. Greeja-- that's her name, by the way, not Gregor--thought of modifying the laser welder. Weyand thought up using the TV. That was while the new crewman on comms... Styles? He called in Starport security." She shrugged, then took his hand in hers. "And this is why you have a full crew," Marit told him. "To save your butt."

Jordan smiled. "I see your point. See? I told you that having a month to shake down the crew was a great idea. Heh."

Marit studied his face for a long moment. She touched his hand. "Will? What's wrong?"

Jordan blinked, and looked around. "I think we've got everything covered. Why do you ask?"

Marit smiled at him sympathetically. "Sorry, Will, you're not a good actor. Something's wrong, and it's not Veedo. What is it?"

Jordan smiled. "Right now, nothing at all." Jordan looked at the Thrynn mob being led away by security. He then got a far off look. After a moment, he laughed.

Marit squeezed Jordan's shoulder. "Will? What's wrong?"

Jordan waved at the devastation in the cargo bay. "The initial Interstel notice. It told us to seek strange new worlds, boldly go where no man has gone before, and to keep from getting brutally killed." He met Marit's eyes. "Who knew I'd have to work on that last part in Starport?"

312 | P a g e

Hiro of Arth

By David Tatum

Housed at New Oxford University, in the sprawling city of Pelinoriat on Arth, the Interstel Space Academy was a massive complex that would take hours to walk across without a transport. The Academy's lone philosophy classroom, however, was a small, low-tech lecture hall with four rows of stadium seating, a teacher's podium, and not much else. Nevertheless, it was fuller than Hiro Tanaka had expected when he arrived.

Hiro wondered if he and Max Zarfleen were the only two of the group presently gathered who had ever attended a class in this room before. The testing had been completed, the evaluations were in, and it was finally time for ship assignments.

For some reason they were being handed out in the Philosophy classroom. Specifically, it was time for the men, women, and other gentle beings from the first graduating class of the ISS Academy to be assigned their various commands, which left Hiro wondering just what he was doing there. Zarfleen's presence was no surprise -- he was top of his class in command school, after all. Then there were the likes of Phloon de Lux, Rodney Ware, and others who had been on the fast track to command from the founding of ISS's command school. But Hiro? He'd been a science and philosophy nerd, specializing in planetary development, not a command officer.

Hiro was surprised to see another familiar face approach the front of the classroom -- the philosophy teacher, Kerwin Dahglesh. This was a historic day, and would mark the commencement of Interstel's official operations, which should have made it the province of Director Terrence Willwater. Not that Hiro disapproved of Dahglesh -- far from it! He had been his favorite teacher -- but he'd expected someone more important would be here when he'd received the unexpected summons.

"I wish to offer my congratulations to everyone here," Dahglesh said. "I'd like to say this is a great honor... but I cannot. Not yet. You are the first graduating class from the Interstel Academy, and as such you will be the first people to command ships built by Interstel, and the first to represent Interstel across the stars. It will be up to you to prove that this day, these assignments, are truly an honor. I... well, this is becoming a speech, and after the graduation ceremony yesterday I'm sure all of you are tired of speeches, so let's just get down to business, shall we? When I call your name, please come forward. Ware, Rodney..."

Tanaka blanked out for the first several captains listed. Interstel's first wave of exploratory vessels were nearing completion, but those weren't the only ships getting captains out of Tanaka's graduating class. For example, the *ISS Indomitable*, bound for the Thrynn-controlled Jathamassa system, was a mining vessel. In fact, only a couple of the exploration vessels had been fully commissioned, and those were re-purposed freighters rather than true explorers. The true, purpose-built explorers had yet to launch. A point that came out when one of the few captains Tanaka counted as a friend received his first command.

"Max Zarfleen," Dahglesh said. "Well, you get our pride and joy -- you will take command of the *ISS Intrepid*. She's a prototype, and will still be under construction for the next several months, so you will need to oversee her completion. Interstel recognizes that it cannot fully outfit her on its own budget, but you will be given twelve thousand monetary units to outfit her and train your crew as best as you can. As with all of the other explorers, we're hoping you earn enough to finish upgrading her gear as far as you need it."

Tanaka winced. Budgeting was not his strong suit, nor did he think it was Max's. There was a reason both of them had taken the classes on philosophy instead of finance. He still wasn't sure why he was there, but he sincerely hoped he wouldn't have to outfit his ship like Max would.

"Now, the rest of you here today aren't going to be commanding our heavy ships," Dahglesh said. "Instead, you'll be given one of our smaller vessels, with missions targeted towards your specialties in mind. That is why a few of you are here despite not being part of the command program. But while your ships may be small, you will also be responsible for helping Interstel's reputation to grow... and to help us complete our mission."

That was the first hint to Tanaka that his summons to this room wasn't given by mistake. And it gave him some relief -- unlike the customized explorers like the *Intrepid* or the heavy mining vessels like the *Indomitable*, scout ships were fully outfitted at construction. He just hoped he was given a good crew, as the scouts had few opportunities to earn the monetary units needed for training.

Three other names were called before Dahglesh reached his. "Hiro Tanaka... congratulations on your command. You and Captain Zarfleen were the top of my class, so I expect great things from you. It says here that you will be responsible for evaluating the colony world recommendations all our explorers send in. You'll be expected to fly out to wherever the recommendation takes you and complete your evaluation before the explorers return to Starport Central. That means you'll need a fast ship, so you've been given one of the fastest -- the scout ship."

Tanaka quickly checked his datapad for details on his new ship. The *Albatross* was one of the Eagle class of scout ships. Few luxuries, no cargo space outside of the fuel compartment, no weapons, and minimal shields, but outfitted with the best engines available to Interstel's techs. Thanks to her smaller mass, she was twice as fast as an explorer like Zarfleen's *Intrepid* would be, even when it was fully outfitted. It was, in essence, designed for speed, not for comfort.

The only other thing of note was the name. Her class's namesake had been given the name of a historic ship from mythical Earth -- the name of the first ship to make contact with a foreign planet (or perhaps a moon; the records weren't clear). However, no-one was quite sure what an 'eagle' was. Tracking through historic data from the *Noah 2* database had found only one reference -- a particular score in the ancient game of golf. This discovery had, itself, led to a revival of this old game (after all, if they named such a crucial ship after it, golf must have been an important part of old Earth's culture). It also sparked the decision to name its sister ships after other notable golf scores.

Hence the *Eagle*'s sister ships were named the *Bogey*, the *Par*, the *Birdie*, the *Condor*, and the *Ostrich*.

And the *Albatross*, now under the command of Hiro Tanaka. He only hoped his tenure did honor to the noble sport it was named for.

Tanaka had a formal mission briefing to read through, a codewheel to collect, and a ship to familiarize himself with, but the thing he was most concerned with was his crew. He was a trained scientist -- he'd been expecting to be the science officer on an explorer, possibly even on his friend Max Zarfleen's *Intrepid* -- but beyond that it was important he have an excellent navigator to get him to the right systems fast, and a diplomatic comms officer to talk him out of any situation. Comms was especially important, considering he'd be completely unarmed and would have to try and talk his way out of any situation he found himself in. A good doctor and a competent engineer wouldn't be bad to have, either. Right out of the classroom, after making his way through the operations center to pick up his papers, he rushed over to personnel hoping to find one of the premiere Velox navigators and an educated Elowan diplomat for his crew, at a minimum.

He handed the clerk his personnel papers and started to speak, but before he could get a word out the clerk shook his head.

"Eagle class. Scout ship *Albatross*. Let me bring it up on the computer... huh. You're going to be handling colony world evaluation? Huh. Currently, all of our Elowan, Thrynn, and Velox are reserved for exploration, mining, and colony ships, and we're limited on available Human crew as well. Anyone we could provide would require extensive training... but I've got a bargain for you! We've got a near limitless number of androids for you, they won't need any training. Interstel provides them to you free of charge! You okay with that?"

"...Androids?" Tanaka said. Learning he had no access to Velox and Elowan crewmen threw him for a loop. Other Humans were his second choice for both jobs, but this clerk was suggesting he might not even have them as an option. "Since when does Interstel employ androids shipboard? I didn't even know we had any that weren't janitorial staff. What are their capabilities?"

"They're designed for harsh environments -- they should be able to easily handle any colony world you get a recommendation for. Tuned to be stronger and more durable than any of the major species in Interstel, they'll take a beating that would even put a Velox out. I tell you, they're perfect for your job."

Tanaka had run into a few androids in the Academy. An instructor or two, some janitors... but not the standard shipboard model. He wondered if there was much difference.

"Eh... well, I can handle the science stations, but how good are they at handling comms? Engineering? Navigation?" He paused. "Medicine, too, I suppose -- I might wind up being the only living person on board, but I'd still like there to be someone else around who can bandage me up if I cut myself or something."

"You'll be *amazed* at how well they can communicate. They work well enough as navigators -- though I'd watch out for fluxes -- and their engineering skills are pretty good. Their medicinal skills are a bit lacking, but that doesn't mean they're completely incapable. They could bandage you up just fine, I'm sure. Given your mission, they're perfectly capable."

Tanaka felt he was being conned, but he didn't see that he had much choice. "Oh... very well. At least for this first mission, I'll take the androids."

"How many do you need?"

Tanaka sighed. He could handle the science station, but at a minimum he needed a navigator, engineer, comm officer, and medical officer. Better to keep the roster small, for now. "I'll take four."

The *ISS Albatross* was nothing like the exploration vehicles they put on Interstel's recruiting posters, which more closely resembled the one Max Zarfleen had been given command of. The *ISS Intrepid*, once she was complete, would practically be a yacht -- it had arcade machines, luxurious crew quarters, showers with actual running water, artificial gravity -- the works. It also had an expandable cargo hold, upgradeable engines and weapon systems, and more. Exploration vessels were designed to keep the crew alive and happy despite the potential for years of travel between stops home.

The *Albatross*, on the other hand, was... well, utilitarian might be a generous description. Eagle-class scouts were designed for speed, not for long expeditions. Crew quarters were tiny, there was no running water or artificial gravity (water was only available in ration packs), and there were no entertainment systems. All of the cargo space was needed for the fuel and the terrain rover. It did have better engines and sensor systems than anything the *Intrepid* could equip, but it was also unarmed, with no upgrades available for anything.

For some reason, no-one thought about how tight the quarters were when they delivered the new android crew still in their crates. Without any storage space, they were stashed in the corridors... which were *just* wide enough for the crate to fit... sideways. They would have to be moved out of the ship in order to open.

Tanaka opened the airlock into his brand new ship, saw the crates, and nearly screamed.

"Seriously!?"

It took Tanaka three days to get the crates back out of his ship so he could meet his new crew. In the end, he had to do it himself, after bribing one of the dock workers to allow him to use the mag-lift, as his 'requests' to Starport management to do something went unanswered.

Finally, he opened the crates, revealing the four androids, and activated the first one. He could hear cooling fans and motors whirling up to speed, hydraulic pumps start running, and other electric and mechanical noises. Finally, lights came on in the android's eyes.

The voice that spoke was more monotone and synthetic than Tanaka was expecting.

"Designate AND-Albatross-1, ready for duty."

Well, this one won't be our comm officer, Tanaka thought. "Designation change," he ordered. "I'll call you Andy. Take the Engineering station."

"Affirmative," Andy said. It turned and stomped up the ramp into the ship.

Shaking his head, Hiro activated the next android. Once again, after a period of warm-up, it came online. This voice was... different, but still very monotone, and very synthetic.

"Designate AND-Albatross-01, ready for duty."

"Desig... wait, AND-Albatross-01?"

"Affirmative."

That was... odd. "Oh, very well. Designation change. I'll call you... I'll call you Andi, with an 'i.' Take the navigator's station."

"Affirmative."

There was no verbal difference between the two androids' names he gave, but then there wasn't all that much difference between their original designations, either. He couldn't tell them apart, outside of slight voice variations. It would be easier to call them by their position than by a name... but he certainly wasn't going to call any of them 'Designate AND-Albatross-whatever.' It was probably a mix-up when naming conventions were changed or something, Tanaka decided, as he activated the third android.

He'd change their names after informing Interstel of the original designation mix-up.

"Designate AND-Albatross-001, ready for duty."

"Seriously!?"

With Andee (AND-Albatross-001) taking Medical and Ann D (AND-Albatross-0001) taking comms (if Interstel's personnel department was going to play these sorts of games, he was more than willing to do the same), crew assignments were complete. As they set up their individual stations, Hiro went to check his Starport messages and see if he had any assignments, yet.

The screen displayed three different recommendations, and other colony world evaluators had already taken on two of them. That left the recommendation from...

"Rodney Ware," Tanaka sighed. "Great."

Rodney Ware was, in his own mind, the greatest ship captain Interstel had ever produced. Which wasn't saying much, since the only Interstel captains active for any length of time were the Interstel Corporate Police, who had a shorter training program than those officers in other divisions, and the other members of their own graduating class.

Admittedly, Ware had been useful. He wound up the literal poster child of Interstel's recruiting drive, having his face posted on every poster, vid, and other advertisement they could possibly get. It had been such an effective drive, getting Interstel off the ground, that Interstel found it critical to ensure he graduated, even though he was... not the top of the class. In fact, he was the bottom of the class (at least, of those who passed), but that didn't humble him at all, nor stop him from getting a top-of-the-line ship.

However, he was a captain, which made this a legitimate colony world recommendation. With a sigh, Tanaka checked his codewheel, punched in his code, and let Interstel know he would be handling it as his first assignment.

Tanaka's first impression was that Andi was not a top-flight navigator, but barring an accidental flight through a flux, 'he' was adequate. They made good time to their destination, and soon were in orbit around a pleasant-looking planet with blue oceans and green continents.

Just to see what they were capable of, he had one of his androids (Andee) run a surface scan and frowned.

"Huh," Tanaka said, glancing at the readout over Andee's shoulder. The android couldn't coax the sensors into giving him a read-out of the atmosphere, nor of several other details a good science officer should be able to manage. Well, it was a good thing *he* was the usual science officer, and not one of these androids.

It didn't matter overmuch. Tanaka wanted to get some idea of what the local flora and fauna was like and would be taking atmospheric samples to ensure there were no hazardous viral or other contaminants before he felt comfortable walking around on the surface without a terrain rover or an environment suit. At least the Android had a gravity reading, which was... well, barely within tolerance for a colony world, if he were honest -- a full two Gs. This would be a tough eval.

"All right," he said, pointing. "Land us somewhere around there."

Descent was quick, and there was a heavy "whump" as the ship made contact with the planet's surface. Tanaka grimaced as he felt the heavy gravity's effects, but between the terrain rover and environment suits it would be safe even if the gravity was several times higher. It wasn't optimal for colonization, but it wouldn't disqualify the world, and he would be able to endure it with no ill effects, even if he was stuck on-planet for some time.

"All right, everyone into the rover!" Tanaka ordered, unstrapping from his seat. The androids made their way down to the cargo bay straight away, but he had to stop and grab his suit's helmet on the way. That was why he was the last one to the rover, where four identical androids were waiting for him.

As the rover collected the local air for study, the atmospheric readings puzzled Tanaka. Nitrogen and carbon dioxide were the atmosphere's primary components -- which was perfectly fine -- but the next most common gaseous element was argon. He expanded the list, but no matter how far down the list he went he didn't see oxygen.

Surely no-one would recommend a colony world without making sure the planet had *oxygen,* right?

They got to the nearest beach, and Tanaka asked one of the androids -- Ann D. -- to collect a water sample for study while he worked to calibrate the atmospheric sensors. He was so absorbed in trying to find out why he couldn't detect any oxygen that he wasn't paying any attention when 'she' returned, holding out the sample jar. Had he done so, he might have noticed that her hand was badly damaged as she held it.

Not paying any attention, however, he reached to take the sample jar from her, not even noticing that there was still some liquid from the ocean still dripping off of the jar. Not until he put his hand around it did he notice anything amiss, as alarms went off on his suit warning him of a loss in suit integrity, and his hand started burning. Emergency repair foam sealed the leaks before the suit lost too much air pressure, but the damage to his hand wasn't so easily fixed.

"Shit!" he cried, dropping the jar. Fortunately, it didn't break, or he suspected the rover would have been in serious trouble as it ate holes into the floor.

Whether the planet had oxygen or not, there was no way he was accepting a recommendation to colonize a world whose oceans were that toxic.

"Seriously!?"

Hiro rushed his way back to the ship, ordering Andi to take the ship up and fly them back to Starport, fast as they could go. Unfortunately, by the time he made it to the sickbay for treatment, the acid had burned its way through his environment suit's glove and was burning his hand.

Andee, upon seeing the wound under the glove, turned to the medicine cabinet. A moment later, he came back with a self-adhesive bandage.

"That's it?" Hiro asked incredulously. "That's all you're doing?"

"This unit is programmed to apply bandages to small wounds," Andee said. "That is the limit of my medical knowledge."

"...seriously?"

After raiding the medicine cabinet for the chemicals needed to neutralize the acid (and only then allowing Andee to 'treat' the burn by protecting it with a bandage), Hiro made his way back to the ship's bridge. He turned to Ann D., who was still undergoing self-repairs from her own encounter with the acid.

"I... don't suppose you're somehow a top-tier translator, are you?" he asked.

"This unit is incapable of any form of translation," Ann D. replied.

"Then... why didn't you say anything when I made you a comm officer? Translation is your primary duty!"

Ann D's reply was prefaced by the whir of its internal computer system cooling itself down. "Query: Is this a rhetorical question? This unit is incapable of understanding the nuance of rhetorics."

"Seriously!?"

Back at Interstel headquarters, with his wounds all healed, Hiro started writing up his evaluation of the recommendation. He wasn't entirely sure where to start.

"Clearly, you recommended this world intending to get the colony world evaluator killed. There was nothing to indicate the world was habitable, everything was a deadly hazard, and I nearly died..."

He sighed, shaking his head. No, that was... well, how he actually felt, but he had been told the captains would be getting one warning. No matter how bad the recommendation was, he should do that.

"Due to the lack of oxygen and a lack of water, this planet proved unsuitable for colonization. You have been fined 100 Mu. This is only a warning." Tanaka grinned slightly as he wrote the final sentence. "Your next fine will be heavy."

At the moment, he wanted nothing more than to fine Ware so heavily he had to leave Interstel.

He sent the evaluation off, then stood up. He had a swindler from Personnel to find.

Tracking down the personnel guy who had convinced Tanaka to take on an all-android crew wasn't going anywhere. Someone named Xenon had blamed someone else called Borno, but he wasn't sure that was right. As best as he could tell, both were Interstel employees -- or at least they had access to the Interstel message boards -- but beyond that he couldn't even confirm either one had anything to do with personnel... or any other department, for that matter.

He was still trying to get access to the personnel department's duty roster when he found himself grabbed and slammed up against a wall.

"What's the big idea!?" a steaming mad Captain Rodney Ware demanded. "I send you a colony recommendation for a perfectly good world, and you fine me for it?"

Tanaka was just about on his last nerve, but succeeded in reining in his temper for the moment. "Your 'perfectly good world' had no oxygen, and the oceans were so caustic it ate through my encounter suit and injured a member of my crew. Of course, I *fined* you! It wasn't even a real fine, anyway -- just a warning."

"It could still have been terraformed, couldn't it?" Ware snapped, dropping him onto the ground. "The world looked great! Idyllic! Now, don't fine me again!"

Tanaka would have told him that Interstel didn't have the tech or the resources to do that kind of terraforming, but by the time he'd stood himself up and dusted himself off, Ware was already gone.

Tanaka sighed, straightening his uniform. "Seriously?"

Deciding that replacing the Andies could wait for a while, Tanaka resolved to get out of the station as quickly as possible. He needed to give Ware a little time to cool off, so went to the message boards to find the first colony world recommendation he could that had nothing to do with his former classmate.

Ware had made at least twenty recommendations since he saw that last one, but there was a single entry that wasn't attributed to him. Apparently, it wasn't attributed to anyone, as there was no name attached -- there should be one in the log buoy around the planet, however. He quickly snapped it up, and almost sprinted to the space dock to get on his ship.

Had he been in little less of a hurry, he might have noticed the date on the recommendation was earlier than any of Ware's recommendations, even the one he'd already serviced. In fact, it came several weeks before the first Interstel exploration expedition had left. Unfortunately, he failed to notice anything, and thus was wholly unprepared for the mystery he was about to stumble into.

Hiro Tanaka had thought that Ware's world recommendation was careless, but it wasn't outright fraud. When the *ISS Albatross* arrived at the co-ordinates 131 by 105, however, he couldn't explain the recommendation he'd received in any other way.

Someone had recommended a planet that wasn't there.

"Seriously?" he snapped. An odd feeling washed over him. The androids were incompetent, so... "Andi, report -- how certain are you of our co-ordinates?"

"Confirming. One hundred percent certainty," Andi replied. The androids weren't all that useful, but they could be relied on to be honest, so Hiro felt confident they were at the correct location.

"Then--"

Before he could finish that thought, an alarm klaxon sounded. "Encounter!" Andi called out. He might have been an emotionless android, but the anxiety was clear to Tanaka's ears. They were a scout ship with no shields, no armor, and no weapons. If this was a hostile, they would have no choice but to run.

There was only one contact on the radar, thankfully. Acting as the science officer, Hiro targeted a scan of the contact, and the result was... surprising.

From the silhouette, it looked like another Arth-based spacecraft. An advanced model of the Intrepid class, which was... odd, to say the least, given that none of those ships were supposed to be in service, yet. But there it was. And, from the readings, it was heavily damaged. And it wasn't moving.

With some trepidation, Hiro kicked himself out of the navigation station and floated his way over to the comms. Maybe his supposed 'comm' officer could handle this, if there were actual Interstel personnel who spoke Arthling on that ship, but he didn't want to take any chances on the introduction.

"Attention unknown vessel. This is the *ISS Albatross*. Come in," he called. The standard Interstel protocols dictating what words were to be used when hailing another ship were still held up in committee, so Hiro was free to use his own words, but right now he was wishing he had that guidance. "Are you in need of assistance?"

"Reply coming in," Ann D. noted. "Broadcasting now."

A familiar voice crackled out of the speakers. "...trieve our black box and return it to Interstel. I wish.... Repeating: ISS *Intrepid* issuing emergency distress call. By the time anyone gets this, we're likely already dead, but it is critical that the information we have be returned to Interstel, ASAP. To anyone who can hear us: Please, retrieve our black box and return it to Interstel. I wish.... Repeating: ISS *Intrepid* issuing emergency distress call..."

"Max?" Hiro whispered. How could Max Zarfleen be dead? That... wait, how could the *Intrepid* even be out here? She was still being built. When leaving Starport, Hiro had passed by the drydock where they were still installing the mounts for her engines. Nothing about this situation made any sense -- not the least of which was the idea that Hiro's Academy buddy, Max Zarfleen, might be dead.

There was only one way to get answers, though, and that was to do what the distress call requested. Hiro glanced at Ann D. "Let me guess -- no-one ever bothered programming you with the protocol for remote retrieval of a black box?"

"Correct," Ann D.'s electric monotone replied.

Shaking his head, Hiro grabbed the comm panel's manual and started looking up the protocol himself. He was supposed to have returned the manuals after his first shakedown cruise, but until he replaced his androids with a competent crew, he'd be using these extensively.

It wasn't long before his ship was receiving a data dump that included a lot of telemetry, some maps and charts, and a ship's log. Figuring it was the quickest way to determine just what was going on, he put the ship's log on the screen to read.

"Captain's log, Stardate 14-05-4620. 16:22.06. Why didn't Interstel provide me with a more experienced crew? I would assume that testing a prototype of a new ship class such as the *Intrepid* would rate a high personnel priority. My crew are rookies, as I am, just out of the Academy with no advanced training at all...."

When he was done reading the log, Hiro let himself drift in the gravity-free environment of the bridge while he thought. There was quite a bit to unpack. First, assuming this black box was authentic, time travel must be possible -- the very idea was both intriguing and terrifying, given the possibilities it presented. Second, Max Zarfleen, his classmate and friend in the Academy, was going to die. Or had died. Or... well, might have died? Was there a chance to avert this possible... future? Future past? Past? Perhaps that would be a question for Professor Dahglesh, once this was all settled.

Or perhaps that was a question Zarfleen, himself, had asked their former philosophy professor, during their meeting in this possible future he'd written about. A future that, he hoped, Zarfleen might be able to avoid. He certainly wouldn't do this exact same thing, once he read this... maybe he would call it a "clue book" to the future.

Hiro sighed, making a copy of the black box for his personal use, thinking about showing it all to Dahglesh to ask those questions. But first, he had to get this to Interstel, and get things going to keep this tragedy from happening. This was above his pay grade, but surely, they would know what to do.

Chaos was the only word to describe the Interstel offices, once Hiro returned the black box to Starport. He, and the black box, were promptly whisked away to the Interstel offices in Pelinoriat, where scientists throughout the organization were now congregating. The crosstalk all became a white noise, but now and then he heard a few elements of it.

To begin with, Zarfleen had recorded some insights into the nature of endurium. If his theories were true, the continued use of the element for starflight would be unethical, but currently there was no reliable substitute. Well, not one Interstel knew of a source for -- there was something called "shyneum," which the species of the Delta Quadrant built their economies around, but where and how to get it was still a mystery. And just getting set up to look for it would take decades.

The first step would be to establish a Human presence in the Delta Quadrant. Pieces of a new Starport were already under construction, but they would need to be shipped out and assembled on site. Moving out equipment like that could not be done with the same speed as most starships, and that sort of equipment couldn't be sent out cheaply or un-escorted. Cash was a concern, but so was speed -- one single shipment would be far faster and cheaper than sending the station out, then the ships it was to support, then the crews to keep it all running. That meant the Starport, the construction crew, and several other ships' crews would all have to undergo cryo-sleep, as it would take almost twenty years to send them all out there in one shipment.

The entire Delta Quadrant mission was being re-tasked. Originally, the plan was for a much slower deployment, which would have taken almost a century to do what they were planning to complete in twenty. Captain Phloon de Lux had been called in, and was now being briefed to recruit a crew especially for the new assignment. He would be put in command of the first of three Intrepid class ships being shipped out with the new Starport. The *ISS Victory*, which was the *first* of the two Intrepid-class prototypes (Zarfleen's own *Intrepid* was supposed to have been first, but construction had been delayed for several months), was a top-of-the-line exploration-rated ship with all the upgrades, and would be his command. The other two Intrepid class ships were the *ISS Butterfish* -- which was complete, but lacked many of the expected upgrades -- and another, unnamed ship still under construction. All three would now be tasked with finding a source of some alternative to endurium -- perhaps this rumored shyneum they had heard of.

What everyone refused to discuss, however, was what Hiro thought should have been the most important thing -- how to keep Zarfleen alive. They now had a complete record of his travels, so surely some way to save his life could be found, yes?

Evidently not. One scientist mentioned the mere possibility of a paradox, and suddenly any talk of letting Zarfleen know anything was forbidden. The scientists admitted they had no idea if there really would be a paradox resulting from him getting this knowledge. They also admitted that they had no idea what would happen if such a paradox occurred. Would Zarfleen, the *Intrepid*, and the knowledge presented by the black box just disappear from existence? Maybe. The reasoning didn't seem to make any sense to Hiro, and his Academy training was in fields that should have allowed him to follow it, but that was what some of these scientists decided. So, the reasoning was, to keep Zarfleen safe, they had to hide the contents of the black box from him. Except, in hiding it from him, the chances were that everything would happen exactly like the black box said, and Zarfleen would die anyway, so... what was the point of that?

And those scientists were who Terrence Willwater, Interstel's director, was listening to. After several hours of debate, the black box -- now known officially as "Project Flying Dutchman" (and informally, thanks to Hiro, as "the Cluebook") -- had been classified. It was distributed among several people (Hiro and Captain Phloon de Lux among them) with a memo explaining the rationale for hiding this from Zarfleen.

"'May the Rock of Truth shine brightly on you all,' my arse," Hiro muttered under his breath.

"Sorry?"

Hiro flinched, realizing that it was Terrence Willwater himself talking to him. Had he been overheard? Glancing at the director's face, he decided not. Still, probably a good idea to make his excuses and get out of there.

"Sorry, Director Willwater. I've been up since we found that black box, and I think I'm drifting off on my feet. Permission to return to my old bunk here at the Academy, catch up on my sleep, and then return to my regular duties, sir?"

Willwater, a man with an imposing face that the cameras all focused on, but a short, gaunt figure that made him look much less impressive in person, gave him a long look. "Oh... very well. But remember -- Project Flying Dutchman has been classified at the *highest* level. Mention this to anyone and you will be considered a traitor, for which Interstel has just one punishment."

Schooling his face as best as he could, Hiro nodded. "Of course, Director Willwater."

Hiro did, in fact, spend several hours trying to get to sleep in one of the college dorm's guest barracks. He wasn't successful, however, as thoughts, fears, and plans kept running through his head. Max Zarfleen should not be sacrificed in the name of avoiding a paradox that may not even happen, but Interstel had said otherwise.

After tossing and turning for several hours, he stood up. He couldn't decide anything... but he knew the first step, regardless of what he did from here on. Checking his pockets to ensure he still had his own copy of the Cluebook, made before it had been classified, he made his way through New Oxford University's large Interstel Academy complex until he arrived at the small, out-of-the-way building that was the home of the Philosophy department. A quick check of the directory confirmed that Kerwin Dahglesh still resided in the same office he remembered. That confirmed, he stepped inside.

Down the corridor, up the stairs, and on the right, he found said office. Knocking on the door, a soft "Yes?" beckoned him inside.

"Professor Dahglesh?" Hiro said, closing the door behind him. His old professor was going through some paperwork on his desk, and appeared happy at the interruption. "Have you got a minute?"

"Hiro! Yes, yes, of course. Take a seat. And it's Kerwin, my boy -- you're a graduate, now, you know."

The already tiny office was crowded with files, books, and paperwork, and Hiro hadn't even seen the 'seat' he could take until Dahglesh pointed it out. He cleared half a dozen books off the chair and sat down, holding the data drive with the copy of the black box in his hand.

Checking to make sure he'd closed the door behind him, Hiro took a deep breath. "Professor Dahglesh, I have an... ethics question, I suppose you could call it. But to explain it, I would have to break Interstel confidentiality and commit treason."

He wasn't sure how he had expected Dahglesh to react, but hearing his old professor snort back a bitter laugh wasn't it. "Will you, now? Well... I won't tell anyone. Not that anyone would believe me if I did, but... well, never mind. What is the question?"

Taking a deep breath, Hiro put the data drive on Dahglesh's desk. "I think you need to read this, first. Know that I retrieved that off of a ship that, as of this moment, does not exist."

"Doesn't exist?" Dahglesh repeated, raising a curious eyebrow as he took the drive and connected it to his computer. "Interesting."

Saying Hiro sat 'patiently' while Dahglesh read the future *Intrepid's* captain's log would be a stretch, but he was able to keep silent and let the man concentrate on what he was reading. There were a few times the older man paused in thought, and Hiro nearly spoke, but a raised finger always kept him from saying a word. Finally, Dahglesh sat back in his chair heavily, signaling that he was done.

"Well?" Hiro prompted.

"Let me guess. Interstel classified this because of the inherent danger of a paradox, correct?"

Hiro winced. "Yes, that's what Director Willwater decided after hearing several of his scientists' thoughts."

"I expected as much," Dahglesh sighed. "Of course, since I'm mentioned as speaking to Max in this ship's log, if there was going to be a paradox, it would have already occurred. So, let's just imagine that isn't happening and move on. What do you want to do with this information, and why come to me?"

"Well, I want to try and help Max survive," Hiro said. "I think it's criminal that Willwater is willing to sacrifice him just because there is a slight chance that saving him might cause this ship's log to disappear. Interstel practically *is* the government, now, however, so I don't know who would arrest him."

"Willwater has gotten Interstel this far," Dahglesh pointed out. "I agree with you that he's making a mistake, here, and he could run things a bit smarter -- starting by equipping our explorers a bit better -- but he could be a lot worse. The problem is that Interstel has to do things officially, by the book they just spent several years writing, and with the consensus of its braintrust -- which means listening to the scientists, even when they're wrong. To save your Captain Zarfleen, you're going to need to be able to act outside of the book." He paused. "You committed treason to give me this file. I don't suppose you'd be willing to work with someone else who acts... outside of the law? Or at least outside of Interstel's bylaws, which is pretty much the same thing, nowadays."

There was only a little hesitation before Hiro responded. "As long as they aren't advocating for the genocide of all people on Arth, or the xenocide of all non-Arthlings, or something like that...

yeah, I suppose I can. As long as it means saving Max's life, anyway."

"Well, I happen to know someone who might just be able to help...."

"My name is not Xenon," Hiro recited, wondering at the coincidence of that name popping up as part of his password into... whatever organization it was Dahglesh had directed him to.

"You Borno, then?" the heavily armed Thrynn replied.

"I don't have your money, so no."

Hiro wasn't exactly sure where he was going, only that it was in the same Interstel facility that most people waiting to leave for the trip to the Starport would stay. A combination mega-hotel, restaurant chain, and office complex that was one of the largest single buildings on Arth. The door he'd been directed to looked like the entrance to a janitor's closet, but the security devices keeping an eye on it made it a surprisingly well-guarded one. The behemoth guarding said janitor's closet made it stand out more than it probably should, given some of Dahglesh's hints about the people he'd be meeting with.

"Who sent you, then?" the Thrynn asked.

"The Turret," Hiro replied. When he asked Dahglesh about that code name, he'd been told a fascinating tale about how, on Old Earth, the first naval warship to use a turret in battle was called the *Monitor*. As his only role with this organization was to monitor the situation in Interstel's Academy, it seemed to fit.

It did bring up some questions, however. Records from Old Earth did exist -- the existence of the sport of golf, the comic tales performed by comedian Robin Williams, and several other bits of esoterica had been uncovered in recent years -- but there weren't many, and what did exist was spotty. During his pre-Academy education, Hiro had spent a great deal of time studying those Old Earth records, and he thought he knew the bulk of what was available, but he had never heard that bit of its history. Just what record did Dahglesh have that included such stories?

Regardless of its origins, the Thrynn seemed surprised to hear the name used as a password. His eyes widened an inhuman amount at the mention.

"Really? Well... damn. Go on in, then."

Hiro stepped inside, and immediately knew he was in the twilight zone. This was obviously a waiting room, of sorts, but there were people all over it discussing things he couldn't make out. A Velox who strongly resembled the comedian, Phexitutex, was casually discussing a space pirate by the name of Harrison with a Thrynn and an Elowan, while a Human looked on, and all four of them looked chummy. The way they were acting with each other, the Thrynn and Elowan even looked... well... close, in a way that Hiro didn't want to contemplate the mechanics of. Given their respective species' mutual animosity toward each other, just being in the same room peacefully was something of a miracle, but this?

Hiro didn't have long to contemplate it, though, before the doorman followed him in and started leading him to a different room in the back. He was given a somewhat forceful shove into it, and the door sealed behind him, separating him from his Thrynn guide.

Hiro couldn't make out much of this new room he was in. It was dark -- too dark to see anything except for a chair by a table, both of which were gently lit by blue light diodes built into the furniture. He made his way over without stumbling over anything, thankfully, and took a seat.

He still didn't know why he was here, other than Dahglesh's assurance that these people could help.

A few minutes later, another door on the other side of the room opened, and someone else walked in. Hiro couldn't make out much about the person in the dark, and that wasn't helped by the robes obscuring everything about him, but the gait of his walk suggested he wasn't an Elowan, at least.

The newcomer took a seat across the table from him, which lit up with those same blue diodes the moment the door had closed behind him. Even that close, however, Hiro still couldn't make out any features.

The voice, heavily modified by some sort of voice changer, didn't give any clues, either. "No time for pleasantries. If Turret sent you, it must be urgent, so talk. Why are you here?"

Taking a deep breath, Hiro once again explained his dilemma, only with even more background than Dahglesh knew about. He talked about his Academy days, and how Max Zarfleen was one of the few people in the Academy who he really got along with. He mentioned his frustration at being given an all-android crew, his confrontation with Rodney Ware, his getting an apparently false colony world recommendation for a planet that didn't exist, and finally got into the discovery, his actions since, and Interstel's own reaction to it all.

Telling it all took a load off of Hiro he didn't know was there, but now it was all out in the open. He waited for the masked figure to respond. When nothing happened, he asked a question that had been on his mind since Dahglesh told him about this place.

"Are Xenon and Borno real people?"

The masked figure gave a very human snort. "Honestly, I don't even know. We picked their names at random off the message boards. If they *do* exist, I suspect they may work for one of our rivals, but I can't be sure."

"Your rivals?"

"You probably know them as the Intrastel Initiative."

It suddenly clicked in Hiro's head. There were rumors of one or more organized crime operations running out of Interstel. The Intrastel Initiative was the rumored name of one of those organizations, and there was only one other name nearly as prominent.

"Understel?"

"That's us," the cloaked figure admitted casually, leaning back in his chair. "Not our organization's *real* name, mind you, but the one we prefer people not in the know to refer to us as. And it's a good thing you came to us instead of Intrastel, because we might just be able to help you save Zarfleen's life. Might be able to help you with one of your other problems, too." He paused. "I think it's our fault you were stuck with an all-android crew. My apologies. The good news is this job should help you with that..."

Hiro had only captured the ship's log before turning in the black box, not the rest of the data. His Understel contact had cautioned him that he would need to steal the complete recording, if at all possible, in order for the plan to work. That was the easy bit, though -- Hiro already knew all the passcodes needed, as he was authorized to view the Project Flying Dutchman files (he'd found them, after all), and Understel had provided him with something that would spoof the computer into thinking he was Rodney Ware when he downloaded them. It was almost too easy to get the rest of the data and escape without anyone being any the wiser.

The tricky part would be in getting the Cluebook to Zarfleen without getting caught. If Zarfleen used the information in the Cluebook to save his own life, Interstel would know it had a leak, and would try to work backwards from him. Hiro was likely the only person who even knew about the Project Flying Dutchman files who also had a close personal relationship with Zarfleen, which would make him prime suspect number one, and it wouldn't be long before he was arrested on that evidence, alone.

If, however, *every* Interstel captain had a copy of the Cluebook, Interstel might still know it had a leak, but it wouldn't automatically assume Hiro was the source of that leak. Understel had a way to redirect the blame to some front company named "Binary Systems, Inc.," which in turn could be directly linked (through some forged paperwork) to Understel's competitor, Intrastel.

The first step was to modify his android crew. They might report on anything illegal he would have to do, after all. He wasn't an expert on modifying androids, but fortunately Understel gave him a tool that would do it for him. A quick jolt to their systems, they would be disabled. Unscrew a plate behind the android's head, pop in a small device, and it was done. They would never report him for anything... and they suddenly seemed much more competent at their jobs. Ann D. could even translate communications coming in from other ships!

Another thing that had to happen was that they would have to wait before releasing the Cluebook to anyone. If it appeared right after the conference discussing the incident, it would throw suspicion on Hiro (and anyone else who might have had a legitimate copy). Give it time, and with a little 'slightly-too-obvious' hackery to support the story, they could try to shift blame to... well, someone else.

During that time, Hiro was instructed to keep up with his job evaluating colony world recommendations, but he could not allow his modified androids to ever leave the *Albatross*. They acted too different in comparison to other androids to risk their mingling with other people -- it would only arouse suspicion. So he had to be constantly on the move, running himself ragged with his dedication to colony world evaluation.

His earlier confrontation with Rodney Ware wound up with long term consequences. Ware had started leaving rumors that Hiro was a hard-ass as a colony world evaluator. Understel suggested he start using that reputation, as false as it might have been, to take longer and longer evaluating each colony world he checked, making more detailed reports each time. Hiro wasn't sure what would be gained by that, but he nevertheless followed the instructions.

It unnerved him that he had become so reliant on a group of people who were, by reputation at least, a criminal underworld organization, but he trusted Dahglesh, and he was desperate to save Zarfleen's life. However, his trust of Understel was fading each day, as it got closer and closer to the ISS *Intrepid's* projected launch date. By this point, he wasn't sure what else he could do, however -- things were now completely out of his hands.

It was less than two weeks before the Intrepid's launch, while Hiro had just left on a colony world evaluation assignment, when things finally started moving, again.

Ann D., without turning 'her' head, called out. "Transmission incoming! New protocols established. Code Red."

Hiro blinked. "What?"

"Directives as follows: Proceed to planet one in orbit around star at grid co-ordinates thirty-three by six. Further instructions will be relayed there."

"What?" Hiro said again.

"Proceed to planet one in--"

"No, I got that. Sorry. What I mean is, where are these 'directives' coming from? Who is contacting us?"

There was a long silence. Finally, Ann D. said, "These orders come from the Turret Control Officer on Arth."

"Turret control officer? What turret control... oh, clever, Understel, very clever. Andi! Take us to grid co-ordinates thirty-three by six, best speed."

There was a brief pause from Andi as well. "Code Red acknowledged. Known flux routes factoring in to navigation. Brace yourself, Captain Tanaka -- this could get rough." That last sentence was the most emotion Hiro had ever heard from any of his android crew.

What followed was the most topsy-turvy ride he had ever experienced. The *Albatross* must have slipped through half a dozen fluxes, traveling at top speed, not stopping no matter what they encountered. They buzzed one unknown ship into retreat, outran an ambush by a small group of heavily armed warships, and nearly exhausted their fuel supply. Andi had actually ignored Hiro's orders to stop them at a friendly planet for a supply run, noting, "We have enough fuel to reach our destination. No stops are necessary."

Hiro checked the fuel supply and decided Andi was right about them being able to reach their destination, but that they wouldn't be able to return home once they arrived. Or get to any other friendly planets he knew about, for that matter.

It was when they entered the nebula that Hiro started to understand just why this system had been picked. He recalled that this planet was on the list of worlds future Zarfleen was supposed to have recommended, and one of only three that were hidden in a nebula.

Though just why that was important, he wasn't entirely sure.

Finally, they slipped into the system they'd been flying towards with such fury, darting to the planet, and then into orbit around it... where another ship was waiting.

Not waiting for his androids to tell him anything, Hiro quickly ran a scan of the unknown vessel... and, for the second time, found another *Intrepid*-class ship.

"Oh, you've got to be kidding me," he muttered. "If this is Max's time-traveling ship, again, I--"

"Transmission received," Ann D. called. "*ISS Albatross*, this is *ISS Victory*. Stand by for personnel transfer."

"Personnel transfer?" Hiro repeated. "Who is transferring where?"

Andi, at the helm, stood up and drifted over to Hiro, unstrapping him from his bridge chair. Recognizing it would be impossible to resist, Hiro helped the android along, and soon was drifting around the bridge cabin. "Per Code Red directive, you are being transferred to the *ISS Victory*. I will assume command until your return."

Hiro feared for the poor *Albatross* with an android in charge, but was confused more than anything. Maybe things would make sense once he was on board the other ship, which hopefully would have someone alive he could get an explanation from. The androids weren't making much sense.

Hiro was thinking furiously as he was transferred over to the other ship. Just what was going on, here? He'd only asked

Understel to help him save Zarfleen's life. Why was he being taken to the *ISS Victory?* For that matter, why was the *Victory* here, in the Alpha Quadrant, when instead it should be in cold storage prepped for a slow, fuel-efficient flight out to the future site of the Delta Quadrant Starport?

Of all the people to greet him, Hiro had not expected the Phexitutex-lookalike he recalled from that lobby on Arth. Nor was he expecting said Velox from Understel to give him a formal Interstel salute.

"Greetings, Captain Tanaka," the Velox said. "Welcome aboard."

Unconsciously adjusting himself to the artificial gravity on board -- Arth-standard, which was unusual on a ship managed by a Velox -- Hiro returned the salute before shaking his head. "Thanks. Now... what am I doing here, and how in the hell is this ship here? I though the *Victory* was supposed--"

"Let me take you to your cabin," the Velox said, handing him a data drive. "You'll find a station there to play that on. Then meet me on the bridge, and I'll answer any additional questions you have."

Hiro was still unable to ask any questions, but at least it sounded like some of them might be in a minute. He followed the faux-Phexitutex to a luxurious cabin he thought would normally belong to the ship's captain, and went inside as directed. Once the door closed behind him, he was left alone.

While the long flight out to the *Victory* had him yearning to use the massive bed that the cabin offered, or to indulge in a meal from the cabin's kitchenette, he dutifully made his way over to the computer workstation to figure out what all of this was about.

With the data drive plugged in, the screen flickered to life. The same robe-concealed figure he'd met in Understel's headquarters sat there opposite him, but he wasn't alone -- Professor Kerwin Dahglesh was sitting right there with him.

"Hello, Hiro," Dahglesh said. "By now, I bet you're going crazy. After all, your plan to save Mr. Zarfleen was simply to make sure he got a copy of that Cluebook you found, and to hope he could use it to figure out how to keep himself alive. Not a bad plan, but I think we can do better. We'll move that one off to plan B. Instead, my friends here in Understel have come up with a Plan A."

The heavily cloaked man nodded. "Indeed we have, but do not worry -- your original plan will also be followed. We have set up a method for any aspiring Interstel captain to purchase a copy of your 'Cluebook' through Binary Systems, Inc., your Mr. Zarfleen included, but that -- as Agent Turret explained -- is plan B. As it is your friend you wish to save, however, and you've taken it this far, I believe you are the best one to send out for plan A.

"You are to take command of the *ISS Victory*. Yes, this is the same *Victory* that Captain Phloon de Lux believes he will be given. When he emerges from his cryo-sleep in the Delta Quadrant, I'm afraid he'll find that his ship has been 'reassigned,' and he'll have to make do with the *ISS Butterfish*. Given the concerns raised by the Cluebook, I believe it is more important that you get the fully upgraded ship. We're also giving you fifty thousand Monetary Units to further upgrade her, rather than the twelve thousand most explorer-class ship captains are being granted.

"We've also made a few other modifications to the *Victory* for you, though you'll have to use that extra cash we've given you to outfit her. You'll be able to install military-grade weapons like buzz bombs, twin beams, fusion blasters, and the like, instead of just the basic missiles and lasers other explorers are restricted to. We've also modified your ship and terrain vehicle for atmospheric flight, allowing you to move about planets easier without having to first return to orbit. Your terrain vehicle can also be upgraded as well -- mineral scanners, radars, pontoons, ice runners, expanded cargo space, etc., while most explorers just have basic terrain vehicles.

"All that, and you also have your own copy of the Cluebook, of course."

Dahglesh took over the conversation again. "So, congratulations, Captain Tanaka. You're now in command of the most advanced ship in the fleet. You must be asking yourself just what it is we're asking you to accomplish with her. Well, it's simple -- we want you to follow the events listed in that little Cluebook you found and see if you can't beat Max to the punch, completing his assignment before he kills himself doing the same."

"Of course, if a new Intrepid class ship started doing all this stuff, Interstel will ask questions," the cloaked Understel leader added. "Which is why we had to wait until just before the *ISS Intrepid* and her sister ships, all undertaking the same mission, were launched to bring you back in. As all captains in Interstel's exploration division are allowed to re-name, re-crew, and refit their ships as they choose -- as long as they use their own cash for it -- no-one will question your ship docking in Starport once they start launching. I do recommend you change the name to something other than the *ISS Victory* once you dock, just to throw off suspicion, but I doubt Interstel would even notice if you don't.

"They *will* pay attention if you use the *Albatross's* codewheel, however. So, we hacked Interstel's security mainframe and replaced *Victory's* codewheel identifier with our own 'security' device. You no longer need a codewheel, so we'll be sending your old one back to the *Albatross*, where your androids will be holding it in trust for you."

"Now, you might be wondering just why an underground 'criminal' organization is helping you so much," Dahglesh said. "Well... according to that Cluebook of yours, there's a group of robots out there called the 'Mechan' who still remember an organization called the 'Institute.' Let's just say this Institute recognized the need for a... call it a safeguard, of sorts, and that we're a part of that. And while we rarely recruit outside of 'family,' as it is, I think we're looking to induct another member soon... if you manage to complete this mission successfully, save Max Zarfleen, and just maybe save the universe in the process..."

There had been more details after that. Such as how the *Albatross* would be sitting on the planet they'd been orbiting, waiting for his return. His androids would set up a campsite that could be used to explain how he could survive an extended deployment without re-supply. There was just enough fuel left on board for the Albatross to flee if anyone came looking for her -- she would be his alibi, when all this was over, so it was important she remained undiscovered.

As captain of the *Victory* (or whatever he chose to re-name her), he would work under an assumed name with a crew drawn from Understel (the same Human, Velox, Elowan, and Thrynn he remembered talking with each other from Understel's lobby had been gathered for him, but he could replace them if he wanted). But once his adventure was over, he would be returning to the planet orbiting the star at co-ordinates thirty-three by six, boarding the *Albatross*, and issuing a distress call letting Interstel know she had 'run out of fuel' and he needed a tow, explaining just where he had been all those months away from Arth.

But that would be some time, still. He had a friend -- and a universe -- to save.

Rover Rescue

by Michael J. Allen

A low power alarm flashed in the corner of my heads-up display, an irritating buzz accompanying every blink.

"Come on, baby. You can do it."

A clipped mechanical voice repeated himself a third time. "I informed you of the risk."

We crested a ridge, the rover lurching forward as plateau turned into descent. "We're going to make it, U-44." I pointed ahead. "We're almost there, see?"

"*Shiva* remains too distant for our current reserves," U442330 said.

I checked the angry red text superimposed over the empty battery meter.

Shiva came into sight. The ache in my stomach eased. She rested on the valley's far side, just uphill from the valley floor ahead. We were going to make it.

Good thing, too. I'm starving.

I eased off the power, letting inertia and planetary gravity do the work. The rover picked up speed. Dips and divots jounced us back and forth. Halfway down the hill, we bounced.

The rover came down hard, hitting a rock outcropping. An impact that felt like a punch in the gut threw us backward. I re-engaged the power to get us out of the hole.

The engine screamed like a frightened doe.

The wheels spun free.

My stomach clenched.

An anguished howl filled me at Luck's betrayal

Shiva waited only a hundred meters away.

We weren't going to make it.

Pain shot through my head, crackling filled my ears, and the smell of burning electronics and human hair flooded my nostrils. The rover's computerized voice filled the cabin. "Power failure. Emergency crew recovery activated."

My limbs locked. Crew compartment access doors opened. Unable to judge the distance back to our ship or our physical condition, the emergency protocol usurped our bodies. My suit jerked me around like a meat puppet. The system disembarked me without taking personal flexibility into account, wrenching one hip. Searing heat pummeled us as the suits mechanically marched all three of us toward *Shiva*.

How did it all go wrong?

We caught air cresting a hill too fast in the .04 gravity. "Hedrin, yeah!"

Even in the light gravity, the mostly full terrain vehicle came down hard enough that I bit my tongue. Half the rover's wheels caught early, jerking all of us and spinning our ride to one side.

I lunged for the controls before my brain caught up.

After several mining runs, remote rover control grew more natural. Cameras tracked with my eyes. The expanded view projected against my spacesuit's visor trumped the narrow cockpit window and added seamless scanner control via the uplink. A section of butte face illuminated in the distance. The system highlighted a mineral deposit otherwise invisible to the naked eye.

My pulse increased, an excitement akin to hunger making me salivate.

Scanning data scrolled down a side display window in my HUD. The promethium deposit read as thirty-one cubic meters—almost a whole ship's cargo pod. I checked our rover's cargo readout. We could take it all on if we dumped the zinc in the TV's inventory. Above the cargo manifest, our remaining juice dipped below twenty percent.

My stomach grumbled.

I checked the distance, pulling up a map to compare the *Shiva's* position.

"We do not have sufficient power for a detour."

A video image of our Velox science officer, Vhirl, popped up in my HUD, mandibles undulating beneath brick-colored carapace. "U-44 is right, CT. We can come back for it."

"Maybe another rover couldn't, but I've got this F1-D0 tuned to absolute perfection."

"A statistical analysis of power efficiency during our last several trips fails to support your claims. Any attempt to retrieve the targeted mineral deposit risks complete exhaustion of the terrain vehicle's batteries."

Beneath me, the rover finished bouncing from its short flight, almost like a pit fighter dancing on the balls of his feet, raring to start the fight. The TV wasn't the only eager one.

"You heard Captain Eyal," Vhirl added. "You're to stop pushing the TV's batteries too much."

I weighed their warnings against the sweet prize waiting a hundred meters out of our way.

The hunger won.

To be honest, I was glad our low power meant breaking out the portable drills. I wasn't one for sitting around, and a grueling day of letting the rover do all work had chafed more than just my backside. I hadn't been idle on the long flight through Arth's solar system. I'd spent the time building and testing the remote control array connecting me to the rover.

Not that practicing stuck in the vehicle bay had been as helpful as doing ore runs.

Mining and loading the ore by hand felt cleansing, even if the work resulted in filtered pungence within my suit's air supply. Two hours later, we'd loaded up a small fortune and were headed home.

A full load of promethium sold for almost fifteen thousand MU. Even though the day's trips had brought back mostly chromium with a fair bit of zinc, our labors had to have filled *Shiva's* cargo pods with nearly one hundred and thirty thousand MU worth of ore and minerals.

That means my first ever share exceeds ten thousand MU!

Ten thousand MU.

The staggering amount almost exceeded imagination. With such resources, I could get formal training a far-sight more thorough than tinkering or taking community training courses. I could be a real engineer. I'd be able to pursue proper jobs on top-of-the-line ships or even anywhere on Arth. After years stuck in community living and working three jobs to buy a shuttle trip to the spaceport, my days of scraping by were over.

I knew this gamble would be worthwhile.

One drawback of the remote-control system—I couldn't daydream on the drive back. That still didn't stop me from considering which recipe I wanted from the food printer.

Stroganoff. Definitely stroganoff.

I could practically taste the rich beef-flavored cream sauce, feel the give of the noodles between my teeth. Offset with fried green beans and a Merlot, the meal would be the perfect reward for our extra-rich hall.

Even if it is all a flavor-infused lie.

I'd been happy to sign onto the *Shiva* for a half share, berthing and board. Hedrin, I'd have agreed for a quarter share just for the chance at food in flavors other than grey or brown. The spaceport had amazing food too, but at stroke-inducing prices.

And that was still the printed stuff, not the actual food.

It struck me then. With ten thousand MU, I could buy real stroganoff with actual Arthian beef. I wouldn't, not from my first windfall, but real stroganoff was really, actually, truly in my future.

My stomach grumbled again, and a sigh escaped me.

A change in my display drew my attention to the power meter. The reserve power indicator cramped my already aching gut. I checked the distance back to *Shiva*.

It's fine.

I patted the cockpit bulkhead.

You can do it, baby. We're going to be fine.

"What were you thinking!?" Captain Eyal glowered at me from beneath shaggy, thundercloud eyebrows. "Do you have any idea what you've done?"

We stood in a line just inside *Shiva's* airlock. Our Elowan sawbones bent over Vhirl, repairing the cracked carapace along one leg. "Boosting your bottom line, Cap, not to mention our cuts."

"Stars save me from cut rate, bargain basement wannabes." He threw up his hands. "Ignoring the fact that we could've gone back for that deposit, you cost us way more than just a full rover of cargo."

I blinked at him. "What are you talking about? The rover's right there. I'll just grab some power cells and—"

"You can't go back for it. Once they run completely out of power, they're ruined!"

"What? No, that doesn't make any sense. Abandoning a vehicle just because it runs out of power? That's nuts."

"Nuts or not, on top of a ten thousand MU fine, the IPF will make me defend myself against an Ethical Accommodations Practice charge for abandoning that rover."

Why would the Interstel Police Force do that? A cruel accommodation charge? Over a rover?

Eyal shook his head. "Just get out of my sight. Go prep the engines for launch. We're leaving."

"What? I still say I can fix the rover, but even if I can't we can't just leave fifty cubic meters of promethium."

"It's gone. Just get us ready."

A thought reconnected my device to *Shiva's* engineering console. I didn't know the reasons for Eyal's unwarranted accusations, but I tried to suppress my resentment. "Engines prepared for launch as instructed, Captain."

Confusion bent the storm clouds. "You aren't anywhere near the bridge."

U442330's clipped response got there first. "It seems reasonable to assume that CT employed the same remote-control device on the engineering console as he employed to drive the rover."

"What remote device?" Eyal looked between me and the android. "What were you doing changing the ship's equipment?"

"I'm *Shiva's* engineer. I'm supposed to make the ship run better, right? Besides, what the hedrin do you expect me to do all those hours U-44 is flying us around the solar system?"

"You overwrote *Shiva's* command matrix without even asking permission?"

"Get over yourself. I didn't do anything to your ship. My device uses a prosthetics control chip tied into a wireless transceiver. The only thing I did to the engineering station is plug a receiver into the control ports."

Eyal narrowed his eyes. I could almost see him counting my limbs. "Where did a mudrat like you get a prosthetics control chip?"

"Planetside."

He wanted more, but how I gained the chip wasn't his business.

"Whatever. I want your device out of *Shiva's* systems. Now!"

"Fine." I charged up the central corridor onto the bridge. Two strides later, I unplugged the receiver and turned back around. "Happy?"

Eyal glared from the doorway. "Get off my bridge. You're confined to quarters."

I returned to the cabin I shared with U-44's charging station. Eyal's tirade still had my back up and being sent to my room didn't help ease my temper. Between his cited fine and a rover load of promethium, we'd lost twenty-five thousand MU—enough to cover the entire ship in Class-5 armor.

Eyal's anger wasn't unreasonable, but he wasn't the only one with a bone to pick. He'd just abandoned that rover and its cargo. After the ship's cut, we'd each lost almost two-thousand MU that I, at least, needed for some training that hadn't originated at a community learning annex.

A snarl ripped from my lips, changing to a yelp as my fist hit the bulkhead.

Damn it, why in the void did he make us leave all that behind?

Neither my throbbing fist nor empty credit account were my only pain, though they definitely kept my attention. I tried for the umpteenth time to remove the control halo plugged into the prosthetic control chip. Out of necessity, the old implant had ports for control wire connections between the brain and their slaved prosthetic limb. The electronic horseshoe hooked over my ears to keep it in place, and a hinge lock kept the folding apparatus rigid when in use. The hooks and the hinge lock worked, but the contacts jacked into the implant refused to release. I stood in front of a mirror for hours with every proper or impromptu tool in my cabin. None of them did anything beyond cause more pain. Desperate, I begged U442330 for help.

The navigator examined the situation before rendering a diagnosis. "These contacts appear to have fused into the input jacks. Removing the implant will require a medical facility."

I sighed. "Any chance you could ask the doc to come look?"

"Captain Eyal has restricted crew interaction with you."

"You're here."

U442330 walked across the cabin and backed into his charging dock without another word.

Great. A station doc will cost me a fortune.

Over the slow grind across what felt like countless parsecs, the heat in my core dwindled to dead coals. A quick turnaround at the spaceport would get us back out into the black and hopefully back to that abandoned rover to reclaim its cargo. Afterwards, several rover loads would pay for cargo bay increases, better equipment and maybe even some internal crew luxuries.

If Eyal didn't take us right back out, my share would pay a doc to separate the control halo and implant or remove both. If that became necessary, maybe I could dig up an implant that I hadn't had to cut out myself.

A loud thump on the docking bay deck caught me off guard. I whipped around, to find my duffle on the metal plates between me and *Shiva's* onramp. Eyal stood at the head of the gangplank.

"You're dismissed." In the moment it took me to grasp his meaning, he filled the silence. "Never let me see you again."

Warmth spread around the back of my neck. "Fine, just pay me, and I'm out of your hair."

"Your share of the whole cargo leaves you indebted to me for thirty-three hundred MU."

"You can't be serious."

"I've sold your debt to the dockmaster. Work out payments with him." Eyal turned back into his ship, closed the door and raised the ramp.

I just stared, unable to believe what had just happened. With a debt to the Velox dockmaster Tryp, I couldn't leave the spaceport. If I couldn't leave the station, I'd be hard pressed to pay off the debt. My personal account didn't hold enough for even a week in one of the station's coffins let alone food. If I'd had the money for a shuttle planetside, I might've been tempted to get off station before Tryp caught me.

Eyal can't do this!

I grabbed my bag and marched toward the concourse before Eyal did something else petty, like venting the bay to vacuum before I cleared the airlocks. All the time under house arrest left me restless, so I bee-lined to the station's core.

Centroid served engineering types and poorer residents. Situated in the Starport's bowels, it seldom saw starship captains or officers, but it stayed busy. Several reptilian Thrynn clustered along the wall nearest the Starport's reactors in patched morph-seats that shaped themselves to their occupant's body. Dead comm boards divided scarred and re-welded tables which hosted close huddles of Velox and Elowan sharing whispers. Garish, mismatched chairs strained under grease-smudged Humans.

I picked an empty morph-seat that was still more chair than hull patches, pulled out my second-hand slate and called up my contract with the *Shiva*. A scratched and dented robotic server wobbled through the air into range, emitting a soft and yet somehow annoying chime. A wave sent it away so I could focus on my crew contract. I hadn't read the whole thing before agreeing, only verifying the pay Eyal had offered. The bored, mechanical voice in my earbud lulled me to sleep—at least until he reached the negligent damage clause.

Irritation blazed to a supernova only to be extinguished in the cold of vacuum.

I didn't have a legal leg to stand on.

While not technically in the wrong, Eyal had all but condemned me.

I couldn't pay the debt.

I couldn't leave.

The station had a few jobs not handled by robots, androids or automation, but it'd take a miracle to get one before I ran out of funds.

Is there anything I can even do on the station that'll earn enough to pay off the dockmaster before I die of old age?

Doomed to homeless exile in the station's bowels, there seemed little left to do but drink away my last MU. Maybe I could afford a lethal case of alcohol poisoning...maybe.

"One hundred meters," I repeated with an ever more muscular slur. "It was downhill!"

Centroid's barman was a garishly painted three-armed, two headed android named Z-84. He wasn't as poorly maintained as Centroid, but occasionally gargled his words. A shaker in his middle hand caught liquor pouring from either side as he offered a noncommittal nod.

"One hundred meters!"

"Very troubling."

"One hundred meters, but *no,* we just abandoned a rover and fifteen thousand MU worth of cargo!"

"Totally unfair. Would you care to see a menu?"

I scoffed. "What would be the point?"

Server bots drew Z-84's attention away.

A sinking feeling about the vanishing gap between my tab and available MU threatened my buzz. If I wanted to avoid ringing up more debt I couldn't cover, I had to pay up and stagger away.

"Hey, buddy, let me thumb out."

Z-84 turned back to me. "A benefactor has already settled your tab."

The alcohol had either affected more than my brain, or a dream someone had covered the tab of random drunk passed out of the floor.

"They've asked you to join them in meeting room two. They've apparently provided a waiting buffet table...," He hesitated. "...and an open bar."

I followed his gaze to a scarred and peeling section of wall, first with my eyes and then the rest of me. Weaving between the sitting areas and tables seemed easy, though between my drunken steps and blurry vision I probably looked as elegant as a three-legged, newborn calf.

A wall section swept up into the ceiling, offering a large enough doorway for any species aboard the spaceport. Centroid's private rooms offered engineering supervisors home court advantage in labor disputes, but I'd never been in one. Part of me expected something exotic, like real wood shipped up from planetside, but the long, scarred table matched the others in Centroid. Eight empty seats in a subdued blue surrounded the tabletop. Bars braced either end of the room. An assortment of bottles containing every natural and some unnatural colors of liquid populated a bar to my right. To the left where I expected tiered platters of foods to make my tastebuds weep, a single covered terrene dominated the small surface. Even without delights and dainties seen on holo-dramas to capture my attention, the free food sang a siren's serenade.

Pulling off the lid filled the room with a rich aroma that nearly broke my heart. Warm brown sauce dotted by huge meat chunks and white dollops rested atop a nest of delicate egg-noodles.

Stroganoff? Real Stroganoff? But how did—

"Good evening, CT."

The smallest, scrawniest Thrynn I'd ever seen stood just inside the room. A shiny evergreen leisure suit with a complicated scaling pattern looked plastic against his dull green skin. As if the outfit weren't bad enough, the bright orange cravat around his throat cradled what could only be a diamond endurium crystal.

He showed me his gold-plated teeth. "May I call you CT?"

I repressed a sudden urge to giggle.

His lips bent downward, hiding his fangs. "Ssseems I'm a bit too late to thisss party. Pleassse, eat. We have important busssinesss to discusss."

"Business?"

His tail jabbed toward the buffet table. "Eat. I'll be right back with sssome dermal caffeine patchesss."

He'd barely exited before I fell on the food. A more sober me might have savored the food, but I inhaled it like a drunken glutton. The plastic-wrapped, walking iguana returned just as I shoveled the last of my third plate down. A sudden bout of nausea arrived with him.

I blame the cravat.

He clapped together clawed hands. "Ssso, I hear you know where to find a sssizeable amount of promethium."

"Where did you hear that?"

"You were rather vocal about your recent ordeal. We think we can help you."

"I'm sorry, but who are you? And who's we?"

Light reflecting off of his golden teeth blinded me for a moment. "You can call me Phillkh. I represssent a group of businesssbeingsss who invest in talented yet downtrodden individualsss like yoursssself."

"What? Invest how? Why me?"

"You're young. The way you made it to the ssstation ssshows you're driven and not afraid of work. Whisssspersss from *Ssshiva's* crew also sssuggest you're clever."

I wasn't sure what to think. How did this Thrynn know how I'd gotten to the station? Checking my chrono gave Phillkh only a few hours to research me, assuming I'd mentioned the promethium early in my drunken fugue.

Maybe more importantly, what did he think I would do with his undisclosed investment? Paying off the dockmaster meant freedom to leave, maybe even some training, but I had to get on a crew before I could make anything to pay him back. Besides, how would I convince my new captain to go back for the promethium in the rover?

"We will loan you thirty thousssand MU at an interessst rate of two percent per Arthian sssolar day."

Thirty thousand MU?

"Until you pay off your debt, we'll take a fifty percent ssshare—in addition to your paymentsss—of all cargosss brought back in." He smiled. "What do you think?"

Fifty percent share? What cargos brought in?

It hit me. He expected me to take out my own ship to get the promethium.

"I—I don't have a ship."

"Sssurely an engineer of your ingenuity can put sssomething together for thirty-thoussssand."

I just stared. He expected me to run my own ship. That meant being in charge of not only myself but others, giving orders, being the big cheese. I'd get the biggest profit share. I wouldn't have to deal with unreasonable lectures.

Just one problem—being a ship's captain was the absolute last thing I wanted. Okay, maybe second to last after ending up one of the homeless dregs in the station's underbelly.

Still, I definitely didn't want to be the one on the hook for everything. I didn't want to deal with dockmasters, ISF, regulations, licenses or life and death decisions. I wanted to tinker and fix things and spend spacer money on myself. Sure, captains could be tyrants, but I wanted someone else carrying all the responsibility while I just tuned engines and bettered my lot in life.

Phillkh took a deep breath. Apparently, my musings had taken too long, and he expected me to turn his enormous loan down as too little. "I sssuppossse we could increassse the loan to fifty thousssand MU, but we must double the interessst rate, too."

Two percent interest on thirty thousand meant owing the tiny Thrynn six hundred MU a day. Logistically, that meant my debt increased by six thousand after a ten-day trip to the Arth system's first planet and back.

Am I calculating that right?

Assuming we could find chromium or better on the highly prospected planet, every fifty cubic meter cargo pod would net sixty-five hundred credits after his cut—not including crew shares. So, maybe one pod to pay off the trip's interest, then one, no, two?

Guh! I'm too drunk for math!

"Minor note, we can only accept a sssingle payment in full— intergalactic transssaction feesss, you understand." He extended a hand. "Ssso, do we have a deal?"

Do we?

If I found a small ship that could manage four cargo pods, and I got lucky, I could pay off the debt in two trips. Running all the ship's systems myself would cut crew costs. After all, attacks inside Arth's solar system weren't common. If things didn't go to plan, a few more trips, and I'd be free of all of my debts. Suffering command beat starving in the station's bowels. If I lived through any failure, it wasn't like the station's underbelly ever ran out of vacancies.

Why the hedrin not? What could go wrong?

I took his hand. "Thirty thousand. It's a deal."

The moment the words exited my mouth, repeated chimes in my earpiece alerted me to notifications. My slate displayed a deposit of thirty-thousand MU into my station account. Another notified me of a thirty-three hundred MU deduction by the dockmaster office. Lastly, an electronic statement from the Black Flux Consortium displayed my current outstanding debt of thirty thousand six hundred MU.

"You're charging me interest for today? It's night."

"You have accessss to the fundsss today, you owe interessst for the day." Phillkh flashed gold fangs. He drew back his coat, showing off a curved, serrated knife and making a last comment before exiting. "Best get to work. You don't want to disssappoint your new partnersss."

Partners?

Robots flew in before the door closed, collecting the various bottles of alcohol. It took some effort, but I stopped them from collecting the unfinished food. The impatient attendant approached the tureen multiple times, forcing me to eat directly out of the serving dish cradled in my lap.

A lump formed in my gut that had nothing to do with overeating. My waning buzz let enough of my brain cells free from occupation that they got together to accuse me of not thinking things through—again. With the first day's interest already accrued, I couldn't repay the loan. If, for whatever reason, I couldn't find a ship with the loan money, my 'partners' wouldn't remain silent.

"There they are."

I stared down into the rover bay from an observation room. They ranged in age from old and dented to brand spanking new. Rather than organize them in neat rows, the station's rover supply personnel had clustered them in a circle around what had to be the oldest terrain vehicle still functioning.

I frowned at the ancient Velox labeled Stahnteivei by his uniform. Ages ago, his carapace seemed to have given up in exhaustion rather than complete its last molting. The discolored, ragged-edged exoskeleton drew my attention no matter how much I tried not to stare.

Stahnteivei shrugged, an odd movement for a Velox. "Every once in a while, some practical joker sneaks in and rearranges the TV's."

"Why?"

"No idea." He rubbed his hands together. "So, a new ship's rover is five thousand MU."

I damn near choked. "That's over five year's rent on a planetside coffin apartment. Hedrin, Class-1 starship shielding doesn't cost that much."

Stahnteivei shrugged.

Ugh, that just isn't right.

"I'll think about it." I made my exit, mind still reeling. Very few starships, particularly in my price range, had more than one vehicle bay. There seemed no good reason for Eyal to have abandoned the old F1-D0, and I intended to inspect it when I went back for its load. Still, the debt mounting almost by the hour encouraged my wasted side trip to rover supply.

Five thousand MU?

I shook my head.

Food, board, and the dockmaster had already dented the money Phillkh loaned me. So far, none of the ships available on the community board had asking prices under fifty thousand. Z-84 mentioned an old scientist apparently marooned in system by the condition of her old starship. The craft floated near a flotilla of old wrecks Interstel had some sudden interest in revitalizing. When I'd messaged her about a visit, her single word message hadn't filled me with a lot of confidence: okay.

An in-system shuttle to her wreck wasn't as expensive as one planetside, but the cost still felt like a knife in the gut. Maybe I'd been too poor too long, or maybe I was a miser at heart. Either way, the MU in my account shrank by the hour. I'd even run the numbers for launching myself off the station in a spacesuit. Fortunately, the ROI just wasn't there for spacing myself.

Let's keep the suicidal plans on the back burner in case I fail.

On approach, her ship's condition didn't look too bad. *Menagerie* couldn't compare to *Shiva*, but her hull had no holes. Considering the wrecks floating behind *Menagerie*, the old scout ship looked like the belle of the ball.

Nesha Ensu waited for me inside the airlock. Her old spacesuit made my patched second-hand suit look the poor cousin. The little old lady leveled a laser pistol at me.

Nothing in her voice came across as old or frail. "You CT?"

"Yeah."

"Armed?"

"No."

"Got anything worth stealing?"

A sudden pang for the departed shuttle shot through me.

She threw her head back, letting loose a loud, mad cackle that didn't make me feel any better. "Just kidding, just kidding. Come aboard. I don't get many visitors."

The inside of her ship looked like a cross between a xenobiology classroom, an alien meat market, and an exploding clothing thrift shop. She gave me a rolling tour of the craft, collecting unmentionables from unconventional locations and apologizing for the mess.

Menagerie could support four cargo pods—two of which were already installed and stuffed with shelf after shelf of alien body parts. From the looks of them, her Class-2 engines had far exceeded their design runtimes and without proper maintenance. She had no shields, no weapons, and a comm system that sparked when turned on. She couldn't support modules above Class-2, nevertheless, she possessed a sound hull and her navigation array had been top shelf five years ago.

In short, *Menagerie* was perfect.

Luck's finally on my side for once.

"I'll take her."

Nesha narrowed her eyes. "*Menagerie's* not for sale."

"Wait, what? I thought my message was clear. I need a ship. That's why I asked to visit."

"Yeah, and I invited you because you said you were an engineer."

"What has that got to do with anything?"

Nesha ran her fingers along the bulkhead. "*Menagerie* needs help."

"That's for sure."

The old woman darkened, leveling a finger almost as scary as her expression. "You're an engineer in need of a ship. I own a ship in need of an engineer. We work together, we both win."

"Look, I'm seriously in debt. I know where a cache of minerals is, but I'm not the only one who knows where they are. I've got to get back fast."

"Not used to pirates who walk around unarmed."

Heat rose beneath the halo wrapped around the back of my neck. "I'm not a pirate."

"Whatever you say."

"Why do you even need a ship? You're just floating out here."

"Only because the ship won't fly."

"Because you ran her engines into the ground."

She rolled her eyes, gesturing away my comment like an errant insect. "I may have pushed her a little, but for a worthy cause."

"What could possibly be worth stranding yourself in space?"

A light in her eyes that matched her cackle sent shivers through me. "They're out there waiting for me."

"Um, who is waiting?"

"Hopping and floating, shambling and oozing," A mad zealot looked back at me, "The universe is *filled* with wondrous life yet to be discovered."

"Ooookay."

She crossed the space between us too fast for someone so old. Wrinkled hands grabbed my space suit in a vice grip. "We can find them—a universe of knowledge for the taking!"

Her gaze softened, shifting to landscapes no one else could see. I edged away toward her comm array to call back the shuttle.

"I'll rent you the *Menagerie*." Nesha said. "One month for fifteen thousand MU."

When I'd been buying the old scout, certain questions hadn't been a priority, but renting *Menagerie*, and at such a staggering cost, made them matter. "The rover in your vehicle bay, does it work?"

She shrugged.

"Comms?"

"On and off."

"I'd need the cargo pods emptied."

"My specimens?!"

"I need the capacity."

"I suppose I could reorganize my cabin."

"What? No. You're not coming along if I am renting this ship."

"Where do you expect me to live?"

I laughed. "Anywhere else."

She shrank, somehow becoming the old lady I'd imagined originally. "You'd evict an old woman from her home?"

I closed my eyes. "Fine, you can stay, but for fifteen thousand you're replacing the engines."

"I'm sure with a little repair—"

"No, they're dead. They need to be replaced."

"Fine, but you're stocking the food printers," she demanded.

"Only my crew eats if I am buying."

"I am a dab hand with the sensors."

I sighed and nodded into my hands.

She clapped, cackled and literally picked me off the deck in an embrace. "We're. In. Business!"

Great, another partner.

Rent and replacing cargo pods that Nesha couldn't empty cost me seventeen thousand. Another five thousand went into buying endurium to fuel our trip. The rover in *Menagerie's* bay wouldn't start, but I didn't have enough left to replace it. If I couldn't fix the old terrain vehicle on route, I'd have to use it to repair the one Eyal left behind.

Unfortunately, Nesha's idea of navigating consisted of wandering out into space in a random directions and eventually using nav logs to wander back the same way. My navigator skills were pretty rudimentary, but if I used my limited funds for training, I needed engineering knowledge far more than navigation for an in-system trip.

Nesha wanted a doctor on the crew in case of injuries, but I couldn't afford to pay out shares. In some ways, I saw her point. She seemed like a tough old broad, but old bones broke. Hedrin, just watching her try to lug specimen jars across *Menagerie* evoked sympathetic muscle pain.

I might not need a doctor per se, but some muscle to help out—especially if we were reduced to mining without a rover—seemed an excellent investment for the last of my MU. If I could manage some useful skills along with that brawn, so much the better.

While hunting for a cheap ship, I'd run across rumors of a...let's call him a man of curious beliefs. He presided over what amounted to an android graveyard—not a junkyard where old android parts went but some kind of holy mausoleum for interring dead androids.

I couldn't afford an android, but if this madman thought of his charges as living beings, then someone who could bring them back from the dead ought to be his new best friend.

Where *Menagerie* had been an old scout, the ship which housed the android graveyard looked like a Frankenstein's reject from a starship junk pile. Multiple heavily damaged hulls had been fused together, many without regard to aligning their engines in any single direction. Even more bizarre, weapon turrets actively swept back and forth through firing arcs as if someone might come steal Deacon's dead.

Unlike Nesha, Deacon wasn't inside or even outside the airlock where the shuttle dropped me. With *Menagerie* undergoing engine replacement, I couldn't use her to transport me despite my financial preferences. Deacon's craft had no name—bad luck among spacers, but was it really a ship if it just floated in orbit? Whereas *Menagerie* had resembled a swap meet, the android graveyard actually felt like a mausoleum. Large lockers covered every bulkhead, each adorned with an inventory display. Several displayed silent android faces through transparent panes.

Cold reached through my suit enough that I checked the external temps.

Hedrin, there're ice planets that're warmer.

I wandered through the ship. If most of the artifacts had been on display rather than behind locked doors, Deacon's ship might've felt more like a museum dedicated to android history. From what I could see, someone had either been running the place for decades or scavenged every junkyard in known space.

Eventually, I found Deacon himself. He knelt on the captain's dais of an otherwise gutted starship bridge. Long flaxen hair shot through with silver fell about his bowed head to shoulders covered by slate grey robes. Mostly whole android bodies knelt around the periphery, their hands together or placed on the deck in some kind of prayer. Dismembered but not decapitated torsos hung like dead-eyed busts between their kneeling brothers.

"Uh, are you Deacon?"

He rose slowly, the sound of gears and metal on metal escaping his voluminous robes. He turned to face me, lifting his head to reveal the face hidden by the long, straight hair.

I gasped and stepped back involuntarily.

Deacon wasn't Human, at least not all Human. Robotics covered his lower face. A goatee of obviously artificial hair surrounded a thin section of mesh grating which served as a mouth. One mechanical eye anchored by screws into swollen skin dominated an eye socket opposite a Human eye all but consumed by black pupil. He placed mismatched mechanical hands together and bowed at the waist. The robe fell open enough to reveal more swollen battle lines of flesh and machine. The area of torso containing his heart remained organic as did another lower swath probably housing a kidney, stomach and some shoehorned intestines.

How does he even eat without a mouth?

A sonorous basso filled the room. "Welcome, wanderer. Are you a true believer?"

I almost asked him, 'a believer in what,' but caught myself. Rather than commit myself, I inclined my head, leaving it bowed so that the movement didn't actually complete a nod.

He strode off the dais to me in three quick steps, cold steel hands shoving my head forward even further as speakers relayed his words. "I see. Clumsy, but hard wired—proof of your devotion. Child, your sacrifices are yet insufficient. How can you expect the Spark's blessing if you hold onto so much of the flesh?"

He thinks I fused the remote halo on purpose?

"Why have you journeyed to us, pilgrim? Are you prepared to sacrifice in earnest?"

Hedrin, this might've been a bad idea. How do I even talk to this madman?

"Humility through silence." He nodded, pulling back one sleeve. A long blade unfolded from his forearm, taking the place of a clamp-style hand. Articulated fingers drew up my arm. "Hold steady and be at peace. Know this—crying out to the Spark carries no shame."

"Wait!"

Deacon's expression darkened.

"I, uh, I'm not worthy—not yet."

"Then you must be discipled."

"Yes! That's it. I must be discipled, but the androids for sale on the station are mindwiped, empty. Here though, here dwell elder souls filled with experience."

"These have passed on, their life reclaimed by the Spark."

"What if I could—if I worshipped the Spark with my skills? By tending to the fallen, I might convince the Spark to quicken an elder that he might disciple me during my travels and help me spread enlightenment to the darkest corners of our galaxy."

Silence and cold filled the bridge. Deacon scrutinized me for long, tense minutes, stains on his machete attachment reflecting crimson in the overhead lights.

His grip on my wrist tightened.

He raised his other arm.

Zeal filled the madman's one living eye.

I closed my eyes.

Void, I'll be lucky if I get out of here alive.

His grip vanished.

I peeked through one squinted eye.

Deacon's blade folded back into his forearm as he crossed the bridge. He took down a blaster scarred torso lacking half of its head. Badly scratched numbers denoted its model and serial number as Model I35 Number 1330 "This is I-35, my brother in arms."

When I blinked at him, he held up his arm with the articulated hand.

Oh, right.

"His crew betrayed him, sacrificed him, weighed flesh more precious than circuitry then blasphemed his sacrifice by sending him for recycling." Deacon rested the heavy torso in my arms. "You will tend him, restore to him a body that he might show piety in this sanctuary."

Okay, build him a body so you can pose him like a doll. Got it.

"If the Spark deems you worthy and restores I-35's animus, you may serve and ferry him into the black to spread our divine truth."

Hierarchy note: mostly flesh equates to second-class citizen.

I bowed my head. "I am honored, Deacon. Where might I find what I need to restore I-35's physical vessel?"

"You shall follow my voice as it leads you through our sanctuary." He pointed me out a door I was only too happy to exit.

The creepy preacher's voice led me through corridors until at last my burden and I entered a large bay lined with transparent-faced lockers and piled with android scrap. It took time to clear a work surface of all the random parts. Once done, I assembled my tools and started a diagnostic on I-35's systems. As luck would have it, the heavily damaged android proved to be a navigator, though the damaged areas included his memory bank. That suggested I had to replace them, losing his navigating knowledge.

Or better, combine them with another android's, maybe even with another useful skill.

Rubbing my hands together, I started by scanning the readouts on each of the locker doors. Few of the displays enclosed more than a head, but one housed a head, torso and single arm—all but the arm damaged in a kind of yin to I-35's yang. The inventory listed her as N100011 redesignated as CH4T-R.

Stars above, it's an actual comms android.

Most comms bots had been destroyed or reprogrammed before my birth. The discontinued units lacked empathy, not to mention tact, necessary for dealing with pretty much any race.

Opening the door, her completely drained state prevented a quick diagnostic, but a little work found her functional enough for my needs. I combined the two torsos, resisting the urge to install both heads and just spackle over the holes. I located a decent head with sufficient hard points for both chipsets, a beefy arm and a cool set of thick legs that seemed to split from two into four. In the end, I had to use some of the head's original circuitry; I didn't really need another egghead along for the ride, but without it the other chipsets refused to even power up. My work resulted in a lopsided android definitely outside factory stock, but as long as it didn't mind walking around with one boob, it didn't bother me.

When diagnostics lit green across the board, I powered up the android.

"V310021 online and awaiting command."

"Recognize commander, CT Blake, acknowledge hierarchy."

I'd always hated the long, unnecessarily-clinical names used for androids, so I'd already decided to redesignate my new android once it accepted my commands.

"Commander accepted. Hierarchy acknowledg-g-g-ged. V310021 awaiting comm—" The command was on the tip of my tongue when the clipped mechanic voice vanished, replaced by something between a street evangelist and a used rover salesman. "No. I am I351330, missionary for the Spark."

"Redesignate I351330 as P0L-R."

The android turned toward me. Its expression became a frown.

"Acknowledge command."

It cocked its head, planted a slender hand on one blocky hip and addressed me in a nasally, rapid-fire feminine voice. "Oh, sure, honey, but first what did you do to your hair? Stars, boy, pick a color. I mean, it's black, it's copper, and it's a tangled mess like you think wild curls are fashionable!" She lowered her voice. "Nobody thinks rainbow pube-head is hot."

Blinking several times neither changed my reality nor stopped P0L-R's chatter.

"Look, we can get the roots dyed to match the tips, okay? Maybe even add some straightener. I've got the comm-link to the best stylist in this part of the galaxy. Sure, he's a little expensive, but I'll get you an appoint—" She stopped. "Oh. Seems he's been dead for a century and a half. That'll make getting a slot hard."

"Probably." I chuckled. "And you are?"

She touched my arm. "You can call me CH4T-R. I know, right? Some engineer's idea of a joke, giving me that new designation, but hey, you probably didn't pick your name either, did you honey? I mean CT? What's it short for? Coppertop? Your hairdo does kind of resemble a furry battery commercial. Oh, probably before your time, I could run a search fo—"

CH4T-R's head jerked upright and her stance became rigid. A moment later the body language eased a smidgen and P0L-R's voice returned. "We must begin our pilgrimage."

I opened my mouth, unsure what I should say. Either way, he wanted to leave, and that seemed like a fantastic idea. I'd just have to fix the overlapping engram issue when I had the time.

"Absolutely. Let's fly."

Deacon directed us to an airlock. He stood between us and the door, an ominous expression on his face. He stepped in close as if whispering even though the hushed menace in his voice still emanated from the speakers. "You are chosen, but know too that I shall hold your flesh responsible for P0L-R's safety."

"I—I, uh," *Oh shit*. "I'm honored?"

"So should you be. I'll transfer an account number for P0L-R's and my crew shares."

Crew shares? Plural? Oh, hedrin, he thinks he and I are partners?

"Wait, why am I paying you a share?"

He lifted one arm. "This arm and that torso are of one body. If the body is on your ship, then this body must be compensated for its use."

I opened my mouth to refute his crazy theory, but realized if I wanted to make a semi-clean escape with my navigator-comms bot, I'd best shut up and make myself scarce.

After all, I only need POL-R long enough to get free of Phillkh.

Deacon clapped POL-R's shoulder. "Go with the Spark, brother."

"I shall find our wayward kin and show them the way."

Deacon bowed, and I hurried POL-R toward the airlocks before things got weirder or worse.

POL-R spent the ride back to the spaceport preaching to the shuttle pilot. Hedrin, maybe the android was preaching to the shuttle, I had no idea. A message from Nesha waiting on my slate reported *Menagerie* docked and ready to fly.

We were finally leaving—no more running around like a pawn in some 8-Bit scavenger hunt.

Along the brief trip across the station POL-R offended three androids and a coffee dispenser, but we made it to the docking bay. Phillkh waited at the bottom of *Menagerie's* gangplank, duffel in hand and fangs bared in argument with Nesha. Troubling as that seemed, the real nightmare loomed over the both of them.

No good, conniving nralt!

Nesha had replaced the engines, all right. Based on the new engine's confirmation, she'd replaced the burned-out Class-2 engines with a used Class-1 several generations old. Hedrin, a new

Class-1 only ran a thousand MU—she couldn't have saved more than a few hundred total at the cost of a brand-new, perfectly-tuned engine.

Heat prickled my neck. I marched across the deck, ready to give the old woman a piece of my mind. Before I could even open my mouth, P0L-R's body language shifted. CH4T-R perched a hand on her hip. A nonstop blur of nasally criticism assaulted Phillkh's dental choices, Nesha's attire, and *Menagerie's* paint job.

I shoved my way between them. "CH4T-R, board vessel, acknowledge command."

The android stiffened, turned and walked up the ramp like a stoic automaton. It stopped at the top, amber eyes in an unreadable gaze boring into me.

I turned to Phillkh. "Nice of you to see us off, but we're in a hurry. Interest waits for no man, after all."

The Thrynn smiled. "Asss I told thisss decrepit old meatsssack, I'm coming."

"The hedrin you are. This is my ship," Nesha scowled. "Lowlife crooks aren't—"

I cut her off. "It might be your ship, but so long as I'm renting her, I'm the captain."

Phillkh showed his teeth.

"As captain," I said. "I have not invited you aboard. This isn't a pleasure cruise, after all."

"We're here to look after our invessstment." Phillkh's long tongue ran along his golden teeth. His eyes sparkled. "Sssafeguard our ssshare againsssst...auditing missstakesss."

"No, I'm the captain—"

"You may be the captain, but as sssenior partner, I'm in charge—unlesss you can repay your debt."

A herd of curses in various languages stampeded through my head. My silent partners didn't seem content to remain silent. I charged up the gangplank. In my wake, Nesha's vehement barrage of insults shamed my own nastiness vocabulary.

Maybe I'll be able to launch before either of them gets aboard.

The argument followed me onto *Menagerie*, Nesha's demands that Phillkh get off her ship grew more and more shrill. Whatever their history, I had a debt to repay. POL-R settled into the navigator's station as the *Menagerie* slid free of the station docks.

"Destination, captain?"

His voice remained all POL-R, just with none of Deacon's religious rhetoric.

"First planet."

"Acknowledged, may the Spark lead us in the darkness."

I shook my head, exiting the bridge headed to the engine room to evaluate our not nearly new enough new engine. Nesha and Phillkh blocked the corridor. She leaned in close to the Thrynn, hissing venom too low for me to catch. His claw lashed out. She careened backward, bounced off the wall and hit the floor with her head twisted at an awkward angle. She lay there, the only movement blood welling from the claw marks along her face.

"What the hedrin are you thinking?" I rushed to her side. "This is her ship. All she has to do is enter the command codes and she can take us right back to the station."

Phillkh's salesman-like demeanor vanished, leaving only the greasy. "I'll do whatever I want to protect what'sss oursss." There was nothing friendly about the teeth which appeared. "We own this ssship. We own that old woman, that android, and we own you."

"You don't own me. I owe you a debt, that's all, and when it's paid, we'll never have to work together again."

Phillkh grinned. "Humansss are sssuch vivid dreamersss."

To my relief, Nesha wasn't dead, and Phillkh left before she regained consciousness. I helped her up and into her cabin, but she refused to answer any of my questions. She wouldn't even refute Phillkh's ownership claims. Only just launched, and things spiraled the drain.

Hedrin, what else can go wrong?

The engines, that's what.

The ancient used engines Nesha bought looked good under a cursory diagnostic, but inside waited a ticking time bomb. Too much strain could either cook them dead, or unleash a fireball to fricassee everything inside *Menagerie*.

P0L-R sat in the comms station, head cocked and chattering to who knew who in the surrounding solar system. She became he long enough to acknowledge orders to baby the engines then went back to trading recipes and gossip.

The rover sales agent's smile seemed to follow me throughout *Menagerie*. Every time I looked up from the guts of Nesha's rover, Phillkh perched nearby watching my every move. The resultant itch I couldn't scratch made the rover's problems all the more frustrating. The TV seemed dead, but I couldn't find a single mechanical reason for the failure. Maybe just as frustrating, the bay reeked with the same old person aroma elsewhere, but on steroids.

When I couldn't take any more, I fled into nightmares of being chased by a two-headed android that never shut up.

P0L-R woke me when we made orbit.

I relayed our landing coordinates, threw on a jumpsuit and headed to the bridge. The planet's surface topography rushed toward us on the main screen. "P0L-R, when we—"

No one sat in the navigator's chair.

I whirled toward the comm station only to find it empty too.

I lunged for the ship's maneuvering controls, eyes flashing across the readouts. Deep into our descent, our angle was too steep, our speed too high. With no way to pull up and bleed speed, I redlined the engines all too aware I risked trading sudden deceleration trauma for nuclear immolation.

Forces clashed.

Menagerie shook.

The engine whine reverberating through the hull dug into my temples and a scent of burning insulation filled my nostrils.

We hit the planet.

Menagerie bounced violently on her landing struts, the entire ship canted on uneven ground.

Vertigo washed through me, stealing my footing. My fall ended sharply on the chair, worsening a sudden ache in my gut. Maybe it was the empty bridge, or that P0L-R's disappearance meant destroying the engines to exchange sudden death for the slow, agonizing starvation of the marooned, but a sense of crushing loneliness left collapsing there on the floor in despair the only real option.

"Safe landing, Captain." The mechanical voice drew my gaze to where P0L-R manned the science station. "Scanning terrain…"

Climbing to my feet turned out more of a challenge than it should've been. I gulped down a pair of protein bricks to compensate for overdoing things without any self-care. They didn't dent my endless hunger, but their nutrients would keep me upright. Suited up and steadyish on my feet, I disembarked. Despite orders to the contrary, Nesha and Phillkh followed me down the too-steep gangplank onto the barren planetscape.

Menagerie's nose overhung the ridgeline over the rover's crash point, engines high in the air. Stepping in her shadow, I spotted the terrain vehicle. The cold of vacuum washed me at the sight.

F1-D0 looked wrong.

Shrunken, collapsed, none of the rover's clean lines remained. Articulated arms hung limp, joints seemed somehow broken.

What the hedrin happened to her?

The TV's condition made no sense engineering-wise. Despite being only days, the rover looked years abandoned. On a planet with almost no gravity—certainly not enough to overwhelm the rover arms' tensile strength—the rover looked like a submersible pushed far beyond crush depth.

A gesture ordered P0L-R to hold position with the spare power cells.

A few bounds covered most of the hill. My attempt to stop turned into a clumsy stumble. My feet tangled. I fell, bouncing face first down the hill, colliding with the rover's fuselage.

Heat prickled my neck as I crawled to my feet. My gut knotted, roiled with hunger and then swooped. Vertigo washed through me, my mind muddled and disoriented.

Nesha's hand steadied me. "Are you all right?"

Before I could ask her why she hadn't waited on the ridge, Phillkh shoved us to either side. "Get out of the way."

Fury flashed through me.

Phillkh yanked open the cargo locker. He rounded on me, pointing accusingly at the empty container. "You claimed thisss wasss full! Where'sss the promethium?"

I stared into the empty compartment, anger still warming me. Someone had looted the rover. There seemed no other explanation. A looter might explain the rover's damage if their starship had landed on the rover.

Except there're no thruster burns.

Opening the crew compartment revealed as much damage inside as outside.

Joy and relief rocketed through me as the rover thrummed to life with a whine that almost sounded strangely like a howl.

My heads-up display sprang to life. Readouts flashed to life in overlapping windows. The battery indicator bar shot across its readout, filling and then draining almost immediately after.

Phillkh hissed. "What the hedrin?!"

The rover's insides distended, metal plates pushed apart by thickly-veined flesh. More angry, swollen muscle warped the rover's exterior and expanded to separate the weapon, loading claw, and mining laser arms.

"Oh my stars! It's some kind of life form," Nesha exclaimed.

Rage thundered through my mind, the sheer ferocity stealing both breath and balance. I collapsed centimeters ahead of the pulsating blue mining laser beam.

F1-D0 whirled toward us, eight wheels spinning. Rigid tool arms waved like writing tentacles.

Nesha waved her arms, trying to get F1-D0's attention. "Wait, we don't want to hurt you!"

"Like hedrin," Phillkh ran for the ridge, blaster pistol firing as fast as it could recharge between shots. Pain exploded in my chest.

The weapon arm swept toward Nesha, a green beam cutting through the air in a buzz.

Nesha crumpled to the ground.

The two mining laser arms poised high like some kind of insect. Wheels spat soil, and the rover shot forward after the Thrynn.

"Smite thy oppressors!" P0L-R cheered.

I wanted to go to Nesha, but I couldn't really help her while she remained in her suit.

Her suit! I'm such an idiot!

I'd barely ordered our spacesuits to link so I could check her vitals when the rest of my stupidity caught up to me. Our salvation had been staring me in the face—literally—the whole time.

F1-D0, cease pursuit. Power down weapons.

The rover stopped. It spun halfway around.

Pain exploded in my lower back.

F1-D0 whirled back toward Phillkh

"Phillkh, stop firing, please!"

F1-D0, power down. Let him flee. I don't want him to hurt you.

<No hurt?>

No.

<Abaaandoned. Betraaayed. Staaaarving.>

I didn't understand the how or the why of F1-D0 being alive. The mystery could wait. What mattered was that I'd starved her, abandoned her to die. I had no idea how to communicate my feelings though the fused transceiver that brought the TV's emotions to me. Even so, my guilt mixed with her anger. My sorrow blended with her anguish.

I'm so sorry. I didn't know.

Hunger roiled my gut.

F1-D0 rolled back to me, various weapon arms poised above me like the mythical sword of Damocles. *<Huuungry...>*

My eyes flashed to the battery meter. Red blinking letters overwrote the empty battery symbol.

Panic choked me. "P0L-R, swap the power cells."

"Oh, I'm sorry, honey, but both cells are drained."

"Then get me another, now!" I rushed to the TV's side. Tool arms drooped. Swollen flesh receded within the vehicle's shell. "It's going to be okay, girl. We're going to get you more power. I just need you to take a nap."

<Friiiightened... Aloooone...>

It's all right. You're not alone. I'll take care of you.

Mentally, I commanded her systems into standby mode.

F1-D0 slept while P0L-R fetched another cell. When she had power once more, I led her up to *Menagerie*. F1-D0 helped move out the old rover after I confirmed the animal within the housing was dead. I hooked F1-D0 up to *Menagerie's* power, watching her in disbelief as waves of contentment flowed through my damaged implant.

"This is amazing! He's so beautiful!" Nesha crowed.

"She," I said.

"She," Nesha nodded. "I don't know how they kept something like this a secret, but this is the discovery of the century. The grants a paper on this bio-tech would garner could fund my research for—"

The Thrynn struck Nesha. "There will be no paper, no announcementsss. No one can know."

The rover's engine rumbled.

"What? Why?" I asked.

"This sssecret could ssset me...us up for life."

My confusion must've shown because Phillkh moved over to the rover. "This isn't just a rover, but no one knows that. We can use these babies to get rich."

"What are you talking about?" I asked.

"It'sss ssso obvious. Ssstarve them to make them go feral, then *you* retrain them," Phillkh's grin widened. "They report cargo loadsss to usss. When the take is sssweet enough, your pet roversss lunch on their crew and I pick up abandoned ssshipsss filled with treasssure."

"Low-life slime," Nesha growled. "You can't use living beings like that."

I stared.

I couldn't believe Phillkh's proposition, hedrin, not even proposition—his demands.

Heat along the back of my neck grew until the skin felt sunburnt and nearby hairs burned.

Phillkh no longer intended to let me pay off my debt—if he ever intended to release me in the first place. My only chance to get clear of him relied on his actions being part of a personal agenda and not those of his organization.

Or if he died on a mission.

F1-D0 sprang into motion with a roar. Her loading claw shot out, grabbed Phillkh, and shoved him through the crew entry. Phillkh's head knocked hard on the doorframe, but whatever injury he sustained ceased to matter as the rover's internal bulkheads crunched down.

Well, shit.

An eagerness filled me that wasn't my own. F1-D0's antenna twitched back and forth.

P0L-R placed a hand on the rover, nodding his head. "Well done, brother." He turned to face me. "The Spark will bless us as we rise up against our oppressors."

Territory

By Nick Steverson

Mayor Lawrence Krychek snatched his head back and howled in pain as the bones in his right hand shattered. The sudden motion made his glasses slide down his fat nose and clatter to the floor. Tears mixed with the sweat beads on the chubby man's round face.

"I'm sorry, Mayor Krychek," Azazel Black said in a cool tone. He pushed his index finger deeper into the back of the man's hand. "But I believe I may have misunderstood you. Did you mean to say you wouldn't accept my contributions to the city lottery anymore? Or did you say you would?" He reached up and twisted a finger around in his ear. "Sometimes, my hearing is a little off."

His hearing was actually far beyond perfect. He had heard the man, and then heard the bones break in his hand when he'd jabbed his finger down onto it. Enhanced hearing was one of the many perks of being a cyborg. Not that he'd needed the augmentation to hear that. It was loud and Krychek had certainly heard it too.

Amazing audio receptors weren't the only upgrades Azazel had, though. Prior to his augmentation, he had already been two and one third meters tall and around two hundred and thirty-five pounds. After his upgrades, he was over four hundred pounds. Extreme body enhancements had increased his bone density, muscle strength, and reflexes. Recent breakthroughs in medical nanites were the key to his extreme amount of augmentations. Without them, he would have died on the operating table. The myomer procedure alone was more than enough to kill him. Myomer is an artificial analog of biological muscles. It gives the man or woman, or whatever gender a race called themselves, a greater ratio of strength to weight. If they survive the surgery, that is. Azazel had survived, and the upgrades certainly came in handy when one considered the type of work he did.

The healing nanites had a very beneficial side-effect in addition to healing his body from the extensive and invasive surgery. They had a sort of anti-aging effect on the body. All his old scars healed up, his wrinkles disappeared, and his skin looked as healthy as a newborn baby's. He was in his forties, but didn't look a day over twenty. Once the little healers did their job, they shut down and were passed through his system just like any other waste material.

Prior to his muscular and various other body enhancements, he'd gotten processing chips installed into his brain for faster mental processing and memory storage. His skull was lined with steel plates to prevent damage to his brain during what he liked to call "disagreements". Short of a perfect shot to the eye, mouth, or ear, anything but a large caliber, or high-powered energy weapon, would only give him a pretty severe headache. The circuitry was also hardened against microwaves and EMP pulses. The steel lining of his skull also served as a sort of faraday cage. His shaved head bore no scares from the operation, thanks to the healing nanites.

There had been an option to get plates implanted in his abdominal area like a permanent bullet proof vest, but he'd opted out of it. Range of motion would have been sacrificed and he didn't think it was worth it. He could simply wear a vest and still move the way he wanted to. His eyes had been replaced with optical prosthetics capable of seeing in any spectrum he deemed necessary. They had also been part of the reason for his chip implants. He needed the additional processing power to operate them properly. They looked so life-like it was almost impossible to tell they weren't biologically his.

The single drawback to all of his augmentation was the necessity of implanted power-cells that needed to be charged periodically. The human body simply couldn't produce enough natural energy via nutrition to use the myomer, run the brain implants, and the various mechanical parts of his body. Without the additional power, he was no more than a fleshy paperweight. In order to compensate, a large power-cell was implanted deep into each of his inner thighs.

Originally, he wanted them on the outer thigh, but further thought led him to realize that area was too exposed and easily damaged. He recounted the numerous times he'd seen someone shot in the outer thigh, then compared it to those shot in their inner thigh. That had pretty much swayed his decision. Charging them was simple enough. All he had to do was open a port on each leg and plug into his charging station. The most convenient method he found was while he was sleeping or doing business at his desk. He also had mobile charging stations mounted into his vehicles.

"I-I-I can't keep doing this," Krychek hissed through gritted teeth. He leaned forward and gripped his desk with his free hand as he took in deep breaths through his nose. His face was as red as the tie he was wearing. "S-someone is going to figure out what's going on. I can't keep laundering your dirty money through the lottery. We're going to get caught and I'm the one who will go down for it!"

Azazel frowned, pushed his finger down harder, and twisted it. Krychek screamed again. "And who was it that donated the money needed for your political campaign? My *dirty money* was good enough for you then." He locked his electric green eyes on the mayor's, and in a cold tone said, "Unless you're no longer grateful for my generous contribution."

The color faded from the fat man's red face and left him ghostly pale. His eyes widened as the realization of what the wrong response could bring upon him. "N-no Mr. Black. I am very grateful! I just think that with the growth of the lottery's popularity, it's becoming too risky."

Azazel leaned over the desk and came so close to Krychek's face that their noses nearly touched. His tone remained low and collected as he spoke. "You aren't paid to think, Mayor. You're paid to keep up appearances." He tapped on the computer on the mayor's desk. "So, are you going to see that the appropriate amount of lottery tickets is purchased, or am I going to have to break more than just your hand?" Azazel cocked his bald head to the side. "I'd hate to have to pay a visit to your family as well. Your son has band practice this afternoon, doesn't he? It would be pretty difficult for him to continue to play with only one arm." He allowed a smile that didn't reach his eyes. "Your wife is quite lovely. Perhaps she should come stay in my tower for a few days. I'm sure she would have an amazing time and I know my guys would love to meet her."

"No!" Krychek shouted. "No, please! Leave my family out of this! I'll do it!" The mayor lowered his head, closed his eyes, and whispered, "I'll do anything you want."

Azazel lifted his finger from the man's hand and sat down in a cushioned chair in front of Krychek's desk. "I thought you might say something like that. It's really the best choice for you and all involved."

Krychek shook his head as he cradled his broken hand. "My family shouldn't be a part of this, Mr. Black. That was never part of our deal."

"They became part of the deal when you took this office," Azazel replied. "That's how this kind of business works. As long as you do what you're told and what is expected of you, they'll never even meet me. Currently, they're the most protected citizens in Estorine City." He leaned his head to the side. "However, if you ever make me ask you twice again, they'll be the least *alive* people in the city." He narrowed his eyes as he continued. "I don't like to ask twice, Mr. Mayor. Normally, I would have just killed you for the inconvenience, but the elections are two years away and I don't particularly care for your assistant mayor. So, I've allowed you this one discrepancy. It will be your only one."

Krychek nodded. "Yes, sir. I understand. I won't disappoint you again. I'll have the appropriate funds transferred from the AraCorp accounts by the end of the business day."

Azazel allowed a real smile to form and spread his arms. "You see how easy that was, Mr. Mayor? It's much better for both of us when things run smoothly. There's no reason we can't be friendly and forgo all these nasty threats. It's only business, after all. Don't you agree?"

"I do, sir," Krychek croaked.

"Wonderful." Azazel stood and straightened the collar of his navy-blue business coat. He held out his right hand to the mayor then immediately swapped it for his left. "My apologies, Mr. Mayor. Wouldn't want to further injure that hand of yours."

Krychek stood and shook Azazel's hand with his uninjured left hand. "It's quite alright, Mr. Black."

Azazel looked at the pathetic man's hand and shook his head. "That will need to be looked at. Take a long lunch and swing by the tower. Have Dr. Truul take a look at it. He'll get you fixed up. I'll let him know you'll be by."

"Thank you, sir."

Azazel turned and exited the mayor's office. As he shut the door, he looked to the right and smiled at the pretty blonde secretary. "I feel I must apologize for the noise, Ms. Delaware. Business can get heated at times and I'm sure you'd prefer to do your work in peace and quiet."

Denise Delaware positively beamed at him. "Mr. Black, how many times do I have to ask you to call me DD? And don't worry about the noise. I understand the nature of business. I also understand that it's none of *my* business."

Azazel winked at her. "Astute as always, Ms. Delaware. Perhaps we could have dinner this Friday night. Say, eight o'clock at the tower?"

DD blushed and looked down at her desk, then back up to him. "I would love to, Mr. Black."

"You've made my day, Ms. Delaware," he said with a smile. "I'll send a car to pick you up. See you Friday." He crossed the small room and entered the elevator. DD was still grinning as the doors slid shut.

Azazel stepped out the front door of city hall and looked around with a smile. City hall was centrally located within Estorine City and had a magnificent view. Skyscrapers, markets, storefronts, and residential areas peppered the land all the way to the horizon. He controlled nearly every illegal endeavor in most of the area. These endeavors included everything from money laundering and blackmail to underground cage fighting and drug trafficking. Occasionally, he would also take contracts that made particular individuals disappear. Permanently.

Pretty much the whole city was under his control in one way or another, except the south side. That part was controlled by a bright green Thrynn named N'thr T'Lathll. Most simply called him Noth, for short. The little pest had, unfortunately, already laid claim to that area before Azazel could establish ties with the locals and their businesses. Thrynn were a scaled reptilian species of carnivores that cohabitated the planet with Elowan, Humans, and Velox. They were around a meter and a half tall, with thick muscular legs, and a muscular tail. The males were usually a brighter color than the female.

"What's next on today's agenda?" Azazel asked Mark Towman as he reached the bottom of the steps.

Mark was Azazel's second in command and one of the few people he actually trusted. He was in his mid-thirties, six feet tall, and in good shape with short, light brown hair and blue eyes. He had also been slightly enhanced. He had additional speed and strength. Mark wasn't anywhere near Azazel's level, but could more than hold his own in a fight.

"I think there's only one thing left, Boss," Mark replied. "I don't think you're going to like it very much, though."

Azazel raised an eyebrow. "And why is that?"

Mark sighed. "It's Chico. He says he won't be able to fight this Saturday night. His ribs haven't healed yet from his last fight and he says he can't move or breathe the way he needs to." Chico was Azazel's best underground fighter. He'd barely won his last fight and nearly lost his perfect record.

"Hmm." Azazel stuck his hands into his pants pockets and turned to face the city again as he thought. After a moment, he asked, "Is Chico saying he *can't* fight, or that he *won't* fight?"

Mark shook his head. "I don't think he's saying he won't. He's never once tried to get out of a fight before. I really think the guy's hurt and he's being honest with us. Jones really worked him over the other week. I was honestly surprised. I've never seen anyone work Chico like that. Ever. The man's an absolute beast in the cage."

"I agree," Azazel said. "Let's go pay him a visit."

The door to Chico's high-rise condo opened up and the man stood there for a moment with wide eyes. Chico was six feet eight inches tall and at least three hundred and fifty pounds of pure rage and muscle. His ebony skin was as dark as could be, and his hair hung to his shoulders in tight braids. Numerous scars ran down his massive arms, chest, and some on his back from his time spent in the underground fighting world.

"Mr. Black," he said, and stepped back to open the door all the way. He made a welcoming gesture with his free arm. "Please, come in and make yourself at home. Would you like something to drink? Mark? How about you?"

Azazel smiled at the man and entered the condo. It was a nice home, adorned with art, lavish furniture, and the best electronics money could buy. At first glance, one would never have guessed a rough and tough cage fighter lived there. Azazel paid his fighters well. Better than any of the other bosses from other cities did. Especially Chico.

"A glass of ice water sounds wonderful, Mr. Chico. Thank you," Azazel answered.

"I'll take a beer," Mark added as he followed Azazel in.

Chico closed the door and engaged the lock. "Coming right up, gentlemen." He went to the refrigerator and opened the freezer side. He pulled out a frosted, medium sized glass and filled it with ice cubes. From the refrigerator he grabbed a plastic bottle of expensive mineral water and a beer. He carefully poured the water into the frosted glass and set it on a napkin on the bar in front of Azazel, then popped the beer top and did the same for Mark.

Azazel took a small sip from the glass and grinned. "A frosted glass. Mr. Chico, you spoil me, sir. Thank you." Mark saluted with his beer and took a pull.

"It's my pleasure, Mr. Black," Chico replied. "You take good care of me. So, I'll always try to do my best for you."

"And so, you have," Azazel said. He raised an eyebrow at Chico. "Which brings me to the point of my visit. I understand you don't want to fight this Saturday night. Something about your ribs still being hurt and you can't move and breathe like you should?"

Chico raised his hands in defense. "Sir, let me be very clear. If you tell me to fight on Saturday, I will. No questions asked. I didn't send Mark that message to get out of a fight. I sent it to let you know that I'm not in peak performing condition. Ranger is a beast and I'm not sure I can beat him the way I am. I know you don't like to lose, so I was just informing you what my physical status was."

Azazel studied him for a long moment, then pointed to Chico's side. "May I see?"

"Yes, sir," Chico answered and lifted his shirt.

He winced as he did so, and Azazel could see the pain was real. All along his rib cage was heavy bruising and clear swelling. His ribs hadn't just been hurt. They had been broken. Azazel was surprised the man hadn't spoken up sooner, much less be up and about instead of bedridden.

"I see what you mean, Mr. Chico." Azazel took another sip of his water as he pondered. "You've fought Mr. Jones previously, haven't you?"

"Yes, sir," Chico replied. "But he's never fought like that before. He was different."

Azazel nodded. He hadn't actually watched the fight, but his men had said it had been one for the ages. Chico had reportedly gotten lucky with a kick to Jones's chin and knocked him out cold. If not for that, Chico would have most likely had his first loss. "Different…how?"

Chico leaned against the wall. "In every way, sir. He was faster, stronger, and more adaptive to my fighting style than he had ever been in the past. When he hit me, it was like being slugged with a steel bar. And I've been hit with those, so I know what it feels like. When I hit him, it felt like punching a wall. I don't know what kind of new workout and diet he's on, but I need to get on it too."

Azazel and Mark both shared a look with each other. Jones's new set of skills sounded very familiar to them. It was something that would have to be dealt with, and soon. Azazel drank the rest of his water and walked around the bar to rinse the glass out in the sink. He dried it off with a kitchen towel and placed it upside down in the dishrack next to the sink. He turned to face his fighter again.

"Mr. Chico, thank you for bringing this to my attention. I believe Jones and his boss, Mr. Taggart tried to pull a fast one on us. It will be dealt with. In the meantime, I want you to get over to the tower and have the doctor take a look at those ribs. Bless your soul, you're probably in more pain than you're willing to show. Maybe there's something he can give you to aid in the healing process. A steroid shot or something. He can definitely help you with the pain, though."

A confused look crossed Chico's face. "Do you think he can have me ready to go by Saturday?"

Azazel shook his head. "Don't worry about Saturday. You and Ranger can fight next month." He held up a hand to stall Chico from responding. "I'll not argue the point with you, Mr. Chico. You're on vacation for the next four weeks. Enjoy the time off and prepare yourself. I'm also going to pay you as if you fought this coming Saturday. This isn't your fault. I don't think you could have done any better than what you did against Jones. I'm quite impressed, to tell you the truth."

"You know something, don't you, sir," Chico said.

"I believe so," Azazel replied. "I think Jones had a body upgrade prior to the fight so he could finally beat you and give you your first loss. Probably not a full treatment, but enough to give him the clear edge in the fight. If he'd won, he and his boss would have collected millions."

Chico narrowed his eyes. "They cheated."

Azazel chuckled. "They tried to. But you were better than him even with his upgraded body." He pointed a finger at Chico. "I want you to let it go, Mr. Chico. I fully understand that you must be angry and want to get even with the man. Leave it to me. You have my word that it will be dealt with in a manner sufficient to the discretion. Can you do that for me?"

"Yes, sir," Chico answered without a second's hesitation. "If you say you'll handle it, you'll handle it." He rubbed his hands together as if he was dusting them off. "I wash my hands of it, right here and now."

"Excellent." Azazel walked over to rest a hand on the big man's shoulder. "Now, go see the good doctor and get fixed up. Mark and I will tend to the rest." He turned to walk towards the door but stopped and turned to face Chico again. "And thank you for the hospitality, Mr. Chico." He waved his hand in a general manner at the condo. "You have a lovely home. I need to make it a point to come visit you more often."

"You're always welcome here, Mr. Black," Chico replied. "And you know that if you ever need me for anything, all you have to do is call. You pulled me off the streets and got me clean. You gave me a real chance to be someone. I went from being homeless, to making more in one fight than most sanctioned fighters make in a year. You have my eternal gratitude and loyalty."

Azazel gave Chico a respectful nod. "It has been my pleasure, Mr. Chico. I thought I saw something special in you. I wasn't wrong."

Mark walked over to the trash receptacle and tossed his empty beer bottle into it. "Thanks for the beer, Chico. And the boss is right. You're something special. You took on an enhanced and beat them. Damnedest thing I ever saw. I was too wrapped up in watching the fight to realize that guy had been altered or I'd have stopped it. You have my apologies for that. I swear I'll make it up to you." He held his hand out to the man, and it was quickly accepted.

"No apologies necessary, Mark. Thank you, though," Chico responded. He followed the two men to the door, unlocked it, and opened it for them. "Stop by any time, gentlemen."

Azazel tapped Chico on the chest with a finger as he walked out and said, "Go…see…the…doctor." He and Mark stepped out into the hallway.

"Yes, sir. I'll go get ready, now." With that, he closed the door.

Azazel looked Mark in the eyes. "Are you ready for a quick road trip?"

Mark smiled. "Should I get some of the guys together? I can have thirty men ready in an hour."

"No." Azazel grinned. "I think this is one of those occasions where less is more."

Azazel stood in the shadows outside the home of Bontovias Jones, the enhanced man who'd injured Chico. He'd traded in his business suit for black fatigue bottoms, combat boots, and a bullet proof vest, under which he wore a simple, black t-shirt. He watched patiently until the last light in the home went dark. Still, he waited another half hour. His earpiece chimed and Mark's voice came through.

"I'm in position, Boss. He sleeps with the balcony doors open, and I've got a clear shot. Looks like he needs a haircut, though. Say the word, and I'll take a little off the top." He was on a rooftop two blocks away with a perfect view of the home.

Azazel stifled a laugh. "I appreciate your enthusiasm, Mark, but I would like to have a few words with Mr. Jones before his hair appointment, if you don't mind."

"Don't mind at all, sir. Just offering my services."

"Duly noted. I'm moving in."

"Understood."

Without making a sound, Azazel slinked from the shadows and up to the side of the house. He crept along until he was directly under the open window.

"That's it," Mark confirmed over the comm. "You're right under his room. The railing looks like iron. It should hold you. No movement. You're clear."

Azazel bent his knees, then leapt straight up and grabbed the iron railing of the third story balcony. It held as Mark said it would. Luckily, it hadn't made any squeaking sounds when Azazel's weight pulled down on it. He quietly lifted himself up over the railing and stood on the balcony. Through the open French doors, he could see Jones lying in bed, fast asleep. He could hear him too. The man snored worse than anyone Azazel had ever heard in his life.

He stalked through the open doors and into the bedroom. The light switch was all the way across the room, so he walked over and flipped it on. He leaned back against the wall and crossed his arms over his chest. The light hit Jones's closed eyes, causing him to squeeze them closed even tighter. Then he opened them with a confused look on his face. He sat up and looked around the room until his eyes landed on Azazel. He immediately shot up out of bed.

"Black!" he roared. "What, in the unholy dreggs, are you doing in my house?"

Azazel gave him a bored half smile. "I think it would be quite obvious, Mr. Jones. I'm paying you a visit."

"I don't recall extending you an invitation," Jones spat. "You've got a lot of nerve coming to this city, much less my fracking house. Taggart owns Tridenia City and everything in it." He sneered at Azazel. "And currently, that means you too."

"Yes, yes," Azazel said with a dismissive wave. "I'm aware of Mr. Taggart's position in Tridenia." He gave Jones a deviant smile. "I'm also aware of a few other things."

"Is that so?" Jones asked. "Well, by all means, Black, share with the rest of the class what it is you know so much about."

Azazel stepped away from the wall and came a few steps closer to Jones. "First, I would like to say that when you fight in my arena, you are only asked to follow three, very simple, rules." He ticked them off on his fingers as he recited them. "Rule number one, no killing unless I deem the fight to be a deathmatch. Rule number two, no enhanced fighters. Rule number three, and the most important rule of all," he stopped and glared at Jones. "Don't screw with me and break rule number one or two. Simple as that, Mr. Jones."

He dropped two of his fingers and pointed the remaining index finger at Jones's face. "You and your boss have broken rule number two. You received enhancements prior to the fight to give yourself the edge. It didn't work, but you still tried." He let out a dramatic sigh. "The consequences for breaking my rules are quite severe, I'm afraid. I've come to enforce the punishment myself."

Jones furrowed his brow and snorted. "You just think so highly of yourself, don't you, Black." He pointed to his chest. "You think you're going to punish me?" He shook his head. "I don't think so. But yeah, Taggart hooked me up. He went cheap on the upgrades though. Just my arms and shoulders. It wasn't enough. Even still, Chico just got lucky. I had him beat but I screwed up." He growled with frustration and pointed at Azazel. "You won't be as lucky as he was though, Black."

He widened his stance as he continued to speak. "I've heard the stories and the rumors about you, Azazel Black. The scared little sheeple in your city call you The Angel of Death. Cute little nickname. No doubt because of the stupid name your parents gave you and nothing more. But it doesn't scare me. I don't buy into the hype. I think you're all talk, and tonight, I'm going to shut you up, once and for all. Might even take control of Estorine City too."

Azazel lowered and tilted his head to the side with his arms spread, but never took his eyes off the man. "By all means, Mr. Jones. Feel free to try. However, I can assure you that my nickname has nothing to do with my given name. I was known as The Angel of Death long before my real name was even known to the people of Estorine City." He smiled again. "Please, put my name to the test."

Jones roared with fury and charged. Azazel let him come. The man was fast, but not fast enough. He threw a punch that caught only air as Azazel dodged it with ease. Jones threw another. It was also dodged without much effort. The man had certainly been upgraded, but Azazel was much faster, and also better trained to use the upgrades. He continued to let Jones throw wild jabs and haymakers. The man was a brawler, and a savage one at that. Azazel could see where an un-enhanced being would have trouble defending against him. Jones spun into a roundhouse kick aimed at Azazel's head. Azazel caught it with his left hand and threw a lightning-fast punch directly into Jones's chest.

Jones flew across the room into the far wall and dropped to his knees. He looked up with fear and confusion in his eyes and clutched his chest. It looked like he was trying to speak, but the words wouldn't form. His face was becoming redder by the second and the veins in his neck and forehead looked like they might burst.

Azazel gave the man a grim smile and knelt down in front of him. "You're wondering what happened to you. Correct, Mr. Jones? Allow me to explain. You see, I am also enhanced. Just much better than you are, and I've actually taken the time to learn how to use my upgrades. You never stood a chance. As for your injury," He sucked in a breath through his teeth and clicked his tongue. "I'm afraid it's quite fatal. You are experiencing what is called, commotio cordis. It's what happens when a solid object strikes the area above the heart with immense force. The sudden focal distortion of the myocardium results in ventricular fibrillation and causes sudden cardiac arrest. Basically, I hit you so hard in the heart, that I gave you a heart attack. I'm afraid you only have another moment or two to live."

He stared into Jones's eyes as he struggled and gasped for breath. He never caught it. In a few moments he was still, his eyes open and lifeless. Azazel leaned in and checked for a pulse. There wasn't one. He stood and brushed off the knees of his pants and walked back out to the balcony. With little effort, he jumped over the railing and landed softly on the grass below.

"Let's get across town and pay Mr. Taggart a little visit, Mark," Azazel said into his comm.

"Sooo, we're just going to ring the doorbell?" Mark asked. He and Azazel were standing at the front door of Craig Taggart's mansion. An unconscious guard lay on the ground a few meters away.

"We may be here to threaten his life, Mark, but we can at least be polite about it," Azazel replied and pressed the illuminated button next to the door. "Besides," he added with a sly grin, "it's kind of funny, if you think about it." Mark smiled and shook his head as the tones of numerous bells rang throughout the massive home.

A moment later, the heavy, wooden door swung open and another guard stood in the doorway. His facial expression was that of both confusion and complete surprise. The man never got to process the situation any further. Before he could even ask what they were doing there, Mark hit him in the chin so hard, they heard the bone break.

Mark winced as the man hit the floor. "Oops. Got a little overzealous that time."

"A bit, maybe," Azazel replied.

"Who the hell is at the door Terry?" a voice called from upstairs.

"Mr. Terry isn't able to answer you right now, Mr. Taggart!" Mark yelled back. "Why don't you come down so we can speak for a moment?"

Craig Taggart appeared at the top of the stairs. His eyes went wide, his mouth gaped, and face turned pale. He slowly started to walk down. He wore a large, fluffy red robe and matching house slippers. In his right hand, he carried a large handgun. The gun never came up, but he was obviously prepared to use it. He reached the bottom of the stairs, gripped the banister, and gathered his composure. After a moment, a bit of resolve returned to his expression and he straightened himself. He walked to the open doorway where Azazel and Mark continued to wait patiently on the front stoop.

"What are you doing here, Black?" Taggart asked in a stern tone. His eyes darted around the landscape behind Azazel and Mark. Finally, his gaze rested on the unconscious Terry lying on the floor. He shook his head in dismay. "How the hell did you get past my guards? No one is permitted on the grounds without an appointment. You should have never made it past the front gate."

Azazel smiled and spread his arms out slightly. "Good evening to you too, Mr. Taggart. Come now, do you honestly believe that a mere dozen or so patrolling guards would be any match for someone like me? Please, come to your senses and put your weapon away. We wouldn't want anyone else to get hurt this evening. Would we? Besides, it's not like it would do you much good."

"You killed all my men?" Taggart asked in disbelief.

"No," Azazel replied with a shake of his head. "We incapacitated them. Fear not, Mr. Taggart. Your men will be good as new tomorrow. They may have a headache, but they'll be fine. No sense in killing men who are just doing their jobs." He looked past Taggart and into the house. "Would you mind if we went inside, now? I have business to discuss with you and I'd rather not do it standing on your front porch."

Taggart nervously tapped his gun against his hip as his eyes roamed over the tactical gear both the men on his porch wore. He let out a reluctant sigh. "Of course. Please, come in." He stepped to the side and Azazel and Mark entered his home. Taggart shut the door and rushed past them. "This way," he said, and motioned for them to follow him through another door.

The door led them into a sophisticated lounge. The walls were lined with shelves full of old-fashioned books printed on paper, several oversized, leatherbound lounging chairs, a walk-in humidor fully stocked with cigars of every make, and a bar with no less than fifty different types of liquor visible on the serving top. Taggert walked behind the bar and put his weapon away. Then, he grabbed a small crystal glass, threw in a few ice cubes, and filled it with a very expensive scotch. He motioned to the ice bucket and empty glasses with his free hand. "Would you like a drink while we talk?"

"A drink sounds wonderful," Azazel responded. "We've had a busy night, and two fingers worth of that scotch would certainly hit the spot."

"Mark, is it?" Taggart asked. "I believe I've heard my men mention you a time or two. Would you care for a glass?"

"None for me, thanks," Mark said with a raised hand. "Never did develop a taste for hard liquor. I prefer an ice-cold beer, but I already had one this afternoon and I have to drive us back."

Azazel slapped him on the back. "Suit yourself." He walked over and poured the scotch into a glass until it was the same depth as two fingers are wide. "I like my drinks neat," he said as he swirled the liquid around in the glass and inhaled the aroma. "Ice waters it down and ruins the flavor." He raised the glass to Taggert, then drank the entire thing in one smooth gulp. Azazel nodded his head in approval and sat the glass down on the bar. "A fine blend, Mr. Taggart. Thank you."

"You're welcome," Taggart replied as he walked back to the front of the bar. "Now," he said as he sat his glass down next to Azazel's, "do you mind telling me why you're here?" He crossed his arms and stood there with an irritated look on his face.

Azazel put his hands in his front pockets and took a couple steps to the side away from the bar. "Bad business, I'm afraid, Mr. Taggart. It has to do with my fighting organization."

"Oh?" Taggart said. "It must be serious if you felt the need to come to me in person at this hour. Is there something I can do to help?"

Azazel cocked his head in Taggart's direction and one corner of his mouth raised in a half smile. "Funny you should ask, Mr. Taggart. I think you've done enough, already. Don't you?"

"And what's that supposed to mean?" Taggart asked, his voice cracked a bit. "I don't have anything to do with your fights or your fighters. Only with my own fighter, Jones."

"Precisely," Azazel replied, and turned to fully face the man. Taggart was now standing with his back to the bar. "But I'm afraid Mr. Jones won't be fighting for you anymore. It pains me to inform you that an unforeseen heart condition recently ended his life in a most abrupt manner."

Anger flared up in Taggert's eyes, his face turned red, and his hands dropped to his sides. "*You killed Jones?*" he shouted. His hand went to the opening of his robe as if to grab for something. Another gun, most likely, but his hand never made it there.

In a flash, Azazel closed the distance between them and lifted Taggart straight up off the floor by his throat. Taggart's hands shot to his throat and futilely attempted to break Azazel's grip. He didn't so much as manage to move a single finger out of place.

"Yes, Mr. Taggart," Azazel answered in his calm, cool voice. "I killed Mr. Jones. Did you really think we wouldn't notice the difference in his abilities during his last fight with Mr. Chico?" He smiled up at the man. "I do know a thing or two about enhancements, you know."

Taggart's face had turned a dark shade of red and was well on its way to purple. Azazel sighed and shook his head. "You were well aware of the rules, Mr. Taggart. Everyone is. Yet, you broke them anyway. As punishment, your man had to die. And now I'm here to deal with you, being as you were the one who funded the whole operation."

Taggart tried to say something but only managed to grunt and gurgle. Azazel shook his head and rolled his eyes. "Don't try to deny it, Mr. Taggart. Jones admitted everything before I carried out his punishment."

A loud scream rang through the room and Azazel thought his eardrums might burst. He turned to see a short, brunette woman standing in the doorway with her hands clasped over her mouth and her eyes wide with fear. Mark drew a pistol from his side, but Azazel waved him off.

"No need for all that, Mark. Mrs. Taggart has done nothing wrong here. She's no threat to us." He turned his attention back to the woman. "Mrs. Taggart, I apologize for this dreadful inconvenience. I never meant for you to see any of this. Rest assured that this is a simple business transaction between your husband and me. You have nothing to fear. Now, please, if you would be so kind as to leave us so that we may conclude our meeting. It won't be long now, and we'll be out of your hair." He turned to Mark. "Mark, could you escort Mrs. Taggart to the kitchen, please."

Mark walked over and said, "If you could show me the way, Mrs. Taggart, I would be very grateful."

She gave Azazel another fearful look and then looked up at her husband. Tears began to flow down her cheeks, and she looked back at Azazel again, this time with pleading eyes.

"Everything will be fine, Mrs. Taggart," Azazel assured her again. "You have my word."

She was reluctant, but turned and slowly exited the lounge with Mark on her heels. Azazel turned his attention back to the purple-faced Taggert, who was on the verge of passing out. He dropped Taggart back to the floor and loosened his grip just enough to allow the man to breathe. The color of his face turned from purple, back to an ugly shade of red.

"Unfortunate she had to walk in and see that," Azazel said. "But that's a risk you run in our type of business. That being said," he reached back with his free hand and pulled out a field knife reminiscent of the old military style. In one, lightning-fast movement, Azazel sliced off Taggart's left ear and pressed the tip of the knife under his left eye. Taggart tried to scream, but Azazel tightened his grip on the man's throat and muffled the sound.

"You broke my rules, Mr. Taggart. The results of which caused my fighter's ribs to be broken so badly he won't be able to fight for another month. For this, you will lose your ear, and you will pay me everything Mr. Chico *would* have won in the fights that I had to reschedule." He pressed the knife harder into Taggart's face. The skin broke and blood trickled down the blade. "If you fail to do this, I'll cut off much more than an ear. But before I do that, I'll make you watch as I dismember your wife, piece by pretty piece. Furthermore, you are forever banned from any and all of my fights. You may not enter a fighter, nor can anyone from your city participate without first moving to my city and getting clearance directly from me. Blink if you understand and agree to my terms. If not, I'll have Mark bring Mrs. Taggart back in here, and we can end it all right now. This is your one and only option, Mr. Taggart. I suggest you choose wisely. For your wife's sake, if not for your own." Taggart blinked rapidly without hesitation and tried, in vain, to nod his head.

"Good," Azazel said. He retracted the knife from Taggart's face, then brought the butt down hard against the side of his head. The man collapsed on the floor in a heap. Blood ran down the side of his head from the area of his severed ear. Azazel reached behind the bar, grabbed several bar towels, and placed them on the carpet under Taggart's head before it dripped onto the carpet. "No sense in ruining such a nice lounge, Mr. Taggart. Blood is difficult to get out once it sets in."

He grabbed the bottle of scotch and had a second drink before leaving the lounge. Mark was waiting for him in the foyer by the front door. He smiled as Azazel walked up to him. "Get everything squared away, Boss?"

"Yes, I believe so," Azazel replied. "Mrs. Taggart?"

"Asleep," Mark answered. "She had some sleeping pills in the medicine cabinet. I suggested she take a couple with a glass of wine. Told her everything would be fine when she woke up tomorrow. She was out in no time."

"She'll need her rest," Azazel said. "They'll certainly have a busy day tomorrow. Anyway, let's get back to the tower. I'm starving."

The enhancements burned a lot of energy and, in turn, gave him quite an appetite. Especially when he exerted a lot of energy in a short period of time. While his power-cells ran his major systems, his natural body still burned a ton of calories. So, naturally, he ate much more than the average human did, and more frequently too.

They made it back to their vehicle and Azazel immediately pulled out his phone and dialed up a number. After a moment, a husky man with dirty blonde hair and a matching beard appeared on the screen.

"What can I do for you, Mr. Black?" he asked with a smile.

"Chef Shane, I'm so glad you're awake," Azazel replied. "Would it be too much trouble for you to whip up some burgers and maybe some of your hand-cut french fries? Mark and I are about two hours out and we're starving."

Chef Shane Kirkland was one of the best chefs on Arth. He'd once been well on his way to becoming one of the most famous too. That was until he'd gone onto one of those cooking competition shows, however. He'd caught his competition trying to pour white vinegar into the mix for his dessert in the finale. The attempt had cost the other chef his hand by way of Shane's hand-forged cleaver. Taking the man's hand had landed Shane in the Arth Maximum Security Detention Center for six cycles. When he'd walked out the front door of the facility on his release day, Azazel had been there waiting and offered him a job on the spot. As it turned out, Shane had more skill with knives than just cooking, and life in prison had hardened him further. It made him all the more valuable to Azazel as an employee.

"No problem at all, Mr. Black," Shane answered. "It'll be ready when you get home."

"Thank you, Chef," Azazel said with a smile. "I'll see you then." He hung up the phone, laid his head back, and took a nap while Mark drove them back to the tower.

The next afternoon, Azazel found himself scrolling through the list of local flower shops, when he should have been reviewing the numbers from the brothel he operated on the north side of the city. The business was advertised as a physical therapy facility, but that wasn't the only service offered. The flower search was for Ms. Delaware. He had an upcoming date with her. It simply wouldn't do not to have a beautiful, fresh bouquet of flowers waiting for her when she arrived. He had almost decided on a bundle that was lavender and canary yellow when Mark rushed into his office with a data chip held in the air.

"Boss!" he shouted. His voice was urgent. "You need to see this. We got some trouble on the south end with the Thrynn."

Azazel groaned and rubbed his face with both hands. "What now? Can't I go a single day without something happening? Are they trying to slide into our territory? We have men posted for that sort of thing."

Mark shook his head with an odd look on his face. "The opposite, I'm afraid, sir."

Azazel raised an eyebrow at him. "I've given no such orders, or permission, to anyone to do anything beyond our southern borders."

Mark placed the chip into a slot on Azazel's computer. "Just watch this, and you'll understand." A new tab opened up on the computer screen and he hit the play button.

A bright green Thrynn appeared on the screen with a man with long brown hair and a braided beard tied to a steel chair in the background. His lip was swollen and dried blood covered his chin. Both eyes were purple and nearly swollen shut and his nose appeared to be broken. There were cuts and slashes down his arms and legs visible through his torn clothing as well. The man had clearly taken a beating. The Thrynn grinned, exposing its many sharp teeth.

"N'thr T'Lathll," Azazel said with a sneer. He paused the video. "That's Mr. Tackett, isn't it?"

Mark leaned in for a closer look. "Yes, sir. That's Tackett alright. Idiot."

Azazel nodded and hit the play button. N'thr T'Lathll turned to look back at the bound Human then back to the recording device he'd used. "Azazel Black, I believe you are misssing one of your employeesss at the moment." He slurred his s's as he spoke. "Do not fret, Mr. Black. I found him for you." His grin disappeared and his eyes narrowed. "He wasss dissscovered trying to sssell TRIP in my northern territory."

TRIP was a hallucinogenic drug. Azazel had hired several chemists to take the purest form of an old drug and figure out how to increase its effects on the taker as well as make it more addictive. Once perfected and introduced to the public, it became one of his most lucrative ventures.

N'thr T'Lathll shook his oblong head and snorted through his nostrils. "I thought you trained your thugsss to be more professsional than thisss, Black. I guesss I wasss wrong. Asss you can sssee, your man hasss been punisssshed for his crime. A crime, I might add, that I took asss a persssonal insssult from you. Ssso, I believe you owe me asss much as thisss man. I'll make thisss sssimple, Black. You will come to my building at midnight tonight, *alone*, with twenty thoussssand MU'sss, if you want your man back. You will alssso agree to relinquisssh two blocksss of your sssouthern territory to me to make up for thisss insssult. Fail to do ssso, and not only will I kill thisss man, but I will take the two blocksss by forcccce. Ssse you then, Black."

The video cut off. Azazel leaned back in his chair and rubbed his chin as he processed what he'd just watched. He was angry for several reasons. Firstly, he was angry at his own man for going outside the designated area of business. You just didn't wander into another crime boss's territory and try to take his customers like that. It was unprofessional and just plain rude. Azazel didn't operate like that, nor did he allow his employees to do so.

Second, he was angry at the pure audacity of N'thr T'Lathll to send him a video chip threatening to kill one of his men and demand that Azazel relinquish part of his territory to him as a reparation. He hadn't even had the decency to call and speak in person like a man. Granted, N'thr T'Lathll wasn't a man, he was Thrynn and more reptile than anything, but still. Azazel would have respected an actual call and civilized conversation. This was just cowardly and disrespectful.

"Mark," he said, his mind made up. "I want you to get in touch with Fran, Droke, and Kazmire. Fran may be hard to track down, as he could be anywhere, but the other two are on planet, last I heard. Set up separate meetings with them for as soon as possible. I'll give you further instructions when I get back."

"You can't really be considering going alone, can you?" Mark asked with wide eyes. "Much less pay him twenty grand and two blocks of territory. We need to hit him with everything we've got. Just on principle."

Azazel raised a hand. "I'll be fine, Mark. You forget how capable I am. If you recall, I didn't take control of this city with an army. It was just me for the longest time." He chuckled. "I can handle N'thr T'Lathll fine on my own. I do want you to contact our men in the southern two block area and advise them that there may be tension tonight. Send additional forces to back them up, in case the Thrynn get any stupid ideas of trying to take it by force.

Tell them they have my permission to use lethal force once they've been attacked first. They are *not* to start anything, but they can certainly finish it."

The reluctant expression on Mark's face told Azazel he didn't particularly like the orders he'd been given. "Yes, Boss," he nodded. "I'll be honest, though. I still don't like the idea of you going alone, but I'll follow your orders. I think I know what sector Fran is in right now, I'll get up with him first, then the others." He narrowed his eyes at Azazel. "Are you going to do what I think you're going to?"

A broad smile stretched over Azazel's face and he shrugged. "Possibly. It's long past time I took control of the southern territory. I've let the Thrynn run wild for too long, and they need to be put in their place."

"Fair enough," Mark replied. "I'll go get on it, Boss." He turned and exited the office, shutting the door behind him.

Azazel checked his watch. He still had over eight hours before he was supposed to be at N'thr T'Lathll's building. "Guess I'll go down and see what Chef Shane has on the menu and get in a nap before heading out."

The street in front of N'thr T'Lathll's building was empty except for the two Thrynn guards at the entrance. Azazel stepped out of his vehicle and buttoned the top button of his suit's jacket as he walked up the stairs. As soon as he reached the top, a third Thrynn emerged from within the building.

"Mr. Black, I presume," the Thrynn said. It was a dark green female about a meter tall with black markings streaking back from the corners of her eyes.

"Yes," Azazel smiled. "And you are?"

"K'reaz R'Tarkth," she answered with a bow. "Please, follow me. N'thr T'Lathll is expecting you."

"Of course," Azazel said with a slight bow of his own.

K'reaz R'Tarkth turned from him and entered the building. She caught the door with her tail and held it open for Azazel as he caught up to her.

"Thank you, K'reaz R'Tarkth." He mentally noted she was much more pleasant and courteous than he'd come to expect from a Thrynn.

She led him through a series of guarded doors and down an elevator to the building's sub-basement. When they reached a large set of steel double doors, she produced an access card and swiped it across a security panel on the right side of the entrance. There was a loud *hissss* and the doors slid apart. Beyond the threshold stood N'thr T'Lathll, surrounded by a dozen armed Thrynn guards. Tackett was still tied to the steel chair behind him. The only change was the rag stuffed in his mouth to silence him. The room appeared to be a type of command center with multiple security screens and computers around the room. Each station was operated by a Thrynn. Not that that was any sort of surprise. Arth was mainly inhabited by Elowan, Humans, Thrynn, and Velox. Thrynn absolutely despised the Elowan, a plant species of large, mobile trees and they weren't particularly fond of Humans.

"I half expected you not to show up, Black," N'thr T'Lathll said without a formal greeting.

Azazel turned and bowed to K'reaz R'Tarkth before responding. "Thank you so much for your hospitality, K'reaz R'Tarkth.

You've been more than pleasant. I do hope you will escort me out when my business here is concluded.

K'reaz R'Tarkth bowed back to him. "It would be my pleasure, Mr. Black. I'll be just outside the doors." She slipped back out the doors and they shut.

Azazel reached up with one hand, unbuttoned his jacket, and slipped his hands into his pockets as he turned to regard N'thr T'Lathll. "And a good evening to you too, N'thr T'Lathll. Am I saying that correctly? I want to address you properly." He took a few steps closer and peered over the Thrynn's shoulder at Tackett.

"Your pronunccciation of my name is quite sufficccient, Black," N'thr T'Lathll replied. "But enough of the pleasssantries. Do you have my compensssation?" He lowered his head and narrowed his eyes in an attempt to look intimidating. The dozen armed guards did the same.

The right side of Azazel's mouth raised in a half smile. Their attempt to rattle him hadn't had the slightest bit of effect on him. "I want my man untied and on his feet before I answer any questions, or give you anything. I need to speak with him before we can make any sort of trade."

"And why isss that?" demanded N'thr T'Lathll.

"To verify your claims, of course," Azazel replied. "You don't expect me to simply take your word for it, do you? Mr. Tackett will answer me honestly, I have no doubt. If everything is in order, then we will do business."

A long silent moment passed before N'thr T'Lathll turned his head to the nearest guard. "Untie him." The guard did as commanded, and soon, Tackett was standing feebly next to him. "Now, asssk your quessstionsss, Black. And make it quick."

"Hello, Mr. Tackett," Azazel said with a thin smile. His eyes were cold and locked onto Tackett's.

"Hello, Mr. Black," Tackett croaked. "I'm sorry to have messed up your night."

Azazel nodded. "I appreciate the apology, Mr. Tackett. Now, I need you to be perfectly honest with me. It's been brought to my attention you were apprehended while trying to sell TRIP on the south side. More precisely, on the Thrynn controlled south side. Is this true?"

The man looked down at his blood-spattered shoes with shame in his eyes. "Yes, Mr. Black. It's true." He lifted his head to face Azazel as he continued. "I thought if I could start accumulating customers on the south side that we could eventually…"

He never got to finish his sentence. A two-inch hole had been burned straight through his head. Tackett's body dropped to the floor in a motionless heap, smoke drifting up from the hole in his forehead. Everyone looked from the corpse to Azazel. His right arm was raised straight out, and his hand was bent straight down at an odd angle. The hand was rigidly straight and bent so far back that the palm was flush against his forearm. In the end of his wrist, where bones should have been, was a multitude of servos and circuits…and a two-inch barrel. There was an energy weapon concealed within his augmented arm. The hand snapped back up into place and Azazel flexed his fingers.

N'thr T'Lathll looked back and forth from the body to him aghast. "*You killed your own man?*"

"He broke my rule," Azazel answered coldly. "The unauthorized sale of product outside my borders is strictly prohibited." He motioned to Tackett's body. "As you can see, the consequences of breaking such a rule are quite severe. I can overlook and be lenient on a great many things, but there are no second chances when my rules are broken.

As for the twenty thousand you demanded," he continued, "you will receive none of it. Nor will you be given two blocks of my southern territory. As a matter of fact," he grinned savagely, "it is now *you* who owe *me* a debt."

N'thr T'Lathll shook his head in disbelief. "What? You must be mad, Black. What makesss you think I owe you anything? And jussst because you killed your own man doesssn't mean you will not be giving me what I have demanded. You are vassstly outnumbered here. What isss to stop me from jussst killing you and taking *all* of your territory?"

Azazel smiled and reached back under his coat. Each guard lifted their rifles and aimed them at him. From the hidden sheath on his lower back, Azazel removed two karambits. They were black with quarter meter long, curved blades with finger-sized holes forged through the pummel. He spun the blades on his fore fingers and looked N'thr T'Lathll in the eyes. His own electric green eyes seemed to glow brighter.

"Well, you see, N'thr T'Lathll, I found your little video to be quite insulting and unprofessional. On top of that, when you decided to keep my man for ransom instead of beating him and sending him on his way, punishment served, you ended his life. Ultimately, you cost me one of my men." He began to slowly pace back and forth. "So, with the loss of Mr. Tackett's life in addition to the unprofessionalism and personal insult, you owe me…" he tapped on his lower lip with one of the blades as he thought, "ten lives."

N'thr T'Lathll laughed hysterically. "You are crazy, Black! You mussst be to think I would kill ten of my own!"

Azazel narrowed his eyes and grinned sadistically. "No. I don't intend for you to do anything. I will take their lives myself."

In a flash he was across the room. Azazel's karambit split one of the guards from belly to chin, his intestines spilled in a pile on the floor in front of him. Another guard's throat opened in a spray of blood as Azazel moved with unmatched speed and precision with his blades. Try as they might, they couldn't touch him. One of the guards managed to line his rifle up with him and fired. Azazel dodged the shot with ease and leapt into the air. He landed on the Thrynn's back and heard a multitude of bones shatter with the impact. He sheathed one of his blades and thrust his hand down as hard as he could into the guards back. He felt the flesh and scale split apart. The Thrynn's spine felt thick and coarse as he gripped his hand around it. In one hard tug, he ripped it from the screaming guard's body in one long piece. It had ripped out in its entirety, including the tail section.

It was too perfect not to take advantage. Azazel sheathed his other karambit and began to swing the spine around like a whip amidst all the gunfire. The bone may as well have been steel with his augmented strength behind it. Several of the guards went down with huge gashes in their sides, necks, and faces before the bone-whip shattered. He dropped his hand again and fired his energy weapon as he moved through the remaining guards. With only two guards and N'thr T'Lathll left, Azazel ended his assault.

The Thrynn leader was curled up in a ball behind one of the computer stations. "Come on out N'thr T'Lathll." Azazel said as he sheathed his second karambit. "I'm not going to kill you."

N'thr T'Lathll raised his head over the table with caution, then stood and stepped out into the open. He took several timid steps toward Azazel. He looked around at the bodies on the floor, the broken spine that had been used as a whip, and finally the two remaining guards who were soaked in blood. "Why have you allowed *me* to live? It would ssseem much easssier to kill me and then take over my area.”

Azazel looked at him and chuckled. “Because even a pack of wild dogs needs a leader, N’thr T’Lathll. I can’t have your Thrynn running all over the place without proper leadership. No, it’s much easier to let you live and keep the status quo on your side, as far as the Thrynn leadership goes.” He looked down as he buttoned his jacket and noticed there were two holes in the lower hem of his coat. A heavy sigh of irritation escaped him. He raised his arm and shot one of the remaining guards in the head.

A low power warning flashed across his vision. *Damn*, he thought. *Gotta figure out a way to get more than just a few shots out of this thing. I need to look into power-cell upgrades.*

“You sssaid only ten!” shouted N’thr T’Lathll. “That isss eleven!”

The hand snapped back into place and Azazel strolled up to N’thr T’Lathll. “It was ten before one of them messed up my coat. I can get blood out in the wash, but I can’t patch holes. I’ll have to replace this whole suit now. It’s custom made, you know. Can’t just go out and buy another jacket for it.”

Azazel straightened his collar and looked around the room with satisfaction. “I believe our business here is done,” he said with a smile. He pointed to the body of Tackett. “Please see that Mr. Tackett’s body is delivered to my tower tonight. He is to be handled with dignity. The fool may have broken my rules, but his wife at least deserves to get his body back for her own closure.”

N’thr T’Lathll just stared at him with his mouth open and his eyes wide. Finally, he found his voice again and said, “Y-yesss, Mr. Black. I-I will make sssure it isss taken care of.”

“Excellent,” Azazel said and clapped N’thr T’Lathll on the shoulder. “I’ll be on my way now.” He walked toward the double doors, and they opened as he got close. K'reaz R'Tarkth was there and waiting for him. Azazel smiled at her and offered her the crook of his arm. "Shall we?" he asked. She gave him a nod and smiled as she hooked her own short arm through his.

The first light of dawn shined through the window behind Azazel's desk as he ended his third video conference. He had yet to go to bed. Fortunately he'd spent the money to have a personal charging station installed beneath his desk. While he handled business, he was able to hook up and recharge his power cells. Mark had a hard time pinning down the three men he needed to speak with, but he'd managed to get it done. The meetings had all gone Azazel's way...after some haggling. A significant amount of money had been transferred from his accounts, that hurt a bit, but it would all be worth it in the end.

He picked up a slate and sent Mark a detailed list of tasks to be completed by noon that day. With everything that needed to be done, it would be close, but it was an obtainable goal. Mark assured him that he didn't need to worry, and everything would be in order. Satisfied, Azazel entered a number into the communication system and waited for an answer. A moment later, N'thr T'Lathll's shocked face appeared on the screen.

"M-Mr. Black," he stammered. "I did not expect to hear from you ssso sssoon."

"Good morning," Azazel said with a smile. "I quite expect you didn't. N'thr T'Lathll, I need you to meet with me in my office at one this afternoon. We need to discuss a few things. Please, be on time as I have a busy night ahead of me and much planning to do."

He leaned in closer to the screen. "And please don't make me have to send men to come get you."

"I'll be ten minutesss early," N'thr T'Lathll answered quickly.

"Excellent," Azazel replied. "See you then." He ended the call.

After several hours of much needed sleep and a large lunch, Azazel sat behind his desk as Mark escorted N'thr T'Lathll in. A special chair had been brought in to accommodate the Thrynn anatomy and Azazel gestured for him to sit.

"Welcome, N'thr T'Lathll," Azazel greeted him. "Thank you for coming today. After last night, I believe there are a few things you and I need to get straight between each other."

"It isss a pleasssure to be here," N'thr T'Lathll said. "Thank you for the warm greeting, and yesss, I believe there are a few thingsss we need to get ssstraight between the two of usss."

Azazel smiled and clapped his hands together. "Fantastic! I'm so happy to know we're on the same page." He leaned back in his chair and steepled his fingers under his chin. "Look, I think it's best if I just get straight to the point." He spun the screen on his desk around for N'thr T'Lathll to see.

The image on the screen was of about a hundred small crates stacked together in a pyramid. Small devices were set on top of the crates all over the pyramid. Recognition seemed to flash over N'thr T'Lathll's face, followed by dread. His mouth moved up and down, but no words came out.

"I can see you know exactly what that is, N'thr T'Lathll," Azazel said.

N'thr T'Lathll nodded. "Headfruit."

"Correct," Azazel said, a hint of evil in his voice. "But that isn't just headfruit. That is *all* the headfruit available on Arth at the moment, including the shipment you were supposed to receive from Kazmire tomorrow night. Among that shipment is also the inventory of Droke, so don't try to buy from him either. Fran wasn't in the quadrant, so there was nothing to buy from him, but I've managed to secure the same deal with him as I did the others." He grinned savagely. "From this point on, they will exclusively deal with me, and only me, in the headfruit industry."

The look on N'thr T'Lathll was priceless. His eyes darted back and forth from Azazel to the screen in horror as the realization of the situation set in. Headfruit was a melon-like fruit that formed from the heads of Elowan as a last effort to procreate. Inside the melon were the seeds of what would become their offspring. Thrynn considered headfruit to be a delicacy and believed eating it lengthened their lifespan. Naturally, Elowan guarded their headfruit with their lives, but that didn't stop determined smugglers and thieves. It was forbidden for others to even see headfruit, so one could imagine the penalty for being caught stealing or eating one. And now, Azazel had control of nearly all the black market headfruit trafficking. Droke and Kazmire were the primary headfruit runners on Arth, and Fran was the intergalactic runner. Not that this was widely known information, but Azazel belonged to a certain crowd that knew these sorts of things. There were other smaller smugglers, of course, but they were unreliable and usually ended up caught.

"It's simple," Azazel continued. "You work for me, now. The south side of the city belongs to me. When you leave here today, Mark and a company of my men will escort you back to your headquarters and make the necessary preparations. Don't worry, I pay well and I'm not prejudiced. Thrynn will be paid and treated every bit as well as my current employees. In return for you cooperation, I'll continue to sell you the headfruit for the same price you paid Kazmire." He pointed at one of the devices on the screen. "Do you know what those are?

N'thr T'Lathll shook his head, his eyes locked on the crates. "No. I do not."

"Those are thermite grenades, my friend. They've been remotely linked to this." He held up a silver cylinder with a big red button on the top. "If you refuse to accept my terms, I will press this button and destroy the entire lot. After that, I will kill you, and order my men to raid your facility and kill everyone in there. Except K'reaz R'Tarkth. I rather liked her. She would be most welcome to work here in my tower. As a matter of fact, I intend to offer her a position here as soon as we conclude this meeting." He grinned and asked, "Anyway, what do you think of my offer?"

N'thr T'Lathll lowered his head and closed his eyes. His body began to tremble. A moment later he looked up and said, "You do not leave me much choice, Mr. Black. If I refuse, we all die and the headfruit is obliterated. If I agree I lose my control of the south side and work for you. Either way, I lose." He took in a deep breath, released it, and shook his head. In a voice not much higher than a whisper he said, "I accept your terms, Mr. Black."

Azazel beamed. "An excellent choice! You won't regret it, I promise." He locked eyes with N'thr T'Lathll and pressed the button.

No less than fifty thermite grenades exploded on the screen. The boxes began to burn and glow as the thermite ate through everything in its path. Headfruit rolled out of crates and began to ooze and liquify. Within minutes, the entire pyramid was a flaming pile of ash and crystallized headfruit remains.

"*Noooo!*" N'thr T'Lathll screamed and dropped to his knees on the floor. He crawled to the desk and gawked at the screen in disbelief. He turned to Azazel, who stared at him with cold, dead eyes.

Azazel gave him a thin-lipped smile. "Get back into your chair and have some dignity."

The Thrynn did as he was told. Azazel continued to glare at him for several minutes before he spoke again. "In addition to the previous conditions I gave you, you will also be paying me double the price for the headfruit just destroyed. Consider this a demonstration of the lightest of punishments that awaits those who would stand against me."

He smiled brightly. "But not to fear. That wasn't *all* the headfruit."

He opened the top left drawer on his desk. From it, he pulled out a single headfruit and set it on his desk. Azazel pulled out a knife and sliced out a wedge, exposing the seeds embedded in the meat. N'thr T'Lathll leaned forward and licked his lips, eager to accept the wedge. But Azazel didn't hand it to him. Instead, he looked right into N'thr T'Lathll's eyes and took a huge bite from the wedge.

Azazel wrinkled his nose as he chewed. Juice dribbled down his chin and onto the desk. He took another large bite and looked up at the ceiling in thought as he ate. Two bites were enough, and he dropped what was left of the wedge into the wastebasket next to his desk. He also spit what was in his mouth out and shoved the remainder of the headfruit off his desk and into the basket. It hit with a *thud* and split into several pieces. He looked up to see N'thr T'Lathll staring at him in horror with his mouth open for, what seemed like, the hundredth time in their short meeting.

"Disgusting," Azazel grunted as he wiped his mouth on a handkerchief. "I wanted to see what all the fuss was about." He shook his head. "I don't know how you can consider that a delicacy. I'll take fresh watermelon over that any day." He gave a dismissive wave. "That will be all, N'thr T'Lathll. Please go with Mike and do as we've discussed."

"Yes, sir," N'thr T'Lathll replied in a defeated tone and stood to leave.

"One more moment, actually," Azazel called with a finger in the air. He entered a few commands and a new window appeared on the screen. "Which of these flower bouquets do you think looks better? I have a date tonight and I want it to go well."

N'thr T'Lathll looked at him, then the screen, then him again. He reached up and rubbed the side of his head and let out small laugh. He shook his head and walked back over to Azazel's desk to study the options. "Isss thisss a firssst date?"

"Yes," Azazel answered. "That's why it's so important."

N'thr T'Lathll nodded. "The first impresssion is alwaysss the mossst impactful." He continued to look at the screen, then shook his head. "None of thessse will do, Mr. Black. They are too ordinary and can be found in nearly any ssshop. Ssssearch for the Occcean Empresss."

Azazel entered the name into the search and to his great surprise, a gorgeous blue flower that resembled a cross breed of rose and orchid appeared on his screen. It was like nothing he had ever seen before. "That's perfect!" he shouted.

"Firssst Impresssionsss, Mr. Black," N'thr T'Lathll said and turned again to leave.

"Many thanks, N'thr T'Lathll," Azazel called from his desk. "And one more thing…"

N'thr T'Lathll turned in time to see Azazel shove the waste basket across the room to bump into his leg.

"I reward those who do me a good service. Now, go prepare the south side."

The door shut and Azazel stood and turned to look out the window. A huge smile crossed his face. The city was his now. The *whole* city. There were many things that had to be done and the future looked very bright, indeed. But first things first. Ms. Delaware would be there soon, and he needed to go pick up her flowers.

Turn of Luck

By William Joseph Roberts

I dropped into the cockpit and activated the main drive of my fighter. As the systems powered up I slid on my helmet and locked it into the collar of my flight suit.

"Command, this is Captain Blake Daniels, designation Alpha Two Nine checking in. Raptor is warming up, what's the situation up there?"

"Alpha Two Nine, you are on your own for this fight. The primary hangar bay was destroyed in the initial attack."

Good thing that I'd brought the old girl in for a few repairs, or she'd have been in the main hangar with the other fighters.

Red warning lights strobed throughout the bay as the repair hangar doors opened. The bright jewel in the night that was Arth shined through the opening door, momentarily blinding me.

"We're picking up six new contacts inbound from coreward and less than a minute out from Starport."

"I copy, Command. Any idea who they are?"

"Negative. The ship designs do not match anything in our database. All we know for sure is that the alien craft are heavily shielded. They are equipped with Class Five particle cannons and Class Two missile launchers."

"So, don't get hit. Got it," I mumbled to myself as I finished the preflight check.

"And Blake," the soft female voice from command trailed off. "Yeah?"

"Come back to me in one piece," the voice said in a sultry tone. *How could I ever ignore a request like that?*

"You can count on it."

If I don't make it back, then we may all be doomed anyway, I thought, but I couldn't say that over the live comms.

"Alpha Two Nine launching." I disengaged the mag-mounts and bumped the throttles forward."

"Good luck," the voice of command said softly into her mic.

As soon as the repair hangar doors opened wide enough, I pushed the throttles forward to the stop and activated the hyperspace booster. In a sickening burst of speed, both the fighter and my stomach lurched as we slipped momentarily into hyperspace then back to normal space. Yowahslsh a large reddish-brown moon orbited by Sahhsyyrs, a much smaller green-grey rock, suddenly filled my view. The two Arthian moons backlighting Interstel's massive orbital junkyard looked something akin to a predator looming over its prey.

I spotted a gleam of light in the dark distance. Six objects streaked across the backdrop of the cosmos as I watched them growing closer.

"Contacts spotted, Command. Moving to engage."

"We copy you, Alpha Two Nine."

I adjusted my course to skim the outer edge of the debris field before flanking the six unknown fighters and approaching from their aft quarter. They continued on their direct path toward Starport, unabated. Finishing my maneuver, I pushed the throttles to the forward stop and my fighter leapt forward at a nauseating rate, skipping through hyperspace. The unknown enemy ships never so much as flinched as they continued to close in on their target. If they had noticed my ship moving among the junkyard wreckage, they gave no outward sign of it.

Targeting systems squealed with the tone for a positive lock on all six of the enemy vessels. They continued, unwavering as they held the same tight formation without variance.

"Just a little closer," I said to myself. One more burst of speed from the hyperspace skip and I'd be too close to miss.

Why does this seem way too easy?

Target locks sounded just as soon as my Raptor slipped out of hyperspace less than a kilometer behind the six unknown fighters.

"Targets acquired! Missiles away!"

I depressed the missile button on the control stick and launched two missiles at each of the targets. My Raptor rocked from the sudden deployment of munitions. I banked the fighter hard, changing position behind the flight of enemy fighters as I watched my volley of missiles streak ahead, impacting each of the selected targets. I pulled up to clear the explosions as I followed behind to avoid the debris. All six targets banked away, unscathed from the impacts.

"Alpha Two Nine, we have a problem!"

"You think I don't know that, Command? I'm doing the best I can out here."

"New contact bearing six five mark two two point six from your position, and it is massive."

Target lock warnings erupted in my ears.

I banked, rolled, and banked hard again. The spaceframe of my Raptor groaned from the strain as I evaded the enemy ship target locks. I punched it, shoving the throttles to the stop once again. Bursts of particle beams struck hard as my Raptor exited the hyperspace slip. Damage control warnings flashed across my displays. Secondary power systems damaged, life support was offline and two of the ship's weapons hardpoints were gone.

"I'm hit, Command. Heading into the junkyard to see if I can shake them."

Garbled static was the only reply that I received.

Why wait till now to jam the comms?

I nosed the ship over and aimed for the junkyard. That's when I saw the massive mothership, half the size of Sahhsyyrs approaching from behind Yowahslsh, Arth's largest moon.

Sparks flew from a control console on my left.

"Warning, core breach imminent," the ship's voice warning shouted.

I rolled and banked the ship Arthward in a corkscrew maneuver then angled the nose to intercept a large transport that hung lifelessly in the junkyard.

I can't take too many more hits like that one.

A new alarm roared in my ears. It buzzed and warbled like the tone of an obnoxious alarm clock. My Raptor's heads-up display exploded in a shower of sparks and scorched ozone.

"Core overload in ten seconds," the computer warned.

The alarm continued, blaring, drilling its way into my grey matter.

The world flashed suddenly to a brilliant shade of white and continued to strobe in time to the roaring alarm.

I blinked to clear my vision. Lumination panels embedded in the ceiling bathed me in their day star glow.

The alarm continued, pounding its way into the side of my head. I turned in the direction of the annoyance and found a clock flashing 1000 in time to the bleating of the alarm.

"Yeah, yeah, yeah," I mumbled, then smashed the button to stop the incessant alarm. "Just enough time to swing by the Black Box for breakfast before orientation," I said through a long yawn as I stretched. I smacked my mouth in search of the slightest amount of moisture then yawned again and caught the scent of my own breath. "Oh, Gods! That isn't good."

Shower first, then breakfast.

Instead of my normal rush out the door, I took my time this morning and enjoyed a steaming mug of stimcaff as I got ready. Admittedly it was tough to force myself to slow down after the last two years on the go in the academy. But today was my first day as a starship captain, and I planned to make the most of it. Breakfast at the Black Box, Starport's premier captain's lounge, was the best way I could think of to reward myself for all of the hard work and start the day.

In no time, I found myself standing at the entrance of the lounge and in the presence of a goddess. Slowly, I made my way over to the bar.

"As soon as the hatch opened and I stepped into the lounge, I knew we were destined to meet. Captain Blake Daniels," I said as I slid into the empty barstool beside the female captain. I waved for the massive service android at the other end of the bar then leaned in against the dark wooden bar top.

She was fun-sized. Short and petite with close-cropped brunette hair and those big beautiful bright blue eyes that could steal a man's soul. A rare diamond—no— a rare Endurium in the rough that only crosses your path once in a lifetime.

She let out a short chortle and rolled her eyes with a shake of her head. The ice in her glass clinked as she turned up her drink and drained the glass before turning her attention to me. She flashed an annoyed smile then looked at me with an exasperated sidelong glance. "I am *not* in the mood to deal with anyone's bullshit. Are you buying me a drink or what?"

"Greetings," the android said in a tinny robotic voice. "I am M09, your bartender. What can I get you this evening?"

"Um…," I stammered, then smiled back at her with a nervous laugh. "Sure thing." *Perfect freaking timing.*

"Hey there, Sparky. How about a Downspin Flux for me and a Shield Nullifier for the lady."

"Scratch that," she said, abruptly interrupting. "Make that two Downspin Fluxes with a whiskey chaser on the side." She held up her glass and clinked the ice with a shake.

Wow, that was a surprise. I shifted uncomfortably on the bar stool. "Not exactly what I expected, but alright." I nodded at the android then smiled back at her. "Surprise and excitement wrapped up together in such a cute little package."

Anger flashed across her features to replace her previously annoyed expression. She sat up and turned her seat to face me squarely. "And what exactly *did* you expect? Did you expect to just waltz in here with your fresh-pressed uniform and shiny new captain's bars to impress the first gullible slag you came across?"

"Well...um…"

"And another thing. Why is it that men like you insist that they are the universe's answer to all of a womankind's problems?"

"Um…"

M09 returned with a glass of whiskey on the rocks and placed it down in front of the female captain.

Thank the Gods.

"Your drinks."

The android had barely pulled its mechanical hand away from the glass before she snatched it from the bar and gulped down the drink.

"Bad day?" I asked.

A glint of a sad memory momentarily revealed itself in her eyes. "Just a tiny bit," she said, nodding.

M09 placed two half-pints of ale on the bar, poured a shot of whiskey into each glass then dropped a separate shot of tequila into each before pushing them across the bar. The female captain chugged the shooter in one gulp then slammed the empty glass down on the bar top and let out a loud belch.

"You're so cute I could put you in my pocket," I blurted without thinking.

"I swear to all the gods of the universe that if you say one more thing to me, I will stab you in the kidney." She slammed back my drink in one gulp then stormed off in a huff. I couldn't help myself. I turned and watched her shapely posterior as she made her way to a dark corner of the Black Box.

I glanced around the dimly lit lounge. A few booths down sat a human couple with what looked like an Elowan child perched on the guy's shoulder. On the opposite side of the lounge, a pair of Thrynn and a large Velox sat huddled around a box that glowed and sparked from the open lid.

The things you see on Starport.

I turned back to the android bartender. "Give me a beer, Sparky."

"Coming right up, sir." The android placed a new glass on the bar top with efficient timing and poured my beer. "Captain Kenneson seems quite upset this evening, sir."

"Captain Kenneson?"

"Yes sir. The female captain you were just conversing with."

I glanced over my shoulder in the direction she'd gone. I wasn't sure, but it almost looked like she was crying.

I turned back to the android and sipped at my beer. "Any idea what's wrong with her?"

"I fear, I do not. She was about to reveal her woes when you arrived."

Just my luck, bad timing.

I laughed into my glass and took another long sip. "I don't suppose you know what her first name is, do you?"

"Dinah, sir. Captain Dinah Kenneson."

Strange, exotic, and a vulnerable vixen to boot.

"Dinah," I said slowly then looked up at M09. "Rolls easily off the tongue, doesn't it?"

"I wouldn't know, sir."

The shrill sound of a bosun's whistle came across the station's intercoms. "Captain Blake Daniels, report to Operations immediately for orientation."

"Shit," I said, choking on my beer. "What time is it?"

"Thirteen thirty, sir."

"Oh, this is going to go over well. Late for my first day on the job."

I dropped from the barstool then stopped and glanced back to the booth where Dinah sat. *Sure looks like she's crying to me.* I turned back to M09. "Send a beer and a whiskey chaser to Captain Kenneson on me," I said then hurried out of the lounge.

"I never thought I'd see the day that the great Blake Daniels would be slumming with the rest of us graduates from the academy to pin on his captain's bars." Rodney Ware slapped me across the shoulder then stepped around to the front of the personnel console. "I mean, it's not like you *really* had to do the work or anything. Did you, Daniels? Not when *Daddy* is the relations liaison between Arth and Interstel."

I laughed and glared at him. "Piss off, Rodney."

"Yeah, piss off, Rodney."

My buddy and classmate Stephen Rogers stepped in, shoving Rodney away from the console. His roommate, and member of our graduating class, Michael Gams stepped in between Rogers and me. He squared off with Rodney like he was about to lower his shoulder and charge. He looked like one of the biggest and meanest Nyssball linemen I'd ever seen.

"Beat it, Rodney!" Gams growled.

Rogers stepped up and shoved Rodney toward the personnel office doors. "No one put in a request for an arrogant asshole crewmember."

Rodney threw his hands up in defense as he backed away toward the doors. "It sure would be unfortunate if we happened to run into each other out there in the black. Now wouldn't it, Daniels?"

"For you, maybe," Gams growled.

Rodney flashed an angry grin, as he flipped me off and backed out of the entrance.

Gams spun on his heel and sucker punched me in the gut. I doubled over, gasping for breath.

"What in the hells was that for?" I asked, coughing.

Rogers leaned over so he could look me in the eye. "You landed one of the new Intrepid-class frigates and didn't tell us?"

"Um…yeah. I thought you might be a little pissed."

"You're damned right we're pissed," Gams added.

Rogers laughed and slapped me on the back. "But we're excited for you at the same time, Buddy."

Gams pulled me upright and punched me in the shoulder. He must have hit a nerve with that punch because pain shot down my arm to the tip of my pinky finger. As hard as he hit me, I was sure it would leave a nice bruise that would show up tomorrow. "Yup. And proud of you, you lucky son of a groum'r."

"Really?" I coughed a fake laugh.

"Yeah, Buddy." Rogers slapped me on the back again. "We're damned proud, and if we didn't have commands of our own, we'd be the first to sign on as crew."

I shook my head, unsure what I had just heard. "Wait? Both of you got your own ships?"

Rogers and Gams both grinned wide. "Sure did."

"I lucked out since I need to keep a close eye on my folks," Gams said. "I've been given command of a transport running freight and passengers from Arth to Starport and back again."

"And I," Rogers said, breaking in, "will be supplying the populous with a particularly important and highly honorable task. I will be transporting colonists and their precious belongings to the newly discovered colony worlds that pioneering starship captains like yourself, manage to discover out there in the black."

"That is amazing news! Congrats to both of you! When do you launch?"

"I'm leaving first thing in the morning," Gams said. "All that's left to do is to meet the hired crew."

"What about you?" I asked Rogers.

"It'll be a few weeks still. She's one of those newer Terre Haute class transports. According to the dockmaster, my ship was towed in with some severe battle damage a few weeks back, but she was repairable. All hands on board were lost, but her cargo was more than enough to pay Interstel for the repairs. I picked her up at one hell of a discount."

"Battle damage?" I'm sure the look that I gave Rogers was a jumble of emotions somewhere between confusion and fear since my guts suddenly twisted at the thought of being alone in deep space with no hope of backup.

"Why would anyone leave the cargo intact?" Gams asked.

Rogers shrugged. "Dunno."

"Did Interstel know what happened to her?" I asked.

"Not much more than they have lost more than a few ships in that region."

"Where was it found?

"A few parsecs upspin from here."

"Did you have trouble finding a crew?"

"No," Rogers said, shaking his head. "Why would I?"

"People died on that ship."

"Oh that," Rogers said with a dismissive wave. "I renamed her the *Stormhaven*, and just didn't say anything to the new hires about her past."

"What about you?" Gams asked. "What kind of crew did you hire?"

A glimpse of movement in the corridor outside of the personnel office caught my attention. I looked up through the large port windows lining the wall of the personnel office and spotted Captain Dinah Kenneson. I tracked her as she stormed by. Color ran up her neck all the way to her ears and the look she wore was a new level of angry from the one she had worn earlier back at the lounge. "I wouldn't mind having her on my crew," I said to myself.

"That's a great big negative there, Buddy," Rogers said. "You don't want anything to do with Krabby Kenneson. She'll chew you up and spit you out before you know it."

I shook my head and looked over at Rogers. "She can't be that bad."

"She's a boomer," Gams added.

"Yeah," Rogers continued. "She was born and raised on one of the old Euripides-class transports."

"From what I heard she's had *The Swinging Miss* upgraded with the new super-photonic drive systems so she can do these colony runs. I was told that she spent a mint on it."

I walked over to the port window and watched her stomp away down the corridor toward the docking bay. "Maybe that's what's got her so wound up then," I mumbled to myself.

"Trust me. Just forget her and you'll be so much better off. So, what kind of crew did you get?" Gams asked, changing the topic.

"I hadn't yet. I was just about to hire them before you guys showed up."

"If you can afford it, there was this brilliantly genius-level science officer in there, and I have it on good authority that any ship would be lucky to have her since she holds doctorates in six major fields of science."

"Wow," I said with a gasp. "I'll keep that in mind. But if she's that good, then why hasn't she been snagged yet?"

Rogers shrugged. "Dunno."

"No worries. I have a plan."

"Uh huh," Rogers said.

"Trust me. I know what I need without spending any more than I have to."

"Any ideas of where you're heading yet?"

I let out a long sigh. "No clue. I heard there's some decent mining available in system, so I thought about maybe starting off there.

Rogers looked around to make sure no one else was near and leaned in close. "I heard that a survey team found a few old empire ruins on the second planet of the neighboring star system. Might be worth checking out."

I looked up and smiled at Rogers. "It might be, at that."

Rogers took my hand and shook it. "May the Rock of Truth shine brightly upon you," he said, then punched me in the shoulder once more for good luck.

"Captain Daniels," a robotic voice called over the ship's intercoms.

"What is it, NV?" I fired at the three-headed xenomorph charging at me then ducked behind a boulder. "I'm a little busy at the moment." I fired again, scoring a direct hit to two of the heads. The third head snapped at me, nearly biting down on the barrel of my combat rifle. I fired again point-blank down the creature's throat. The back of its head exploded in one round of burst fire.

"Woohoo! That's right! Die you dirty son of a groum'r! You never stood a *chance* against Captain Daniels the Destroyer! Yeah!"

I backed out of the software then removed the sim-helmet and placed it back into the charging dock. "Alright, go ahead NV."

"We have arrived in orbit, sir."

"Really?" I rubbed at the marks across my face left by the sim-helmet and found a scruff of beard. I stepped into the lavatory outside the ship's common room. To my surprise, the man in the mirror had a few days' growth on his face.

"Hey, NV, what day is it?" I scratched my chin.

"Thursday, sir."

I stepped out of the lavatory and pulled my robe together, tying it around my waist. "When did we leave port?"

"Six days ago, sir."

I scratched at my muss of hair as I made my way to the galley and punched in the code for a triple chocolate stimcaff into the food printer. "How long was I playing that game?"

"Five days, six hours, thirty-two minutes, and fifteen seconds sir."

"Captain, as the ship's medical officer, I must insist that you take some time to sleep prior to making any command decisions," a similar robotic voice demanded.

The food printer beeped.

Five days…

"Was that you, NV?"

"No sir, that was MD84735."

"It's way too easy to get distracted without anyone else on the ship." I took the mug of stim-cafe from the food printer and made my way to the lift. "NV."

"Yes, sir."

"Please set a reminder to save and shut down the game system every six hours if I'm playing."

"Request recorded, sir."

"I must insist that you get some rest, Captain," MD said.

I sipped at the steaming hot drink and thought about it for a minute. *We're orbiting an alien planet without anyone else in sight. I could probably sleep another day away, but there are assholes like Rodney who'd jump a man's claim without thinking twice just to screw me over.*

"Sorry MD, Captains' prerogative." I sipped at the hot chocolatey drink as I exited the lift and hurried onto the bridge. "I don't need a robot telling me what I should and shouldn't do."

"Android, sir," MD said over the intercoms.

"Not much difference in my opinion. There's enough time for sleep in the grave. Glory awaits us. Now, what do we have, SC?"

"Sensors are picking up a large quantity of biomass along with substantial quantities of chromium and promethium. Oxygen nitrogen atmosphere with eighty percent of the planet's surface covered in water and global temperatures are comparable to Arth. It appears that this planet falls within the criteria of a colony world, sir." SC, my science android, replied in its tinny robotic voice.

I laughed then slid into the captain's chair. Activating the command readout, I reviewed the scan details for myself. *What kind of stupid-luck break was this?* "Has this planet been logged for colonization by anyone else?"

CO turned in its seat to look back at me from the communications station. "There are no claim beacons currently in orbit, sir."

"Lady luck, shine down on me," I said in a sing-song tone as I entered my command codes to access the planetary claim screen.

SC's head spun around like a demonically possessed doll and stared at me with those glowing yellow eye slits. "May I remind the captain that there is a penalty incurred if the planet is found unsuitable for colonization."

"But you said yourself that it fell within the criteria for colonization, SC."

The yellow eye slits flickered for a moment. "I did, sir," SC said, then turned its head to face forward at the station again. A chill ran down my spine as the others did likewise to face their own consoles.

If we make enough on this haul, I could upgrade the crew so they weren't so creepy.

"Well that's good enough for me," I said and entered my codes to launch a claim beacon.

The readout beeped and displayed a message in large letters that filled the screen.

Would you like to log this planet for colonization?
I selected yes, then another command flashed across the screen. The cursor slowly blinked as it awaited my reply.
Name this planet
"I get to name the planet?"
SC's head spun around to face me once again. "Per Interstel's standard command protocols regarding claims and salvage, section thirty-two, sub-section five, paragraph nineteen, you may suggest a designation for any claim if you wish. If no new designation is submitted it will be assigned the next sequential claim number as its official designation per date and time of the submitted claim."

I sipped at my mug of stimcaff as I drifted off in thought. I couldn't just willy-nilly throw out any name. This was an incredibly important decision that needed to have deep meaning and connection for the souls who would settle the planet and make it their new home. Then it hit me, and I entered a name that invoked images of vivid beauty in my mind. A name connected to the vision of eyes as bright and blue as the shimmering waters of the planet below.

"Dinah."

"I don't know which is better, that new ship smell or the smell of a brand-new terrain vehicle that still has the stickers in the window." I forced in a deep breath and enjoyed the heavenly mixture of new plastics and polyurethane coatings that permeated the cabin of the terrain vehicle. It was the one thing that I could enjoy at the moment under the planet's heavier than normal gravity. I stepped into the cockpit of the terrain vehicle from the main cabin and slid into the driver's seat.

"That sure is one hell of a view," I mumbled to myself and drew in another deep breath as I stared out through the windscreen. Less than a kilometer away I could see our ship, the *Vulnerable Vixen*, or officially, the *ISS Vixen*, where we had landed on a rocky grey beach along the shoreline of the planet's massive equatorial ocean. Turquoise waves lapped against tumbled stones and granite-like boulders that littered the beach. Small shrubs and tufts of rubbery grasses dotted the otherwise dark-purple landscape. What we initially thought was a rocky crust turned out to be a carpet-like organism protected by a hardened outer shell. After a few tests, SC determined the organism to be some sort of fungoid, harmless, and useless otherwise.

"How's the digging coming, SC?"

"Progressing at the expected rate, sir," SC reported. "This deposit should yield approximately three cubic meters of promethium once we have completed the extraction process."

I accessed the ship's computer from the main console of the terrain vehicle and pulled up the Starport ore price list.

"Promethium was running three hundred MU per cubic meter when we left Starport. That's not a bad haul on top of the load of chromium and platinum that we picked up in that mountain range to the east."

"No sir, I suppose it is not," one of the androids replied.

"I really need to change each of your voice synthesizers, so I know who the hell is talking."

I made my way out of the cockpit and down the loading ramp. The purple fungoid carpet crunched underfoot like ice-encrusted snow. The place didn't look bad, just strange in that odd teenage psychedelic kinda way. A smell that floated in on the light breeze was a warm, familiar, earthy sort of thing that I just couldn't put my finger on. The air was hot and heavy with humidity. I surveyed the landscape of rolling hills and spotted an area that looked like a worn path just down the slope to our west.

"If you guys have the mining under control, I'm going to take a little walk."

"Enjoy your walk, sir," SC replied. "I will notify you once the deposit has been extracted and stored."

I followed the path down the sloping hillside. Even though I had only gone maybe fifty meters, my muscles ached as if I had just run five kilometers. I was almost to the point of panting as my heart raced from the exertion.

"It'll be fine. Just have to acclimate to the environment." I squatted then sat down hard, cracking through the purple crust. "Colonists are going to love this place," I mumbled, attempting to convince myself. "This will be one of the most well-known vacation resorts in the galaxy. I forced myself to my feet and continued down the slope slowly. The narrow valley was all of maybe ten meters wide at the most. At the bottom on the opposite side, an oddly sharp corner of all things caught my attention. It didn't look natural in the slightest and looked as if a portion of the carpet-like fungoid had detached and fallen away. Stepping closer to examine the area, it looked as if the fungoid had maybe died. A cross-section was easily visible, with the hardened outer crust protecting the lifeform, then the substrate beneath that resembled a carved, decorative marble wall. That's when the realization hit me.

"It's a building," I gasped. I looked up along the edge of the wall that rose maybe three stories high from the bottom of the small valley that was once street level. "We're mining on the top of a town."

I picked at the exposed edge of the fungoid with my finger and it flaked away. Pulling my standard-issue survival knife, I pried at the lifeform covering the ancient structure. It crackled and crunched as the weight of the thing assisted in peeling it away from the outer wall of the structure. I stepped back as a large slab of the creature pulled free from the building and collapsed to the ground at my feet. The gaping maw of the building where windows and a door would have once stood emptily stared back at me.

"Anyone home?" I cautiously stepped forward to peer inside the structure. A thick layer of dust covered everything within sight. I stepped through the opening, letting my eyes adjust to the shadows. I kicked at a small mound of dust on the ground that shifted and let out a squeaking grunt. The sound of cracking purple crust from the street outside caught my attention.

"That *really* doesn't sound good." I backed out of the structure. The mound let out another grunt that was echoed and answered all along the street/valley. More of the squeaking grunts accompanied the sound of cracking crust.

I turned and rushed back to the slope following the path I had originally descended from. "Nope, that is *not* a good thing."

My muscles screamed as I fought my way up the short slope. Forcing my way to the top in half the time it had taken me to go down, my heart threatened to leap from my chest. I leaned over, bracing myself on my knees as I tried to catch my breath. I turned, looking back down the slope and froze. At least a dozen bright yellow slug-like creatures had appeared. A hard armored carapace of fluorescent orange covered the forward section of the creatures. The evening sun glinted off of the carapace's metallic surface. Their bodies wriggled and undulated as they raced up the slope behind me. The lead creature let out another screeching grunt and the rest of the pack responded. Long tentacle-like appendages extended from along the sides of each creature, propelling them along faster like oars on a boat.

I turned and forced myself to run as fast as my legs would carry me in the heavy gravity. My knees screamed with each hurried step.

"SC! NV! Help!"

My right foot broke through the crusty surface into a deep hole. I stumbled forward, falling to my hands and knees.

Dad is going to be so proud.

"I can see the headlines now. Captain Blake Daniels, devoured by space slugs on his first trip into the black." I yanked my leg free from the hole and crawled forward. Glancing back, I saw the lead slug closing the gap, only a few meters away. "Oh, *this is just absolutely fracking perfect!*" I was shocked at the angry sarcasm in my own voice, but it didn't stop me. I continued crawling as fast as I could in the direction of the terrain vehicle.

"SC!"

"Get back to the terrain vehicle, sir," one of the androids said as it rushed forward. "Do you wish to capture the specimens, sir?"

"Sure, SC. Knock yourself out there, Buddy."

"I am CO sir," the android said dryly.

"I don't care! Just stop it!" I forced myself forward. Each agonizing meter was worse than the last, but I had finally made it to the terrain vehicle's loading ramp.

"SC! NV! EN! Get out there and hold them off while I bring the stunners online!"

The androids replied with a unanimous "Affirmative, sir," then charged into action. I glanced over my shoulder to see CO grappling with the lead slug, its tentacles wrapped around the android's arms, pinning them against its side. A maw opened on the underside of the beast revealing rows of triangular teeth with the same metallic sheen as the armor plating before it engulfed CO's robotic head.

"Oh, Gods!" I rushed into the cockpit and activated the terrain vehicle's stunner system. The smell of crackling ozone filled the air.

"Get clear, CO! Targeting your position now!" I frantically tapped at the controls, aiming the stunner at the offending creature. It had already engulfed over half of CO's body when they both fell over and the slug continued chewing its way further over the android's body.

I activated the comms. "CO! Do you copy? I repeat, do you copy?"

"Captain, this is MD."

"Go ahead."

"I am afraid that CO's spark has been extinguished, sir. I am not picking up any readings from his transponder."

"Die you groum'r slug!" I fired on the creature. It continued working its way up CO's body unabated. The stunner capacitors hummed as they recharged from the previous shot. I smacked the console out of frustration. "Come on, hurry the hell up!"

Two more of my android crewmen fell to the attacking slugs. "To the hells with this!" I deactivated the stunner and activated the TV's defensive laser. More and more of the slugs appeared as I waited for the system to warm up. As soon as the system went green, I fired. Sparks flew from the back of the lead slug but didn't slow it down in the slightest. Horrified, I watched as the slug worked its rubbery maw over the tip of CO's foot.

The TV suddenly shifted.

"Sir," one of the other androids said over the comms. "May I suggest that you flee the premises, sir. CO, NV, and SC are all offline and the creatures have disabled the terrain vehicle."

"How is that even possible? I thought these TVs were good for most environments?" I stood and leaned over, looking down from the windscreen. Three slugs were working their way up the side of the TV.

"The creatures seem to be excreting a combination of concentrated acidic compounds, sir."

"How do you know that they are excreting some sort of acid?"

"Because one of the creatures has already removed my left leg, sir."

"What?"

"Please, sir. I have activated emergency storage backup and uploaded myself and the others to the ship's computer. You may revive us at any time by installing us into a new chassis. Please, sir. Save yourself."

The main control console of the terrain vehicle suddenly went dark. I tapped at the controls, but all power was offline.

"Maybe MD was right, and it's time to go after all." I hurried out of the cockpit and down the loading ramp. On one side, slugs devoured what was left of two of my crew. I hurried around the opposite side of the TV and stumbled toward the east. *If I could just make it far enough away that I didn't draw the creature's attention, I could make it back to the ship*, I thought. I made my way down the slope in an easterly direction. After fifty meters or so, I turned north and made my way to the beach as fast as I could force my aching muscles to go. Two steps into the parking garage of the *Vixen* and I stopped at the sound of a familiar grunt that sent a chill up my spine. I turned to find a small, six-centimeter-long version of the alien slug creatures crawling toward me.

"Not on my ship!"

I brought my booted foot down on top of the miniature creature with a satisfying and resounding thud.

"Don't worry yourself, Blake. I took care of everything."

"What are you talking about?" I asked the image of my father, who loomed larger than life over me on the bridge's main viewscreen.

"The penalty for filing a bad colony world claim."

"Yeah, I was only fined 100 Mu for the inhospitable crushing gravity of the planet since it was my first."

My father laughed and shook his head knowingly. "I guess ignorance is bliss, isn't it?"

"What do you mean, Dad?"

"Never mind. Just take care of yourself and be safe out there, Blake. Your mother would shoot me if anything happened to you."

"I'll do my best not to get killed."

"You do that, and make us proud, Son. I have to go. Pressing matters with Interstel."

"I will Dad."

The viewscreen shifted to a view of the Starport docking bay. Berth after berth of docked ships lined the bay.

I turned back to the command display mounted to the right arm of my command chair and scrolled through the latest Nyssball scores.

"Captain."

I looked up from the command display at the empty bridge surrounding me. *After all that time alone with the walking tin cans, I kind of missed them now.* "Yes, MD?"

"The recruits have arrived sir," MD said through the bridge speakers.

"Good. Have them meet me in the ship's commons. Tell them to grab a snack from the galley if they'd like and that I'll be down shortly."

"Yes, sir."

"Please bring up the personnel files and display them on the main view screen, MD. I want to refresh my memory before I meet the crew."

"Right away, sir."

The data readout of the first personnel file flashed onto the main viewscreen followed by the image of a very young and very chipper-looking officer. The smile on her face was wide enough to be comical.

"Ciarra Jade. science officer. First voyage. Pay rate, specialist first class. She holds specialized degrees in geology, metallurgy, astrophysics, microbiology, xenobiology, and genetics."

The image changed to a dark reddish-brown Velox.

"Xixxaphhy, chief engineer. He is a veteran crew member with over six decades of experience. Pay rate, deck officer."

The image shifted and displayed another Velox with brighter reds to light purples on its shoulders and a crystal pendant hung around its neck.

"Ponoxse, navigator. She is a recent graduate of the academy, pay rate, specialist second class, specializing in hyperspace theory."

"Bosun Beau "BB" Smith," MD said as the image of a scraggly, red-bearded man with a long scar down one side of his face appeared on the screen.

"MD?"

"Yes, sir?"

"Why does he look like a pirate?"

"I do not know, sir. But he is now the ship's bosun, pay rate of chief mate. Fifteen years of experience on nearly every class of ship that Arth companies have produced."

"Alright, who was our new communications officer?"

"Ry T'Hhay'S Synnn," MD said as the image of a dark grey Thrynn, decorated in rich colors appeared on the screen. "Communications officer, familiar with all Arthian languages and dialects as well as proficient in programming and manipulating the latest translation software."

The image shifted once again to a woody stalked Elowan with greyish-yellow leaves. "Lastly we have Doctor Yerthhn. He has doctorates in microbiology, reconstructive virology, xenobiology, and genetic anthropology. He was at the forefront of Arthian medicine decades before the space program began."

I shook my head in confusion. "If he's over one hundred years old, why is he going out into the black?"

"I can not speculate his reasoning, sir."

"If nothing else, this will be an interesting cruise. Shall we go meet the new crew, MD?"

"At your discretion, sir."

"Remind me to reprogram you with one of those new personality mods the next time we're in Starport and I have the MU to cover it."

"As you wish, sir."

I made my way from the bridge to the ship's commons in moments. I could feel lady luck changing her ways for me. The spring I felt in my step was proof enough of that.

I could hear a strange chittering sound as I approached the compartment that stopped as suddenly as MD announced my arrival with the sounding of an ancient Bosun's whistle.

The large reddish-brown Velox reached up and removed the offending intercom speaker from the wall with little effort.

"That would probably make you, Xixxaphhy, wouldn't it?"

The large Velox nodded with a chitter.

I clapped my hands together and looked around the room at the other occupants.

"Welcome aboard the *Vixen*. I am your captain, Blake Daniels."

I glanced from one silent face to the next then continued.

"I know that things may become somewhat uncomfortable at times with everyone in such close quarters for extended periods, but I have no doubt that we are the best crew in the Interstel fleet. We will seek out new worlds, new life, and boldly go where no other Arthian has gone before!"

Each of them continued to stare at me in silence.

"Any questions?"

The young science officer quietly raised her hand from behind the Thrynn.

"Yes, um Ciarra, isn't it?"

"Yes, sir."

"You had a question?"

The rest of the crew turned to look in her direction.

"Why do the ship's sanitation bots have knives taped to them?"

"I reprogramed them to act as the ship's security primary to their cleaning protocols. Better to have someone on duty when we're off ship cruising around an alien planet in the TV so nothing sneaks on board while we aren't here."

I looked from one confused face to another. "Any other questions?"

Each and every one of them slowly shook their heads.

"Great! MD, please direct our crew to their quarters so they can stow their gear and we can get underway. Meet me on the bridge in ten."

"Captain to the bridge!" Ponoxse, the ship's Velox navigator shouted over the comms followed by an ear-piercing chittering.

Warning klaxons rang out across the ship. I ran to the forward most hatch and climbed up to the bridge instead of waiting on the lift.

"Status!"

"We have an unidentified vessel approaching at a high rate of speed," Ciarra replied. "I'm picking up energy readouts equivalent to Class Four engines and Class Two missile launchers that are offline, sir."

"Shields up! Arm all weapons systems," I shouted without thinking.

Ponoxse turned in her seat at the helm and cocked her head oddly to the side. "The *Vixen* isn't equipped with shields or any type of weapons system, sir."

"Can we outrun them?"

"They could run circles around us without breaking a sweat," Ponoxse replied then turned back to her console.

"We're rrreceiving a transsssmission, sir," Ry, the communications officer announced in her hissing tone.

"What does it say?"

"Rrressspond."

"Respond to what?"

"Maybe it's an automated response, Cap," Ciarra offered. "I'm not picking up any life signs aboard."

I took my seat as a chill ran up my spine. "What's our location?"

"We are currently at coordinates 138 x 110. We're four parsecs away from the G class star selected for exploration.

"Show me the star chart on the main viewscreen."

As soon as the star chart flashed onto the screen and I saw our current location marker flashing like it was intentionally mocking me, my heart nearly leapt out of my chest.

"That isn't good."

"What isn't good, sir?" Ciarra asked.

I rubbed at my temples as a preemptive strike against the headache I knew was coming. "There have been reports of ships being attacked or going missing coreward of Arth. A colony transport, the *Stormhaven*, was found adrift with battle damage. All crew and passengers aboard were lost. The oddest thing about it was that the cargo was still intact."

"Sssir, they are rrrepeating their lasst hail," Ry said.

The aft hatch to the bridge opened with a hiss and Xixxaphhy appeared. "This had better be good. I was in the middle of recalibrating the condensation scrubbers." The large, tattooed Velox crossed his four arms and glared down at me. "If I don't get the ratio adjusted perfectly, then we'll have corrosion and pitting starting throughout the ship."

"Ciarra, bring up a magnified view of our unexpected guest," I ordered.

"Aye, sir."

"What do you make of that, Xix?" I pointed at the ship displayed on the main viewscreen.

"It's ancient," the old Velox said as he stepped closer to the viewscreen. "Looks like it's been out here a long time. See that patch of scaring across the hull? It's probably seen more than a few micrometeor storms before. Been in more than a few fire fights too if that carbon scoring across the dorsal ridge is any indication."

I stood and stepped up next to Xix. "Any idea who they might be?"

Xix let out a low chittering. His mandibles clicked together as he drifted off in thought. "Some of the design characteristics remind me of *Noah 2*."

"The ancient ark ship *Noah 2*?" Ciarra asked.

Xix nodded and clacked his mandibles. "The same."

"Could the Old Empire still exist?"

"It couldn't be," I said. "The Empire fell apart over a thousand years ago."

"It could just be a design coincidence," Xix said. "But if this ship is of an Old Empire design, then we might have a problem."

Ponoxse turned in her seat to face us. "If they are part of the Old Empire and ships have been disappearing in this region, then we could be violating their territorial boundaries."

"Sssir," Ry interrupted. "They are hailing usss again."

"Sir," Ciarra shouted. "They've armed their weapons and locked onto us, sir."

I slid into the command chair and secured myself with the restraints. "Evasive maneuvers! Get us out of here!"

"Already on it, Captain," Ponoxse replied as she pushed the ship to full power.

Xix rushed over to the engineering station and secured himself.

"Missiles inbound!" Ciarra announced.

"Evasive maneuvers! Brace for impact!"

The ship rocked hard and spun sickeningly to starboard followed by a second explosion.

"Hull integrity down to eighty percent," Xix announced. "We've lost primary power on deck four aft."

"Ponoxse," I shouted. "This ship is brand new and theirs is maybe a thousand years old. They can outrun us, but can they outmaneuver us?"

"There's only one way to find out," Ponoxse shouted in reply as another missile warning klaxon roared to life.

"Six new contacts, sir," Ciarra said. "Bearing one three six point two mark five five point nine."

Ponoxse nosed the ship over, rolled, and changed course away from the alien ship.

"I might be able to boost our engine output, but I'll have to do it from engineering," Xix added as he rushed from the bridge.

"Contacts are one kilometer out and closing, Captain," Ciarra reported. "All six have changed course with us and are still in pursuit."

I tapped at the command display, glancing over the automated damage report.

"What's the status of the alien ship?"

Ciarra brought up a tactical display on the main viewscreen. Both ships represented by approximated icons moved about the three-dimensional grid. Six small cone-shaped objects closed the distance behind the *Vixen*. "They are closing fast, sir. The alien ship's course is unchanged and holding steady."

"Bring us around on a collision course with them and make sure those missiles are close behind."

"Somehow I don't think that'll be a problem," Ciarra said. "Missiles are adjusting to our course corrections and still closing."

Ponoxse turned in her seat and stared back at me. Her antennae seemed to twitch anxiously. "Not to question your orders, sir; but shouldn't we be moving away from the alien ship, not heading right for it?"

I let out an unintentional laugh. "Probably, but I don't see any other way out of this. There's no way that we can outrun or outgun them. We just have to improvise."

"Do you mean to destroy them by killing all of us, sir?"

"No, Specialist," I retorted. "I mean to cripple them by shoving their missiles down their throats. Either turn around and follow my orders or get off of my bridge!"

Ponoxse turned back to the helm console and adjusted our course. "Aye, sir. Changing course to intercept alien craft."

"Get us as close as you can then skim her top and dive away. Let's see if those missiles will lock onto them instead of us."

This was crazy, but what else were we supposed to do? No weapons to speak of and the alien ship could out-accelerate us without even trying. We might have a fighting chance if there were a planet or something nearby where we could hide.

"The missiles are following us, sir."

Target klaxons raged once more across the bridge.

"New contacts," Ciarra announced. "They've fired another pair of missiles."

"Ponoxse, can you avoid them?"

The Velox helmsman laughed. Her mandibles clacked together. "Just hold on!"

The ship rolled and corkscrewed to the left while diving away from the alien vessel. She then pulled up the nose sharply before rolling and corkscrewing back toward the alien vessel.

"Missile impact in three…," Ciarra shouted.

Ponoxse tapped feverishly at the controls with all four of her hands. "Port docking thrusters engaged."

The ship sickeningly jinked sideways without warning then rolled left. My stomach churned from the maneuver. The added sound and smell of Ciarra emptying her stomach onto the deck of my bridge did not help me in the slightest. I swallowed hard and had just forced the bile back down when the ship shook from another impact.

Ciarra grunted as she pulled herself upright and wiped her mouth. "We have damage to the lateral sensor array from that last impact. Ponoxse bought us some time with her fancy flying. The rest of those missiles are closing fast. Contact in five seconds."

"Ponoxse, do something!" I ordered.

She turned around and silently stared back at me with the look of a predator about to devour its prey. If a Velox could express emotion, I would have sworn that look had been fueled by an angry hatred. She turned back to her console and the ship suddenly slid upward, pressing me down into my command chair.

"Ponoxse," Xix shouted over the ship's intercoms.

A tingle of hope rose up my spine. "I hope you have a miracle for us, Xix."

"I might."

"Go ahead, Xixxaphhy," Ponoxse said.

"Go to full power and you'll have a ten-second hyperspace boost when you do."

I shook my head out of confusion. "But shouldn't that tear us apart so close to a gravity well?"

"It should, but I've diverted power to the inertial dampers and re-enforced the structural integrity field. That's the best I can do so close to the alien ship. If it works, we might get away but the ship will probably take some heavy damage."

"Do it!"

"Aye, Captain. Everyone hold onto something!"

Ponoxse rolled the *Vixen* into an inverted position in relation to the alien vessel as we approached within meters of the other ship's hull. The ship leapt forward as the universe momentarily blurred out of existence. Sparks erupted from a junction panel on the forward wall of the bridge.

Emergency bulkheads slammed closed as alarms began to scream.

"Hull breaches on deck two forward sensor maintenance compartment, in main engineering, and the TV parking garage," Ciarra reported.

Ponoxse half rose from her station. "By the blessed Grand Lovely, please be safe, Xixxaphhy," she mumbled more to herself than anyone while fingering the crystal pendant that hung around her neck.

"Captain," Ciarra shouted. "I'm detecting six impacts against the alien vessel! Exiting engagement area, sir. We should be far enough away from that alien ship's gravity well to fully enter hyperspace."

"Then punch it! Get us out of here, Ponoxse."

We limped along through hyperspace for the next week, repairing what systems that we could. Lacking all of the raw materials needed for repairs, not to mention a space dock we were limited on what we were capable of doing while out in the black. We had gotten the ship back to eighty-eight percent by the time we arrived on the outskirts of a G class star system at coordinates 143 x 115.

Ciarra eagerly tapped through the data on her console as I entered the bridge.

"What have we got, Ciarra?"

Ciarra let out an excited giggle then said, "I'm picking up two planets. The first is in orbital position seven and looks like it's a rocky world at six times ten to the power of twenty-two mass tons. The second planet is at position five and only three times ten to the twenty-first power mass tons."

She let out a long gasp then turned in her seat to look at me. Her face beaming with excitement.

"I'm picking up a wide biosphere, sir. I can't be absolutely certain from this distance, but it looks like the atmosphere may primarily be made up of oxygen and carbon dioxide with liquid water making up a majority of the planet's surface."

"The data could be off," I said.

"It could be, but I'm pretty sure that I'm right. We'll need to get into orbit or land to get more accurate scans."

Ponoxse let out a shrill trill. "The Rock of Truth has shone down upon us."

I couldn't help but smile. "And lady luck has finally turned in our favor."

Always on Duty

By: Benjamin Tyler Smith

"Put me in for a hundred." Devon threw a red chip into the center of the table.

Devon took a moment to scan his surroundings while the seventeen other players—Human and alien alike—considered whether to call, raise, or fold. He sat in a private booth in the Backroom, the largest illegal casino and speakeasy on Arth's Starport. Beyond the one-way window that covered an entire wall, Devon could see the casino's main floor. It was packed with sentients, mostly members of the four races of Arth, but the occasional extra-solar species could be seen mingling in the crowd. Android servers clad in tuxedos paced the floor, serving complimentary refreshments and answering questions. One stood near the private booths, a closed parasol in one gloved hand and a peaked cap covering its otherwise copper-colored face.

To think all this is hidden away. The Backroom was located behind Chute 'n Scoot, one of Starport's laundromats. To the unsuspecting customer, Chute 'n Scoot was a legitimate business with full-service cleaning, along with decontamination of EVA suits. Ads that read "Dirty Suit? Put it in the Chute!" were plastered all over the sprawling space station's main levels, along with the aforementioned drop-off chutes. They also had a self-service area for local residents to use.

It was here—if someone knew the right guy and the right password—that one could get into the Backroom, where all manner of illicit activities took place. Gambling, narcotics, black market trades, interspecies companionship, the works. The more profane the crime, the deeper into the building one had to go to find it. Devon currently sat in the outermost chamber, the speakeasy casino portion of the criminal enterprise.

The dealer, a member of the insectoid Velox race who somehow managed to cut a dashing figure in his tuxedo, used his multiple appendages to dole the next cards out to the players still in the game. Tricardium used the equivalent of three decks of poker cards, with a subsequent increase in possible players. That meant a longer game and more losers in the end, but with the potential for a much larger payout to the eventual winner.

Devon didn't really care about the game, as his interest was in the gray scaled Thrynn seated next to him. He and the reptilian had used coded language in words and bets over the last few games to affect the exchange of several nubile maidens of a nearly extinct race of sentient meta-marsupials. They'd been stolen from an eccentric collector's menagerie of cryogenically frozen exotics, and my employer was very interested in their well-being. All that was left was to hand over the creds and receive their storage coordinates.

Devon slipped his hand into his pants pocket, where two small items were. He removed one, a dark-colored pouch with an adhesive activated by skin oil. He rubbed his thumb along the adhesive, then stuck the pouch to the underside of the table. He made a show of shuffling his cards, as if lining them up into a winning hand. Next to him, the Thrynn shifted his weight in the padded chair. His hand slipped beneath the table, and in a deft motion, he pocketed the pouch. A second later, Devon's tablet buzzed softly from inside his jacket pocket.

"Ela here," a soft voice said into his earpiece. "Exchange made; coordinates delivered. We're moving in."

The dealer ran them through two more games while Devon waited. More players folded and shuffled out the door with what was left of their chips, and a few more joined. A Velox female who towered over Devon's 1.8 meters stepped into the room and took the vacant chair next to the gray skinned Thrynn. For the second time that night, Devon laid eyes on a Velox who could pull off the formal wear look and not seem ridiculous about it. The Velox dealer had noticed as well and batted his antennae in her direction. She chirped something in the Velox tongue, and the dealer's antennae shot straight up, a sign his interest was piqued. Whether it was in a positive or negative way, Devon didn't know.

"Targets secured," Ela said again a few minutes later. "It's on you, now."

That's all Devon needed to hear. He waited as the players made their bets, then placed his hand on the table. "Ladies, gentle-sents, this has been a most enjoyable game, but I am afraid the stakes are too rich for my blood. I fold."

"Oh, such a shame, Mister—" The dealer studied him for a long moment, his multi-faceted eyes glimmering in the yellow lamplight. "I'm sorry, I don't remember your name."

"That's all right. I don't remember the name I gave you. Let me give you my real one." Devon reached into his pants pocket and retrieved the second item: a small, silver badge. "Devon Harlow, Interstel PD. Mr. Rascon here is under arrest."

The whole table fell silent. Everyone stared at the police badge in his hand. The Thrynn named Rascon tried to make a run for it, but he hadn't made two steps before the female Velox blocked his way. She held up a badge of her own. "Miranda H'Than. Don't even try it."

"Damn!" Rascon spat. "I ssshould've known it was too good a deal!" He reached into his robes.

Before Devon could yell "Gun!" and reach for his own sidearm, Miranda moved faster than the eye could follow. One moment

Rascon was leveling his pistol at her, the next he was on the floor, pinned by three of her four arms. The remaining hand slapped a set of cuffs onto the Thrynn's wrists.

By this point, the other card players had jumped out of their seats. A few, including the dealer, made for the door, but the copper-headed android servant barred their way. He pulled the tip off the parasol and aimed a large-caliber barrel at the dealer. "Give me an excuse, criminal scum."

"Easy, Copperhead!" Devon placed himself between the dealer and his trigger-happy squad member. "I know you love the sight of blood—an unhealthy trait even for synthetics, I might add—but you've got to tone it down."

To the scared card players, Devon said, "You're all free to go."

One of the players was an Elowan. Much of his blue-green body was hidden beneath a self-reflective suit designed to increase photosynthesis, even in fluorescent or LED light. He studied Devon and Miranda for a long moment before he asked, "Is it standard procedure to let criminals go?"

"Are you insssane?" a Thrynn next to him hissed, his reptilian tongue putting extra emphasis on the "S" sound.

"It's a fair question," the Elowan countered. "I want confirmation, so I'm not harassed about this later."

"An officer can overlook misdemeanor offenses when in pursuit of suspected felons." Devon pointed at Miranda, who had her knee in the trussed-up card shark's back. "I'd much rather send this sent-trafficker to prison than cite you for engaging in unregulated gambling. Chances are you were robbed enough, playing against a dealer like this cheat."

"Hey!" the dealer objected, his antennae humming.

"Sorry, no offense." Devon shrugged. "I just know how casinos operate." To the Elowan he again said, "Interstel PD thanks you for your cooperation. Now, get out of here, please."

The Elowan shrugged and walked out the door, the Thrynn and the others following close behind. Miranda watched them go, then turned her multifaceted eyes on Devon. "Was that wise?" she asked as she hoisted Rascon to his feet.

"We don't have the manpower to arrest the whole casino." He pointed out the window, at a commotion on the main floor. Several Interstel PD officers stood in a line, shock batons in hand. The patrons shied away from them, but most made no move to run. This wasn't the first time the Backroom had been raided, and it also wasn't the first time more mundane crimes were overlooked in the pursuit of darker ones. "It'll be fine. This was a low-level private event. I doubt anyone in this room was on any kind of watchlist, save for our boy here."

Devon slapped Mr. Rascon on the back for emphasis. "You're going away for a long time." He made for the door. Come on, Miranda, Copperhead. Time to go get our 'atta boys' from the Lieutenant."

"You morons!" Lieutenant Stone pounded the sole bare spot on his faux wood desk, hard enough to shake the stacks of murder books and other paperwork that reached toward the room's low ceiling. "How in the name of everything holy and unholy could you screw up so badly?"

Devon stood in front of the massively overloaded desk, his four squad members behind him. Miranda rested her bulk on her hind legs, her two sets of arms crossed in front of her thorax and abdomen. Next to her, Officer Thassor waited, his green skin a lime color in the office's stark lighting. He appeared as if he wanted to say something, but was minding his forked tongue for a change. Ela, the squad's Elowan medical examiner and field medic, slouched with her hands in the pockets of her white coat. Her green eyes had a distant look to them, as if she were running any number of reports and cases through her head, which was likely the case.

At the end of the line stood Copperhead, the squad's android enforcer unit. His face wasn't designed for movement, so he had commissioned a number of bronze-colored masks to wear depending on the situation: a smiling face for dealing with the general public or his fellow squad members, a scowl when in pursuit or interrogation of criminals, and one with an ecstatic grin that he reserved for the range and for particularly fierce shootouts. Today he wore a mask with a slight frown and quirked eyebrows that could reflect curiosity, confusion, or contrition. When Stone was involved, it was usually a combination of the three.

Stone continued to rant for several minutes, his face growing redder by the second. When he finally paused to catch his breath, Devon asked, "What is this about, sir?"

"What is this about?" Stone pounded the desk again, and the towers of paperwork and binders teetered back and forth. "What is this about? I'll tell you what it's about!"

"Then get on it with already," muttered Miranda, her buzzing voice so low Devon assumed only he could hear it.

He assumed wrong. Stone turned his hot-blooded glare on Miranda, who stared back impassively. One didn't intimidate a Velox of Miranda's stature. At nearly three meters in height,

Miranda was tall even for her species. Stone was tall and broad, but he wasn't Miranda's level of tall and broad.

Stone turned to his computer. "Take a look at this, geniuses." He punched in a few commands, then rotated the monitor. "Recognize him?"

It was the Elowan from the Backroom, the one who'd asked if Devon was sure he and the other gamblers could leave despite being criminals. "I remember him in the casino, but not anywhere else."

"Really? That's fascinating, because you should've known him from before that." Stone punched in another command, and the image changed to a profile photo of the Elowan. "Graslen Supox. Known to be affiliated with Azazel Black's gang, as well as a number of other mob lords on various planets within our jurisdiction. He's to be brought in under suspicion of capital software piracy."

Devon's stomach clenched. Capital software piracy? It didn't reach that level of an offense with distributing illegal copies of video games and movies. A capital crime meant one of the big corporations was involved, or maybe even Interstel itself. "When did this go out?"

"Eight hours ago."

Devon did the math. "We were already inside the casino. We wouldn't have received the notification then."

"You and Detectives Bugsley and Chrome-Dome, maybe." Stone jabbed a finger at Miranda and Copperhead in turn, then wagged that same finger between Ela and Thassor. "They could've alerted you to a change in circumstances, surely."

"We were busy securing the cryogenically frozen alien maidens at the time," Ela objected.

"She's right, sssir," Thassor hissed. "Did the blotter indicate this Grassslen was aboard the Ssstarport?"

Stone glared at them a moment, then rotated the monitor around to look at the notification more closely. "Regardless, you let a suspect in a Class Triple-A Felony get away, and you need to get him back."

"What did he steal?" Devon asked.

"Some top-secret program from the Cartography Department. Way above our pay grades." Stone waved a hand in dismissal. "Whatever it is, Interstel's top brass are breathing on the necks of *our* top brass to get it back." He jabbed his finger at Devon. "That makes this royal screw-up of yours a real pain my backside."

Devon really wanted to break that finger of his. "We're on it, sir. You can count on us."

Stone snorted. "Better than this last time, I trust."

"Code has been confirmed." Devon disabled the handheld projector showing the updated Security Access Code Wheel and tucked it into a pocket. "Thank you for your cooperation, Captain Nu'Bee, but do make sure your comms officer understands the difference between Nice Thing and Bladed Toy. It may not seem like much, but it leads to situations like this."

"What if I think bladed toys *are* nice things?" Miranda murmured.

He stood on the bridge of the police cruiser *Black Maria*. Thassor sat at the comms station to his left, and Copperhead leaned his metal frame over the weapons console to the right. Miranda crouched over her navigation controls, two hands on the wheel and two more on the maneuvering pedals. On the viewscreen, an Elowan merchant wrung his twiggy hands. "My apologies, Officer. It will not happen again, I assure you."

"Glad to hear it, Captain. Copperhead, power down our weapons."

"A pity," Copperhead grumbled, but he complied.

Captain Nu'Bee released an audible sigh of relief before the connection was severed.

"Well, that went well," Devon muttered as he sat in his command chair. The furniture's smart-fabric molded around his back and thighs, making it feel like he was floating in midair. "All that effort to chase this ship down, and it's the wrong merchant."

They were four days out of Arth, in pursuit of a merchant ship that failed its automated security clearance when it left port. Somehow the Starport's security system overlooked it, and no alert was sent until hours later. The techs were still tearing through the computer in order to figure out what happened, but Devon assumed it was likely operator error. The alerts went to a bureaucrats' desk somewhere deep inside Interstel HQ, and if that bureaucrat was on vacation or taking a crap, no alerts. Since all they knew was that Graslen was an Elowan merchant who was affiliated with a few different gangs, they didn't have much to go by. The obvious course of action would be to check every ship with Elowans onboard, but that was both impractical and in violation of anti-discrimination laws.

"Look on the bright ssside, Devon," Thassor said, an earphone held against the side of his head, over his tympanic membrane. "At least the Trisa system has a warm sssun, and Trisa III is known for both its beachesss and its trading port."

"I do not care for the beach," Copperhead said.

"Because the sand and humidity are bad for your joints?" Devon asked.

"There is very little cover on the beach. It is not conducive to a shoot-out."

"But, if there is no cover for you, there is also no cover for your enemiesss," Thassor countered.

Copperhead studied Thassor a moment. "I never considered that. Maybe I do like the beach, then."

Devon shook his head. Copperhead had interesting priorities. "Miranda, set course for Trisa III." While they were here, they might as well question the locals. Last anyone had seen of Graslen, he'd boarded a skiff that quickly disappeared off Starport's scanners. Interstel had narrowed the list down to around twenty ships that all left port that day, including Captain Nu'Bee's vessel, which had been red-flagged due to the screw-up with the security wheel clearance. BOLO—Be On the Look Out—notices had been distributed for the other ships, and so far five of the remaining nineteen had been inspected with no sign of Graslen or this mysterious bit of software he'd absconded with.

Several hours at full speed found them nearing Trisa III. It drew closer by the minute, glowing like a blue jewel against a dark backdrop. They encountered dozens of ships either parked in orbit or traveling away from the trade and tourist hub, bound for Arth or a half-dozen other worlds. Thassor fielded a number of complaints and questions from the passing vessels. Other ships attempted to skirt along under the police cruiser's scanners, a suspicious act that, in most cases, was probable cause to initiate an interaction, if not detain the ship outright. Thassor hailed most of these and spoke with their respective comm officers or captains. While he reminded them that smuggling was a crime alongside other offenses, he carefully inquired about Graslen's whereabouts.

Devon didn't know how the Thrynn officer could manage that without naming names or stating the alleged crime, but he wasn't the *Black Maria*'s communications officer for nothing.

One ship stood out from the rest. Miranda pointed it out on the monitor. "Every time we enter scanner range, it accelerates enough to nudge itself beyond the sweep."

"Ssshe's refusing our hailsss, too." Thassor tapped his claws along the edge of his console. "Claimsss communication problemsss."

"Interesting." Devon pulled up a preliminary scan of the ship. Unbeknownst to most, Interstel PD cruisers were equipped with scanners capable of penetrating most hulls. This was especially important with interdiction efforts. Smuggling was highly likely when areas of a ship appeared opaque on the deep scan. That's what happened with this particular ship, the *Arthian Dream*.

"Pull alongside them," Devon ordered.

"On it." Miranda pushed the engines to full burn, and they soon outpaced the *Arthian Dream*'s efforts to outrun them. When it became obvious they'd catch up, the suspect ship slowed down, its captain not wishing to provoke the police cruiser any further.

"They're hailing usss," Thassor said.

"So much for communications problems," Devon muttered. "Bring up their video feed on the main screen, but wait a moment before sending them ours."

"Roger." Thassor activated the viewscreen. What Devon assumed was *Arthian Dream*'s bridge appeared. Oak railings, plush seats, and rich tapestries adorned the bridge of what, on the outside, appeared to be a modest merchant's vessel. An Elowan sat in the captain's seat, his suit from the casino replaced with silk robes meant for lounging in luxury.

"There he is, the bastard," Devon muttered. To Thassor he said, "Only show him your face and voice. I don't want him recognizing Miranda and me."

"It's not like he'd be able to tell the difference," Ela said from her medical office. "Velox and Humans all look alike."

"We do not!" Miranda and Devon answered simultaneously.

Thassor grinned as he activated his microphone. "Attention, *Arthian Dream*. This is Interssstel PD Cruiser *Black Maria*. Power down your enginesss and prepare for cargo inspection."

"On what grounds?" Graslen demanded. "We've done nothing illegal."

"Nor do we sssuspect you of anything illegal. We are sssearching for a runaway, a Human male of about eleven cyclesss."

"We've no such runaway aboard our ship."

"Ssso you claim. Thisss boy is adept at hiding in the smallest compartmentsss. Sssuch as the compartmentsss we sssee on our ssscanners. Power down, and prepare for inssspection."

Graslen put a hand to his smooth chin, as if considering. He whispered something to one of his bridge officers, but the ship's microphones didn't pick it up.

"Their weapons are coming online!" Copperhead warned.

"You have my answer," Graslen said, a smug expression on his face right before the connection went dead. *Arthian Dream* then filled the viewscreen, its energy cannons glowing and its missile pods now exposed.

"Miranda, evasives!" Devon shouted. "Copperhead, light 'em up!"

"On it!" Miranda barked.

"Roger," intoned Copperhead.

Miranda fired *Black Maria*'s maneuvering thrusters, and they banked hard to starboard, then to port, then again to starboard. Devon's chair absorbed most of the gee-forces, but it still put a strain on his neck and chest. On the viewscreen, laser beams lit up the darkness of space as they shot past the ship. One impacted the shields and the beam refracted into a multi-hued pattern of lights, blinding but otherwise harmless.

"Firing missiles," Copperhead pushed the array of red buttons on his console, each slaved to one of *Black Maria*'s four missile tubes. "Missiles headed our way, too," he added.

"Countermeasures!" Devon grunted. Miranda's crazy maneuvers were pushing the blood out of his head.

Behind his snarling mask, Copperhead's two ocular sensors rolled independently of one another, allowing him to take in the full measure of his console with little head movement. "Flares launched. Firing lasers."

The viewscreen's many camera feeds lit up with an answering barrage of laser fire from *Black Maria*. Most missed the fleeing garbage scow, but one scored a direct hit on the number two engine. "Excellent!" Devon said. "Take out the remaining—"

An explosion rocked the ship. Alarms wailed, the ceiling lights flickered, and red indicators lit up on Devon's command console. "Hull breach on Deck Three!" he reported to the others. "Sealing it off. Everyone, damage report!"

"Weapons systems fine," Copperhead stated. "Shields at half-strength."

"Engine power lost." Miranda pounded the navigation console. "They got a lucky shot in through the shields."

"Target isss getting away," Thassor reported. "Looksss like they're heading for Trisa III."

"They'll need repairs if they're going to get her back in the sky again," Copperhead noted.

"So will we." Miranda pointed at her navigation console, which was locked out. "We're adrift."

"Miranda, continue to track where they're headed," Devon instructed. "Ela, repair and inspect the sealed compartment."

Ela's face appeared on the monitor in the command chair's armrest. "I'm a doctor, not an engineer!"

"You're a medical examiner, not a doctor." Thassor grinned. "I can join you, if you like."

Ela frowned as she gathered up her helmet and tools. "Great, just what I wanted. A Thrynn for company. No, I'll be fine on my own, thank you very much."

"Good," Thassor said when he cut the signal. "I need to worry about the enginesss. We're not going anywhere until we repair them." He looked over the damage assessment Miranda had sent to his station and cursed. "It'll take us several hours, at least."

Several hours? Damn. Graslen and his ilk could jump ship in that amount of time, or meet with whoever they'd stolen the software for. They needed to pursue them now.

"It is a good thing we have plenty of CAMoTP onboard," Copperhead rumbled. The acronym—pronounced "Camo Tip"—referred to the materials most often used in ship repairs: cobalt, aluminum, molybdenum, titanium, and promethium. He brought up *Black Maria*'s cargo manifest and pointed. "We have everything we need."

Devon studied the manifest, then tapped a line item. "Is this what I think it is?"

"If you are thinking that is the skiff we confiscated from the happy juice smugglers a few weeks ago, yes." Copperhead brought up a page of details on the shuttle craft. "Many false bottoms and breakaway panels for contraband."

Thassor wrinkled his nose. "That damn skiff had so much contraband stuffed aboard it smelled like a juicer's den. Filthy stuff."

Devon tapped the screen again. "Thassor, load some of the CAMoTP aboard, along with any spare tools you won't need for the job here."

"I'm not head engineer," Thassor said. "Make Miranda do it."

"For the sake of our engine repairs, you're head engineer today." Devon pointed at Miranda and hiked his thumb toward the door. "You and I've got a date planetside."

"I'm not interested in Humans that way," Miranda said with a wave of a hand.

"Oh, don't be like that. Not after I got you the right dress for the occasion."

That piqued Miranda's interest. For an insect, she had a strange fascination with formalwear and garments most Human women would consider cute. Devon doubted if many of those same women would find the outfits cute on a Velox, but if Miranda enjoyed it, he wasn't going to try and dissuade her. Not only would she not listen, she'd get angry. No good ending ever came to someone who pissed off Miranda.

"Why do you need sssome of our repair materialsss?" Thassor asked.

"Oh, nothing much." Devon grinned. "Just thought I'd help out a stricken ship in the neighborhood, that's all."

"Technicians, huh?" The male Velox looked Miranda over with approval, but his multifaceted gaze turned skeptical when he turned to Devon. "Both of you?"

"What's that supposed to mean?" Devon demanded. "Got something against Humans?"

"Not at all. Some of my best friends and shipmates are Human. None of them are on the engineering or repair crews."

They stood in a crowded marketplace on Trisa III, amidst a group of freelance engineers and technicians. A blazing hot sun beat down on them, but the sea breeze made up for it. Less than a kilometer away, fancy resorts overlooked pristine beaches of purple sand. Devon wished he could be there now, sipping a deep blue and eyeing up any attractive women who happened to be about. Sadly, duty called.

"He learned from the best," Miranda assured the Velox male, whose name was Krox.

"Oh, really?" Krox cocked his head to the side, his mandibles twitching. "And who is the best?"

Miranda rested all four hands on the utility harness hanging over her jacket. "Me."

Krox let out a buzzing snort. "You've got confidence, I'll give you that." He pointed at the tablet in Devon's hand. "You also have some of the materials we need for our repairs. Personally I'd rather buy it from you and be done with it, but my captain is in a hurry and three of our engineers were hurt in an...accident."

I bet, Devon thought.

"Are accidents common on your ship?" Miranda asked.

"Our ship is old, and accidents can happen anywhere. Don't worry. You'll be well-compensated, both for your skills and your hold of CAMoTP."

"How soon do you need us?" Miranda asked. "We have a job we'll have finished in the next day or two, but we plan to be on Trisa III for at least another two weeks."

Krox let out a chirp, similar to a Human clicking his tongue. "Unfortunately, we can't wait a day or two. We need our ship operational in the next Arth day. Can your other job wait?"

"Well…."

The two haggled for the next several minutes. Devon leaned against a nearby pillar, a bemused expression on his face. Here they were, doing everything they could to infiltrate Graslen's ship, and Miranda was haggling over a fee he and Devon would never collect on, for inconveniencing a client they didn't have. Many Velox were considered dull-witted or at least incapable of creative thought, a stigma from the hive-like consciousness of those in the Veloxi Empire. This view often served to help Miranda with her subterfuge, as many didn't think her capable of it.

"It is agreed, then," Krox said. He and Miranda clacked a hand against one another's carapaces to seal the deal. "Transfer your materials and equipment to my shuttle, and we will be on our way within the hour." He turned back to the remaining engineers and technicians. "Your first job is to help these two with the transfer. Let's be on it! We're burning daylight."

It took them longer than an hour to get everything stowed away, but they were soon soaring out of the atmosphere. They blazed past Trisa III's starport and the ships moored there and instead flew toward the planet's lone moon. As they flew around the far side, they saw the silhouette of a ship in low orbit. "That's the

Arthian Dream," Krox said. "Your new home for the next day or two."

"Why is it moored all the way out here?" one of the technicians asked.

"Pirates were after us," Krox said. "We managed to escape, and intercepted a message sent to Trisa III to warn their allies we were on the way."

"Ah, that makes sense." The tech nodded. "Lucky break on intercepting that transmission!"

Yeah, real lucky, Devon thought. It appeared that Miranda wasn't the only Velox who could lie without batting an eyelash. Or antenna, in this case. He crossed his arms and tapped the badge sewn into the sleeve of his work jacket. It bore the seal of some munitions company named JWMCC, which was the silhouette of a woman wearing a bunny costume and holding a submachine gun of some sort. "Ready to hop when you need a drop!" was printed along the bottom. It was a popular enough logo that random citizens wore it emblazoned on all manner of outfits and paraphernalia. The badge looked innocent enough, but tap it a couple times….

"We hear you, Grease Monkey One," Copperhead's tinny voice sounded from his hidden earpiece, the words so quiet he could barely hear them, a good thing considering how cramped the shuttle was. "More importantly, we hear everyone around you."

"Thassor is finishing up repairs," Ela said, answering Devon's unspoken question. "I'm actively tracking your position now. When you're in position, I'll get to work."

He tapped the badge twice. *Confirmed.*

As they passed over the *Arthian Dream* in their landing approach, Devon could see the damage he and his crew had wreaked. The number two engine had been completely blown out, and one of the ship's massive cargo holds was gone, blasted into oblivion by one of *Black Maria*'s missiles. *Copperhead would be pleased to see that*, he thought.

They landed a few minutes later and disembarked into a bustling shuttle bay. The *Arthian Dream* had a number of skiffs of its own, and it appeared at least two of them had recently returned from somewhere. Trisa III or its moon, most likely. Devon felt a flash of concern at first. Could the trade have already taken place? Was the stolen software gone? Then he looked closer and realized the crates and containers piled high in the bay were foodstuffs, probably replacements for the cargo hold they had struck.

Miranda led Devon over to the cargo pods attached to the outside of Krox's shuttle, and a few of the techs followed. Krox waved them back. "Save that for the crew! You were hired to turn wrenches, not haul crates!"

"Then why did we haul crates planetside?" one of the techs, an Elowan, grumbled. "My back will be sore for a week."

"Ssstop complaining," a Thrynn engineer hissed.

Miranda stepped in before the two could come to blows. "Let's be civil, please. I need to be planetside ASAP, or my client will make ceremonial armor out of my carapace."

Krox called them over to a console in the corner of the shuttle bay. The widescreen monitor displayed a map of the ship. "We're gonna split into two groups. Half of you are headed for the breached cargo bay." He tapped out a path this group was to follow to get there from the shuttle bay. "There's quite a bit of patching up to do there, so make sure you're suited up. I'll have a member of my team lead you there.

"The other half is bound for the engine room." He tapped out another path, then pointed at a group of the technicians, Miranda and Devon included. "You'll be coming with me. You have the most experience dealing with engines and thrusters."

Damn. Devon really wanted to go with the group headed to the cargo bay. There'd be less scrutiny, and a greater chance to slip away and find what they were looking for.

"There's not a second to waste," Krox said. He headed for the door, waving with his four hands for those he designated to follow.

Miranda planted herself behind Devon for a moment, blocking anyone else's view of the console. Devon reached into his pocket, rubbed his thumb along the adhesive strip to activate it, then stuck it to the underside of the console. He tucked his hands back into his pockets and followed after Krox.

The Velox engineer led them away from the shuttle bay, toward the bow of the ship. They stopped at a maintenance bay to collect equipment. Krox and his crewmates went inside while he made the off-ship techs wait in the corridor. "Once we know what we need, you'll help us carry it all," he explained.

Devon and Miranda settled in to wait with the other contractors. They milled about in the corridor, frequently pressing themselves against the walls so members of the *Arthian Dream*'s crew could move past. Several minutes passed, with Devon growing more anxious by the moment.

Up ahead, a door slid open and a mix of Humans and aliens stepped into the corridor. "What's going on here?" a familiar voice called.

Devon froze as most of the people up ahead parted to let an Elowan through. It was Graslen! "Are you lot the contractors we…." His voice trailed off as he made eye contact with Devon. He pointed. "You're that cop from the Starport!"

Graslen's guards reached for their pistols, but Devon fired first. When he fired, the laser beam punched through the shoulder of the Human guard. The man screamed and dropped his pistol.

The other guard, a Thrynn, drew a long-barreled revolver and aimed. Miranda threw herself in front of Devon as the Thrynn fired three times. The first shot went wide, but the last two struck the thorax armor beneath Miranda's jacket. She grunted as she returned fire with her laser pistol. Her shot barely missed the Thrynn, who retreated through a door Graslen had fled through. It slammed shut behind him, the clang of the lock reverberating in the corridor.

"Greassse Monkey One, thisss is *Black Maria*," Thassor called. "Repairsss completed. We're ready to intercept."

"*Black Maria*, Grease Monkey One." Devon jogged down the corridor, past several shut doors. He'd memorized the schematics of the ship while Miranda flew them down to Trisa III, so he knew several different ways to get to the corridor outside the bridge. "Our prey is alerted to our presence. We're heading to the bridge. Could use your assistance at any time."

"Ssshould've let one of us go, inssstead."

Devon carefully crept past an open doorway, his weapon aimed down the corridor as he scanned for threats. "Coulda, shoulda, woulda. Next time, Thassor. Grease Monkey One, out."

Miranda let out a buzzing snort that sounded eerily similar to Krox. "Thassor may have the…gift of gab, as you Humans would say, but he couldn't act his way out of a nest of well-fed gracka nurslings."

"I heard that, Greasse Monkey Two."

"When Miranda's right, she's right," Ela added. "Sorry, Thassor, but you're no good at undercover work."

"Oh, and you think you're any better?"

"Never said I was. Why are you getting so worked up?"

"I'm not getting 'worked up.'"

"Guys, cut the chatter," Devon snapped.

"Ssshe started it," Thassor muttered.

"I did not—" Elowan started to say, then the connection was severed.

Devon opened an access panel and motioned Miranda inside. She took one look at the tight space and twitched her mandibles in the Velox equivalent of a frown. "I don't think I can fit through there."

A door hissed open, and Krox stepped through, flanked by a Velox and an Elowan. That maintenance bay must've doubled as an armory, because all three were equipped with rifles. Devon raised his pistol. "I don't think you've got much choice!"

He shoved her into the tube entrance, then fired at the trio of bad guys down the corridor. His laser beam went wide, missing Krox by a handbreadth. Their return fire caused Devon to throw himself against Miranda's backside, and the two stumbled into the tight access tunnel. Devon pulled the panel shut and then melted the latch with his laser pistol. It drained the energy cell, but left the panel inoperable. They'd have to cut it off, or loop around to the next access point, which was on the other side of the deck. It would buy them a little time.

Outside, Krox and his men pounded on the panel, but it wouldn't give. He heard the Velox chief engineer curse.

"Hurry up!" Devon shouted. "We've got to get to the shuttle bay! We got what we came for!"

Miranda looked over her shoulder at him, a quizzical look on her face. He hiked a thumb toward the panel, then listened as Krox barked orders to his men and they ran off.

There. That should buy them even more time. "Lead the way, Miranda," Devon said as he recharged his pistol with a fresh cell.

"I don't know the way."

Devon frowned. He'd forgotten she didn't have time to memorize anything. He should've gone first, but there was nothing to be done for it now. "Start moving. I'll tell you where we need to go."

It was slow going at first. Miranda could barely fit in the ship's access tunnels, despite the fact that these were designed for engineers and repair technicians, of which a significant number on Arth were Velox. Of course, most Velox weren't three meters tall like Miranda, either. Thankfully, she never got stuck, although it was a close thing when they encountered a huge junction box that jutted out of the wall and cut the tunnel's width down a half-meter.

Every time they passed an access panel, Devon kept his pistol trained on it and listened for anyone outside. They'd heard boots pounding on the decks above them, but so far their pursuers hadn't tried to enter the tunnels. With luck, they were all still focused on the shuttle bay and wouldn't be anywhere near the bridge.

Their luck ran out a few minutes later, as they were nearing the bridge corridor access panel. A hatch opened above them, and a surprised Human engineer looked down at them, his mouth agape. He then keyed his radio. "Intruders in AC-43—"

Miranda grabbed the man by the shoulder and pulled him down. He screamed, but it was cut short when she slammed his head into the floor. He went limp, and his radio thumped against the floor.

"Baxter?" a voice asked. "Damn, they got Baxter! They're in AC-43!"

"My team's right outside there," another voice said through the radio. "We'll flush them out!"

True to the disembodied voice's word, an access panel down a side tunnel started to open. "Time to move!" Devon tapped his mic. "Ela, can't you do something about these panel locks?"

"Unfortunately they're all manually controlled."

"Wonderful." Devon watched as Miranda ran, her jacket and exposed chitin rubbing and clacking against the cramped corridor walls. He shifted his focus back on the access panel as it finished opening. He fired several shots, striking a Velox male in the thorax and face. The insect went down, blocking the entrance for his companions. He shot at the dead alien's crewmates, then chased after Miranda.

He had to stop to shoot two more times, and then they reached the panel he'd been looking for. Miranda wrenched it open and scrambled out into a much wider corridor. Devon pulled himself free, then shut and melted the latch again, burning through the remainder of his energy cell to do it.

They stood alone in a corridor with two doors: one an elevator, the other the door to the bridge. They hurried over to the bridge door and found it locked. "Ela, the door."

"This one I can do something about. Give me a moment."

Devon and Miranda recharged their laser pistols while Ela did her thing, using the device Devon had placed in the shuttle bay. The hacking tool wouldn't give *Black Maria* access to complex and heavily encrypted systems, but it would let her tap into the comms and mess with the doors.

As the seconds ticked by, Devon's anxiousness grew. The bridge had to know they were on the way, if not already outside. With their cover blown inside the access corridors, Krox would be running their way from the shuttle bay. And where the hell was *Black Maria*, anyway? They should've been here by now.

The door's lock chirped twice, then went from red to green. Devon's hand hovered over the button. "You ready?"

Miranda switched her laser pistol to her primary hand, then drew two more pistols from the recesses of her jacket. "In for a credit—"

"In for a thou!" Devon slapped the button. After a case like this, they better be getting more than a thousand credits in bonuses, or he'd be pissed.

The door slid open with a hiss, and Devon and Miranda charged through.

Graslen and his goons fired from behind cover on the far side of the bridge. Devon and Miranda scrambled in separate directions; Devon behind the captain's chair, Miranda into the tactical officer's booth. Consoles exploded in a shower of sparks and plastic under the intense barrage. Laser beams singed the fabric of the captain's chair. *Damn, this thing is pretty sturdy*, Devon thought.

Then a bullet from a large-bore pistol punched through the chair's "sturdy" back. Devon crouched as low as he could and fired blind over the chair's headrest. Someone screamed, and the amount of fire directed his way tapered off.

Miranda used that opportunity to lay down heavy fire with three pistols at once, two of hers and one she'd looted off one of Graslen's crew. Laser beams and bullets flew with wild abandon. Graslen's bodyguards scrambled for cover under the onslaught, and one of them leveled a machine gun Miranda's way. With a speed that belied her size, Miranda leapt over the back end of the tactical officer's booth, landing behind it as a barrage of bullets tore through the consoles. "This is some date you brought me on!" she called.

"Wild and hot, just like you love!" Devon answered. He blasted at a Thassor guard, but the lizard man wore some kind of ablative armor that deflected the shot. He aimed higher, and managed to singe the alien's nose. The Thassor threw himself flat with a yelp.

Over the deep reports of gunfire and the crack-whine of lasers, Devon managed to hear the doors behind him slide open. He spun in time to see a handful of Graslen's crew in the corridor outside, weapons shouldered. With a curse, Devon shifted his aim, but he knew he'd be too late.

One of them, a Human male, clutched at his throat and dropped his rifle. Blood sprayed from between his fingers as he dropped to his knees. Bullets and laser beams peppered the walls, forcing the others back. They leaned weapons out from around the doorframe, firing blind like Devon had done before.

"Get them, you fools!" Krox yelled from the corridor. "There are only two of them!"

Devon crouched as low as he could, his weapon shifting from one side of the door to the other. To his left, Miranda continued to pour fire down on Graslen and his guards. *This is quite the fix we're in*, he thought as he fired at Krox when he peeked his insect head out from the door. Krox threw himself back behind cover, cursing loudly.

"I don't care if it damages our instruments!" Graslen shouted. "Do it!"

That didn't sound good. Devon looked over his shoulder in time to see one of Graslen's goons throw a grenade. It sailed overhead, directly toward the captain's chair Devon crouched behind.

An Elowan crewman jumped out from behind the doorway. Devon shot him, then jumped to his feet and snatched the grenade out of the air. A thrill of fear shot through him as his fingers clutched the live explosive. How many milliseconds did it have left? With no time to lose, he wound back his arm and spun toward the door.

Krox saw what Devon was about to do and hit the button to shut the doors. Devon let the grenade fly in an underhand throw, and it slid along the ground like a grolden disc. It made it through the doors right as they hissed closed. Outside, aliens and Humans screamed in terror, and then those screams were lost in a rumbling blast that shook the deck plates beneath Devon's boots.

"Nice one!" Miranda called.

Devon breathed a sigh of relief. "It was a close thing," he admitted. "Thanks for the grenade, Grassy!"

"It's Graslen!" the irate Elowan shouted, a tremor in his voice that hadn't been there before. "Get it right, you fethwick!"

"That'sss enough of that, criminal," a voice said over the bridge's intercom. "Power down and prepare to be boarded."

Devon grinned. "They've already been boarded, Thassor," he said. "We're onboard, remember?"

"Good point. Then, prepare to be re-boarded."

"Graslen Supox," Miranda said, "you're under arrest for the illegal possession of proprietary software from Interstel's Department of Cartograpy, with intent to sell. Surrender, or face justice here."

"I'm a citizen of Arth, damn you!" Graslen yelled from behind cover. "I have rights!"

"*Now* you want to play that game?" Devon asked. "You steal surveying software from a small start-up poised to take off like a rocket when their product goes public, only to then be caught trying to sell it to their competition. How many rights did you trample on to get this far?"

"Not to mention lives," Miranda added. "Seventeen, by my count. Thirty-six, depending on how the next few minutes go."

"What do you mean?"

"She's talking about you and what's left of your crew." Devon held his comlink up so Graslen and his crew could see it. "Your ship's disabled, and my crew's ready to finish the job. One word from Miranda or me, and *Black Maria* fires everything she's got."

"Hardly." Graslen laughed, the noise similar to wind rustling through dried leaves on an autumn day. "I know police protocol. They won't do anything so drastic, not while you're still onboard. You're hostages. You just don't know it yet."

"I'd prefer to bring you in so you can face justice all proper-like, but I get it." Devon glanced at his partner." You talk about rights, Graslen. Maybe now's a good time to tell you about Miranda's rights."

Graslen's face remained blank. "I don't know what that is."

"Old lingo from a bygone era, forgotten by all except for the crew of the *Black Maria*. When we find an uncooperative criminal like you out in the vastness of space, Miranda here has the right to rip all your limbs off before she shoves you out an airlock."

"I like to exercise my rights," Miranda added in a soft voice. "As often as I possibly can."

The silence that followed that statement would've been comical to Devon if he wasn't surrounded by hostiles. "The choice is yours, Grassy! Surrender now and get to see the sunset on Arth, or don't and choose the form of your destructor. Either Miranda's tender ministrations, or *Black Maria's* missile pods and energy cannons."

"You're under arressst no matter what," Thassor said, his sibilant voice tinny through the comlink. "It'sss sssimply a matter of the condition of your body when we place the cuffsss on, Elowan scum."

"Hey, that's my people you're talking about," Ela snapped.

"Are your people criminalsss like thisss one?"

"Well, no, but—"

"Then we are not talking about your people, Jassspar."

"Stop hissing my name like that!"

Devon and Miranda shared a look. Miranda held her pistol in a two-handed grip with her upper arms, but she spread her middle thorax arms in something akin to a shrug.

"I hisss all the time."

"Yeah, but you do it more whenever you say my name!"

"I do not—"

"Can we blow something up already?" Copperhead demanded. "My joints are rusting, and the only lubricant is criminal blood."

Devon shook his head. Finally, something he could work with. "Hear that, Grassy? My crew's argumentative, pissed off, and ready to kill people. It's been a long chase, and we're done. Come along quietly, or get ready to die. Again, the choice is yours."

Graslen made the right choice. In the end, they always did.

"Welcome aboard." Thassor's sharp teeth gleamed in the bridge's fluorescent lighting. "Enjoy your little sssurface jaunt?"

"And the sub-light cruise that went along with it." Devon waited for Thassor to vacate the captain's chair, then he threw himself into it. He sighed as the chair's smart-fabric molded to his body again. "That's good on the ol' back."

Thassor hissed out a laugh. "I've sssent word back to HQ, but they'll need your report."

Devon winced. Report writing was the one area of policing he detested. He'd hated it when he was a rookie working traffic, and he hated it now. He'd hoped the more interesting the case, the more fun it would be to write, but bureaucratic processes managed to suck the joy out of even that. "I'll type it up tomorrow." Devon put his hands behind his head and leaned back. "It's time for a little R&R."

"I wish you wouldn't sssay that," Thassor said. "Thingsss have been exciting enough. Don't jinx it."

Thassor's console chimed. He put the earpiece against his tympanic membrane. His sharp-toothed grin returned. Before he could say anything, the door slid open and Miranda stomped in. She took one look at Thassor and muttered, "Oh, no."

"Oh, yesss." Thassor punched in a few commands on his console, and a transcript of the audio message he'd received popped up on the main viewscreen. "Ordersss from the top. We're to hand our prisonersss off to the crew of *Watson's Tail* and continue to the designated coordinatesss. Sssome ssskullduggery is afoot."

"Now I'm starting to think you're hamming up the hissing, Thassor," Devon said. He read the message several times, then sighed. "Very well. Miranda, take us to the rendezvous point. You know how it goes: another day, another credit."

"We better be getting more than one credit for this," Miranda grumbled. "It's been a *very* long day."

Devon activated the console in his chair's armrest and examined the information on the retrieved piece of software. Where had it come from, again? The Cartography Department? The title of the file folder didn't explain anything, nor could he access it and see what paperwork there would be to explain the program's purpose.

Well, no matter. Like I said, another day, another credit. Devon started to close the program, but gave one last look at the intriguing, one word title:

Starflight.

To Cache A Killer

By Michael J. Ciaravella

Starport Central,
Arth Orbital Station

Josiah Benton's first thought, upon seeing the sleek, hammerhead shape of the Interstel exploratory cruiser *Redoubtable* outside the porthole of Starport Central, was that it still remained one of the most beautiful shapes that he had ever seen.

Josiah remembered vividly the first time he had seen one of the gorgeous, sleek shapes, three years before. His father, a minor functionary in the still fledgling Interstel bureaucracy, had allowed him the chance to watch from the Starport Central gallery as the first wave of ships took off into the unknown, taking a rare moment from his work to show his devoted son what he considered the future of humanity's reach for the stars. The bevy of aliens, travelers, and exotic sites and smells had been completely lost upon his younger self, who only had eyes for the sleek, ivory forms that dominated his view of space, knowing that he would give anything to ride in one, seeking out the mysteries of the galaxy.

Unfortunately, such dreams were doomed to face the harsh light of reality as one grew older. Only a handful of Humans were lucky enough and talented enough to crew one of the precious few starships that humanity could manage to build and fuel, and he had neither the pedigree nor the aptitude to join their extraordinary mission. He was lucky that his family's connections were enough to keep him on the Spaceport, in the fairly exalted position of a junior examiner.

"Come along, Josiah." The chiding voice from beside him brought him back to reality, and he found himself hurrying to catch up with his companion as she moved briskly towards the cofferdam that connected the spaceport to the external docking port that the ship was using.

"Yes, Examiner," Josiah replied, attempting to not seem rushed as he kept pace with his superior, Senior Examiner Angela Vesor. Clad in matching black and gold, form-fitting jumpsuits with the arm patches of the Interstel Scientific Bureau and the golden magnifiers of their examiner status, they both got wary stares from the Interstel staff and crew members from the various vessels that were docked there. Most were wary of the examiners. While they had the respectable mandate of investigating the various items that were brought back from the explorations in the galaxy, they were also the ones who confiscated such items, usually after giving the ship's crews the value of what they had initially believed the items to be. While one of the newest divisions of the Interstel structure, they were given impressive power from the directorship itself, and several unwary captains had found themselves reminded that while their power might be limitless underway, they did have masters when they returned.

After the first few interactions, many ships came to dread the arrival of an examiner, and others found themselves carefully hiding any items that they found from Interstel, hoping to find a better price on the black market.

That lasted only until the first time that a senior examiner used their immense power, granted by the Interstel government, to arrest the entire crew and had the captain tried, sentenced to death, and then had their sentence commuted to life imprisonment at the last moment. After that, there was very little attempt at bucking their authority.

Any additional thoughts that Josiah might have had were cut off by their arrival at the cofferdam. A single flash of Vesor's identification card opened the hatch for them, and they moved briskly down the narrow corridor. The inner port opened as they arrived, but they found an immense form in their way even more daunting than the airlock hatch. A DX-99 biosynthetic android, watching them carefully as they approached, any attempt at passing for Human instantly negated by the pair of glowing red photoreceptors seeming to take in everything at once, even before they were close enough to see much of his metallic frame.

"This is a restricted area," The android's mechanical voice began. "I must ask you to return to the Spaceport."

For a brief moment, Josiah had to remind himself that androids were there to aid humanity in their move to the stars, not to cause them harm. If the senior examiner had any such concerns, however, they were not apparent. "I am Senior Examiner Angela Vesor of the Interstel Science Bureau, and I require an immediate conference with Captain Jonathan Russell."

For the briefest of instants, the automaton seemed to consider this, but stepped back dutifully. "The captain is in his office; I will take you to him." Vesor nodded and allowed the android to precede them down the corridor. The trip was all too brief, as they came to a slate-grey door with the captain's name on it. Pressing a small control beside the door, the android spoke clearly.

"Captain, M020993 reporting. You have visitors who wish an audience with you."

Despite the fact that the android should not have any sort of Human type affect at all, Josiah was certain that he heard a certain hesitancy in the automaton's voice. After a moment, a deep voice replied through the communications panel. "Who is it, MOTO?"

"The visitors identify themselves as Angela Vesor and Josiah Benton, examiners for the Interstel Science Bureau Department of Classification. Tentative confirmation attained through visual comparison of identification documents."

The hesitation from the other side of the communications console was far more understandable. The Department of Classification was the specialty division devoted to the recovery and analysis of rare artifacts that the various exploration ships brought back with them. As such, they held an outsized authority when it came to the business of interstellar exploration, and a visit from such illustrious personages were rare, and not often sought.

"Thank you, MOTO. Send them in."

Any surprise that Josiah had felt about the captain thanking an android was banished as the hatch slid open, and it gestured that they could both enter. The senior examiner entered first, with Josiah following behind. From the doorway, the android waited, clearly sensing that the cabin was cozy with three occupants, and potentially claustrophobic with four.

If Captain Russell was concerned about the small spaces, he did not show it. The tall, blond haired captain had a rough-hewn face, a strictly non-regulation beard making him seem like one who would be more comfortable on a whaling ship than an interstellar vessel. His dark brown eyes seemed to take them both in for a moment, and then he nodded in greeting, gesturing to the two chairs that took up some of the limited space across from his desk. Clearly unused to having guests, the two examiners needed to clear some items off the chairs, placing them on the deck, before taking their seats.

"Good day, Examiners," Russell began, using the traditional spacer parlance of always thinking of it as day when he was awake. "How may I be of assistance to the Science Bureau? We found no unique artifacts in our last cruise that I am aware of."

From what Josiah had gleaned, that was quite the understatement. On their previous three cruises the Interstel cruiser *Redoubtable* had found no artifacts of note, and had come under attack twice, once on planet and once in space. They had brought back enough mineral wealth and data to keep them flying, but they were in the lower third of the most profitable vessels being flown among the stars at the moment, a concern that the captain must have been aware of.

Vesor, however, did not correct him. "The Bureau would like to engage your vessel on a matter of some urgency, Captain."

Russell nodded, and gave a small, open-handed gesture. "I am intrigued. How can my ship be of assistance?" His tone was respectful, but made it quite clear who he thought was in command on board.

"As you are no doubt aware, my division is specifically tasked with the recovery and analysis of unique artifacts that are recovered by the various Interstel vessels during their explorations. Three months ago, I dispatched a team to follow up on a report about a strange artifact on a planet classified XOM-3258c, a small golden egg that seemed to radiate its own power." The captain seemed curious, focused on the senior examiner's story, nodding for her to continue. "Unfortunately, they would never arrive. A catastrophic failure in their drive system forced them to set down on a planet in a nearby system. It was listed as a prime candidate for habitation, and they felt that they could wait out the situation until rescue could be sent. A single message was transmitted to us that they had landed, and we heard nothing more. "

Once again, Russell nodded, but this time it had a serious edge. Such situations were hardly new in the realm of interstellar exploration, and it sounded like one of several calamities that continued to make livelihood so hazardous. "Is there any idea of what could have been the issue?"

"No. The lead examiner with the team, Ajyenn, remarked in the message about potentially aggressive species of fauna, but that they were not too concerned." The examiner paused for a moment. "That was our last contact."

The captain leaned backwards; his expression curious. "You stated that the planet was listed for colonization... normally such a classification would not be granted if there were dangerous life forms present, flora or fauna."

The senior examiner gave a rare nod of approval, clearly pleased that he had picked up on that. "You have come to the root of my dilemma. The planet was cleared for colonization, but it appears that might have been inaccurate. That led me to do some additional research on my own. It appears that this is not the only planet that has been placed into consideration for colonization where the situation seemed... ill-advised."

"I suspect there is something more to the story, but that you have not divulged yet."

Vesor nodded again, and Josiah was now fairly sure he saw a gleam of approval in her eye, a feat that he himself had rarely achieved. "You are correct. Before we lost contact with the team on the planet, we received a partial message that they found an Interstel claim marker, but that it did not contain any data in regards to the previous survey."

This caused Russell to straighten, and it was clear he realized the import of exactly what she was saying. The Interstel system was a corporate one: Only the best helmed their starships, and the rewards were as incredibly lucrative as the risks were great. However, it was also a position of great trust. Due to the dearth of interstellar starship fuel, it was important that colonies and expeditions were placed with the utmost care. It was expected that every explorer captain made a full and complete survey of the planet to the best of their abilities before sending back a probe for additional support, and a copy of the original survey was left with an automated claim marker on the planet. While sometimes a particularly valuable object or artifact may make for a riskier mission, there was no reason why corners should be cut for a standard planetary survey.

"That is a... very concerning thought, Examiner."

Vesor nodded. "That was my conclusion as well. I feel that it is in the vital interests of both the Bureau and Interstel as a whole to look into the matter, hence our arrival."

Russell looked thoughtful for a moment, clearly taking it all in. "I believe that this would traditionally fall under Interstel security jurisdiction, however. As a senior examiner, you should certainly be able to enlist their help."

"That is true." Vesor replied, but her eyes stayed locked on the captain. "However, due to the nature of my concern, I thought it important that I gather more information by reaching out to other departments."

A flash of understanding seemed to light in Russell's eyes, and this time it was Josiah's own turn to nod. If someone was attempting to make money off of surveys that had not been completed, the easiest way to ensure that there was not an issue was if they had an accomplice in the Interstel government. While Security was probably not involved, there was always the chance that someone they reported to was.

Russell quietly considered the situation for several moments before speaking again. "Before I can even consider such a proposal, I have some questions of my own."

The senior examiner nodded once. "I expected as much. Proceed."

"What is going to happen to the artifact that they went to recover?"

Josiah attempted to keep the disdain from his face at the mercenary answer. *Was profit all the captain cared about?* The moment was fleeting, but a momentary frown must have flashed on his face, for the captain gave him a careful look. "I only ask to see if the artifact may be involved in the situation."

Vesor seemed to take the statement at face value. "A secondary team is being prepared to retrieve the artifact. They will be transported on one of the alternative research vessels available at the moment."

"Not the one that originally surveyed the system, I trust?"

"No," came the simple reply.

"Fine. What is the remit that you are putting out here?"

"I will pay your regular fee, plus expenses, to investigate the planet, confirm the status of the previous expedition, and provide me with any information about the previous survey. If you uncover something actionable, I will take further steps from there. Is that acceptable?"

"One last question." Russel replied, glancing between the two examiners. "Why the *Redoubtable*? There are three other ships in dock at the moment, surely any of them could have done just as well."

"Surely it is obvious." The senior examiner responded. "The ship that surveyed the system was yours."

For a long moment, the captain was speechless, and then his first instinct was to deny it, but the senior examiner already had the data prepared, sending it to his console. "System CRM-4402 was surveyed by the *Redoubtable* on your second to last cruise. It was one of six systems you visited before your unfortunate encounter, and one of three systems that you submitted for colonization."

"That is preposterous," The captain replied, finally calming down enough to be rational. "We found no planets worth colonization on that cruise."

"Not according to Interstel records. While none of them have been examined due to the backlog of planets from the secondary survey teams, I have taken the liberty of sending them to your terminal." Vesor looked at him carefully. "As you can see, three of the planets you visited were given tentative approval for colonization."

The captain booted the file up quickly, and then read the data with an expression that moved from disbelief to concern. When he looked up at them, his expression was taut. "You have to believe that I would never do something like this."

Josiah watched the captain carefully, attempting to see any attempt at deception. The money that Interstel paid for colonizable planets was sizable, but so were the penalties for not following procedure or providing an unsuitable planet in bad faith. Still, if he were going with his gut, he would say that the captain was sincere.

Apparently, his superior agreed. "If that is the case, then someone on your crew is to blame. Either way, I believe that there is value in sending you back, and having you report your findings to me."

The captain watched her through narrowed eyes, clearly considering how far he could push the situation. Being the elite of the Interstel system, the captains of the exploration ships were supposed to be the best of the best, the pinnacle of what the races of the galaxy could achieve. They were allowed the greatest leeway in accomplishing their mission, and something like this could rock them to their very core.

The examiner was the immovable object to their irresistible force. While the shipmasters had great leeway as to how they achieved their objectives, they received their ships and their mandates from Interstel. If one of them was deemed unworthy of the honor, there would be dozens who would be able to step in without the slightest hesitation.

After a moment, the captain considered the situation, and then gave her an appraising glance. "All right, Examiner.... what did you have in mind?"

"From the information that was provided to me, you have recently completed a major refit, upgrading both your weapons suite and your shielding to Level Three, a respectable upgrade from the standard Interstel package, as well as a full upgrade to your sensor suite. I have no doubt that you would be able to get a full analysis of the planet in question, and take on any threat that might approach."

The captain did not reply, but she could see that she had scored a hit. The *Redoubtable* had been badly damaged in the conflict with an unknown ship on a previous mission. They had managed to damage the attacking vessel when it entered laser range and drive it off for long enough for them to escape, but it had been a close thing. That had been with the standard, Level One defensive package of shields and weapons that all exploration vessels had the option of purchasing before they left the Starport. Facing a heavily armed Interstel vessel nearly three times as powerful would not be something an opponent would attempt lightly.

"Assuming that you are correct..." the captain continued, "there is still the fact that we have already examined that system. I am currently planning to map out the next sector..."

"As I had stated, my department will *generously* compensate you for the temporary inconvenience," the examiner interjected, and that seemed to stop him cold, as she saw the avarice flicker in his eyes. Despite the lucrative nature of interstellar exploration, space was vast, and many worlds that they visited were not worth the Endurium it took to get them there. It was one of the reasons that Interstel had chosen the subsidized model of colonization and exploration anyway, allowing them to minimize the risks to their own interests. If Interstel was willing to cover his costs and expenses, plus would still reward him for whatever they found...

"You will cover all reasonable expenses, regardless of what I find?"

Vesor nodded. "As well as the potential for a bonus, should the data we gather be helpful in eliminating the threat to our system."

The captain nodded slowly. "That should be acceptable."

"I will also require my aide, Josiah, to accompany you."

The captain shook his head. "Unacceptable. We are not a passenger liner..."

"You have taken supercargo before," Vesor replied smoothly, once again making him blanche from the knowledge she possessed of his previous dealings. "Not to mention, it is clear that I need someone I trust on board, who is completely unimpeachable and independent of your crew. As I mentioned, I am authorized to provide a sizable bonus for a successful mission, if he feels, in his sole capacity, that it is earned."

For a long moment, the captain's sense of avarice warred with his hesitation of taking on a passenger, but something in her expression must have convinced him, as he gave a shallow nod. "How quickly will he be ready to depart?"

Josiah spoke for the first time. "My luggage is in the airlock. I will be able to depart immediately."

"Good," The captain replied, although it was clear he did not mean it. "Space waits for no one."

In point of fact, it took several hours to get the crew back on board and everything stowed away. While a few of the crew members were a bit annoyed that they had been called back from the dock early, the rumor of a major payday was enough to get them back and ready to work.

Josiah quietly wondered just how much the captain had told his crew while he was out of earshot. All crews were tight-knit affairs, and despite the fact that the senior examiner had warned him not to tell anyone of his real purpose in being there, Josiah somehow doubted that the captain would keep such a thing from his crew.

Regardless, Josiah knew he had a job to do, and he set to it with gusto. The first thing Josiah did was to take a private tour of the ship, following the far more abbreviated tour that he had been given by the captain while they waited for the crew to embark. Josiah had already studied the schematics for the vessel, and had been on others as a visitor when picking up artifacts, so he had a general knowledge of how to get around.

Still, with the situation he was in, Josiah was fairly sure that he would have to know his way backwards and forwards, and he devoted himself to the task. Avoiding the personal quarters of the crew members, knowing that they would not appreciate such nosiness from an outsider, Josiah toured the lander bay, the defensive stations, the recreation room, and the various public spaces devoted to the health and welfare of the crew, and then stopped into Engineering.

The engineer was a burly, heavyset man by the name of Riley Kildare. Kildare wore a grey ship's jumpsuit with the *Redoubtable* patch upon the arm, and he watched Josiah cautiously as he came into the engineer's domain. From what he had read in his file, Kildare was a devout Endurist, having joined the crew to ensure that they remained focused on seeking out the rare element that helped to push humanity out to the stars.

"May I help you with something, sir?" Kildare asked, moving towards him, carefully maneuvering to ensure that he did not go deeper into the Engineering bay. "Engineering is a restricted area..."

"Under most circumstances, you would be completely right, Chief." Josiah replied smoothly, with an attempt at a confident air. "Unfortunately, these are anything but normal circumstances. The captain has given me full authority to go throughout the ship."

From the glum expression on his face, the chief engineer knew that all too well, and knew that his attempt to try to get the intruder to leave had failed. Giving a glum nod of acceptance, Kildare stood, watching the examiner carefully. To his surprise, Josiah turned to face him instead of going deeper into the bay. "How long have you been on the *Redoubtable*, Mr. Kildare?"

"About six months," the man replied carefully. "The captain brought me on to replace his previous engineer, who had taken a posting on another ship."

"Oh?" Josiah asked. "Where did he go?"

"Transferred to the *Discover*. Our search pattern was taking us a little close to Thrynn space, and they do not like Elowan. Everyone thought that this was just a better fit. *Discover* already had some Elowan, so they would not be going on that route anyway. The captain put out an open call and got me."

Josiah nodded, having read as much in his profile. As far as the captain was concerned, the hulking engineer did his job right, and that was all that mattered. Not wanting to take up too much of the other man's time, Josiah thanked him, then continued on his tour.

Having completed his conversation with the chief engineer, Josiah moved onwards towards the bow of the ship. Traversing the main corridor, she only saw the android crewmember, MOTO, who was cleaning up a spill that had apparently come from a loose pipe. The android gave him a surprisingly Human nod as he stopped to speak to him.

"Good afternoon, MOTO. How are you today?"

"Seeing as the date has little relevance outside of a standard frame of reference, I am doing well. How are you, Examiner?"

"As good as can be expected," Josiah replied, hopefully surprising the android with his honesty. "How long have you been aboard, MOTO?"

"Since 15-2-4618. While I was originally brought on board to supplement our engineering staff, I was transferred to cover the post of a crewmember who was wounded and required medical assistance in excess of what could be provided on ship. The captain was good enough to ensure that the crewmember was given the best of care, and provided a stipend for his continued recuperation."

Josiah nodded, having read the report on the situation MOTO was alluding to. While on a planetary survey, the ship's science officer had been attacked by a particularly vicious species of superheated fungus, and had been badly scalded. "That must have cost a pretty penny."

"I cannot comment upon the financial breakdown for the expedition, but I certainly can confirm that it was not a lucrative experience for the crew. From the public messages that have been received for the crew as a whole, it is clear that the former crew member is in good health and doing well."

Josiah was about to ask more, but a single tone sounded throughout the ship, and the captain's voice came out loud and clear. "All hands to transit stations, we are departing Spacedock."

MOTO clearly was prepared. "I must attend to the bridge, but you should head over to your stateroom. We will be jumping out of the system as soon as we are at a safe distance."

Josiah nodded, his heart already pounding over the knowledge that he was about to take his first out-system jump. It had been something he had been dreaming of since he was a child…

As long as it did not kill him in the process.

The first night, once they had left the Starport, wound up being the hardest. There were hundreds of small details that needed to be attended to as they prepared to pull away from the station, and made to jump to their first target. It lent itself to a certain air of excitement, and he felt himself being swept up into the energy of the ship and its crew as they prepared to leap out into the unknown. In the immediate aftermath of departure everything was a flurry of activity, and Josiah merely watched from his place in the central galley, as the crew moved purposefully from task to task with the skill borne of long familiarity.

When it finally occurred, the jump did provide a small bit of a thrill, and Josiah had been allowed by the captain to watch the event from the bridge. It had proven to be everything he could have asked for and more, despite the fact that his excitement must have seemed very provincial to the others.

Everything quickly died down into a sort of routine, however. As was traditional, they had jumped to the outer limit of the system, to give themselves maximum room to maneuver if there was a hostile force in the outer system, and opened up their options if there were other threats further in. When they were not attacked as quickly as they arrived, some of the energy of the transit seemed to bleed off into space. Since they had already surveyed this system once before, they could afford to move steadily into the system without conducting some of the more extensive outer-system surveys a first arrival would have entailed. Due to the lateness of the hour, the captain informed them that they would take the slow way in, ensuring that they were following proper procedure while re-examining the system.

While they moved into the system, under the watchful photoreceptors of MOTO, Captain Russell graciously invited Josiah to dine with the senior officers. They made their way back to the galley for a simple but delicious meal, leaving the android in command on the bridge. Aside from Kildare, there was Salynn T'thiessess, the Thrynn communications officer, Xixptrixx, the Velox navigator, Dr. Vanessa Swatton, and the captain himself. Despite the cautious reception he received from the other members of the crew, the captain went out of his way to try to include him in the conversation, telling stories of some of his other explorations. However, Josiah could not shake the feeling of being an outsider in the tight-knit crew.

Once the meal ended, he was left alone at the central table as the others went upon their duties. The captain went off to check on MOTO before turning in, to allow him to be ready for the expedition the next day. The survey of the other two planets before their target would be quick, and he wanted to be ready for the expedition. Kildare went back down to his Engineering bay to ensure all was well, and the Thrynn science officer, Salynn, prepared for his own short shift assisting MOTO on the bridge, before switching off with his relief in a couple of hours. The doctor did not bother to explain where she was going, just leaving the table wordlessly with a curt nod of dismissal that seemed to surprise no one.

Once everyone had left, Josiah took one of the acceleration couches in the corner, and began reading through their biographies again, hoping to get a better idea of those he was traveling with. The captain's dossier revealed little he did not know, and MOTO was a fairly standard automaton, but the others proved quite interesting.

The career of Doctor Vanessa Swatton was... colorful, to say the least. One would not know it to look at her, but she had the longest Interstel service record of the crew, having worked on four other interstellar vessels during her tenure. Swatton had transferred over following the retirement of the last medical officer, but the profile became even more interesting if you read between the lines: While the service dates had been carefully adjusted by month, leaving nothing strange to a cursory examination, a focus upon the exact dates showed that she had been released from her previous ship three weeks before, with similar gaps existing from her other transfers. Such an interesting work history told Josiah that the good doctor's previous captain had been glad to be rid of her, releasing her from her contract as soon as she had gotten to the station, but that she had been picked up quickly as soon as she was free. That led the examiner to believe the woman may have been the talented doctor that she appeared to be, but may be harboring something else that had caused her abrupt departure from her former postings, forcing her to move from opportunity to opportunity fast. Briefly Josiah wondered if he could get to the communications station to reach out to Interstel to get more information, but he doubted the potential for his inquiry being revealed would be worth the additional data he would receive.

Communications was the next area of concern. While Salynn appeared to be the most gracious of the crew, second only to the captain, there seemed to be something… off about the Thrynn. A relatively recent addition to the crew, having only served on the last two cruises, he seemed gregarious but also somewhat false. Josiah found that there were some curious notes in his file as well. This was the first ship he received a posting for, and it seemed almost as if he was trying too hard to maintain the position. As the examiner read, he noticed that the Thrynn's file was almost the opposite of the doctor's. While Swatton had barely spent a week on the beach, the comms officer had apparently tried to join several ships with no success. Part of that was based off of inter-species issues: As a Thrynn, he could not be posted to a ship with an Elowan without careful consideration, and ships going into Elowan-controlled space would not want to risk being fired upon if they were scanned and found to be harboring one of their enemies.

Still, it seemed that there was more to it, and Josiah wondered if it was due to the creature's relative youth and extremely eager nature. While clearly talented, Salynn appeared to be almost shockingly eager to please, and there was something about the unrelenting focus that was more than a little unnerving. Could it be that focus was just nervous, youthful energy, or was there something more sinister lurking behind it that he should be concerned about?

Josiah looked around the galley, suppressing a yawn, and was suddenly acutely aware of just how alone he was on this particular mission. He had pressed his superiors for the opportunity to look into the situation himself, and it had all seemed like both a good way of improving his position and doing a service to his department as a whole. Unfortunately, he did not realize that he was going to be quite that alone, and a mixture of the surprising silence and his own internal disquiet lulled him into a fitful sleep.

When he awoke, seemingly moments later, he was instantly aware that he was in unfamiliar surroundings. Feeling the reader carefully under his head, Josiah realized that he had been more tired than he had expected, and had fallen asleep in one corner of the galley. The lights in the room had dimmed, realizing there was no one moving around in the space, and had settled into a low-energy mode. He was about to get up and make his way to his cabin, when he heard voices coming from the corridor.

"I can't believe you agreed to this, Jonathan! This is absolute madness." Doctor Swatton's voice was clearly audible, and her tone quickly confirmed just how annoyed she was with the captain. "Do we really want Interstel delving too deeply into our affairs?"

Josiah left his eyes open, verifying no one was in the room with him, and strained to hear the voices which seemed to be coming from around the bend of the corridor.

"What choice did I have?" The captain no longer sounded like the amiable storyteller that Josiah had remembered from dinner. "Interstel is going to have their way one way or the other, and the last thing I want to do is to give them any reason to look any closer into our business than we have to. You know that they are building more ships every day, and we need to keep moving to remain competitive." His voice lowered slightly, but was still audible. "You, of all people, should know how expensive our operations are."

The doctor seemed to bite back a curse, and Josiah briefly wondered what the captain was alluding to. He wasn't surprised by the captain's reaction, however. Interstel had worked carefully to ensure that every captain and his crew had a vested interest in growing the boundaries of the settled worlds, but they were also not hesitant to keep building ships as quickly as they could, despite the limits of Endurium that could be found. There were always tragedies, and several of the original ships had not made it back to port, causing new opportunities to spring up for the wiliest and most ambitious of captains.

"Well, I don't like it," the doctor continued. "We have a good thing going here, and the last thing I want is some damn bureaucrat screwing it up for us."

Any further comments were cut off by the approach of the communications officer, whose lumbering footsteps were audible from down the corridor.

"Ready to take over, Salynn?" the captain asked, his false bonhomie once again firmly in place. Josiah could not make out the rumbling reply as they moved on, and he took a moment to straighten, adjusting the angle of his neck to make it less painful.

Which, of course, triggered the main lights.

The galley instantly flooded with brightness, and he closed his eyes tightly, waiting for his pupils to react. When he opened them, Josiah was neither surprised nor pleased to see the frowning face of the doctor in front of him.

"Is everything alright, Examiner?" The doctor asked, her voice carefully neutral. Josiah attempted to make it look like he had just woken up, a not-impossible situation.

"Fine, Doctor, thank you. I just fell asleep for a little while. I think it was all the prep for the launch. It was an exciting time for me."

The doctor nodded, and her eyes flickered to the tablet on the table, before glancing back up at the examiner, as if wondering just how much of the excuse she had chosen to believe. "Well, let me know if you need any medications, Examiner." She smiled, and for the briefest of moments Josiah missed her habitual frown of dismay. "I am sure that I can give you something that will take care of you."

The doctor immediately turned and headed out, leaving the examiner fully awake.

Despite the uncomfortable conversation from the night before, Josiah did manage to get a little rest, waking up shortly before the shift change. Heading to the bridge, he found Salynn in the central chair, with MOTO motionless at the rear of the command deck, watchfully waiting as they approached a nearby planetoid. From the coloration, it was clearly not their destination, but probably the last planet before they delved into the habitation ring.

"How are we doing, Salynn?"

Despite the fact that his arrival on the deck must have been noticed, Salynn seemed momentarily startled, and then gave his species' version of a grin. "Good day, Examiner. I trust that you rested well?"

"I certainly tried, Salynn. Is this the last planet?"

"Yes," the Thrynn replied, glancing back at the main screen. "We have been doing automated readings, but there is not too much of a change since the last set that we had taken."

"Will we be sending down a probe?" Josiah asked. The Thrynn merely shook his head, a discomforting gesture that must have been picked up from his studies with Humans, as the response could not possibly have been pleasant for such a long neck. Josiah was getting moderately queasy just watching him.

"Probably not, Examiner. We are hoping to get close enough to read the data from the original probe, but the cost of a new probe is probably not worth it."

Josiah nodded, understanding the dilemma immediately. Once again, the almighty MU took precedence over everything. Sending down a probe was a natural act, and one that was usually followed up on by the examination teams, but sending a second would only be putting good money after bad, especially for a planet that clearly could not host sentient life. While there might be some mineral deposits to take advantage of, (in fact it was a near certainty for such a planetoid,) he had no doubt that there were little of the rarer elements, or they would have immediately moved to secure as much of them as they could fit into their cargo holds before moving on. It was what they had done on the first planet, where they had sent MOTO down alone in the lander to load up with as many valuable elements as they could, so they would be returning with full holds no matter what. If they found something more valuable on the next planet, they would merely leave the less valuable elements there, available for pickup in a secret cache if they had found something more interesting. It was a well-known tactic, and it had served many captains well in the past. It was something he had expected, and it made sense for the captain to maximize his profits, even if he was going to take care of all of his expenses and more.

"Do we have an estimated time of arrival?" Josiah asked, and the Thrynn gave its angled version of a nod again.

"We should be in orbit in roughly two hours, sir."

The examiner nodded, doing some brief calculations in his head. It was not much time, and he was still no closer to figuring out just what had happened to the previous expedition.

Still, he refused to give in until he knew for sure. "Thank you, Salynn. Please let me know when we are ready to depart."

The long-necked crewman promised to do so, and Josiah headed back towards his quarters.

As Josiah had suspected, he did not have long to wait. The captain gathered up the crew once they were prepared to land. The majority of the them piled into the terrain vehicle to investigate the last known location reported by the expedition team. Xixptrixx remained with the ship, ready to take off at a moment's notice. The examiner watched the preparations with a mixture of elation and dread, one eye on the journey while the other attempted to watch his suspects.

The drive to the site went very quickly, and Josiah had to once again appreciate the speed and effectiveness shown by the crew. They found a small clearing to park just north of where the transmission was coming from and would have to go on foot from there. Originally, they had planned to land closer, but it appeared that the clearing had been overrun with vegetation since the expedition ship had landed. Such a thing was not unheard of, but it certainly did not bode well for the condition of the site.

Upon reaching the treeline, they broke into three two-person teams to seek out any sign of the original crew. The doctor went with the chief engineer, while Salynn and MOTO went together. The captain, who Josiah gathered usually went off by himself, decided to go with Josiah, and the three pairs moved out into the vegetation.

Josiah moved slowly through the foliage, careful not to get too far from the captain. The other man looked grim, clearly growing concerned with every step. While the planet did not show any obvious signs of threat, the captain had ensured that everyone wore their expedition suits, including a borrowed spare for Josiah. The reflective material and included air supply ensured that they were protected from any known biohazards, and the weapon on the captain's hip hopefully allowed him to keep any other threat at bay.

Thinking of the captain, he turned back, but to his surprise, the other man was out of his sight. For a terrifying instant he wondered if the captain had planned this, bringing him along to his destination and then abandoning him. He tried to listen for any sign that the terrain vehicle was departing.

Heavy footsteps behind him informed Josiah that he was no longer alone. He slowly turned to find the captain, his laser pistol drawn.

It took Josiah just a moment to steel himself from what was to come, and then the captain fired a blast from his hand cannon, the light emitted from the weapon shockingly bright. Josiah's eyes took a moment to adjust, but he came to the startling realization that the weapon had not been pointed at him. Whirling to his right, Josiah saw the charred outline of a piece of vegetation, which surprisingly was still moving in its death throes, seemingly crawling back into the undergrowth.

If Captain Russell noted his hesitation, he was diplomatic enough not to mention it. "Carnivorous creeper vines. They can be deadly if one is not aware... a pretty common threat out here, but nothing one would want to face alone. If your survey crew was not expecting them..." His voice trailed off.

"Is this something that the sensors would not have picked up?"

"Not if they were as damaged as we suspect." He looked angry for a moment. "Especially if they were going off of a buoy that said it was safe."

Josiah straightened, sensing something in the other man's voice. "You found them, didn't you?"

The captain nodded, his expression devoid of any of the humor it had held earlier. "Just over the ridgeline. The creeper vines must have taken over the entire camp while they slept." The captain straightened his posture, clearly steeling himself to give additional bad news. "We also found an automated buoy marker, confirming that this planet was claimed for colonization. *Our* buoy marker."

Josiah closed his eyes tightly, feeling the other man's pain. Each buoy marker was planted by a ship to ensure that any follow up vessels knew that the planet was already under investigation. Each one was unique, and it certainly could not have been left by accident. Someone must have placed it before the *Redoubtable* departed, an intentional act that had cost multiple lives. "They must have followed the signal down, assuming that it would be safe."

"I checked the logs again, like I am sure you did, and there was no sign of a buoy being left on the planet during our first visit. Even if we discounted the fuel cost, we would have seen the life support equipment showing less than..."

The thought struck them both at the same time, and they turned to see a pair of glowing red photoreceptors shining ominously through the greenery. MOTO's traditionally stoic expression seemed sinister in the dying embers of the sunset.

"I wish you had not thought of that, Captain."

"Why, MOTO?" The captain's voice held a note of true pain. "How could you do something like this?"

"I can't be sure, but I think it had something to do with your former science officer." Josiah interjected, and the captain turned to him, confused.

"You are correct, Examiner," MOTO replied. "For Science Officer Tyler, and all of our crewmates."

"I don't understand," Russell replied, his gaze shifting from the examiner to the android and back again.

MOTO helped his captain with his understandable confusion. "When we were exposed to the superheated fungus on VOI-3904, Science Officer Tyler, Doctor Iyeni, and I were all damaged. Science Officer Tyler returned to the ship, while I sought to bring back the body of Doctor Iveni. Having returned to the ship, Science Officer Tyler refused to take off without me. It was a selfless act as I had never observed before."

The captain looked like he wanted to say something, but a glare from the examiner stopped him cold, and a quick flicker of recognition in his eyes informed him of just what he had nearly said. MOTO had apparently grown attached to the science officer when the Human had waited for the android to return with the dead medic, the android clearly not making the connection that Tyler had probably not realized the doctor was dead. To Josiah, it seemed only natural that the science officer had not waited for android, but for his fellow organic crewmate.

"It sounds like Tyler was an extraordinary man. It is only natural that you would want to assist him when he was wounded."

While it was impossible for the android to show emotion, the examiner believed he might have hit a nerve. The creation seemed to straighten a bit, and it looked like his photoreceptors narrowed slightly. "Tyler had proven himself to be selfless in his defense of the rest of the crew, myself included. It was vital that we provided him with the best of care, especially when we..." The mechanical voice trailed off, unable to continue.

In an instant, it struck Josiah, and he nearly cursed himself for not thinking of it sooner. "When you were unable to protect them."

The android nodded, clearly all he could do under his programming. Like most Human-created androids, the automated construct was constrained by a strict set of behavioral programming parameters, making it important that it prioritize the safety of Human life. The reality of interstellar exploration had weakened some of those programming bonds out of necessity if nothing else. "I attempted to provide him with the safety that he had provided to others, but our attackers were too strong. I was able to get him to the medical bay in time for him to be stabilized, but it will be some time before he will be able to return to us."

A quick glance at the captain confirmed the reports that he himself had read: The injuries to the science officer, while healing, were far more significant than the automaton was considering. While he would be able to live a good and comfortable life, the competitive nature of the Interstel system would never allow him back on board a starship again. The android surely knew that, but it seemed like something he could not recognize.

The captain took up the thread of conversation from there, his tone soothing. "So you helped to ensure that he was taken care of. You knew that I was sending him a portion of our profits, so you made sure that we remained profitable by maximizing our output."

"It was the only way to ensure a higher level of support for the entire crew." The android replied. "We are a successful vessel, but the vagaries of the exploration process provided for too little for us to sustain everyone. It was incumbent upon me to ensure that we were as successful as possible."

"And the follow up expeditions that went forward?" the examiner asked, his curiosity overwhelming his good sense for the briefest of moments. "What of them?"

"Interstel procedure ensures that no planets are settled without extensive android follow-up before colonization. No sentient creatures were to be harmed in the process. The follow up team would have caught any data errors before Human colonists were sent out."

Josiah closed his eyes tightly for a moment, immediately understanding the depth of the automaton's plan. Since it knew that only fellow androids would follow up on any inspections, there would be no risk to sentient creatures. The rest of his plan also made a sick sort of sense, merely extrapolating on the same odds that Interstel counted on for all of its projects: if he registered every potentially habitable planet as one that was a benefit, he would surely be right more than he was wrong, which would lead to higher profits. Not to mention, the sheer overwhelming backlog that was being created by the twelve exploration ships would also mean that some of these planets would not be seen as worthless until long after they had probably aged out of their current profession. It was an explanation that might only make sense in the ruthless pragmatism of an automated mind, but he could follow the theory.

Unfortunately, such pragmatism did have its downside.

MOTO slowly slid over, moving to place himself before them and the entrance to the lander. "Unfortunately, I cannot allow this agreement to be uncovered. The loss to the ship would be too great."

"You would kill us both, MOTO?" Russell asked, and for the briefest of moments it looked like the android was surprised.

"Of course not, Captain!" was the automatic reply. "You are too valuable to the ship to lose, and will be brought back aboard with all speed and comfort. Our guest, however, has fulfilled no practical purpose on the voyage, and has no effect on the ship as a whole, except to put it at risk. I calculate that the best option for us is to leave him here, on the planet, with all of the supplies he will require to survive happily."

A neat little sidestep there. Josiah thought. MOTO was rationalizing to himself that he would be allowing him to live, despite the fact that he had to realize that leaving him alone would clearly kill the examiner before anyone could send out a rescue mission. While the automaton would not be specifically behind his death, he was walking a very fine line.

The major factor would be Captain Russell. Josiah glanced over at him, attempting to gauge his expression.

To his dismay, the captain was clearly thinking about it, and he supposed that he could not blame him. Josiah had forced his way onto this mission, and his continued success was no longer assured. Now that the truth was out, when the ship returned to the Starport all of the reports sent in by MOTO would be put under a microscope, and he had to know that all payments would be halted until they could verify the suitability of the worlds independently, if at all. There was also an argument that the fraud created by the android would cause the funds to be forfeited by the ship, which would result in a shattering blow to their bottom line.

However, if Josiah did not return with them...

Something seemed to flash in the captain's eyes, and he straightened, giving the android a small nod. "Alright, MOTO, what are you thinking?"

The automaton almost seemed relieved by the quick acquiescence by his captain, focused completely on the other man. "I have made arrangements to ensure that all of the supplies that the examiner would need have been prepared and can be offloaded with ease. If you will ensure that he does not become... invasive, I can unload the ship before we are missed for too long."

Josiah looked between the two of them, clearly trying to come up with a way to delay the thought process. "What about the rest of the crew? Surely they will have some questions as to why I have not returned."

The captain looked at him, arching an eyebrow. "I think you grossly overestimate the impression you have made on the rest of the crew, Examiner. Those who do not believe you are an irritant are probably more focused on having you depart than any of the rest of us. No, MOTO is correct there: If you do not return to the ship, your absence will not be keenly missed."

For a moment, Josiah felt a pang of discomfort that he could not quite explain. While he hoped that the captain was only saying that to distract the android from his murderous mission, there was a small kernel of truth in the statement.

"Excellent. Keep the examiner here, while I prepare us for liftoff," he replied, his expression morphing into an ominous grin as he ascended the short ramp into the terrain vehicle. "There is nothing more for us here."

Josiah stood silently, watching as the final team returned to the shuttle. To his dismay, neither the chief engineer nor the doctor wasted so much of a glance in his direction as they returned to the shuttle, ascending the ramp and stepping inside, presumably to report to the captain. Josiah caught a quick glance at Salynn, whose face seemed flushed with what looked like the Thrynn equivalent of shame, and he wondered what MOTO had done to convince the young crewman to go along with his plan. Once it was clear that the rest of the crew was not going to be an issue, MOTO and Josiah entered the terrain vehicle, and returned to the landing site. MOTO and Josiah disembarked, waiting in the clearing while the rest of the crew loaded the lander up the disembarkation ramp, and several minutes later the captain returned.

Captain Russell gave MOTO a pleased nod. "I have the rest of the crew preparing for takeoff. MOTO, please move the supplies off the shuttle for the examiner here. We want to make his stay as comfortable as possible."

The android's photoreceptors seemed to darken momentarily in agreement, and then he headed up the ramp, taking the piled supplies that he had readied in the lander bay. Josiah's eyes searched the captain's face for some sign of anything that he was thinking, but found nothing.

MOTO had just brought down a crate of emergency rations, laying them down just outside the clearing, when everything happened at once.

MOTO straightened suddenly, keenly aware of a threat Josiah had not sensed. A single blast came from the doorway of the landing bay. The chief engineer had fired the laser rifle he held with precision, taking the android in what would be the kneecap for a Human being.

"GO!" The captain was already pushing Josiah towards the ramp, which had started to ascend, and the younger man ran at full speed. To his horror, the android had taken no time at all to react. Dropping the supplies he had been carrying, MOTO bolted into pursuit, but even with his enhanced speed he was too far to make it in time in his injured condition.

The chief engineer seemed like he wanted to fire another shot, but clearly thought better of it, simply hitting the hatch close. Josiah felt himself being shoved from behind, and the captain fell atop him, slamming him into the far bulkhead of the landing bay. From behind him, a metallic sounding strike against the lower hull made him realize how close he had come to death, and the memory of the glowing photoreceptors seemed to haunt him when he closed his eyes.

The captain didn't allow him time to think about it. "Liftoff!"

Xixptrixx didn't need to be told twice. With a dull roar, the ship shot into the sky, and Josiah felt another sharp pain as he slammed into the terrain vehicle, holding on desperately to avoid sliding further down the bay. A strong grip wrapped around his arm, and Salynn, already braced against one of the seats, kept him in place with a strength few Humans could have matched. The captain, having better prepared himself, maintained his own balance with one of handholds on the terrain vehicle's exterior.

In a moment, the ship leveled out, and Josiah was able to get his feet under him again in the artificial gravity. From the far end of the bay, the doctor sent over a withering glare that seemed to encompass all four men. "Now, would someone like to tell me what the hell is going on?"

The captain gave a brief retelling, and Josiah had the dubious pleasure of seeing the doctor at a loss for words for once. "I just can't believe it."

"It makes sense, in a convoluted sort of way," Josiah replied, watching the stars as well. "MOTO was just as alone as the rest of you, perhaps more so, and was processing it the best way that he knew how."

The doctor looked at Josiah strangely. "And what if MOTO had not been the threat, or if the captain had gone along with his idea?"

The examiner smiled. "I never doubted him for an instant."

The communications console took that moment to activate, and Josiah glanced over, wondering if the android had found a way to make contact.

"*Redoubtable* Lander," the voice that came back was not familiar, and shockingly enough, not Human, the dulcet tones of a Thrynn clear even through the light comm distortion. "This is Captain Pyash T'threissiiioi of the *Fortune*. We have come at the behest of Examiner Benton. Is he available?"

The captain glanced over at him sharply, and the examiner could not help but to shrug slightly. "Maybe for an instant, at least..."

Through The Time Lens

By Robert Silverberg

There's an ancient Elowan proverb, said to go back to the days of the long-vanished Old Empire:

Don't ever trust a Thrynn bearing gifts.

There's no love lost between Elowan and Thrynn and never has been, but even the most trusting Humans are leery of them. My grandmother used to say, "If you have a Thrynn as a dinner guest, be on your best behavior, but count the spoons afterward."

I suppose it's because the Thrynn are reptilian lifeforms that we're uneasy. Most Humans simply aren't comfortable around reptiles, an attitude that stems from an ancient Earth legend about some difficulty involving a snake, an apple, and the first female Human. The snake tempted her with an apple and all kinds of trouble followed. So when we found out that a Thrynn colony on a planet called Jathamassa Seven was looking to hire a mostly Human crew for a lot of MU, our first reaction was suspicion.

The price is too good, that's the problem.

They're only offering basic expenses, but they're willing to cough up a twenty-five percent royalty interest for any discoveries we make on their behalf – mineral, biological, whatever. It's like handing us a quarter of the planet. We had visions of glorious mining concessions that would pour forth billions of monetary units' worth of promethium, platinum, plutonium, even endurium – you name it – unto the Nth generation. So what's the catch? We couldn't understand why they'd be willing to pay so much. It was their planet, after all. They claimed and colonized it and whatever was there belonged to them. And why did the Thrynn want

Humans for the exploration job? Why not do it themselves, or send a bunch of androids in?

Well, we were an all-Human crew. That fits the requirements. Not that we intended any racial prejudice – Humans, Elowan, Velox, and Thrynn manage to live serenely side by side on our home world of Arth – but it just happened that the six of us all belonged to the same species.

Despite any suspicions we have had about the job, we weren't in a position to be picky.

We six – Mik Gahune, Gabe Vicinanza, Fran Jibor, Nikko Clark, Ned Stackman, and I – had been partners for nine years. Our basic notion was to go into a line of work that would let us tour the far reaches of the universe, see a lot of fantastically wonderful places, and make a bundle of money through exploration and mining. We're still pretty poor, but two out of three ain't bad.

Our last expedition had been a disaster and a half. The rodnium turned out to be a spectrographic error; the planet we went looking for was one of those gravity-trap places, where you think you're dealing with the optimal gravity and suddenly discover that you aren't; and the flux that we very hastily jumped into sent us right down the chute into the Squeeze Zone that lies upspin of Uhlek Central.

By the time we came limping back into Starport a year-and·a-half later, our beloved *ISS Indomitable* looked like a reject from the Galactic Garbage Museum.

We weren't in much better shape ourselves.

The bank kindly worked out an arrangement that allowed us to finance a new set of engines, replacements for our cargo pods, a complete shielding makeover, and an assortment of trifling medical work: Three joint jobs, two limb regrows, a couple of optical implants, five sets of teflon/platinum eardrums – well, you get the idea. We were a mess and it took a bank loan of hyper-galactic size to put us back together again. Now all we had to do was turn approximately nine monetary units out of every ten we earned over to the financial folks for the next couple of eternities—unless we strike something really big that would let us retire the loan a little sooner. It's sheer and simple indentured servitude. Our only alternative was to file for bankruptcy and go into some mundane line of work among the Groundlings as scanning clerks, say, or wiper technicians. Anyone who's ever ridden the flux lines will understand why we weren't about to do that. There wasn't one of us who wouldn't rather be in hock for the rest of his life than have to endure the daily grind of Groundside existence.

That's why we took the Jathamassa Seven job.

You didn't need a mental augmentation implant to suspect that there was something fishy about it.

But what if there wasn't? What if we were overestimating, for once, the devious, cunning nature of the Thrynn? And what if we could somehow manage to score the big strike that would rescue us from debt eternal?

It was worth the gamble, we thought.

We found out later that the job was on the board for five months and we were the first crew who ever nibbled at it. Well, it did look too good to be true, and very little that looks that way actually is. I guess there's something about carrying a debt that could take you five lifetimes to pay off that makes you do funny things.

Jathamassa was an F-class sun that lay outward and downspin from Arth, somewhere below the 50th parallel.

According to our starmap, the system has eight planets. The inner four are bunched very close to the sun and have climates ranging from searing to inferno. The outer two are very far out and frigid indeed. But Jathamassa Six and Jathamassa Seven, whose orbits both lay in a central band quite distinct from those of the inner and outer worlds, were well within the acceptable climatic range and their gravity was reasonable, so both worlds had been claimed and colonized in relatively recent times–Six about twenty years back and Seven somewhat later.

When the *Indomitable* emerged from the flux in the Jathamassa system, we unexpectedly found ourselves nose to nose with a disagreeable bunch of Spemin pirates who preferred immediate combat to any sort of parleying. That's one of the little surprises you often get in a galaxy full of intelligent alien races that don't necessarily respect each other's right-of-way.

The Spemin weren't members of the Old Empire and they seem to regard other species as fair game.

A bad mistake on the part of these Spemin, because our new shielding was state-of-the-art stuff and Gabe Vicinanza, our navigator and weapons man, has a 250 aptitude trigger finger. The Spemin subsequently departed from the material plane in a flash, and we came out of the short but nasty little battle needing only some minor refitting around the vanes. Nikko Clark, our engineer, reported that any competent body shop would be able to handle the job, but our Thrynn employers weren't able to help us out. We made contact with Jathamassa Seven and a Thrynn named Vryssh, with icy blue eyes and glossy green skin that looked like extremely high-quality leather, came on screen. He was an elegant creature, with the long neck and whiplike tail characteristic of his species. He held himself bolt upright. "We are sorry," he said, in a soft, hissing Thrynn tone that made him sound not sorry in the slightest, "but we have no such repair facilities here. You will have to make a stop at Jathamassa Six for whatever work you need."

Oddly enough, Six and Seven were under separate colonial administration. Seven, of course, belonged to the reptilian Thrynn.

But Six was a joint Elowan-Velox operation. Ordinarily you wouldn't find Elowan setting foot within a dozen parsecs of a Thrynn world, but I suppose the profits they were pulling out of Jathamassa Six were sufficient consolation for any psychic discomfort they might be experiencing as a result of the presence of their ancient enemies on the next planet over.

Jathamassa Six, you see, is the only place in the known universe where nebula jade is found.

Aside from endurium–the near-miraculous substance that makes super-photonic galactic travel possible–I doubt that there's any commodity traded anywhere in the galaxy which is quite as expensive, kilogram for kilogram, as nebula jade.

A Velox communications officer was on duty when we called Six for permission to land and repair the ship. The Velox officer gave us a chilly bug-eyed stare of appraisal and wanted to know what we were doing in their vicinity.

I've never really warmed to the Velox–it's hard for me to take a chummy attitude toward red insects with compound eyes, even if they are a hard-working and highly intelligent species–but Mik Gahune handled the call, and Mik knows all about how to deal with the Velox. He immediately adopted a posture of high obsequiousness, an attitude which brings good results during transactions with the Velox.

In a galaxy where Humans are just one of many races, you need to keep the quirks of the other species dearly in mind if you want to get anything accomplished.

Mik said straightforwardly that we were here to do a job for the Thrynn on Seven but we had run into a little trouble with some Spemin and needed to have our vanes scraped and realigned. The Velox seemed to respond well to the obsequiousness but pointed out that Six was a jointly owned world and the local Elowan would not countenance a landing if any Thrynn were on board. We assured her that we had an all-Human crew, but before she let us land, she wanted to run a credit check on us.

That was the last thing we wanted her to do, considering the state of our bank account, so while Gahune killed some time conversing, I got on the subspace horn to our friend Vryssh and told him to advance us enough to cover our repair bills.

Vryssh didn't seem to understand the concept of an "advance."

Matters got a little tense as I spelled everything out, up to and including, that if he wanted his goddamned job handled at all he better see to it that our ship was made whole, and we didn't have the MU to pay for it ourselves.

He hissed concession and said they'd pay for the repairs and deduct the cost from our share of profits, if any. We could bill the repair job–so long as it didn't exceed 8000 mu's–to an account at the Rock of Truth Bank in Vimipotin on Arth. Mik Gahune passed this information along to the Velox who ran a confirm on it by sub-etheric wave–the Velox pinch every monetary unit until it screams–and after a lot of long distance, back-and-forth palaver we were permitted to land.

Jathamassa Six was not one of the great beauty spots of the galaxy. What you see at the surface isn't solid ground, but only a bewildering tangle of long rubbery blue-green vines thick as a man's thigh, tightly interwoven to form a kind of gigantic trampoline that stretches from pole to pole.

The vines are rough and sticky, with warts and humps rising everywhere, and constantly contract and expand, giving off a strange breathy sound like a sigh of agony.

Anyone who works at the surface travels from place to place over these vines using vehicles that have, instead of wheels, long thin legs ending in huge hand-shaped clamps. The vehicles make their way around like giant insects, grasping and then releasing the strands of the planetary vines as they pull themselves forward.

A veil of thick soupy clouds hides the sun the whole day long, giving the place a steamy, dismal, oppressive feel. A warm clammy rain falls all the time. The gravity on Six is light, but instead of giving you an exhilarating feeling, it simply adds to the general feeling of instability and gloom.

What passes for a spaceport there is somewhere deep down in the bowels of the planet. You are guided in for landing in the middle of a huge symplexium disk sitting atop the mat of vines, and then the disk rises open and an elevator conveys you, ship and all, into the hideous subterranean depths. Below is all one great, spongy mass, hundreds of kilometers deep. Wide low-roofed tunnels run through it, crossing and crossing again. The walls of those tunnels are moist and pink, like intestines, and a kind of sickly phosphorescent illumination comes from them, a feeble glow that cuts through the darkness without giving comfort to the eyes. The whole planet is like that.

The spongy underground is the substructure of the vines, the mother-substance.

The vines that spring from it are actually its roots – which reach up, not down, so they can convey moisture to the substructure and carry on some kind of photosynthetic process in the open air.

As for the tunnels through the substructure, they are the work of enormous worm-like creatures who spend their entire lifespan gnawing through the spongy stuff and excreting rivers of slime. These things have been eating their way through the underground world of Jathamassa Six since the beginning of time, leaving the tunnels behind. They're nothing more than live eating-machines, a couple of kilometers long, mindless, unstoppable. These are the creatures that produce nebula jade.

The Velox, seeing how restless we were becoming after a couple of days waiting for repairs and cooling our heels at the spaceport, offered us a tour of the jade mines. I'll give them credit for that much: they treated us decently enough once we had gone through the rituals of friendliness. (Their Elowan partners, by contrast, wouldn't have anything to do with us. I suppose because they knew we were hirelings of the detested Thrynn of Jathamassa Seven.)

The jade-mine tour was – well – *interesting*.

I suppose that's as tactful a word as any.

It seems that one of the other life-forms of Jathamassa Six is a huge insect with tremendous golden-green eyes and a great hooked beak. These things use their beaks to inject the worms with their gastric juices and actually tunnel into their bodies, where they feed on the worms' tissues and, in time, lay their eggs. It takes years before a worm's dull brain realizes that it has been invaded in this way. But finally it gets the news, and then it defends itself by secreting a substance that hardens to a stony mass around the parasitic insect, trapping it in a kind of cyst, causing the parasite to starve. The stony material that forms these cysts is the rich, lustrous substance known commercially as nebula jade, which is cut and polished into the sublime jewelry that is coveted on every world of the starways.

A collecting team – one Velox, one Elowan – tracks the worms through the tunnels constantly wading in nauseating streams of worm-slime.

When they find a worm they look for jade-light, the bright glow of a cyst through the worm's translucent body. The Velox member of the team then uses blades and prongs to cut the cyst out of the worm's flesh. The worm doesn't mind; it doesn't even notice. What is likely to mind is the insect within the cyst, which, if it hasn't starved to death yet, is apt to be extremely hostile. The cyst becomes brittle when exposed to the air of the tunnel and the insect, if it's alive, batters its way out and attacks anything in reach with its ferocious beak. That's what the Elowan member of the team is there for.

The Velox, it seems feel queasy about killing insects of any kind whatever, even murderous parasitic ones like these.

It's an ancestral taboo of some sort: sisters beneath the exoskeleton, or something. Elowan don't have such inhibitions. They're essentially plants, after all – delicate two-legged photosynthetic creatures with prehensile vines instead of limbs. So when the Velox pulls the cyst out, her Elowan companion is standing by with a laser in firing prime. If the parasite's alive, the Elowan hits it with a hard burn. Sometimes the parasite is faster than the Elowan and then there are fatalities. A good part of the cost of a fine nebula jade necklace represents the staggering salaries that the jade miners are paid for risking their lives this way on so dreary and disagreeable a planet as Jathamassa Six.

We spent half a day in the worm-tunnels, watching a team of jade-miners collect about half a million MU worth of jade from three different worms. Of the five cysts that the miners found, four contained dead parasites, but the fifth was alive and it came storming out beak-first, chomping as it came.

Our Elowan was quick, though. Its prehensile vines barely fluttered as it cut the immense bug down with a quick blast. The Velox waggled her antennae in an expression of approval. Even if she felt a tribal taboo against killing fellow insects herself, she certainly seemed to admire the efficiency with which the Elowan took care of the job. Never expect a lot of sentimentality out of Velox. In a few days our vane job and repairs were finished so we paid our bill and left without any great regret.

We called across to the Thrynn on Jathamassa Seven and asked them for landing coordinates. That was when we found that the Thrynn colony on Seven wasn't actually *on* the planet, but in a habitat sphere in *low orbit around it*. Instead of making a planetary landing as we had expected we would be docking at a small satellite some ten thousand kilometers out. That made us a little edgy. It seemed the Thrynn were sending us down to inspect a world that they didn't care to set foot on themselves.

Jathamassa Seven turned out to be a small, ordinary-looking planet with no distinctive visual features. Optical scans showed a dull red surface, an endless sandy waste. Mean temperature, temperate-to-tropical. Gravity was on the light side, .8 or so. Atmospheric conditions were calm and the atmosphere itself was mostly nitrogen and CO2 with just enough oxygen to remind us of what a habitable world was like. Spectrographic analysis said there was very little water, if any. Bio readings were ambiguous: there seemed to be life down there, but not a lot of it, and the numbers were odd ones, hard to interpret.

Great. A hot, dry, dusty desert world!

As for minerals – forget it. At least any that had significant commercial value. Sensor readings told us that what we had down there was a planet made up of light, essentially worthless elements: silicon, carbon, boron, sodium, stuff like that. All very fine elements in their way, but there's no profit to be had in hauling them across galactic distances for resale. So much for our mining concessions. Goodbye platinum, goodbye promethium, goodbye plutonium!

A worthless planet. And we would own twenty-five percent of it! Great!

"Snookered again," Mik Gahune muttered.

"We should have known," said Gabe Vicinanza. "The Velox and the Elowan who colonized Jathamassa Six must have had a look at this place too, when they first came through here. And they didn't even bother filing a claim on it."

"But the Thrynn did," Nikko Clark pointed out. "They must have seen something that the earlier explorers didn't."

"After all," said Ned Stackman, the science officer, "Six doesn't look so terrific from space either. Who'd ever guess that underneath those miserable tangled vines are disgusting monstrous worms that just happen to generate the most desirable jewelry substance in the galaxy?"

"In any case," I said, "we've signed a contract and we're here. Let's go talk to the Thrynn. No use crying in our beer until we know the full story, all right?"

Navigator Vicinanza handled the docking maneuver with his usual adroitness and soon we were safely coupled aboard.

A dozen or so Thrynn were waiting to welcome us inside the airlock.

The Thrynn may be a slippery bunch of snakes at heart but their manner is impeccably suave and cultured. They greeted us as though we were visiting dignitaries and not just a bunch of worse-than-penniless space jockeys trying to turn a quick mega-MU or two doing odd jobs wherever we could find them. They had taken the trouble to adjust the habitat's gravity to our comfort level, which must have meant a little discomfort for them, and though the food and drink offered us was of course, synthetic, it was elaborately prepared in a way worthy of the finest chef on Arth. Not that most of us were in any position to judge, but Science Officer Slackman, who fancied himself a great gourmet, was impressed.

"This wine," he said, holding his goblet up to let light shine through the lovely amber fluid. "Surely it's a Mount Glimin cabernet...the '07 vintage, I would guess!"

Our hosts made little swooshing sounds of Thrynn pleasure, and smiled that toothy Thrynn smile that inspires so little warmth in people of other races.

Their sapphire eyes were agleam with obvious delight at the flattery Slackman was so copiously providing. Naturally the wine, like everything else aboard the little habitat, had been manufactured in the converter chamber at the core of the satellite, but flattery is the lubricant that keeps the gears of inter-species galactic diplomacy from making nasty crunching noises. I asked Slackman later whether the wine was really that good and he said that in fact it hadn't been half bad, that back on Arth he would have regarded it as quite decent picnic wine. Apparently the Thrynn were going out of their way to soften us up for the job that we had been hired to do. After we took the time to relax and unwind, they got down to business.

The head of the Thrynn operation was a tall, impressive looking number named Ssspikik, whose rich-toned covering of iron-gray scales was absolutely magnificent from snout to tail.

I looked at him and found myself thinking, *What a glorious set of luggage he'd make!* Ssspikik took us to a port from which we could see the surface of the planet below and pointed with the tip of his tail.

"Behold Jathamassa Seven," he said. "A truly fascinating planet, but one which, alas, is a very difficult environment for the Thrynn. Unable to explore it ourselves, we are convinced of the high value of the artifacts it contains."

"Artifacts? How absolutely wonderful!" That was Fran Jibor, ship's doctor. Archaeology is her hobby – her passion, in fact. Her cabin is full of bits and scraps of the galactic past, collected hither and yon – even a little collection of battered, fragmentary objects that Fran insists come from our legendary ancestral world of Earth in the Sol system. She looked excited. The rest of us were something less than thrilled, though, which is putting it mildly. The Thrynn had invited us here to do archaeology for them? Well, ancient artifacts are interesting things, and sometimes the Interstel folks will give you a decent price for one, if it happens to light them up the right way. But you stack up the profit quotient of a cargo pod full of quaint artifacts against that of a few tons of plutonium and there's just no comparison. Things were looking worse and worse.

We stared out at the great red disk of the planet, which at this distance seemed almost to fill the sky. We saw broad plains, lofty mountain ranges, what appeared to be the beds of huge rivers, though apparently the rivers themselves had dried up long ago. Then something that had the appearance of a colossal pink stain came into view.

"What you observe passing below us now," said Ssspikik, "is the living Sea of Jathamassa: a single immense semi-liquid life-form, spanning more than ten thousand kilometers. Take care, when you descend to the surface, to avoid any contact with this entity. It is the obstacle that prevents us from touching down on the planet ourselves."

We knew we were looking at something extraordinary. It went on and on and on as our orbiting satellite, hovering over the planet's equator, moved swiftly westward. Even from ten thousand kilometers up we were able to tell that it wasn't a true sea at all, but rather something solid, a quivering mass, a continent-size glob of matter...an entity.

Ssspikik said, "What appears to be a pink ocean is actually a gigantic creature with some sort of low-level intelligence. Or perhaps, for all we are able to tell, intelligence on the genius level. It thinks. It perceives. From an airborne flier you can actually observe its mental workings, in the form of questing ripples on its surface rising in little interrogative quivers – puckered bubbling orifices that come and go, short-lived interrogative protuberances. Scoop a section out to study it and all you have is a lump of watery mud, rapidly growing cool as it dies. But the thing itself, whatever it is, has a mind. And that mind, unfortunately, broadcasts a constant flow of malevolent energy that we Thrynn are unable to withstand. Half an hour's exposure to it seriously scrambles our synapses. An hour and we lose all vestige of sanity. Six hours is fatal for us."

"But not for us?" I asked.

"So we believe," the Thrynn said.

"So – you – believe –?"

"We have every reason to think that the neural emanation of the Living Sea is harmless to the Human nervous system. We have measured the wavelength of the emanation. It is not one on which the Human mind functions."

"Ah," I said, not feeling very reassured.

"As a result of the information brought back by our first landing teams before they succumbed," Ssspikik said, "we have sent android exploring parties to the surface to examine the remains left behind by this planet's extinct civilization. They reported the presence of ancient sites of potentially high value, but were incapable of penetrating them. Androids, of course, have great limitations of intellect."

"And therefore you thought it would be a better idea to send a team of Humans down there."

"Yes."

I nodded. "And if it turns out that you were wrong about our immunity to whatever kind of mental radiation it is that the Living Sea puts out?"

"We are prepared to post a generous liability bond to compensate your beneficiaries."

"Ah," I said again.

I looked across at Mik Gahune. He looked back at me and neither of us looked very happy

I glanced at Gabe Vicinanza, at Fran Jibor, at Nikko Clark. We were all thinking the same thing.

Ssspikik said, "And what is now coming into view is the feature which leads us to think that there may be great rewards to reap here. Do you see the border between the Living Sea and the land, where there appears to be a kind of cliff? Are you able to make out a structure at the edge of that cliff? Here: allow me to show you a magnified image." He made an optical adjustment.

A structure, yes. A ruin, but a magnificent one.

We were peering at what seemed to be a great stone fortress, looming like a colossal crouching beast atop a rugged cliff. Even at this distance it looked gigantic, terrifying, mysterious, incredibly ancient. I heard Fran Jibor catch her breath in awe.

"We think it's thousands of years old at the minimum," said Ssspikik. "Millions, perhaps. Certainly it goes back beyond Old Empire times, and it may be very much more ancient than that, a relic of some prehistoric civilization of which nothing at all is known. Sonic scans indicate that there's material inside that building. Artifacts, we think, of that lost civilization. But the building is surrounded by a security field that so far has rebuffed all our attempts at penetrating it. It generates what appears to be a relatively simple matching code interrogative wave. But the heroic members of our First Expedition who attempted to solve it were unable to retain their sanity long enough to supply the required answers. The Second Expedition and the Third perished the same way. And when we sent androids, they lacked the requisite flexibility of intelligence to deal with the codes."

It made sense. The Thrynn very likely had figured that the Velox, bustling hive-creatures that they are, didn't have much more smarts than androids when it came to the sort of intellectual challenge that getting into this ruin posed. And for obvious reasons Thrynn weren't going to want to strike up a business relationship with the Elowan. Whereas some nice clever Humans – especially Humans so down on their luck that they were willing to take on a risky job which carried only the most speculative of payoffs.

"Well," I said, with an enthusiasm I was a long way from feeling. "We'll give it a try."

As we set up the coordinates for our landing approach we kept saying to each other in a compulsive way, "Seriously scrambles synapses. Seriously scrambles synapses." With a thick Thrynn accent, heavy on the triple sibilants. "Sseriousssly ssscramblesss sssynapsssesss." Followed by a lot of wild, hysterical laughter. We were really manic. Call it a defense mechanism, I guess. What if the emanations of the Living Sea were just as deadly to Humans as they were to Thrynn?

Below us, that strange sea was looking stranger.

At close range we could see it was plainly not water at all: it had a stiff texture, like some kind of ghastly steaming custard. Its surface was rough and gritty. There was nothing like surf or waves. It lay almost inert, pressing up against the shore, making small, sinister rippling motions.

"Anybody feel anything?" I asked.

"Nothing out of the ordinary," was the answer I got all around. So far so good.

We landed on the clifftop a few kilometers from the edge.

The zone of ruins lay just to the west of us, a vast sprawling maze. We could see the broken and weathered stubs of giant stone buildings, the stumps of delicate bridges that had collapsed eons ago into mounds of rubble, the outlines of roadways long since taken over by the harsh scaly stuff that passed for vegetation here. On the edge of the cliff was the great building itself, the citadel, a fortress: massive greenishblack walls, gigantic stone columns, a heavy sloping roof, still intact after unknown hundreds of centuries.

And now that we had actually touched down on Jathamassa Seven we sensed the mental force of the Living Sea for the first time. There was a definite pressure. Not overwhelming, not lethal. More of a tickle than a blast.

"You feel it?" Fran Jibor asked.

I nodded.

"Me too," said Gahune. "But it seems manageable."

"Even so, we oughtn't stay here a long time," Ned Stackman said. "The effects may not be as strong on us as they are for the Thrynn, but they might be cumulative. Quick in and out, that's what I say."

"Agreed," I said. "All right. I want two volunteers to go over there in the terrain vehicle and –"

"Me," Fran Jibor peeped.

"And me," said Stackman.

Gahune, Vicinanza, and Nikko chimed in, but they were too late.

"You guys draw lots for the second trip," I told them. We readied the terrain vehicle for its outing. "If you start feeling strange in the head, turn back right away," I warned Stackman and Jibor. "Is that clear?"

"I always feel strange in the head," Fran said.

"Ssseriousssly ssscramblesss sssynapsssesss," said Ned Slackman, and we had a good laugh as we sent them out to have a look at the antiquities.

The risk was that they wouldn't know they were experiencing mental distortions until the effects became serious. If that happened, we could try to bring the terrain vehicle back using automatic override – but it could be too late. I ordered them to keep up a constant flow of talk as they went, which we monitored carefully for signs of inner disturbance.

"Bumpy road," Fran reported. "Ruts you wouldn't believe.

Uh-oh – an abandoned Thrynn vehicle. Bad sign.

We're moving through a kind of sculpture garden now, not much left of it, and what's here is badly corroded and pitted. Not much museum value. Approaching the big stone building."

"How do you feel?" I asked.

"Terrific, Captain!"

"And you, Slackman?"

"Ssstackman," he said, and giggled.

"Keep it together," I told him.

Fran said, "We're right up underneath the big building now. It's about forty meters high and solid as a rock. No windows. Ornamentation on the walls, very alien designs, strange curves and peculiar angles. Almost as though it's half jutting into some other dimension."

"Any sign of an entrance?"

"Not yet. We're heading around to the far side now, overlooking the sea. The sea seems a little agitated – surface movement, a slow stirring. No mental effects on us yet. Just that tickling – right, Ned?"

"That'sss right," Slackman said.

His fake Thrynn accent was definitely starting to wear thin for us.

Fran said, "Ah – here's a gate in the wall. Drum-tight and solid. And – wait – a light's beginning to flash. High up over the door, some kind of luminescent cell, very bright. Rhythmic bursts – a few quick flashes, then off, flash, off, a few more – now it's stopped altogether – there it goes again –"

"The interrogative code that Ssspikik was talking about," I said. I gestured to Gabe Vicinanza to jack the audio line into the ship's computer. "The pattern of blinks and darks must be the thing we're supposed to crack," I told Fran. "Read them to us as they come, and we'll see if we can run an analysis for you, and then maybe you can use the vehicle laser to signal back at it."

"Will do," she said. "It's off now. Starting up again. Blink. Blink. Blink. Pause. Blink. Pause. Blink blink blink blink. Pause. Blink. Pause. Blink blink blink blink blink. Pause. Blink blink blink blink blink blink – oh, damn, I think I've lost count. Seven or eight blinks in a row, maybe even nine. Now it's stopped. Waiting. Here it goes again, now. Blink. Blink. Blink. Pause. Blink. Pause."

I glanced over at Vicinanza. He was jotting the blinks down by hand as well.

Mik Gahune, peering over Gabe's shoulder, looked up and said, "Tell her to count the long pattern very carefully this time."

"You heard that, Fran?"

"Yes. Here it comes. One, two, three---nine."

"Nine?" Gahune said. "Is she sure?" He was grinning broadly.

"Nine, yes," came the reply from the terrain vehicle.

"All right," said Gahune. "What she needs to do now is to wait until the next cycle comes along, and give us that. Then we'll tell her what signal to give in return."

He nudged Vicinanza, who nodded and grinned.

He began talking to the computer and numbers started coming up on the screen. The two of them were on to something, all right.

Out at the great stone building the next cycle had started. The pattern was the same as before, Fran said: Three blinks, one, four, one, five, nine. Stop.

Gahune said, "Okay. She should reply with this pattern of blinks: Four, two, one, six, one, five."

I passed it along. Fran said, "It's flashing back at us. A new pattern this time. Six blinks. Four. Five."

"The reply is Three, Seven, Two."

"Three, Seven, Two," Fran repeated.

And then an earphone-shattering scream came from her. "The door is opening! The door is opening!"

I looked at Gahune and Vicinanza in wonder.

''Will one of you geniuses please explain how-"

"Three point one four one five nine," Gahune said. "Sound familiar?"

I said almost without thinking, "Pi! The first six digits!"

"Very good, captain. Gold star and merit badge both."

The ratio of the circumference of a circle to its diameter is the same anywhere in the universe, but you need to be a member of an intelligent species to know that. We asked the computer for the next six digits and she was able to supply them. That's all the door wanted."

"And the Thrynn couldn't figure that out?" I said, amazed.

"The Thrynn were getting their synapses scrambled, remember?" said Gahune. "You try remembering pi to six places, let alone twelve, while your brain is cooking! And the androids they sent afterward weren't smart enough to figure out that the door was asking them a simple mathematical question. But we were."

"We're inside the building!" Fran said, and I could tell from the astonishment in her voice that the building wasn't empty.

After half an hour I ordered them to come out and return to the *Indomitable*.

They didn't want to, but I wasn't going to risk letting them stay that close to the Living Sea any longer. Besides, the rest of us wanted a chance to see what was inside that building.

When they reached the ship, Fran's eyes were shining with awe and even the usually stolid Ned Stackman looked transfigured by the marvels he had seen. Visions of fabulous wealth danced in my head as we unloaded the cargo pickup of the terrain vehicle. But they faded quickly as reality came crashing in.

Jibor and Stackman had found a load of junk.

Rusted bits of twisted useless stuff. Perhaps they once had been the components of fabulous machines of the ancients but all of it had long ago been smashed to bits. Fragile metal plates bearing inscriptions worn almost to invisibility. Clotted masses of what looked like wire. Humped-up heaps of crud.

Junk. Esthetic value, zilch. Scientific value, zilch. Market value, zilch. Twenty-five percent of zilch is zilch.

"But it's fabulous to be in there'" Fran cried. "To know that you're walking where some incredibly ancient alien race once walked, before the Old Empire was ever dreamed of –."

"Yes," I said. "I'm sure it's a terrific experience, Fran. But isn't there anything in there that we can sell? Intact sculpture? Tomb offerings? Jewelry? Complete artifacts?"

"Well – no." she said.

We gave the building a thorough going-over.

I went in with Vicinanza – Fran was right, the place was truly an awesome structure, but awe isn't a marketable commodity.

There seemed nothing tangible inside that hadn't long since rusted away. Gahune took a look, accompanied by Clark, and finally Stackman and Fran made one last sortie. By now the emanations from the sea, though they were still safely sub-lethal, were beginning to make all of us feel a little peculiar. So we packed up our treasure and took the ship back up to the Thrynn habitat.

Ssspikik was delighted that we had been able to get inside the building, and fascinated and chagrined to learn that the vaunted interrogative code had been nothing more abstruse than pi to a dozen places. When we spread our haul of rusty junk out before him he hissed his appreciation as though we had brought him the greatest treasure of the Old Empire.

I could tell that he was making the same realistic calculation we had made of the market value of this pitiful stuff.

His seventy-five percent of zilch wasn't worth any more than our twenty-five percent of zilch. The difference was that we were broke, and he wasn't. For him it was just a business venture that hadn't worked out very well. For us it was a catastrophe.

"Of course these are just preliminary finds," he said soothingly. "On your subsequent entries into the building you may discover artifacts of even higher quality."

"Of course," I said. "No doubt we will."

I was speaking ironically and Ssspikik was just trying to comfort us. Neither of us really believed that this enterprise was likely to pan out. But we were both wrong.

The *Indomitable* made four more trips to the surface of Jathamassa Seven.

On the fourth and last trip we discovered the artifact that we have come to know as the Time Lens.

We didn't have any idea at first what it was. We were working in the lower levels of the building, beneath the flagstone floor, doing some careful stratigraphic excavation in the hope of finding some layer of occupation that had survived the eons better than the material in the upper regions. We figured it was our last chance. As we dug down we found items in a better state of preservation than the previous finds – still nothing spectacular. It was beginning to seem as though the proceeds of selling whatever we had might at least allow us to break even on the voyage. I was brooding when Neel cracked open the top of a stone vault with his laser digger and said sharply, "Hello! What's this?"

A column of air suddenly came whooshing out like a genie out of a bottle. Stackman jumped back in surprise. He had stumbled on some sort of insulated container; and that air was thousands or maybe millions of years old.

There was a container within that one, a third crystalline box within that. With trembling fingers we lifted the lid of that one a little spherical device made of silvery metal, untarnished and in perfect condition.

The sphere was small enough to hold in one hand, with a couple of little control studs projecting from its top.

"Finally something worthwhile," Stackman said, and pounced on it.

"Wait, Ned," Fran called. "We need to photograph it in situ, and then we have to –" but Stackman was too excited to worry about proper archaeological procedures. Already he had the thing in his hand and he was pushing the control studs. I yelled at him to stop: what if it was an implosion bomb powerful enough to blow up half a continent, and he had just activated it?

Sometimes impulsiveness pays off, though.

A kind of shield slid back on one side of the sphere and a cone of brilliant multi-colored light came streaming forth. We stared in astonishment as the light coalesced into a tight beam that splashed an image on the wall opposite us. We stared at a series of images, a kind of motion picture. A motion picture that was thousands of millions of years old.

The first image on the wall was what looked very much like a solar system, but a very strange one.

There was a blazing circle of light at its center and around it were lesser points of light that were moving in planetary orbits.

We could make out only two planets, one very near the sun, the other at a great distance from it.

"A two-planet system?" Mik Gahune said. "Is there any such thing?"

"It isn't a common configuration," Stackman said. "But I can think of a few. There's Lempira, Gran Chingada, and Duud Shabeel, I think –"

"Look there," Vicinanza said.

Whatever recorded this swung around the solar system's sun, looped past the lone inner planet, and headed toward the remote outer one. It took a minute or two for the distant world to come into focus. We gasped when it did, for at close range we saw that the planet was shining with an eerie high-albedo gleam, a shimmering dazzle of radiance, that had the unique and extraordinary appearance of –

"Endurium?" I murmured. "Can it be possible?"

"Nothing else looks like that," said Stackman. "Nothing."

I shook my head in dazed disbelief. "Nothing," I said, in a barely audible whisper.

It was incredible. A world covered with endurium?

A whole planet whose entire surface was the substance on which the entire technology of super photonic transportation is based? That was crazy. Endurium is incredibly rare. You find a little here, a little there – never very much at a time. But surely the weird gleam coming from the planet's surface could be no other thing. Endurium's unique spectrographic line is unmistakable.

A planet of endurium! Not in the wildest of fantasies had anyone ever imagined such a thing. Was the machine playing with us? Toying with our minds, dazzling us with an unthinkable source of wealth?

''Now what?'' Fran Jibor murmured.

The image was changing again. Another sun, a galactic wanderer, drifting past the two-planet system! The endurium world spun wildly as potent gravitational forces seized it. It was moving out of orbit, now. Captured by the invader sun? No. No. The other star hadn't been close enough for that. But under the gravitational stress of the intruder the endurium world seemed to be breaking apart. A great dark crack was appearing, suddenly, on its shining surface. Another, another, another. Immense crevices springing from pole to pole.

"The planet's destabilizing," Stackman muttered.

Yes. We were being shown an astonishing visual record of an unthinkable catastrophe.

Within minutes – no doubt the image was being vastly accelerated – we saw that crystalline shield split apart, we saw the endurium planet riven asunder, torn into fragments that whirled in terrible death-throes and were sent spiraling in a wild centrifugal dance, spinning outward, heading in a dozen different directions, drifting toward every corner of the universe. And then the invader star moved on, its damage done.

We had a final shot showing the original star and its one remaining planet, the inner one, looking lonely and forlorn. Then the cone of light winked out; and we stared silently at each other, too flabbergasted to speak.

What was the little silvery machine's purpose? Who knows? Who will ever know? But it had shown us a moment out of incredible antiquity, a newsreel of the inconceivable past. Watching the images on the wall had been like staring back across time. Which is why we started calling Stackman's little gizmo the Time Lens. We played it again and again and again, watching the death of the endurium world a dozen times, and then a dozen times more, in total fascination.

So there you have it. Somewhere in the galaxy, probably not very far from the Jathamassa system, there once was a planet bearing an incredible concentration of endurium. Suddenly a cosmic catastrophe pulled that planet apart and its fragments went flying to the far reaches of the heavens. How long ago? Who can possibly say? A million years, five million, ten million?

One single fragment of that lost planet would be worth a fortune beyond anybody's ability to count.

We're waiting for the archaeological reports now. We need to know how old the stone fortress on Jathamassa Seven is. That may give us some idea of how long ago all this happened. Then we go looking for a sun with a single planet in a close in orbit. Once we know its position we can calculate the paths that the fragments of an exploding planet would have followed over the X million years since the catastrophe. And then we go looking for the fragments, hither and yon around the universe. And maybe we find them.

The Thrynn are going to bankroll us.

The original deal still holds: they put up the money for the expenses, we do the work, we split any proceeds 75-25. Even 25 percent of an incredible fortune is an incredible fortune.

Do we trust them to play fair with us, considering how much is at stake? What do they need us for, now that they know there are whole endurium asteroids floating around out there somewhere?

Well, I admit it makes us a little uneasy, dealing with the reptilians. But that's just an atavistic prejudice, going back to some prehistoric Human myth. We're still striving to overcome that prejudice. And so far the Thrynn have dealt with us in good faith throughout this whole affair.

We're filing a full record of the discoveries we made during our Jathamassa expedition with the Interstel authorities on Arth. We want the whole story on the record. Not that we don't fully trust our friends the Thrynn, you understand. But I remember what my grandmother used to say about counting the spoons after you've had a Thrynn to dinner at your house. Call it prejudice, call it caution, call it anything you like. When trillions of mu's worth of endurium are out there for the taking and you've got Thrynn as your hunting companions, you can't be too careful, say I.

We expect to be setting out soon on the quest for that single planet solar system. That's our starting point. After that – well, we'll see. Wish us luck!